INN LAK'ECH

A Journey to the Realm of Oneness

ELEYNE-MARI SHARP

Writelighter Books

Printed in the United States of America

First Printing, 2018

WRITELIGHTER BOOKS
P.O. BOX 12
NEWPORT, RI 02840

www.writelighter.com

*With love to my mother, Rosemary,
and to all the mothers before her*

In time and with water, everything changes.

— LEONARDO DA VINCI

PROLOGUE

T HE WIND CHIMES NEXT TO the lighthouse door tinkled softly in tandem, then shook furiously in the island breeze, interrupting the old woman reading from her book. It was hard to believe that Fannie Flagg had dyslexia because she wrote excellent stories and *Can't Wait to Get to Heaven* was one of Seraphina's favorites.

She loved the author's down-home, Southern girl humor and her gift for creating such lovable characters. Seraphina especially enjoyed the name of the heroine in this book: *Elner Shimfissle*. It was a fun thing to say aloud, letting the name tickle her tongue: *Elner Shimfissle.* She changed her voice to a higher key, sounding exactly like a flute, then deepened her tone to the resonance of a tuba. *Elner Shimfissle.* All names should be this fun!

But Elner and her faithful friends would have to wait because a family member was coming home. Humming one of her favorite spiritual chants composed by a famous twelfth-century abbess, Seraphina arose from the white stone bench to enter through the violet door of the light-house. Once inside, she rummaged through the assorted mess of old oil lamps, maps, and clocks until she located her yellow rain slicker with the black duct tape patches at the elbow.

The little rowboat was tied to the wharf, changing colors from red to purple to red as it swayed in the water. Seraphina untied the rope and climbed in, rowing across the waves with the energy of a teenager. Of course, she could have done this the easy way, but it tickled her to do something so incredibly human.

Looking out at the teal waves, Seraphina's ancient intuition confirmed that the visitor was drowning. This knowledge did not worry her because all guests entered through the water portal. She continued to row with great happiness, wondering how a third-dimensional character like Elner Shimfissle might handle the situation.

Seraphina rescued the brown boy from the depths of the ocean, transporting his limp body to the lighthouse for emergency restoration. While the crystals flashed their brilliant light rays of color energy, Seraphina rejoiced and sang of gratitude to the Almighty. Soon the lights dimmed and the boy reconnected to his full Divinity.

"Welcome back, Dear One," Seraphina sang in her angelic soprano. "For a tiny soul, you've had quite the adventure!"

"Did I do well?" asked Prabhakar.

"Very well," said the innkeeper. "When you return to your suite you will find that it reflects your new green aura."

"Excellent!" said the boy. "Only three lifetimes to go!"

Seraphina laughed at his exuberance. "That is correct, but first things first. How does a Loving Pink treatment at the Soul Spa sound?"

"Fine," he said, gazing out the lighthouse window.

"I sense that something is troubling you, Dear One."

Prabhakar could never hide anything from Seraphina, nor did he wish to.

"Yes," he sighed. "As you know, I am most anxious to connect to the soul of my dear father, Sankhar, from my life in India. He needs to know I forgive him. Has he arrived yet?"

Seraphina smiled. "Not yet," the wise woman answered. "He is busy being a teenage girl."

CHAPTER 1

T HE DELIVERYMAN STOOD IN THE doorway, holding the sequined six-foot fishtail as if it was his prize catch of the day.

Glorie Sunday looked up from the glass counter and waved her arms at the hulking stranger in the My Wife Loves Me Just The Way I Am T-shirt.

"Stop! No! Don't take another step!" She pressed the button on the intercom. "Elm, I need you out here!"

On the storage room floor in the back of the store was fifteen-year-old Elm Sunday, sitting cross-legged with her head bowed in deep concentration.

She didn't hear her mother's plea at first because she was too busy painting a nautilus seashell on a drum and needed to be extra careful with her brushstrokes if she hoped to sell it at Sea Angels. Besides its loud bass tone, the drum could be made to sound like the ocean waves by tilting it, which caused the metal beads to scramble inside and create the cadence of the surf. Elm thought it was very cool.

As there was no immediate response from her teenage

daughter, Glorie reached behind the counter for her walking stick, a carved mermaid with a cascade of curls flowing down one side.

"Have an accident?" the man blurted.

"Yeah, I was accidentally infected by a *tick*," she drawled. "Look, the store is opening in twenty minutes and you're blocking my entrance. Could you move that thing out of the doorway?"

He shrugged, leaning the tail against the nearest wall. "That's quite an accent you got there, Lady," he said, wiping his forehead sweat with the back of his hand. "Y'all from the Deep South or something?"

Glorie shot him a look that would have sent most Yankees running. "Yes, I am—from Georgia—and I need you to turn right around and come into the store from the back."

He frowned, staring down at the neon, ocean-themed floor. "What is this place?" he asked, picking up a ceramic mermaid figurine from a wicker table. "Some kind of cutesy mermaid store?"

"Yes, it's Sea Angels and that tail is desperately needed for a birthday party tomorrow and—"

The man wasn't listening because his attention was drawn to an old newspaper article about a young woman who worked as a mermaid at a Florida waterpark. The article was hanging in an aqua blue frame on the same wall where he had set the tail.

"That's my mama," said Elm, who had emerged from the storeroom.

"Oh yeah?"

Elm gave her mother an "I got this" wink and assumed her best customer service persona. She was a thinner, prettier version of her mother with huge sea-green eyes and straight, long hair the color of golden copper. She hadn't made peace with her small breasts, huge flat feet or the freckles that spilled across her pert nose but Glorie said she was nice-looking enough to have modeled for any one of the mermaid prints that hung on the walls.

"She used to be a professional mermaid," Elm boasted. She always thought her mother was beautiful, even after her weight gain. "Down in Florida."

"Yes, many, many moons ago," said Glorie, now a plump, middle-aged woman wearing huge, pink-tinted glasses, dangly starfish earrings, and graying, strawberry-gold hair stuffed under an outlandish, floppy pink hat. "Elm, would you *kindly* show this man how to get to the back from the outside. And that mermaid tail's for the party, so make sure he's careful with it."

Elm nodded. They didn't want a repeat of what happened at the Tessa Baker party, where a mother of considerable size "borrowed" the tail from her daughter, wriggled inside until it burst at the seams and sent sequins rolling all over the place.

Glorie said it was like looking at six pounds of sugar in a five-pound bag.

Like all Sundays in Little Blessing, the mornings were reserved for worship, but the restaurants and store owners were not opposed to taking money from summer visitors, so their doors flew open at noon. Or around noon. Or whenever the proprietors felt like showing up. Elm called it "Wishy-Washy Sunday."

There wasn't much happening at the store at one o'clock, so Elm called The Good Book Tea Room for their lunch order. Twenty minutes later, she returned with sandwiches and fruit-infused waters. She supposed she shouldn't have ordered the pricier lobster roll for herself, but she craved its succulent sweetness. As far as she was concerned, lobster was the perfect summer food and (next to a double dip Triple Fudge cone from Holy Cow Sundaes, the home of Little Blessing's world-famous Divinity Fudge), it was her favorite addiction.

Elm set the lunches on the counter, grabbed two turquoise and Caribbean blue wooden chairs from the front of the store and placed them outside the entrance. Then she lugged a huge stuffed mermaid and plopped it into one of the chairs.

Maybe this will bring people in.

She joined her mother inside for lunch in the arctic air conditioning, where they ate and chatted in the delicious chill, anticipating a stampede of customers seeking immediate heat relief.

They would be waiting a long while. This was beach season in late July and even though the shop was conveniently located across from Moonwater Beach, most sun-worshippers planted themselves on the beach until at least four o'clock or whenever they felt they had achieved ultimate bronze perfection.

Business had been deathly slow since Memorial Day, despite the website promotions and the year-round mermaid birthday parties. A small stage with an underwater backdrop and golden scallop shell throne had been set up in the back of the store. It was still one of Elm's favorite places.

Glorie tapped her pink mermaid pencil so hard on the counter it snapped. It was the third broken pencil that day.

"No more pencils for you, Mom," Elm laughed, wiping up the wood fragments with a paper towel.

Poor Mermie. As if having Lyme isn't bad enough.

Then Elm got an idea. "Hey, wanna play our game?"

"Sure," said Glorie, perking up.

They spent the next two hours watching the windows, guessing the professions of passersby. It was one of the many activities they enjoyed doing together, like singing Christmas carols at church, eating a picnic aboard the *Glorie Hallelujah*, and scuba diving in the ocean.

The door chimes tinkled and three middle-aged women walked in. They had thick black hair, leathery tans, and enormous gold jewelry.

Sand Stabbers! It was the name Elm used to describe women who wore high heel shoes on the beach.

"You got a restroom around here?" The woman speaking had an aquiline nose and graying temples.

Glorie and Elm looked at each other and smiled. It was time to play "let's mess with the tourists."

"No, I'm so sorry, Miss," Glorie lied, exaggerating her Southern drawl. "Little Blessing doesn't provide sanitary facilities for non-residents. Our mayor says it just isn't in our itty bitty budget this year."

"That's ridiculous," said another woman. "Whoever heard of a tourist trap without public restrooms?"

Trap? Elm could only imagine what her mother was thinking.

"Now if you rich Yankee women want to buy some property in Little Blessing—to help the economy, you know —then you could use the bathroom whenever you like, of course. I would be plumb tickled to help you find the town realty office."

Elm played along, without the accent. "But they've closed for the summer. Did you forget that, Mother?"

Glorie winked. "Why, that's right, Honey Child. So I guess you'll have to hold it until the *next* tourist trap, Ladies!"

Two of the beach women scowled and exited, leaving

their friend behind. Elm watched the woman pick up a green mermaid scarf from a shelf and let it drop to the floor.

On purpose.

"What the h—?" Glorie said.

Raising her bejeweled middle finger, the woman laughed and hurried out the door, leaving it wide open.

Elm ran after her like a wildcat on a deer chase.

"Hey, you!" Elm shouted. "Don't you ever come into my store again—*ever*! And who do you think you are, giving my mama *The Finger*? I'll cut that ugly finger right off you!"

The woman slipped inside Holy Cow Sundaes two stores away but Elm was relentless and stood outside screaming.

"And when you know the damn air conditioner is on, you close the door unless you're paying for it. And don't you even think about peeing in our ocean, Lady, or my daddy will arrest you—he's the mayor of this town!"

It was the first time Elm had ever lost her temper in public and she was shaking. She didn't care what those women thought about her because they were disrespectful. But she probably shouldn't have said *peeing* or *damn* because it was not the kind of behavior one expected from The First Daughter of Little Blessing. And God was watching. He was always watching.

When Elm returned to the store, she was surprised to find that Glorie wasn't upset.

"If it isn't my little ol' guard dog," Glorie laughed. "Hey, remind me to give you a treat when we get home."

"You're not mad?"

"Mad? Girl, I'm proud!" Glorie exclaimed, hugging her daughter. "But it's a good thing your grandma wasn't around because I could hear everything you said out there, even with the *damn* air conditioner blasting!"

CHAPTER 2

F OR THE NEXT HOUR, GLORIE and Elm discussed their
town's ongoing problem with tourism. Elm enjoyed
these discussions because she felt Glorie valued her input,
even though she was just a teenager.

Little Blessing had struggled for years against becoming
an official tourist destination. The town did no advertising
with the state's tourism board and, in response, the state
did little to promote the town's beautiful beaches and
summer activities.

And yet the word got out that Little Blessing was the
place to go for fun and sun, especially if one needed
privacy and happened to be artsy or eccentric.

Partying was definitely not on the agenda when the
original settlers landed in Little Blessing in 1648. Led by
Elm's ancestor Reverend George Sunday, they were a
group of proud and pious people whose every breath was
devoted to praising the Almighty.

When it was time to name the streets, the Puritans sought
no further than "The Good Book" for inspiration. They
dubbed the main thoroughfares after the Seven Virtues,

except for Gluttony Road, of course. That unholy street was reserved for the town outcasts, the sinners who wasted their nights drinking ale and playing poker at Gluttony Tavern.

Gluttony Road was the devil's playground. As far as Elm knew, no Sunday ever played there.

IF ANYONE COULD SCARE THE DEVIL HIMSELF IT WAS RUTH Abbott Sunday, a tall woman with salt-and-pepper hair, thin nose, tiny brown eyes, and a no-nonsense attitude. The late reverend's wife wore no makeup or jewelry, resembled a hawk with glasses, and was shoving a stack of printed cards across the sales counter.

"Here's a new batch, Gloria."

Uh oh. Even from her vantage point on the stage, Elm could see the sinner cards.

"Mother Ruth, there's really no room for these."

"Leave them on the counter then," Ruth snapped, her eyes searching for Elm. "Where's Mercy-Faith? Did she run off to the beach? I thought the whole point of her working at the store this summer was to learn the value of a dollar."

Ruth was the only one who called Elm by her given name, the one she insisted upon before Elm was born. In Ruth's opinion, all Christian names should be biblical, even though she married a George.

"Hi, Grandma. I'm back here, polishing the throne."

Elm stepped off the stage to give her grandmother a quick peck on the cheek. "How are you feeling today?"

Ruth grimaced, as if she was in pain. "I'm fine, thank you. I'm glad to see you working, Girl."

"Yes. Today I've been in the storage room painting a sea drum."

"What the devil is that?"

"It's a drum that has all these metal beads in it and when you tilt it, it sounds just like ocean waves. I'll let you see it when it's dry."

"What a waste of time," Ruth huffed. "As if we don't get enough of these blasted ocean waves every day. Gloria, you're not going to allow this, are you?"

Elm glanced at her mother, whose face had turned an angry red. Ruth had plumped down in one of the turquoise rocking chairs outside the entrance, leaving the shop door ajar.

"Good lord, she's gonna scare everybody," Glorie muttered.

She hobbled outdoors and rested her hand on the back of Ruth's chair. "Wouldn't you be more comfortable inside, Mother Ruth?"

Ruth did not yield and continued to rock, assessing the beach scene across the street.

"Those young women should be ashamed of themselves," Ruth said. "There's hardly a stitch on them. And they're flirting with those men! I sincerely hope that Mercy-Faith has more self-respect."

"Well, thanks for stopping by," said Glorie. "I'm sure the other stores are just chomping at the bit for those cards."

Ruth's eyes darted and settled on Glorie's walking stick. "So," she berated. "You continue this charade of having a disease that my doctor says does not exist."

"Well, my doctor says something else and I believe—"

"*And* I understand," Ruth interrupted, "that you've turned your entire dwelling into an insane animal shelter and there's dog filth everywhere. Lord knows you've never been the best housekeeper on the best of days, but my son and granddaughter don't need to live like that. Of course, David would never complain—"

"And he shouldn't," Glorie blurted. "Since he's the one who brought the dogs in the first place."

Ruth was momentarily stunned. "Well, my David always did have a kind heart," she rebutted. "And I'm sure he got it from me teaching him the words of the Lord."

"Well, bless your little heart!" said Glorie, sarcastically.

"And another thing," Ruth continued. "When are you going to stop talking like you just got off the plantation? You've lived here for years. The least you can do is talk like a civilized human being."

Glorie shrugged and went back into the store, closing the door behind her.

"How's Grandma?" Elm asked, dumping the sinner cards into the wastebasket behind the counter.

"Don't ask," said Glorie. "And don't ditch those yet. The woman's not gone until she's gone."

Elm nodded, but stopped what she was doing when she heard a commotion outside.

"Mommy, Mommy, I wanna go in here!"

A little brown-haired girl in a hot pink swimsuit and neon green flip-flops was eager to enter the store but burst into tears when she saw the intimidating, bird-like woman rocking by the door.

Elm quickly assessed the problem and ran outside to rescue the child. "Don't cry," she said, stepping in front of Ruth to lead the girl into the store. "We're open."

Mmmmm, she smells like bananas and coconut.

Good smells were one of the many benefits of working in a store with an ocean-view location. Elm loved the fragrance of the salty ocean, coupled with the flavored suntan lotions the beach people liberally splashed on their bodies. And the daily sweet scent from the homemade waffle cones at Holy Cow Sundaes made it all one very delicious scene.

"Your mermaids are very pretty," the child said in awe.

"Thank you," said Elm, proud to be associated with her mother's vision. Sea Angels was the only shop of its kind in New England. It boasted an abundance of dolls, jewelry, suncatchers, dreamcatchers, books, journals, soaps, signs, mirrors, bedding, furniture, and clothing. And how could anyone not like its shimmering palette of blues, greens, pinks, and purples?

"This one is funny!"

The little girl was holding a chubby rag doll mermaid with blond curls, a starfish covering its navel, and a powder blue and white polka-dotted tail. It was a Krista Owens original and a personal favorite of Elm's.

Delighted, the girl swung the doll in the air, causing the mermaid's long legs to knock over a glass bowl of purple and teal mermaid fin soaps. The bowl shattered and soap tails were rolling in all directions across the floor.

"You *sinner*!"

Ruth was at the scene, shaking her finger at the frightened girl.

"Mommy!" the girl screamed. "Mommy, help me!"

Glorie went to comfort the child while Elm fetched the broom and dustbin from the storage room. At that moment, the girl's mother rushed in.

"Don't you dare yell at my girl, you...you devil witch!" she warned, shoving past Ruth to cradle her sobbing daughter.

"What did you call me?"

Yikes. This can't be good for business.

"Come on, Chloe," the woman said, wiping the girl's tears with a tissue from her purse. "This is a bad place and these are very bad people. They just want your money —let's go!"

After they had gone, Ruth closed her eyes and whispered a quick prayer. It did nothing to change her sour perspective.

"Did you both see how rude that woman was?" Ruth insisted. "And what kind of name is Chloe? Something heathen? I'm telling you, Gloria, tourism is ruining this town and I plan to tell my son, the mayor, he'd better do something about it! Now, where did you put those sinner cards? Get them out here, front and center!"

WHEN BUSINESS CLOSED FOR THE DAY, ELM TOLD GLORIE she would meet her at home, then went outside to the back of the building where she had parked her bike. It had been a birthday present from her parents and she loved its silvery teal color and pretty turquoise basket.

A seagull was perched on the handlebars and she waved it away, inspecting for bird droppings. Satisfied nothing was amiss, she placed a small notebook and pen inside the basket, walked the bike to Charity Street and hopped on.

"Hey, Elm." It was Mrs. Lightfoot, the owner of Holy Cow Sundaes, waving to her from the sidewalk. "Gotta minute?"

"Sure."

Elm watched for traffic as she dismounted and walked her bike to the side of the road. A stout woman with chin-length blond hair, Mrs. Lightfoot was wearing her milk-maid costume, the official uniform of Holy Cow Sundaes. There was a golden halo pin on her ruffled cap.

"I'm glad I caught you. Do you have any plans for this

Saturday? I finally got Pete to take me to Willowtown for our anniversary. They've got an Italian restaurant over there that I've heard great things about and I've been craving some Fettuccine Alfredo, so I was wondering if you wouldn't mind babysitting the kids."

It was no secret that Elm had achieved the title of the Best Babysitter in Little Blessing. She was like a teenage Mary Poppins. The kids loved her because she was fun and imaginative, played games and drew pictures for them, while their parents appreciated her respectful manner and the tidy home they always found when they returned.

"I think I'm available. Can I call you when I get home?"

"Yes, please. And Elm—I know how busy you are so I'm willing to pay double."

Elm had known Mrs. Lightfoot her entire life and had licked her way through the entire ice cream shop menu. "I wouldn't feel right about that."

"Okay, how about I throw in three double-dip Triple Fudge cones along with your regular rates?"

Elm could never turn away ice cream or chocolate, for that matter. "My favorite. Thank you, Mrs. L."

Back on her bike, the breezy ride was exhilarating. She rode down Charity Street, past the white-painted shops with their hanging baskets of red geraniums, past scenic Moonwater Beach, The Seashell Carousel, Sailors Chapel, Faith Camp Meeting Grounds, Sunday Free Library, and the Little Blessing Town Hall & Post Office.

Minutes later, she was pedaling through the Godsend Nature Trails at Purity Park, taking a shortcut around the seventeenth-century statue of Little Blessing founder Reverend George Sunday. Finally, she reached a particular grove of pine trees overlooking the bay and stopped to catch her breath.

Of course, nothing had changed, and why should it? It wasn't like Miss Vi was going to walk away after being rooted in the same spot for over five hundred years. Maybe trees sauntered around in books like *The Lord of the Ring*s or *The Wizard of Oz*, but sauntering (trees or otherwise) was discouraged in Little Blessing because it might give the impression that you were lazy and had nothing to do. In fact, everybody had a purpose in Little Blessing. Even the elderly.

Elm parked her bike next to a stalwart evergreen, grabbed her notebook and pen and climbed the stairs to the treehouse she shared with Snow, her best friend. Once inside, she grabbed a hold of Miss Vi's thick trunk to brace herself before plopping down upon the lavender floor pillows.

It was amazing that nosy tourists hadn't discovered the treehouse, but most rarely wandered off the beaten path, for fear of ticks and bears. There were ticks, of course, but there hadn't been a bear sighting for at least a century. Elm always suspected that Snow initiated the bear tale to protect their little sacred space in the woods.

A violet light was streaming through the hexagonal roof as it always did this time of day. Elm sucked on her pen for a moment, then scribbled her thoughts:

DEAR MISS VI,

Poor Mermie had a bad day. She was in a lot of pain and it didn't help that Grandma came to the store to torture her. Grandma yelled at a little girl who broke a bowl of mermaid soaps. I don't know why Grandma is so mean. Just born that way, I guess.

Anyway, I painted my new sea drum today and can't wait to use it. I'll tell you all about it later, of course.

I noticed you have a new bird's nest. Are you feeling crowded?

Does all that bird chirping wake you up in the morning? It would give me a headache.

I love you and I hope you still love me.

Your friend,

Elm

NOT MANY GIRLS COULD CLAIM THEY HAD A TREE AS A confidante. For Elm, it started when she was eight, when Big Dave shared his "big secret" about a special tree with a mysterious violet aura.

To most people, there was nothing visibly special about "Miss Violet," just one of the many evergreens standing in whispering contemplation. But her father and his best friend, Jason Moontree Smith, were sensitives, which meant that they could see the energy around objects, people, even ghosts. The boys decided she was the perfect hiding place to read their Boy Scout magazines, play games, and plan their future. So they built a crude observation deck from a few boards they had retrieved from a construction site and Miss Violet remained their secret hideout for the rest of their youth.

After Elm and Snow inherited the tree, their fathers surprised them by building a sky roof and windows, and replacing the old rope ladder with a wooden one. They also added a small bookcase and platform bed for reading. The girls were delighted.

With a breezy water view, they claimed the treehouse as their summer camp for chatting, reading, writing, and watching. Miss Violet continued to grow through the center of the treehouse and was affectionately re-christened *Miss Vi*. She became such a beloved part of their youth that Elm never told her father she'd be "hanging out at the treehouse". No, they were "hanging out with Miss

Vi" and Big Dave understood because he felt the same way.

One day, Big Dave presented Elm with a gray metal box and key. "Elm, you can always trust Miss Violet to protect your secrets from humans," he said. "But don't forget that all of the trees around here are part of the Wood Wide Web. They speak to each other. So there are no secrets among trees. Remember that."

Elm placed her finished message inside that same metal box (now hidden inside a tree knot) and locked it with a key from her pocket. Then she lay back against the pillows to close her eyes and absorb what was left of the violet rays.

CHAPTER 3

THERE WAS A LOUD CLANGING from the kitchen when Elm got home.

Glorie stood by the sink watching Big Dave, who was crouched on the floor with his tousled blond head inside a cabinet. Behind him were five dogs of varying sizes, pushing to get a look.

"What's going on?" Elm asked.

"Oh, your father brought home another stray dog."

"Really, Dad? Wow, that's seven."

There was another clang and then Big Dave's face appeared. "Do we have any extra dog bowls anywhere?"

"Yes, we do and no, you're not," warned Glorie. "We have more than enough dogs now and we don't need anymore."

For the past five years (and to Glorie's dismay), Big Dave had been adopting dogs from his pal Jason, the town vet. Each of the pooches was a mixed breed and assigned a number for easier identity. *One* was a red Irish Setter/Golden Retriever, *Two* was a Jack Russell Terrier/Beagle, *Three* was a Lhasa Apso/Poodle, *Four* was a

Labrador Retriever/Hound, *Five* was a Dachshund/Terrier, and *Six* was a Schnauzer/Terrier.

"But this one—you'll really like this one, Mermie," Big Dave promised. *Mermie* was his pet name for Glorie.

"She's a Great Pyrenees mix, real pretty, mostly black, but with a white chin. We'll call her *Seven*."

Elm shook her head and laughed. "That's a surprise."

She knew who was going to win this battle over the canines. Her father loved animals and once considered becoming a veterinarian himself and partnering with Jason, only he couldn't bear to see an animal in pain. In fact, he was so compassionate towards all living creatures that he became a vegetarian before he began first grade and refused to learn how to fish or hunt when he joined the Boy Scouts. Being a vegetarian also made him an odd duck in Little Blessing and the polar opposite of his carnivorous, take-no-prisoners mother.

"Use this," said Glorie, handing Big Dave a blue-and-white china bowl. "It's one of your mother's and I've always hated it."

Big Dave pecked his wife on the cheek, grabbed her by the waist with one hand and filled the bowl with dry dog food with the other.

They're so weird. But I love them.

As a little girl, Elm never grew tired of hearing about her parents' love story, even though she knew it by heart. Glorie had left Humble Shores, Georgia to study marine biology in Florida and ended up being employed as a part-time mermaid at Blue Planet Waterpark to help pay her college tuition.

According to Glorie, becoming a mermaid wasn't the easiest job she had ever had. First, she had to fight the instinctive fear of drowning while wearing a thirty-pound tail strapped to her legs. Then there was synchronized choreography to master, which meant that Glorie had to learn how to keep her feet together while performing underwater somersaults, blowing bubbles, and joining her sister mermaids in oceanic conga lines. As if that wasn't enough, she was expected to wear underwater makeup, keep her eyes open, smile constantly, and hold her breath for up to five minutes.

One day after rehearsing, Glorie was climbing out of the pool. Big Dave stood in front of her in his crisp, white uniform, blocking the sun like the tallest, mightiest tree in the forest.

"You look wet," he laughed, extending his beefy hand.

"You think?" Glorie didn't know who Big Dave was nor how he had gotten past the security guards, but it was obvious that he liked her and the feeling was mutual because she thought he was drop dead gorgeous. At six-feet four inches, Big Dave was a muscular five inches taller with a full head of bushy, golden hair and the largest blue eyes Glorie had ever seen on a human without appearing comedic. A beautiful, gentle bear of a guy.

Dripping, she reached for a towel draped over a deck chair. From that moment on, they would be together in body and soul, like Earth and Water, for the rest of their lives. He became the sturdy rock that she would cling to in stormy weather and she would play the water nymph who delighted him with her giggles, playfulness, and bubbly personality.

Ever since that first meeting, Big Dave had dubbed her his "Little Mermie," although one could see that she was hardly petite. Without heels or tail, Glorie stood at five feet and ten inches. Luckily for her, Big Dave didn't mind tall, curvaceous women with long legs, especially when they had cute freckles across their nose and coppery waves of waist-length tresses. And he loved her infectious laugh and southern accent.

"And the rest is history," Glorie would say.

It was how she always ended the story and Elm would always applaud.

FOR A GIRL WHO HAD JUST TURNED FIFTEEN, ELM THOUGHT she had a pretty cool life. Her father was the mayor, her mother owned a mermaid shop, and they all lived together with their seven dogs on the second floor of the building that housed the marina office and showers.

Tucked away in quiet Creation Cove, they shared their view with up to fifty sail and motor boats claiming summer refuge at Sunday's Marina. There was always something interesting to watch, always something colorful to enjoy. Never once had Elm wished she lived in a spacious home with a grassy lawn and a tree swing in the backyard. Her backyard was the water, an endless vista of beauty and change.

Besides her occasional babysitting jobs, Elm had two part-time jobs this summer—working as Mermie's assistant at Sea Angels and as a dockhand/photographer for Big Dave in the marina office. As a newlywed, Glorie had been unimpressed by its "sailor's man cave" decor. Before its renovation, there had been charts and books stacked higgledy-piggledy on metal shelves, along with broken-framed photographs of boats, assorted boating equipment, and nautical knickknacks. Glorie tackled it as her first project in her newly married life, replacing the old with a new navy couch, end tables, lamps, picture frames, desks, chairs, wooden bookcases, refrigerator, and water cooler.

Wearing her official Sunday's Marina cap, Elm sat at

her worktable in the office, her sea glass booty spread before her. It had been a good haul. She carefully separated the green from the amber shards and was delighted that there were more blue and white pieces than normal.

Darn. Only one red shard this time and no violet.

One day she would find that elusive violet glass. It would be her prize.

Elm picked up one of the smooth green pieces and held it up to the light.

Probably from a beer bottle.

But the flavor she experienced while looking at the color wasn't beer, it was lime.

Like a sugary, sour, candy fruit slice.

Thank goodness she liked that flavor because she had synesthesia and she worked with green a lot!

Taking her wire cutters, Elm cut two 12-inch pieces of sterling silver wire, then crossed them in the center and twisted until the wires were attached. She lay the sea glass on top of the wires and wound the wrapping. She was trying to decide what kind of bail to make when the ship's bell rang over the door and Big Dave walked in, followed by Dogs *Two, Three, Four,* and *Seven.*

"How'd you do?" her father asked, placing his keys and walkie talkie on his desk. The first three dogs took this as a sign that he planned to be in the office for a while so they claimed their spots on the couch and got comfortable. Seeing no room left, little *Seven* went over to Elm, whining for some attention.

Elm put her tools aside and wiped her hands with a cloth before petting the dog. "What a good girl," she cooed.

"Find any violet in there?" Big Dave queried. He was sporting a trim goatee and mustache, which Elm thought made him look even more handsome.

"Zero. Nothing," Elm answered. "And I'm getting

really tired of not finding any, Daddy." It was a favorite color, too, because it tasted like lavender vanilla. "People have been asking on the website if my pendants come in violet and poor Mermie has to tell them 'no.'"

"Well, cheer up," he assured her, picking up his phone and dialing a number. "You'll find it someday."

Elm's desk faced a huge window, offering a picturesque view of the harbor. Per usual, her attention wandered and she'd pause to watch the boats sail in and out of the marina.

Brutus. Joy Ride. Just Ducky. Wicked Winch. Dock Holiday. Dream Catcher.

"Hey, Dad," she said. "Better hold your nose, 'cause here comes *Breakin' Wind*!"

Her father laughed, crossing his eyes as he held his nose.

The ship's bell rang and a tanned man in his late thirties walked in.

"Thank god for air conditioning," he said, removing his sailing cap to wipe his forehead. "It's almost a hundred today."

Big Dave stood up to shake the man's hand. "I'm Dave Sunday, the owner of this marina. And this is my daughter, Elm. You're the captain of *Lady Diana*, aren't you?"

"Yes, I'm Mark Boylston," the man said. He glanced at the dogs sleeping on the couch, then took a seat in the chair next to Big Dave's desk. "Taking a little vacation with the family. Started from Boston and just cruisin' to nearby ports, you know, fishing and seeing the sights. Got a little rough two days ago. My only crew is my lazy eleven-year old son and a wife who'd rather save her nails than bail water."

The men laughed and Elm suspected there would be a

long conversation about boat engines and wives and weather patterns, so she decided to take a break.

"Excuse me, Captain Boylston," she said, covering her sea glass with a cloth and grabbing her camera and walkie-talkie. "Dad, I think I'll go on my rounds now. Do you need anything while I'm out?"

"Nothing I can think of," said her father. "But keep your radio handy, in case I get a craving for something sweet."

"Roger that." Elm loved using radio lingo, even when she wasn't using the walkie-talkie.

No sooner had she opened the door when *Seven* raced to join her. "Oh, all right," Elm said. "But you might regret it 'cause it's real hot out there."

Elm's "rounds" consisted mainly of checking the cleanliness of all the public areas, including the showers, laundromat, picnic area, and swimming pool.

Even though it was her job to tidy up after the boaters (using non-toxic cleaner she had made from coconut oil soap, spearmint essential oil, baking soda, and vinegar), Elm also fancied herself as the marina's official greeter and website photographer. She enjoyed chatting with the guests about their adventures and sometimes they invited her onboard to show off their treasures or play games with their children.

Photography was a relatively new hobby for Elm. It gave her another form of creative expression, also an appreciation for her town and nature. She often brought her camera on her sea glassing excursions and there was a nice picture on the website that Elm had taken aboard the *Glorie Hallelujah*. It showed the harbor with its lush skyline of green trees and a scattering of historic brown, brick red, white, and blue cottages. *Photo courtesy of Elm Sunday.*

Elm quickly cleaned the showers and laundromat, then

snapped a few pictures of her handiwork before heading to her next destination. *Seven* was barking at a snooping white swan with an orange beak. It was gliding along the murky green water, stretching its thin neck as it inspected its larger, mechanical cousins.

Most of the hulls were painted white, although *The Sea Wolf*'s was red and *My Retirement*'s a deep, forest green. Apart from their monotony-white bottoms, the sail covers flaunted a colorful parade of navy, teal, rust, khaki, burgundy, hunter green, and Caribbean white. Each vessel was secured to its slip with a yellow, blue, green, turquoise or mint green dockline as the sunlight bounced off their teak and chrome adornments.

Along the pier were hanging baskets overflowing with fragrant red geraniums, leading to a large patio with picnic tables and barbecue pits which overlooked the marina. Elm was glad she had watered the flowers that morning; otherwise, they would have wilted in the extreme heat. There wasn't much activity in the marina that day, although a few boat owners were sunning themselves on their upper decks.

A seagull in flight dropped a crab shell on the dock and *Seven* scampered off to investigate. In the distance, Elm could see an approaching sailboat with turquoise sails and a Bermuda flag.

It's probably here for the regatta.

"Excuse me!" a woman called out from one of the boats.

Elm stopped and looked up at the boy sitting at the helm of *Lady Diana*. The forty-eight-foot motor yacht looked like a floating garden with a flybridge.

"Yes, ma'am?" She still didn't see the woman.

"I'm Peg Boylston," said the thin woman, peeking out from behind a potted tree on the upper deck. She was wearing a floral two-piece swim suit and mirrored sunglasses.

"Oh, hi, Mrs. Boylston. Welcome to Little Blessing. I'm Elm Sunday. I just met your husband in the office."

The woman smiled. "Yeah, and he's probably still there. He likes to talk about boats. Listen, you got a minute?"

"Sure."

"Not much of a breeze," said Mrs. Boylston. "Any special activities in town today? My boy is getting restless."

The woman's son turned on the radio as if he was trying to drown out their voices. Elm witnessed him tossing something white in the water from his high perch.

I hope the kid isn't littering.

"Well, there's a kite festival going on at Moonwater Beach."

"What's the beach like?"

"Oh, very sandy and very breezy," Elm replied. "And we've got one of the oldest carousels in the country."

The boy must have had supersonic hearing. "I don't want to see no carousel, Ma!" he yelled. "That's for babies!"

"Shush, Trevor!" his mother snapped.

"Well, the kite festival is always a lot of fun," said Elm, staring at the woman's green sea glass bracelet. "It's just a twenty-minute walk from here and they have a competition and some food and kite vendors. I can get you a street map, if you like."

"That would be great," said Mrs. Boylston, noticing Elm's interest in her jewelry. She shook her skinny wrist, stretching her long fingers showcasing bright red nail polish. "Do you like my bracelet? I made it myself."

It was beautiful, quite different from Elm's own sea glass pieces. "It's very nice," said Elm, surprised at the jealousy churning inside. "Too bad there's no sea glass for you to collect around here. There was a sea glass convention this summer and our beaches were picked clean."

But I know where to find more and I'm not telling you.

"Too bad," said Mrs. Boylston. "I've been collecting sea glass at all our ports."

Elm saw Captain Boylston walking towards them on the pier. "Well, I'd better finish my rounds," she said. "I'll drop off the map later. It's nice to meet you, Mrs. Boylston —and you, too, Trevor. Maybe you'd like to go swimming? We've got a nice pool. I'm going there now."

The boy ignored her.

Whatever.

A dragonfly was perched atop of the "Swimming Pool Rules" sign on the white picket gate. Snow had told her that dragonflies represented transformation and were actually fairies, so Elm took a closer look, staring for fifteen seconds.

No, nothing but a darn insect and I'm still me. Wait 'til I get a hold of that Snow Whitedove Smith!

Despite the No Alcoholic Beverages and No Glass Containers rules printed in bold letters on the sign, Elm was annoyed to find empty beer bottles on one of the poolside tables. Two bottles had spilled, leaving an odorous, yeasty puddle.

Elm typed in the combination code to the pool supplies closet and retrieved a paper bag, a roll of paper towels, and a nontoxic glass cleaner. She quickly plopped the bottles into the bag and placed them inside the bin in the closet, then returned to clean the table and take her pictures of the pool from assorted angles.

It's too darn hot.

The sun was beating down with no mercy. Even though the pool water probably wasn't very cool, it did look inviting so Elm removed her brown boat shoes and sat on the pool edge, dangling her freckled feet in the water.

I can't believe nobody's out here.

Usually there was at least one boater sunning themselves by the pool, so she assumed that most of the guests had gone to the kite festival.

The last time we went was when I was eleven.

As part of Little Blessing's Father's Day activities, Elm and Big Dave had flown their homemade stunt kite on the beach while Glorie watched their endeavors from her iron bench on the boardwalk. Someone had entered a giant octopus kite that year and Elm recalled how Glorie had groaned at the sight of the black and purple tentacles flapping in the sky.

Okay, I'm going in.

Luckily, Elm always wore her swimsuit in the summer, just in case she was invited to an impromptu pool party. She bent over, gazing at the clear water against the turquoise floor. Before diving, she remembered her long-time promise to her father, said a quick water blessing and plunged.

I'll only swim for a few minutes or so, just long enough to cool down.

But the water was not cold. Nevertheless, it was freeing, triggering memories of the times when Glorie was teaching her some of her old mermaid flips and how to swim with a monofin. Of course, Elm had outgrown all the mermaid stuff when she was thirteen but she didn't want to hurt her mother's feelings, so she never told her.

I wonder what Mermie would say if she knew there are real mermaids in Little Blessing.

Elm also wondered if she remembered her training and attempted a flip underwater.

Woo hoo! I did it!

The feeling was exhilarating as she swam in the bright underwater, imagining that she was her mother, wearing a teal bra and tail, her red hair flowing with shells and flowers, as she twirled and jumped through hoops before an enthralled audience.

It must be a great feeling to know what you want to do with your life.

Elm had no ambitions, no plans for the future. But sometimes she did long for adventure, something challenging, and maybe even a little dangerous. Something that would get the townspeople to take notice and say, "There goes that Elm Sunday. Isn't she something special? And who is that handsome man with her?"

It might be nice to have a boyfriend.

The closest Elm had ever come to experiencing a romantic interlude was when she was eleven. She and Noah were messing around the newly built condominiums on Serenity Wharf. Curious, they walked through the unlocked front door of one of the units, then hid inside a bedroom closet when they heard a realtor showing the property. That's when Noah made his move. It was just a few kisses but it was enough to cause a lifelong impression.

Fifteen minutes went by before Elm realized there was another body swimming in the water.

Seeing *Seven's* furry paws dog-paddling towards her, Elm's first concern was that the pool had been contaminated and she would be cleaning up dirt and dog hair for hours. She quickly got out and squatted next to the pool ramp, clapping her hands to get *Seven's* attention.

"Come on, girl. Come on!"

The dog obeyed, shaking herself when she reached dry land. Elm wondered how *Seven* had gotten into the restricted pool area and then she saw the hole dug under the fence.

Suddenly, her walkie-talkie squawked.

"Hey, Babycakes. Over."

Oh gosh, how long was I swimming?

She grabbed the radio from the table where she had left it and pushed the button, trying to sound calm and amusing. "May I take your order, Sir?"

Big Dave played along. "Yes. I would like a veggie burger, a side of fries, a chocolate milkshake and a super large hug from the sweetest girl in the world. Over."

Elm laughed, thankful that her father was so easy-going. "Um, I'm at the pool now. Somebody left beer bottles on one of the tables, but I got rid of them. Still cleaning up. Over."

"Roger that," he responded. "Why don't you take the rest of the day off and go swimming? Good day for it. Maybe practice your mermaid tricks? Over."

Elm grimaced. "Uh, negative, Big Daddy. That's kid stuff. Over."

CHAPTER 4

I *SWIM PAST OBSTACLES TO find new treasure.*

Elm was brushing her hair in front of her bedroom mirror when she noticed the latest affirmation card Big Dave had stuck in the mirror frame. It depicted a mermaid kissing a treasure chest.

Elm read the affirmation again, shaking her head. Each time she had tried to "swim past obstacles" in Little Blessing, she had failed miserably, and it didn't help that she had no real talents. She couldn't sing, couldn't dance without stumbling, couldn't draw anything better than stick figures, couldn't play an instrument without sounding like a wailing animal in pain.

She was bad at team sports, too, which she discovered when she tried out for basketball camp the previous summer. She couldn't run fast, jump high or dribble a basketball. And what was the point of her dad nicknaming her Elm when she wasn't even tall enough to reach a basket?

"Daddy, why did you name me Elm?"

"Don't you remember?"
"Tell me again!"

Big Dave would smile, as he always did whenever Elm asked him a question. He told her about how the elm tree was magical, strong, and flexible. It never rotted, not even in water.

As a marina kid, Elm was taught to respect the water, so it was no great surprise when Glorie presented her with *The Hidden Messages of Water* as a homeschooling reading assignment.

Inspired by the book's focus on the consciousness of water and its reaction to thoughts, an eleven-year-old Elm conducted an experiment where she set up a dozen glass jars of spring water on their living room balcony to collect the energy of the water. She taped the word *Love* on half of the bottles and *Hate* on the others.

Seven days later, the bottles labeled *Hate* had turned cloudy, while the water in the *Love* bottles remained clear. Excited, Elm shared her findings with Snow, suggesting they make bottles of positive "moonwater" and sell it to the tourists. Although a great success, the girls had to shut down their little enterprise because many of the towns-people objected to their product's name, claiming it sounded "too occultish."

～

ELM GLANCED UP AT HER STARFISH CLOCK AND FROWNED.
Six forty-five. Already?

She wanted to be out of the house by seven, so she needed to get going. She quickly gathered her hair into a ponytail and picked at her face a little, assessing her imperfections in the mirror.

Why do I have so many freckles? Why don't I have any boobs? Why am I so short? Why do I look like I'm twelve? Why?

Elm sighed, knowing that if her father had been in the room, he would have reminded her that there was always something to be grateful about, even if the situation seemed dire. She thought about this for a moment and decided that, okay, she was glad that she wasn't completely hopeless. She swam like a fish, knew almost everything about the local history, and created beautiful wire-wrap jewelry.

Elm also possessed exceptional marketing sense and this is how she came to own her sea glass jewelry business at the age of fifteen. She named it *Vitamin Sea by E* and Glorie allowed her to sell her pendants and bracelets at Sea Angels and on the company website. Many people sold sea glass jewelry but Elm's were unique because they were the only ones packaged inside genuine medicine pill bottles.

The girl's uniqueness did not end with her jewelry. Since she was three, she could see auras around people and objects, including the violet one around Miss Vi. Elm could also taste colors in numbers and names. Since none of her friends ever mentioned having this talent, she proclaimed herself a freak and kept her synesthesia a secret from everyone except Miss Vi.

THE BEST TIME TO FIND SEA GLASS IN LITTLE BLESSING WAS when the tide was at its lowest, a few hours before the tourists swarmed the beaches. Sometimes tourists would deplete the natural supply with their beach pails or metal detectors, so Elm avoided those areas. Fortunately, Elm had insider access to all the secret coves and locations that were still unspoiled from the grabby hands of visitors.

Her father owned two boats—*Sea Angel*, a forty-foot sloop, and *Glorie Hallelujah*, a small outboard motorboat that he used to transport boaters to and from their moorings.

On this particular early morning, Elm had gotten permission to take the *Glorie Hallelujah* to search for sea glass. She planned to be gone for at least four hours and had already packed up her sunblock, sunglasses, Sunday's Marina sailing cap, two wrapped sandwiches, an apple, and a large water bottle.

"Elm? Are you leaving now?"

Glorie was lying in her white chenille-covered bed, surrounded by four of their dogs. It was where she spent most of her time when she wasn't at Sea Angels, but at least she had a pleasant room, painted in soft coastal colors with natural wicker accents. Glorie and Big Dave maintained separate bedrooms because Glorie often thrashed about whenever attempting a comfortable position where her Lyme disease-ridden body was not in pain.

"Yes, Mermie. Do you need something before I go?"

"Not really. I just wanted to tell you I love you and to have fun today."

"Thanks," Elm said, kissing her mother's cheek. "Do you want me to rub your legs and feet first?"

She was already late, so it didn't matter if she spent a few more minutes taking care of Glorie.

"Oh, would you? You're my favorite daughter in the whole wide world, Elm Sunday."

"Mom, I'm your *only* daughter."

When she had finished, Elm grabbed her belongings and trotted out the door and down the stairs to the brick walkway with *Seven* nipping at her navy dock shoes.

Sunday's Marina was more crowded than usual, due to the upcoming Little Blessing Regatta the following week.

Elm expected most of the regatta crews to be sleeping but there were already a few men and women outside, cleaning and polishing their vessels.

One of the men on the *Bermuda Breeze* was very dark-skinned, which was an oddity in Little Blessing.

Elm had just put her gear into the motorboat when *Seven* jumped in.

"Out!" she cried, but the yapping dog did not leave. "Out! Come on, *Seven*—go home!"

"Can I help?" It was the dark man.

"Um, okay."

Don't stare at him. It's not polite to stare.

He smiled, holding out his hand so the dog could sniff it. Then he scooped the pooch under his arm and set her on the pier, as a red-faced Elm motored out.

I wonder if he's watching me. Go home, Seven. Go home!

Elm decided to forget about the incident, although she frequently looked over her shoulder, leery that others might discover her favorite sea glass spots.

Despite the previous night, the water was amazingly calm and Elm was excited because she usually found a boatload of sea glass after a storm.

Once when she was nine, her cousin Matthew Sunday teased her about taking up an old person's hobby, but Elm didn't care. She knew the water held a treasure trove of secrets and she was certain that one day she would discover something more valuable than old medicine bottles that had been tossed and transformed by nature.

Thank you, Water. I love you.

It was the silent prayer she always said before swimming or turning on the boat's motor, except for today when *Seven* and the sailor disrupted her routine.

"Always send love to the water, Elm," Big Dave had taught her. "Negative thoughts cause pollution."

Approximately two hours later, Elm was eating a tuna salad sandwich at the entrance of the sea cave. So far it had been a good haul. She had already collected a pound of frosted glass shards in the common green and amber colors along the shore line, but she hoped to find at least some rare cobalt blue and red pieces before she returned home.

In the distance, she observed a black seal swimming towards her.

I've never seen a black seal before.

Gray seals were quite common but they were usually visible in the spring.

But it's not spring.

As the figure grew closer, she realized it wasn't a seal, either.

"Hello again."

It was the man who had helped her with *Seven* and he was grabbing the side of her boat.

"Yes?"

Is he following me?

"Of course, I followed you, Priestess."

"What? I didn't say anything."

The man laughed. "No, but your heart did."

Elm probably should have been more cautious because there was no one else around. But the sailor's smile was intoxicating and an inner voice told her to trust him. If she was wrong, she had a boatful of glass as her weapon.

"May I get in? I'm a little tired from swimming."

"Um, okay."

Elm shoved her sea glass aside as the young man swung his body onboard.

"Hello."

"Hi." Elm felt the heat in her face.

Okay, now what?

"Except for the blushing, you look like a mermaid," he said, picking up a green glass shard and holding it up to the sky. "Pretty."

Elm made a grab for the shard, but the man held it away from her, waving his hand in the air. "That's mine," she said, retrieving the glass and burying it in her collection.

The man laughed again. "You *act* like a mermaid, not wanting to share your sparkly things." He noticed Elm staring at his arm tattoo. "You like my tattoo? Tell me what you think it is."

"I don't know," Elm stammered. "Some sort of squid?"

Should I really be talking to this guy? If I screamed, would anyone hear me?

"Probably not, but no worries, Priestess."

He's reading my mind!

"My tattoo is an octopus and a very special one. It is called a mimic octopus. A shapeshifter. It is my totem. Have you heard of totems?"

Elm had never heard of totems or shapeshifting octopuses. But she did wonder if there were some human beings who could change into black seals.

CHAPTER 5

"**H**EY, SNOW, ARE YOU UP there?" Elm was standing at the foot of Miss Vi.

"What's the password?" croaked the raspy voice above her.

"Arachibutyrophobia—and you know it's me." Elm had contributed the new phobia password, based on her allergy to peanuts.

"Don't be afraid. Come on up!"

Elm climbed the ladder and got a whiff of a cold roast beef sandwich before she even saw Snow Whitedove Smith, her best friend since they were eight years old. A husky, athletic girl, Snow had a raspy voice that sounded as if she smoked several packs of cigarettes a day.

"Wait a sec," said Snow, motioning for her to sit next to her. "I just want to finish this sentence."

"Sure."

Elm sat on a pillow and took in her surroundings. Besides Snow's greasy lunch bag, there was a water bottle, switchblade, and amethyst crystal keychain in a little pile. Leaves and twigs were scattered across the floorboards and a stray orange and white cat was in the corner, pawing at an insect.

"How do you spell *thalassophile*?" Snow asked.

"I have no idea," Elm answered. "What the heck is it?" She was studying a squirrel outside the window, who found her equally fascinating.

"It's a person who loves the ocean."

In the distance, Elm could see the *Sea Crystal Ferry* dropping off a load of passengers from High City. The boat trip took two hours each way, but it was a lovely ride and not too bumpy.

"Why don't you try sounding out the word? That's what Mermie always tells me to do when I can't spell something."

"Nah, I've got a better idea," said Snow, grabbing a dictionary from the shelf. "I just hope it's in here."

Elm was still watching the ferry, recalling her first ferry trip when she was nine years old. Mermie had taken her on a field trip to the art museum. After lunch at the museum, they spent a few hours at High City Harbor Park, sitting on the grass and listening to a jazz band perform at the gazebo.

It was a fun day because Mermie allowed her Inner Child to come out to play. At the arcade, she sampled salt water taffy from the taffy machine and shot plastic ducks with water. Then she rushed Elm to the swings, where she showed her how to swing standing up and how to dismount in a back flip without getting hurt. Elm had no idea her mother was so acrobatic.

But that was way before Lyme.

"Okay, I found it," said Snow. "You can talk to me now."

"I'm honored."

Elm looked back at her friend, a member of Little

Blessing's only indigenous tribe, the Moonwaters. Snow had straight, chin-length black hair and eyes the color of melting chocolate. While Elm adored her like a sister, Snow could be pretty aggressive. Elm thought it might have something to do with her daily consumption of meat.

"What's that?" Elm asked, guessing that the notebook had something to do with Snow's Native American roots.

"It's my story," Snow said. She removed her sandwich from the bag and offered her friend a bite, which was refused when Elm saw the thick chunks of beef and solidified fat squeezing out from between the bread slices.

Yuck.

"I'm writing about a girl who's a water carrier in my tribe," said Snow. "I read online about a tribe in Canada who were water carriers. They call themselves Yinka Dene. Yinka Dene—doesn't that sound like music?" She took a big bite of her sandwich, wiping the mustard from her chin.

"Hey, you got any chips?" Elm asked, eager to tell Snow her own story.

"Nah, my brain-dead sister forgot to buy some when she went grocery shopping. So what do you think, Elm?"

The cat was sitting on Snow's lap now. On top of her notebook, of course.

"I guess it sounds musical. But what's a water carrier?"

Snow shooed the cat away and sat up straight, as if she was about to give an important lecture. She enjoyed talking about her heritage and Elm was usually a good audience.

"Water carriers were very important to indigenous people," Snow explained. "They were the women who carried water from the sea so the tribe could use it for cleaning and drinking and stuff. They carried the water in bags made of animal skins."

"Gross," said Elm, wrinkling her nose. Even though she

owned leather shoes, the idea of carrying water in bags that really looked like animal skins was turning Elm's stomach.

"You're such a baby, Elm," Snow chastised. "Look, it was a very spiritual act, and the best thing about it is that no man was allowed to touch it."

With that last sentence, Snow huffed triumphantly. Despite having a much-beloved father and a great affection for Big Dave, she didn't respect men very much. Elm wondered if it had anything to do with Snow being molested by a tourist when she was twelve.

"Hey, you know what? You should be a water carrier!" Elm exclaimed.

"Yeah, and you should be a mind reader," Snow laughed. "I've already decided. When we graduate in two years, I want to join one of those water organizations that helps bring clean water to people in poor countries. And then I want to see if I can get some sort of water group started here in Little Blessing. Our town isn't poor, but water is important to our way of life because we have a lot of mariners and fishermen and I want to teach people how to save the water from pollution."

Elm nodded. Despite warnings of serious fines, she had seen oil dripping from motor boats and visitors dumping their waste into the water at Sunday's Marina.

"Boy, you've got the rest of your life all figured out."

"Yeah, mostly," Snow agreed. "And what about you? Have you decided if you're even going to college yet? Or are you going to become a fancy, performing mermaid like your mom?"

Uggh.

Elm knew Snow was teasing but she hated the idea of going away to college. It was a topic Elm really didn't want to think about or discuss. Except for High City (which was way too big and scary), there were no higher schools of learning close to Little Blessing. This meant she would have to leave home, and she never wanted to leave home. *Ever.*

"Not really. Hey, I'm only a teenager. Why do I have to think about it now?"

Snow gave her the long, disapproving look of a woman far wiser than her years. "Because you need to have a career and you need to plan for it. Unless you think some Prince Charming is going to swoop into Little Blessing and make you his princess."

"You mean like Daddy did with Mermie?" Elm giggled.

"Boy, are you naive. You know that was a fluke, right? And besides, Big Dave met Mermie in Florida, not here."

"I know that." *Jeez, I'm not stupid.*

Snow was still talking. "And your grades are only average, so you probably won't qualify for a scholarship, so that means your parents will have to pay for college and it's not cheap, because you have to buy books and stuff and—".

She stopped, reaching for a paperback book in the bookcase. "Oh yeah. Speaking of books, I read this piece of junk of yours."

Elm reddened. It was a teenage romance called *Sailor, Sailor, Sweep Me Away* by Dreama Arielle.

"You didn't like it?"

"Hell, no, I didn't like it," Snow snorted. "Elm, life is not this take-me-away-from-all-this-or-I'm-gonna-die romantic crap you think it is. It's working your butt off and scraping pennies and putting up with your teachers and your schoolmates and your older brothers and sisters. I can guarantee you no sailor is going to sweep *me* away and it's not gonna happen to you, either, so get real."

"I *am* real," Elm protested. "And it's a good book. You don't know anything."

"The hell I don't," Snow argued, waving the book in Elm's face. "This so-called book has no realism whatsoever. Like, why can't these stupid book authors show teens the way we really are? For instance, most girls pick their zits and have periods once a month and skip school and sometimes get a really cool teacher we can talk to. Why don't they ever write about that?"

"I guess because they don't want to be too boring or gross," said Elm. "Well, I mean the first part of what you said. Not the teacher thing."

Snow pretended to smack Elm across the face. "Bam! Wake up, Sister! And you know what? I blame Mermie and Big Dave for this."

Elm was surprised, knowing that Snow adored her parents. "What did they do?"

The cat was back on Snow's lap and she stroked him. "Yeah, think about it. They homeschooled you until tenth grade and you came out of it with all these fluffy bunny thoughts and I'm telling you, Elm, you're really gonna fall on your butt when you start *real* school in September."

"There's nothing wrong with homeschooling."

Snow's eyes flashed. "No, because you've been on this fun, all-expenses paid learning vacation while I've been a prisoner in the god-awful Little Blessing school system. I'm gonna let you in on a little secret, Elm. Did you know I used to get jealous whenever I heard that Big Dave taught you how to do something cool like sail or tie knots or use the marine radio? Or when Mermie taught you Spanish or how to make mint juleps?"

For once, Elm wished Snow would get her facts straight. "Mermie never taught me how to make mint juleps. I'm underage. And why are you acting like Jason isn't a great dad?"

Snow looked ashamed, but just for a moment. "Yeah, Dad is great but he's got the clinic and not a lot of time to sit down and talk. And I don't have a mom. But you do, and your mom taught you how to cook at a very young age, which has come in real handy these days because that Lyme bug has zapped her energy and your dad isn't always around to help her."

"Yeah, so?"

"Look, Elm, all I'm saying is your parents may have taught you how to survive but they didn't prepare you for all the teenage angst you're going to experience once you get to high school."

Snow tossed the book at Elm and she caught it.

"You're just trying to scare me," Elm countered. "Anyway, I don't think it's gonna be that bad. I know most of the kids from church or Girl Scouts."

"Yeah, you do," said Snow, looking down at the sleeping cat. "And everyone knows you're the mayor's daughter. But when those kids aren't around their parents —trust me, Elm, they're different at school. Ugly things like bullying and judging and competition and social hierarchy are the norm. You'll see, Miss Romance. Lucky you have me and Noah to take care of you."

Noah!

Elm broke out in a devilish grin. "Yeah, and you better watch out, Snow Whitedove, or maybe someday I'll marry that brother of yours!"

Snow wadded up her lunch bag and threw it at Elm. "In your dreams, Sister!"

Elm had finally lost patience. She grabbed a broken branch from the floor, holding it up like a talking stick. "It's my turn now. Snow, I've got something I've been dying to tell you and I want you to listen to me."

Snow appreciated Elm's respect for tradition. "Okay.

Well, you've got a talking stick. I just hope it has nothing to do with a boy."

Elm blushed. "Yeah, it does. I mean, no, it doesn't. I mean, he's a *man*. And his name is—guess what? Royce."

Snow laughed out loud. "Royce? What is he—a car?"

Elm ignored the insult but proceeded to tell Snow about the mysterious dark man who had helped her at the marina. She told her about how *Seven* wouldn't get out of the boat and how she was having lunch and saw a black seal, but it wasn't a seal. And then she exhaled the rest of her thoughts in one dizzying breath.

"He's from Bermuda, I guess, and he's racing in the regatta and he has the whitest teeth I've ever seen and this really cool accent that I hadn't noticed before until he found me by the sea cave. I mean, after the dog thing. He said I looked like a mermaid and he was fascinated by my beauty and he called me Priestess. And then he followed me in his dinghy except I didn't know that he had a dinghy because he hid it in the cove when he saw me, and then he swam over to me and I thought he was a seal. And then he sat next to me and he smelled real good and then I saw his tattoo and it's an octopus and he told me it's his totem and I didn't want him to know that I didn't know what a totem was and he asked me if I knew that an octopus really has six legs and two arms and when something bites off their leg it will grow back even better and they're not really villains and I didn't know that either and—"

"Oh-my-god, Elm—I'm gonna bite off my own leg if you don't shut up!"

The cat meowed and jumped out the window.

"Look. Even the damn cat can't stand it," Snow joked.

Ha ha. You're so funny. Not!

"It's not funny, Snow. And I've got the talking stick, remember? And I'm not finished!"

Snow backed down. "Okay. But I'll have to break tradition again if I don't like where this is going."

Whatever.

"Snow, nothing like this has ever happened to me before. He's a *man* and he smelled real good."

"Yeah, you said that already," Snow said, ignoring protocol once again. "Except you left out the part about him being a stalker."

Elm accepted defeat and rolled the talking stick across the floor.

Thanks for not letting me talk.

"So where is this guy from, Elm?"

"He's on the *Bermuda Breeze*."

"That doesn't mean he's from Bermuda."

"I don't know where he's from," Elm admitted.

Then Snow *went there*.

"Did he do anything to you? Did he touch you?"

Elm searched for words, but she felt numb and maybe a little sick.

"Noooooo. Not really. Except, well, he did—"

"He *did* touch you!" Snow accused.

"No, no," Elm corrected. "He kissed my hand. So it was sort of a touch, I guess."

"It was sort of a mauling, you mean." Snow was shaking her head, annoyed by her friend's naïveté.

"It gave me goosebumps," Elm admitted, recalling the unfamiliar tingles. "And he wants to see me again, Snow. So what do you think?"

"I think you're bloody crazy," Snow answered. "Real stupid, too. Like, maybe I should push you out of this tree and then you'll hit your head and maybe that'll knock some sense into you!"

That was all the motivation Elm needed. She grabbed a pillow and hit Snow on the head, who grabbed another pillow and retaliated until they were both laughing and covered with feathers.

Snow looked at her watch and grimaced. "Shoot. I gotta get home. Let's do our prayer now."

The girls arose, each hugging a section of the tree trunk and chanting:

> *"Thank you for your leaves so green*
> *Stretching limbs so high above*
> *Thank you for protecting me*
> *In your violet aura love."*

As they prayed, Elm closed her eyes and listened to the birds, the insects, the boats in the water, and the whispering pines. She heard her own beating heart quickening as her mind received a clear vision of Royce's face, smiling and beckoning.

So now her best friend knew her secret, which meant that it wouldn't be long before Noah knew her secret, too.

CHAPTER 6

A T SUNSET, ELM WAS WAITING at the Seashell Carousel on Moonwater Beach, leaning against a peeling blue seahorse.

Hand-carved by Phineas Rupert, a summer visitor who donated the carousel to Little Blessing in 1876, its vibrant colors had faded long ago. The seahorse and Neptune were missing a jeweled eye and there were cracks in the scallop shell chariots and a few of the mermaids and dolphins. When Elm asked Big Dave why the town council didn't have it repaired, he said it was because their memories hadn't faded.

"What you see as old, they see as beautiful," he said.

Beautiful. And that's exactly how Elm would describe Royce. *Beautiful.* A beautiful man.

To say she was excited was an understatement. She had told her parents she was going to the movies with Snow but it was a downright lie, and it felt strange because she couldn't remember ever lying to them, except during their birthdays or Christmas when it was important to keep secrets.

So maybe lying to Mermie and Daddy means I'm just growing up. It can't be all bad.

Evening was approaching and people had abandoned the beach in favor of eating dinner or watching the latest feature at Seaview Cinema. The scent of popcorn was so strong that she could almost lick the melted butter from her fingers.

Somebody's whistling.

Elm turned around to see Royce carrying a large piece of driftwood.

"Priestess."

"Hi." *What's his name again?*

"Royce."

"Hi, Royce," she giggled, tasting his name in a synesthetic flurry of vanilla white, juicy orange, and decadent chocolate brown.

"I wasn't sure you would come," he grinned.

"I said I would."

But you're making me nervous.

"Well, I am an older man, you know," he chuckled, moving in closer.

Elm felt dizzy from his intense body heat, causing her to grab hold of the wooden seahorse to keep from falling. Royce grabbed her hand to steady her and did not let go. Her cheeks were burning and there was a strange throbbing in her vagina, like a second heartbeat.

Vagina. What a weird word.

Mermie had insisted on teaching her the correct words for her sexual body parts, which Elm found surprising coming from a woman who wore funny pink glasses and outlandish hats.

Why the heck am I thinking about Mermie when there's this beautiful, wonderful man standing in front of me, holding my hand?

For a few long moments, he stared into her eyes while

her heart pounded with an exaggerated loudness threatening to deafen the sound of the surf. Then he said, "I have something to show you. Come with me."

Still holding her hand, Royce led her to a spot at the edge of the shoreline. There was still enough daylight to see where he was pointing but all she saw was the sand and the surf.

"What am I supposed to be looking at?" Elm asked.

"Your birthday present."

Royce had drawn a ten-foot birthday card with an octopus and the words "Happy Birthday, Priestess".

"Today's not my birthday."

Royce laughed. "Not your physical birthday, but your spiritual birthday. Like the Mimic Octopus, you will change your body into any shape you wish. You will be my apprentice."

Elm shuddered. *Apprentice?* Maybe Snow was right. Maybe Royce was nothing but a creepy old stalker.

"Um, I'd better get home."

He was clutching her wrist now. "Not yet," he insisted. "I have another gift for you."

He led Elm to the center of the sand card, where he handed her a tiny white box. With trembling fingers, she opened it to find a round foil-wrapped piece of chocolate.

"What's this?"

Royce laughed. "Have you never seen chocolate?"

The surf was loud and she raised her voice to be heard. "Yeah, but my parents don't like me to have sugar!"

Why did I say that? It's not even true!

"This chocolate is magic. You'll see. Let me feed it to you."

With the wind and waves behind him, Royce carefully unwrapped the candy and rubbed it on her lips to part them. She bit down, the chocolate coating sliding like butter in her mouth.

Delicious.

What happened next caught her totally off-guard.

Royce's tongue was probing her mouth and Elm surprised herself by allowing it. After a few hot but heavenly moments, he stopped and grinned.

"Now, I've got the cherry," he said, producing the fruit between his teeth.

This was too much excitement for naive Elm to handle. Her knees buckled and she collapsed on the cool, wet sand.

"Aren't you too old to be leaving tree mail?"

Elm was in the treehouse, getting ready to return the metal box inside Miss Vi's secret knot when Noah Skyfeather Smith appeared at the entrance. The way the light was shining on his head like a halo, one would have thought he was an angel instead of an annoying busybody.

"You scared me!"

"You're easy to scare," he said, reaching for the box.

With lightning speed, Elm tucked the box under her rear and hoped he wouldn't grab for it. "Brat," she laughed.

"Bigger brat." He plopped himself down next to her, grabbing her pen from the floor and pretending to poke her with it.

"Would you stop!" she said, shooing him away. "And what are you doing here anyway? What's the password?"

"Nudophobia."

"No."

"Chromophobia."

"Wrong. I like color."

"Eisoptrophobia?"

"What's that?"

"Fear of mirrors," he snorted. "But in your case, it's a good thing 'cause your face would break the glass!"

"Ha ha—and you're wrong."

"Dendrophobia."

She shook her head. "If I was afraid of trees, I wouldn't be in a treehouse, Stupid."

"Bogyphobia."

"Who told you?"

"C'mon, Elm. I've watched you and Snowflake for years," he said, smugly. "I know that you are afraid of the bogeyman and I know where my sister keeps the secret phobia list. And I know other dirty little secrets, so you'd better watch out!"

"Jerkface!"

There was one secret Elm had never divulged to anyone and she hoped Noah was clueless. She had had a major crush on him since she was ten. Two years older than she, Noah was one of the most handsome boys in Little Blessing. He had the same shiny black hair and soulful brown eyes as his sister but was much prettier.

Do guys even like to be called pretty?

"So who's Rolls Royce?"

That blabbermouth Snow!

"Just Royce. And he's none of your business."

"But I thought you were *my* girlfriend, Elm!"

She knew Noah was messing with her. "Since when?"

He's sitting much too close to me. It isn't right. I have a boyfriend now.

"Oh, since our dads were passing out cigars the day we were born. Didn't I give you a ring, Mercy-Faith?"

He knows I hate that name.

"You mean that crummy old dandelion thing you gave

me when I was six?" Elm accused. "I threw it away. It turned brown and messed up two pages in my journal."

Noah put his arm around her and kissed her head. "But you do love me, don't you?"

It didn't feel bad for Noah to hug her, so she let him.

"No, I don't love you," she protested. "I never have."

And that was a big fat lie.

Noah looked doubtful. "Uh huh. Well, speaking of dads, I went to see Big Dave today. I asked him for a job at the marina, just for the rest of the summer and then after school. I want to buy a car so I can take my favorite girl-friend shopping, to the movies or wherever she wants to go."

"You're so full of it," said Elm, pushing his arm away.

Noah had always been a big flirt and she usually enjoyed his attention but Snow had told her she saw him making out with Sarah Lightfoot behind the Holy Cow ice cream store. Sarah's mother owned the store, which made the girl very popular with the boys.

Well, I may not have much experience with romance, but I think Noah kissing another girl should be a definite deal breaker!

"You gotta go," Elm said, grabbing the metal box. "Snow will kill me if she finds out you've been here."

She watched Noah climb from the treehouse. Once she was sure his feet had touched the ground, she replaced the metal box inside the secret knot on Miss Vi's trunk.

Noah was waiting for her. From the condition of his bicycle, Elm was surprised its rust-coated gears still worked. She supposed he did need a car because in a month's time he would be starting his senior year at Little Blessing High and he probably wanted to make a good impression with all the senior girls.

"So what did Daddy say about the job?"

"What do you think?" Noah flashed a teasing smile, looking very pleased with himself.

Elm knew the job was a shoo-in because Noah had known Big Dave his entire life. As his father's oldest friend, Big Dave was family to Noah, like having a fun uncle. He had been Noah's scoutmaster and they both had similar, easy-going dispositions.

And, of course, they both love me.

"That's great," she lied, not sure she liked the idea of Noah being on her home turf. "I guess I'll see you around."

"You'll see me alright," Noah said, moving in for a kiss. "So how about a reward, girlfriend?"

Elm was half tempted but pushed him away.

"Ewww. You're really full of yourself, you know that, Noah? I'd rather kiss—well, I'd rather kiss Snow."

"I'll bet she'd like that," he laughed, turning his bicycle around and motioning her to follow him to the main trail.

"Oh, shut up," Elm said, putting her notebook and pen in her basket. She followed Noah with her bicycle. "Hey, do you know if Snow's at home?"

Noah's eyes scanned her for clues and nodded. "She should be," he said, mounting his wobbly bike. "Dad just hired a Reiki master to help him with the animals and Snowbird's supposed to watch. Want to ride with me?"

"Okay, but no funny stuff," she warned, climbing aboard her own bicycle. "I've got to get back to Sea Angels in a few hours. But I do have something important to tell Snow."

"Yeah, yeah. But first, you had to tell Miss Vi."

Elm blushed because the statement was true. Thanks to tree mail, Miss Vi knew everything there was to know about Elm Sunday.

And the trees were always whispering.

CHAPTER 7

D*EAR MISS VI,*

Royce kissed me again today and he gave me another chocolate-covered cherry and it made my head swoon. Is that the right way to say that? Anyway, Royce says eating the chocolate is one of my initiations as a sea priestess. He's really into this sea priestess thing. I'm not sure what it all means but he's very excited about it and I like him SO much, so I listen. I let him read my palm and he said I have a short lifeline but not to worry because just like an octopus I have three hearts and can change my life whenever I want to. I told him I understood what he was saying but I really don't get it. How can anyone have three hearts?

Royce says I don't know my own power but he can teach me everything I need to know about being a priestess, even when he goes back to sea. I don't want him to think I'm a baby so I just nod my head and eat the chocolate. Of course, I would never tell Mermie or Daddy about this. They'd say I was being drugged or something. Anyway, I love you and hope you're getting all the rain and nourishment you need.

Your friend,
Elm

. . .

ELM AND NOAH RODE THEIR BICYCLES IN TANDEM, HER sparkly silvery teal next to his battered cobalt blue. She loved the pine-scented breeze on her cheeks as they made their way to Moontree's Animal Hospital, tucked away on a sprawling lane in the woods, not too far from the seedier neighborhood around Gluttony Road.

At the top of the lane was a barn-shaped wooden sign with a painted arrow and they turned, cruising down the road until they reached the veterinary clinic.

The converted barn was connected to the Smith home, a modest ranch house where Dr. Jason Moontree Smith and his late wife, Debra Waites Smith, had raised their brood of five—Storm, Autumn, Lily, Noah, and Snow.

The pair walked in and Autumn, a big girl of twenty, greeted them at the front desk. She was recently engaged and eager to talk about it.

"Hey, Elm."

"Hey, Autumn. Is Snow around?"

"I think so. Let me check."

Autumn left the room and was back in a minute. "She says she'll be right out."

"Thanks."

Autumn hadn't forgotten about Noah. "And *you!*" she cried. "Dad's been waiting for you, little brother. Where've you been, anyway?"

Noah was playing with the business cards on Autumn's desk. "Who wants to know?"

Autumn smacked his hands. "The sister who's getting married next spring," she said, puffing out her chest like a pigeon.

"Nobody cares," he said, reshuffling the heartworm

brochures in the wall rack. Then he left the room to see his father.

"Yeah? she yelled after him. "Well, you'll care if you want to be in my wedding party!"

While Elm continued to wait for Snow in the empty lobby, a furry floor show was in progress. Next to her chair was a large metal Please Adopt Me cage with three mewing kittens inside—one calico, one white, and one black. Two of the cats were tumbling with each other as their little brother climbed up the side, looking for a way to escape.

"Hey, Cutie," she said. "What's wrong?"

She leaned over to stroke the top of his little white head through the bars. "Don't worry. They'll find you a good home."

"Hey, Elm," said Autumn, waving her left hand over her desk. "Wanna see my ring?"

"Okay." *Actually, I'd rather play with the kittens.*

"Stop showing off, Autumn," said Snow, dressed in pale blue scrubs. "Nobody wants to see your stupid ol' ring." She whisked Elm outside to an empty parking space.

"Thanks, Snow."

"No problem. What's up?"

"Nothing," said Elm. "Well, something. Maybe nothing. I don't know. I'm not sure why I'm here. Maybe I should go."

Snow pretended to examine Elm's eyes. "Have you been smokin' something funny? You sound crazier than normal."

Elm glanced around and motioned for Snow to follow her to a tree stump in the yard.

"Snow, I really want to talk to you about it but not while Noah's big ears are around—"

Snow laughed and sat on the stump. "His ears are big, aren't they?"

Lowering her voice, Elm said, "Listen, I'm serious. I don't want to take the chance, alright? I'll wait and tell you at the regatta."

"That's cool, but why are you here if you're not gonna tell me why you're here?"

The way Snow put it, it did sound ridiculous but Elm couldn't help it. Just thinking about Royce canceled everything else from her mind.

"Well—uh, Noah said I could watch some woman helping the animals, so I thought I'd check it out."

Snow looked suspicious but didn't persist. "Yeah, she's a Reiki master."

"A what?"

"Jeez, you're sheltered," Snow chided. "She's an expert at Reiki. It's energy healing. This woman—Kat is her name—she just moved to Little Blessing and she's opening an office upstairs at Hallelujah House. She's showing us how to use Reiki on the animals and I'm gonna get some attunements from her so I can become a Reiki master, too. Then I'll help Dad after school."

Elm smiled at her friend's enthusiasm. Before Snow had decided to become a water carrier, it had been her life-long dream to become a veterinarian like her father.

In the examining room, Kat's hands hovered over a sick poodle. A slender black woman with beautiful waist-length hair, her eyes were half open as Jason, Snow, and Elm watched her perform the treatment for ten minutes. When she finished, the grateful pup licked her hand and everyone laughed as he stood up and raced around the room, his tail wagging.

"That was amazing," said Jason, who had just noticed that Elm had joined them. "What do you think of Reiki,

Elm?" He was in good spirits, as always. His personality was much like her father's. In fact, Big Dave had told her that if she was ever in trouble and couldn't find him, Jason Moontree Smith was the man to call.

"Wow. It's pretty cool."

"Elm, this is Kat Corrente," he said. "I think you two have something to talk about."

Elm wondered how Jason had read her thoughts, but shouldn't have been surprised. He had always been something of a mind reader.

Kat smiled and took Elm's hand. "Happy to meet you, Elm. That's an interesting name. I knew a Willow once, but you're my first Elm. Do you like trees?"

"They're okay. There's one I really like. It's a pine tree."

"Interesting energy, too," she said, releasing Elm's hand.

NOT IN ELM'S FIFTEEN YEARS HAD AN IDEA EXCITED HER more. She had already discussed it with Snow and was eager to get to Sea Angels to tell her mother.

For most of the ride, the scenery was a breezy blur until she reached Charity Street. She got her second wind at the corner, took a sharp left to the back of the store building, parked her bike next to Glorie's jeep and nearly ran inside.

"Mermie!"

Glorie was on the phone at the counter, waving at her daughter. "Yes, I know it's past due. Didn't you receive my check?"

Elm waited until her mother finished her call and then pounced. "Guess what?"

Glorie sighed. "You won the lottery and you're paying all our debts."

"No, guess again!"

"You kissed a frog who's really a prince and *he's* paying all our debts."

Elm thought about that for a moment, allowing Royce's regal image materialize for a few moments in her brain.

"No, Mermie. I found you a healer!"

Two days later, Elm and Glorie were at Hallelujah House, taking a short elevator ride to the second floor. Kat met them at the door of The Healing Wave, wearing a lilac tunic and matching trousers.

"Can my daughter stay with me?" Glorie asked. "I'm a bit nervous."

"No problem," said Kat.

She led them to a private, windowless treatment room illuminated by candles. Its desert sunset hue complemented the earthy-brown artifacts and sacred symbols displayed on the walls and shelving. In the center of the room stood a covered massage table and above it was a strange, rectangular light fixture.

"What is that?" Elm asked.

Kat beamed with pride. "It's my crystal bed."

Elm touched each of the nine clear quartz crystals, her fingers buzzing. "Are they real?"

"Absolutely."

Kat invited Glorie to touch a crystal. Fascinated, Glorie asked: "What does it do?"

"It balances your chakras and gives you an overall feeling of well-being," said Kat.

"Well-being, huh? I sure would love to have me some of that wellbeing, Sister!"

Kat laughed and took Glorie's cane, while Elm sat in a

rattan meditation chair in the corner. Kat helped Glorie remove her shoes and onto the padded massage table.

"Mrs. Sunday—"

"Glorie, please. I don't want to be confused with my mother-in-law. She's in a whole class by herself."

"Glorie, then," said Kat. "We'll do a Reiki session first, then the crystal bed."

"Kat, would you tell my mother what Reiki is?" Elm asked. "I told her my version but I'm not a Reiki master."

"Reiki helps clear and balance your chakras," Kat explained. "They're the spinning wheels of energy within all of us."

According to Kat, Reiki was a healing technique of channeling universal life energy into the body. Kat's specialty was Usui Reiki, named after its founder Mikao Usui, a spiritual teacher and healer from Japan. The method included a number of hand positions and symbols.

Kat clapped her hands to activate the tranquil background music of flutes and singing bowls. "So tell me where you've been hurting."

Glorie half-laughed. "Would I sound neurotic if I said *everywhere*?"

Kat smiled. "There's a tightness in your crown chakra," she said, holding her hands slightly above Glorie's head. After a few minutes, she asked, "How are you feeling now?"

"Like something just burst inside my head," said Glorie, amazed.

Kat's hands continued to hover, scanning Glorie's main chakras and paying extra attention to areas that she sensed were physically, mentally or spiritually blocked. At each point, she asked how Glorie was feeling.

When the Reiki had ended, Glorie burst into tears and Elm ran to her mother's side.

"What's wrong, Mermie?"

"I—I don't know," Glorie stammered.

Kat assured them it was natural for some people to cry or laugh at the end of a session. It was part of the detoxing. She gave Glorie a glass of blessed water, saying, "When you are ready, Glorie, we'll start the crystal bed session."

Elm wiped her mother's tears with a tissue. "If this is upsetting you, we can stop right now."

Glorie took a big gulp of water and handed the glass to Elm. "No, I'm ready."

"I'm glad," said Kat. "But first, you'll want to remove all your jewelry."

Elm took her mother's rings and pendant and returned to her chair, watching Kat cover Glorie with a sheet up to her neck, then placing a white silk mask filled with dried lavender buds over Glorie's eyes.

"I want you to set an intention that you are going to feel better now or whatever it is you want your intention to be," said Kat.

"I think I can handle that," Glorie agreed.

"Okay, I'm going to turn the machine on now, Glorie, and all you have to do is just lie back and concentrate on your intention. There will be different colored lights flashing through the crystals—red, orange, yellow, green, blue, indigo, violet, pink, and white. We'll do this for just twenty minutes, but you'll be surprised at how fast the time flies."

Kat flipped a switch on the machine and Glorie heard a soft humming, Kat's slippered feet walking across the floor, and then the treatment door closing.

"You still here, Elm? I can't see through this mask."

"Yes, Mermie," said Elm, propping up the pillows in

her chair. "Do you want me to talk to you while you're doing this?"

"Okay."

"Can you see the colors?" Elm asked, watching the lights flash.

"No, not really," said Glorie. "Just white light."

But Glorie was about to see more than light.

"Elm!" Glorie cried. "Elm, are you there?"

"Yes, I'm here."

"You're not going to believe this but I'm seeing all these heads floating around me. They're men—they have no bodies—and none of them look familiar. Some have mustaches, some have beards. They're very stern-looking, kind of scary. But I'm not afraid."

"That's good, Mermie. I don't want you to be afraid."

Another five minutes passed before Glorie spoke again.

"I see a different man now," she continued, dreamily. "He wants me to drink something from a silver spoon. It looks like dirty water. Yes, I think it is. And there's something floating on top, like algae."

"Is the man saying anything?" Elm asked.

"Yes," said Glorie. "He wants me to let the poison go."

"What poison?"

Kat had said the procedure would be a quick one, but Elm and Glorie were still surprised when they heard her tap on the door.

Kat helped Glorie sit up and gave her another cup of blessed water. As Glorie's head rushed from dizziness, an amazing energy was tingling throughout her body.

Glorie giggled. "Am I stoned?"

Kat laughed and said, "Well, it may feel like you are. But it's not permanent." She suggested that Glorie ground herself by hugging a tree outside the building.

Big Dave was waiting in the lobby to take them home.

As he and Elm escorted Glorie to their car, his wife stopped walking, pointing at a nearby tree.

"Wait a minute—I gotta hug that tree!"

When Glorie was finally in the passenger seat, Big Dave chuckled. "So I'm guessing this was a good experience, Mermie?"

"You bet, Baby—let's do it again!"

CHAPTER 8

T HE LITTLE GIRL WEPT AS *her mother carried her on the winding path, through the German forest, and up the mountain to the monastery. She closed her eyes and buried her face in her mother's neck, not bearing to look at the medieval stone structure which would become her home for the rest of her life.*

While Elm dreamed, the solar-powered, crystal suncatcher hummed in the window, the morning sunlight splattering rainbows across her head. Big Dave stood at the foot of his daughter's lavender and turquoise bed, watching her curl up into a fetal position and clutch her stuffed dolphin in a tight hold.

"Hey, Babycakes," her father whispered.

Elm did not stir.

"Elm."

Still nothing.

Glancing around the room, he reached for the seahorse feather duster next to the aquarium and tickled her forehead. "Mercy-Faith."

Elm scrunched her nose and turned over on her back. "What's wrong?"

"Nothing's wrong," he assured her. "Good morning, Sleepyhead."

"Morning."

With one eye open, Elm rolled over to view the clock. There was a new affirmation taped over its face:

My body is a magnificent Rainbow.

Elm groaned, pulling the covers over her head, knowing full well that she could never hide from "Daddy Lighthouse. "It had been her secret name for her father ever since she was four and had wandered away at the annual seafood festival. Like a beacon, her father's near-blinding grin shone through the crowd, his blond head taller than the rest as he came forth to rescue his sobbing daughter.

While Elm snoozed, Big Dave browsed through her small library of sea glass books. Elm was born on July 19, a Cancer, so she was naturally drawn to the water, which was evident from her collection of water globes and seashells. Like her mother, Elm loved coastal colors and had decorated her harborview bedroom in shimmery hues of coral, lavender, and turquoise.

"Are you still here?" Elm moaned.

"Always," he smiled. "Happy Regatta Day!"

THE LITTLE BLESSING CLEAN REGATTA attracted thousands of spectators during the second weekend in August. For contestants like the *Bermuda Breeze*, it was a respected warm-up race for larger, better-known regattas in Nantucket and Newport.

To accommodate the large crowds, the local *Sea Crystal*

Ferry had extended its service to include four roundtrips from Boston. The first race didn't begin until 11 a.m., but there were other activities beforehand. Registrants checked in at 8 a.m., the Parade of Sail was at 9 a.m., and the food and craft vendors at Purity Park officially opened at 10 a.m., closing down at 5 p.m.

At the end of the ferry ramp, Elm and Snow sat at a long, yellow-draped table under a white tent, passing out regatta schedules and maps to ferry passengers. They were wearing their brand new royal blue polo shirts with the Little Blessing emblems (a cross on a sailboat) on the pocket. Royal blue was a good color for Elm because it tasted like dark chocolate-covered blueberries and she liked blueberry anything.

"I can't believe we got stuck over here again," Snow grumbled as she half-smiled at people. "But we're close to the Fries Guy and the soap lady and I can almost see Miss Vi, so that's something."

"Yeah, I know," said Elm. "But we missed the Parade of Sail because we had to set up and I wanted to see Royce before the parade to wish him luck. Now I can't."

Snow handed a young couple an information packet, then turned to Elm. "Why are you still messing with this guy? He's old enough to be your father."

"No, he's not." Elm hadn't even thought of the age difference before.

"Okay, but he's old, Elm. Like, *real* old. And he's gonna be gone after the race anyway, so then what happens?"

"We already figured it out," said Elm, reaching under the table to retrieve more packets from a box. "We'll talk online. And then he'll come back next year and I'll be older and more mature."

"Mature?" her friend snickered. "You might think so, but you'll still be underage."

A woman with a map in her hand interrupted their conversation. "Excuse me, but where can I find the public bathrooms?"

While Snow highlighted the privies on the map, Elm thought about the weekend ahead and wondered how she was going to see Royce again without her parents finding out.

MOST OF THE SHOPS ON CHARITY STREET WERE OPEN during the regatta, including Sea Angels. Glorie had hired Cassie Hamilton, the daughter of the town's postmaster, Fisher Hamilton, to assist her for the rest of the summer. Cassie wasn't as creative as Elm, but she was always punctual and polite to the customers and willing to don the mermaid costume for the occasional "Under the Sea" birthday party.

"So this is your shop," said Kat Corrente, dressed in a pale green tunic and white capris. "I love the colors."

Glorie beamed. "Thank you. And welcome to mermaid paradise."

Kat laughed. "I can see that." She paused to look at the *Vitamin Sea by E* display and draped a sea glass bracelet over her wrist. "This is pretty. Is the designer local?"

"Very local," said Glorie. "Elm makes them. You remember my daughter?"

Kat placed the bracelet and her credit card on the counter. "I do. Long red hair, sweet energy. Is she here?"

Glorie took the credit card and processed it. "Not today. She's working the information booth at Purity Park."

"Too bad," said Kat, picking up a starfish soap and adding it to her purchase. "Well, please tell her I love this bracelet and I think she's very talented." Kat signed the credit card slip and added, "Oh—and I'm sorry I didn't get to say 'hi' to her the other night."

"The other night?" Glorie was confused.

"Yes," said Kat. "I was walking on the beach when I saw her by the carousel with a man. It looked like she was having a pretty good time."

WHILE SNOW WATCHED OVER THEIR BOOTH, ELM TOOK A bathroom break. She hated the portable toilets—they were hot and stinky and sometimes shared with bees—but they were conveniently located about fifty yards away from their table. Fortunately, the line was short, so she was in and out in less than ten minutes.

Snow seemed okay, so Elm decided to investigate the craft vendor area.

Jewelry. Candles. Soaps. Lotions. Scrimshaw. Sea glass ornaments. Marine photography. Pirate paraphernalia.

Elm stopped when she came to a rainbow display of mermaid tail pajamas for toddlers. She couldn't resist stroking the soft cotton material.

"Hi," Elm said to the woman behind the table. "Do you make these?"

The woman smiled and stood, anticipating a sale. "I sure do. But you're too big for these, Honey. Are you a mother?"

Blushing, Elm said, "I'm only fifteen."

"Well, you never know these days. Anyway, I'm having a special this weekend, just for the regatta. Buy three and get one free."

"Thank you," said Elm, "but I don't babysit anyone

with kids that small. It's too bad because they're really, really cute. Actually, my mom has a mermaid store here in Little Blessing." She reached into her little change purse and handed the vendor a Sea Angels business card. "Please call her. I know she'll go crazy over these."

The vendor thanked her and Elm continued strolling past the kaleidoscope of tents until she had reached The Shell Seer. It was a beautiful booth with a large painted backdrop of a tropical beach.

"Would you like to meet your seashell partner today?"

Elm was startled to find the seer standing next to her.

"Um, I'm just looking, thanks."

"I know you're busy, young lady, but do you have ten minutes?"

Elm glanced at her pink and turquoise watch. She still had some time.

"Okay. But what's a seashell partner?"

She sat across from the seer, whose reading table was a huge nautilus with a mirrored top displaying an assortment of seashells. The pale blond woman was dressed from head to toe in varying shades of turquoise and Elm thought her skin actually glowed with light. Unlike some of the fortune tellers she had seen, this woman was not theatrical or creepy.

"I will show you. My name is Angel, by the way. What's yours?"

Now that I think about it, you do look like an angel. And your name looks sparkly pink with a bit of gold. Tastes like strawberry mousse with candied orange peel.

"My name is Elm."

"Very pretty name," said the seer, moving her seashells across the table. "It's one of my favorite trees." She stopped what she was doing and looked deep into Elm's eyes. "Elm, are you familiar with seashell divination?"

"Never heard of it."

Angel smiled. "That's okay. Well, let me explain. I have a different technique from other readers you might know." She waved her hand over the shells. "You see these seashells? What I'd like you to do, Elm, is to choose three of them and then I will tell you your past, present, and future."

"From the seashells." Elm stifled a laugh.

"Yes."

Elm looked up to see if Snow was waving at her. She wasn't. "Okay. So how many are there?"

"Forty-four," said Angel. "But three of them are meant just for you. Are you ready to choose?"

CHAPTER 9

AFTER THE REGATTA THAT EVENING, Elm was scheduled to babysit the Lightfoot twins, while their mother went to a late night Red Hat Society party at the Good Book Tea Room.

Hannah Lightfoot was the founder of the Little Blessing chapter and so far there were five members. Elm wished Glorie would join the Red Hats because they were always doing something fun and she felt her mother needed some fun to take her mind off her disease. And Glorie liked to wear wacky hats.

Willie and Mary were cute seven-year-olds who had tons of toys and lots of energy. (Mrs. Lightfoot often referred to them as *Vanilla* and *Strawberry* for their different hair colors.) They could be a handful but they were also very sweet and Elm wondered why Mrs. Lightfoot, a widow, never had her older daughter Sarah babysit her siblings in the evening.

I guess she's probably too busy kissing Noah.

Elm didn't like thinking about Noah. He irritated her. She'd rather daydream about Royce.

After she put the kids to bed and washed the dishes, she sat at the kitchen table to write a letter to her very best friend.

> *Dear Miss Vi,*
>
> *You wanna know something? I'm in love. I know I said that about Noah but I was a baby before and now I'm grown up. This is real love. Snow says I need to forget about Royce but I think she's just jealous. She says I've only known Royce for a week, but the funny thing is I feel like I've known him forever. I wish Snow understood that.*

Elm thought she heard someone giggling. Usually, the twins would wake up at least once, but she checked and they were sound asleep. She was heading back to the kitchen when she heard the giggling again. It was coming from Sarah's bedroom so she quietly opened the door and flipped on the light.

Elm was disgusted by the orange bedroom walls and the sight of a half-dressed Sarah lying on her bed with Jordan Hamilton, the postmaster's seventeen-year-old son. Elm assumed the couple had sneaked in through Sarah's bedroom window.

"What are you doing in my room, Elm Sunday?" Sarah screamed. "Get out!"

Elm shut the door, wondering how long Sarah had been home and if Noah knew that Sarah was two-timing him. As annoying as Noah could be, Elm thought he deserved to know the truth.

Not that I really care.

WHEN ELM AWOKE THE NEXT DAY, SHE KNEW SHE HAD TO

find Royce before the regatta. She had to tell him about the seer.

She was out the door by six, making her way down the pier, past an array of sail and motor boats until she found the slip where *Bermuda Breeze* gently rocked.

Royce sat alone on deck in a full lotus pose with his eyes closed, welcoming the golden rays of the sun.

"Permission to come aboard, Captain," she said, saluting.

Is that cute enough?

Royce smiled, opening one eye and then the other. "I'm not the captain, but I'm sure he'd want a sea priestess aboard."

Elm giggled and cozied up next to him. The cool morning turned hot very quickly because the electrical current between the two was instant, like magnets. Being with Royce was an intense experience—she couldn't explain it—but she knew she didn't want it to end. Not ever.

"So, guess what happened to me yesterday, Royce."

"You became more beautiful?"

"No. A woman read my seashells!" she blurted.

"Cowries?"

"There might have been one there, but she had different kinds of shells," Elm said, removing a folded piece of paper from her pocket to read. "I had to pick three of them. For my past, I picked a Sea Biscuit. It means I'm too concerned about what other people think."

"Intriguing. What else did she say?"

Elm was delighted that Royce seemed genuinely interested.

"Well, for my present, I picked the Angel Wing. It's real pretty and it really does look like an angel wing. Oh, and did I tell you that the seer's name is Angel? Pretty cool, huh? Anyway, the Angel Wing says I'm feeling trapped."

"Not surprising."

Elm knew she was speaking too fast again but couldn't help it. *I'm with Royce!*

"And then the shell I picked for my future is—oh, heck, I can't read my own writing. Something about a turkey. Oh, yeah. It's called a Turkey Wing Ark and it means I will be acting badly and must change my behavior immediately."

Royce laughed and smacked his lips. "I've always liked my turkey wings."

Elm bumped against his shoulder and he tickled her. "Seriously, Royce. Do you think I'm going to turn evil?"

He looked deep into her eyes and she thought she would swoon. "I think—" he began, "that evil is a matter of perspective."

"Elm Sunday!"

Noah stood on the pier with his arms crossed. He had on his official Sunday's Marina garb—a crisp white shirt, khaki shorts, and navy cap—and he was glaring at her.

"What?" she yelled.

"I need to talk to you," Noah barked. "Right now!"

"Why?"

"Get off that boat and I'll tell you!"

Annoyed, Elm reluctantly left Royce's side, who had already become engaged in conversation with his sleepy crewmate, Stewart. As she stepped on the dock, she overheard Stewart say something about *jailbait* and Royce's distinct ha-ha-ha-ha laugh.

"What do you want, Noah?" His name usually tasted like sweet caramel corn but it was stale and tasteless today.

"Walk with me," he ordered.

"Why should I?"

You don't own me.

"Just do it, Elm!"

They walked to the opposite side of the marina until they were at the picnic gazebo. Then Noah grabbed her arm and said, "Now what the *hell* were you doing over there?"

Elm made a sour face, trying to shake off his grip. "Nothing. I wasn't doing anything. Don't you have some work to do?"

Noah glanced at his watch. "I've got some time. Listen, Elm, that guy's at least ten years older than you."

"So?"

"So it looks bad."

Elm rolled her eyes. "So maybe I don't care what you think, Noah Skyfeather!"

He finally released her arm. "Well, I care and you should, too, Elm Sunday. You know this is a small town. Everybody talks around here and you're the mayor's daughter."

"So?"

"So you've got to be extra careful of everything you do and say," Noah warned. "Otherwise, it will be a bad reflection on Big Dave and Mermic and your grandmother and all the other Sundays around here."

Elm turned to face the water. "I said I don't care. Weren't you listening?"

Noah was relentless, spinning her around to face him.

"The Elm Sunday I know has always cared. You care about your parents and your friends and your dogs and the marina and Miss Vi and you even care about all those whiny little kids you babysit. I've seen you cry over dead birds and terrorism in the Middle East and when that elf died in that Harry Potter movie. People might say you're skinny and spacey but the one thing—the one thing they never say is you don't care."

And do they ever say you're ignorant and getting on my nerves?

"Well, so what?" she challenged. "I'm fifteen now and it's my life and I'm gonna do what I wanna do."

"Yeah, it's your life all right but you were definitely flirting with that guy—in broad daylight—and it's not right and you know it and I'm telling you to stop it right now or someone might get hurt."

"Oh, I'm so scared," Elm retorted. "Look, you don't own me, Noah. So why don't you just leave me alone and go find your girlfriend Sarah so you can suck on those stupid cow lips somemore!"

Noah's eyes flashed. "You shut up about Sarah. I'm talkin' about you, brat. Just stay away from this guy. And stop rolling your eyes at me. Do you hear me, *Mercy-Faith*?"

Enough with the Mercy-Faith!

"You know what?" she said. "Your girlfriend Sarah is cheating on you!"

Then she turned and ran back to apologize to Royce.

IN THE HEAT OF THE MOMENT, ELM HAD FORGOTTEN THAT voices carry. She didn't notice Glorie sitting at the white cafe table on their second story balcony, typing the content for her website's "About Us" section on her computer.

"Beautiful day."

Big Dave stood in the doorway, wearing a white shirt and khaki shorts, his sailor's tan complementing his clear blue eyes. He saw Glorie's near empty tea cup and asked, "Can I get you a bagel and more tea before I go?"

"No more tea, but a bagel and maybe some juice

sounds great," she said. "Before you go, did you happen to hear our daughter screaming at Noah?"

"No, I guess I missed that," he said. "And I'm sure it wasn't *our* daughter, Mermie."

Glorie sipped the rest of her tea. "Well, all I know is she was yelling at poor Noah over something. I have no idea what it was about, do you?"

"A lover's spat?" he teased, giving her a quick hug.

"Oh, God, I hope not."

Sea Angels is situated in the tiny artists' colony of Little Blessing. Conveniently reached by ferry, we are one of a dozen unique shops and galleries on Charity Street. (The town's only shopping district.)

Sea Angels is located on the ground floor of Hallelujah House, a converted Victorian hotel situated directly across from beautiful Moonwater Beach.

Surrounding businesses are The Good Book Tea Room, Blowhard's Flags and Banners, Little Blessing Art Gallery, Carousel Boutique, Holy Cow Sundaes, Blessed Coffee and Bakery, Saltwater Souvenirs, Ocean Gemstones, Charity Street Candles, Sunday Best Clothing Store, Ye Very Olde Antiques, Vanity Hair Salon, Little Blessing Community Bank, and Seaview Cinema.

The pleasantness of the morning was interrupted by a chorus of screams and laughter below. Glorie leaned over to get a better look at the swarm of children descending upon the picnic area like hungry flies. They were running around the picnic tables while their pot-bellied father prepared the grill to cook steak and hamburgers.

"Here ya go."

Big Dave had returned from the kitchen with a napkin-covered breakfast tray. The honey-nut cream cheese was piled high on her toasted cinnamon-raisin bagel and there was a wooden skewer of fresh pineapple, orange, and cherry in her orange juice.

"Dave, did you ever notice that some people eat hamburgers in the morning?"

"Unfortunately, yes."

She picked up her bagel and took a bite. "I don't know why but it's kind of turning my stomach today."

Her husband grinned. "Are you thinking of becoming vegetarian, Mermie?"

"Maybe," she said, brushing the crumbs from the corner of her mouth. "Oh, probably not," she laughed. "I don't think I have the willpower to join you on the Dark Side."

"You mean 'The Light Side,' right?" he chuckled.

She took another sip of juice. "Whatever you say, Dear."

A few minutes later, Glorie heard the front door close and watched the top of her husband's blond head bouncing along the deck towards Noah, who held a container of coffee in one hand and a walkie-talkie in the other. As they strolled along the pier, one of the boat owners approached them and they stopped to shake hands.

Glorie finished off her bagel and returned to her writing, but it was difficult to concentrate. Despite the early hours, the radio music was annoyingly loud. Two boats —*Mad Max* and *Bite Me*—seemed to be battling for the title of "Most Annoyingly Loud Boat in Little Blessing".

"Good morning, Boating Community! Well, it's Day Two of the fifth annual Little Blessing Clean Regatta, featuring over fifty vessels from around the world, all powered by wind or sun..."

The radio announcer continued his update and then Glorie heard a familiar laugh in the distance.

Her eyes followed the voice and saw Elm sitting on the deck of *Bermuda Breeze*, engaged in deep conversation with a thin, dark-skinned man who appeared to be holding her hand.

"What are you doing with that man, Elm Sunday?" Glorie said to herself. "Stop playing with fire and get your butt off that boat!"

Glorie reached for her phone but changed her mind when she saw Elm waving goodbye to the sailor. Relieved, she swore that she would never allow this man to hurt her little girl.

CHAPTER 10

E LM HAD BEEN SUMMONED.
        Bicycling to Ruth's house, she wondered what
"The Pray Lady" had in mind. Ruth had never been the
loving, cookie-making grandmother type and did not
encourage visits from her granddaughter except for holi-
days and Ruth's birthday.

*She must have heard about what happened at school. She must
have heard about me and Royce.*

Transitioning from homeschooling to public school can
be daunting for most teenagers but Elm's first day at
George Sunday High School was tougher than expected.
The mayor's daughter had gained a reputation as "that girl
who was messing around with that black man at the
regatta."

In every class, Elm was taunted with stares and whis-
pers. Students would trip her in the hallways, throw their
lunches at her, one girl even screamed at her. Elm doubted
she could tolerate this kind of treatment for the next two
years.

Unfortunately, homeschooling was no longer an option

for Elm because her Lyme-diseased mother had been bedridden since Labor Day. Glorie had closed Sea Angels for the season because she was having a hard time reading and often spoke in gibberish. So Elm knew she had to make the best of things at school.

It wasn't easy.

At the end of her first day, Elm was disgusted to find a Bible verse taped to her locker door:

The name of the righteous is used in blessings,
but the name of the wicked will rot.

Later, when they had met up at Miss Vi's, Elm complained to Snow about "the worst day of my life."

"Why do people have to be so mean?" said Elm, munching on an almond butter-smeared apple slice she had saved from lunch. "I'm not hurting anybody. You'd think they never saw a black man before."

"Uh huh." Snow was busy sketching her self-portrait in her notebook.

Elm crumpled up her lunch bag and threw it at Snow. "Are you even listening?"

Snow put her drawing aside. "Yeah, unfortunately. Look, open your eyes, Elm. Little Blessing isn't the most progressive community, you know? The only so-called minorities living here are the Moonwaters and there are only about forty of us. And it's not like you ever knew a black person before this Rolls Royce guy, so don't act like you know everything. People are gonna hate what they don't understand. And what they don't understand, they're afraid of."

Elm thought about Snow's comment as she was riding to Ruth's house. Could Royce be the reason why Ruth had summoned her? Clearly, her grandmother was a judgmental, intolerant person. Had she heard the rumors?

Elm parked her bicycle on the private street in front of the former sea captain's home, leaving her lightweight jacket in the basket. She rang the doorbell and stepped back, recalling a time when she was nine and had been summoned to spend the weekend with her grandmother.

Apparently, Ruth felt it was time to bond with her only grandchild. But the visit proved disappointing. They didn't bake cookies or plant flowers or talk about school or sew dresses for her dolls. Not only was Elm not allowed to sing or laugh or play, but she was forced to spend most of the weekend either reading the Bible or being quizzed on the Bible by her grandmother.

Each night would end with a cold supper and an eight o'clock bedtime. Unfortunately, Elm's slumber would be interrupted by the ghost of Captain Marcus Brewer, the first owner of the house, built in 1811. He never spoke to Elm, but she found it beyond creepy to have a strange old man sitting on the edge of the bed, stroking her strawberry gold locks and humming.

A woman with white hair and a grim expression opened the door.

"Are you Mercy-Faith?" the woman asked, her voice croaking. She wore a pair of bifocals attached to a chain that kept slipping off her nose.

"Yes, Mrs. Cotton," said Elm, nodding to her former Sunday School teacher.

She acts like she doesn't know me. Weird.

"My mother said my grandmother wanted to see me."

"Mrs. Sunday is in the parlor."

When did Grandma get a parlor?

Going inside, the first thing Elm saw was the huge wooden cross that hung on the wall in the foyer, setting an intimidating tone for the entire dwelling, which could have easily been an extension of the old Grace Church of the Ascension with its stark white walls and mahogany floors, doors, and windows. Elm had not ventured far before Ruth's voice thundered from the living room.

"Mercy-Faith, come here!"

Elm was surprised to see a group of stern-looking women staring at her. She recognized them as ladies from the church.

"Sit down in that chair," said Ruth, pointing to a chair in the middle of the circle.

What the heck is this?

Elm sat on the hard chair, painfully aware that the women were glaring. She felt her face burning and looked down at her sneakers, noticing that one of the laces was loose.

"Look at me, girl," Ruth commanded. "I want to see those lying devil eyes."

I'm not looking. I'm not looking.

"Do you know why you are here, Mercy-Faith?"

"No, but I want to go home."

"You will go nowhere," said Ruth. "Mercy-Faith, you are a sinner before Almighty God. You have committed indecent acts with a man of foreign birth and you must be punished."

Punished?!

"Don't you touch me!" Elm screamed, her eyes darting around the room.

"Silence, sinner!" It was Mrs. Warren, the church choir mistress. "Okay, good ladies. Let us turn to our Puritan hymnals and sing Number Thirteen!"

Singing? This is crazy!

There was a ruffling of pages, then Mrs. Warren blew on her pitch pipe, prompting the women to sing:

> "Hasten, O sinner! To be wise,
> And stay not for the morrow's sun;
> The longer wisdom you despise.
> The harder is it to be won."

The women sang four choruses. By the time they reached *"For fear the curse should thee arrest,"* Ruth was standing behind Elm, digging her bony hands into her granddaughter's shoulders. "Sinner girl, do you now repent?"

The pain of Ruth's claws cutting into Elm's skin made the girl angrier. She jumped out of the chair and kicked it across the room.

"Hell no, I don't repent—and I'm leaving, so get the hell out of my way!"

The women gasped, collectively. "Did she just swear at us?" In their ideology, cursing was a great sin.

"Enough of this, Ruth," said one of the women. "It's time Mercy-Faith was punished."

"What kind of punishment?" Elm half-expected the old ladies to wheel out the wooden stocks.

"We're talking about baptism," said Ruth.

"I've already been baptized—as a baby. You were there, Grandma—I've seen the pictures!"

Ruth's sanctimonious expression did not change as two women grabbed a screaming Elm by the arms and rushed her to the bathroom. She continued to scream as they removed her clothing and pushed her into a full tub of cold water, dunking her head several times.

Help me, Daddy Lighthouse! Help me!

Ruth and the other women stood outside the bathroom, chanting: "Repent! Repent! Repent!"

Oh, Jesus, let me die.

The women left Elm weeping in the bathtub. Elm

could hear their muffled voices and the sounds of cars driving away outside.

When she found the strength, she got out and towel-dried, examining the bruises on her body.

Great. Just great.

Ruth was waiting in the living room in her rocking chair, reading the Bible. "Where are you going, Mercy-Faith?" she quizzed, in a somber tone, not lifting her eyes from the page.

I could barely get my clothes on because I hurt so bad and she acts like nothing happened.

"I'm getting out of here," Elm retorted. "And you know what, Grandma?"

"What's that, girl?"

"I'm never, *ever* gonna speak to you again!"

Enraged, Elm pedaled directly to Miss Vi. She had decided to camp overnight in the treehouse because she just couldn't face Big Dave after what his mother had done.

But I don't want Mermie and Daddy to worry.

She dialed the house number and left a message, saying she had left Ruth's house and was spending the night with Miss Vi.

It wasn't until Elm was plumping up the musty pillows that she realized she had not stopped for food. She reached for Snow's old sleeping bag for warmth and looked out the window, trying not to think of her stomach rumbling.

Elm had always loved the dreamy, magical color of twilight. In Little Blessing, it was a violet-gold hue melding into a hazy dark blue. It tasted like root beer. She looked towards the town, illuminated in its electric glow, and considered all the people who were judging her.

Am I really evil?

~

"Breakfast time! Hey, anybody up there?"

Elm wiped the sleep from her eyes and poked her head out the doorway. "I'm here, Daddy. Come on up!"

Miss Vi shook as Big Dave climbed to the treehouse. When Elm saw him, she hungrily grabbed the bag from his hands, pulling out a warm cinnamon sugar donut and shoving it in her mouth.

Laughing, Big Dave said, "Hey, be careful not to choke on that. There's a couple of them in there. And I've got a thermos jug with hot chocolate, too."

"Thank you," Elm said, her mouth full. "Did you happen to bring any napkins?"

"Napkins?" Big Dave reached inside his jacket pocket and pulled out two napkins, wiping the sugar from his daughter's face.

Another donut and a cup of hot chocolate later, Elm was finally feeling human again. And ashamed.

"Sorry about the message," she said, wriggling out of her jacket, which was quite damp.

Her father was staring at the bruises on her arms. "And what happened here?"

"You really don't want to know, Daddy."

"Were you in an accident?"

"Not really. Let's forget about it, okay?"

Unfortunately, Big Dave was not willing to let it go.

"Elm, if someone hurt you, I need to know. Do you want me to call the sheriff?"

"Not if you want to arrest your own mother."

So now I've done it.

Big Dave was stunned, as if the breath had been knocked out of him. "Okay, let's get you home."

They put her bicycle in the van and drove the entire way home in silence.

On Monday in the school cafeteria, Elm recounted the full story to Snow.

"Wow, you're lucky they didn't brand you or cut off your ear," said Snow, devouring an overcooked cheeseburger with greasy fries.

Three boys and a girl stopped at Elm's table, making faces and chanting: "Repent! Repent!"

"Just ignore them," said Snow.

"Repent! Repent!"

Snow threw her tray at the group and they ran away. She finished her sandwich and noticed Elm staring at her.

"What?"

"You said to ignore them," said Elm.

"I never said I follow my own advice," Snow laughed. "Seriously, Elm, those old bats are crazy. And they're abusing you in the name of religion. It's sick."

After finally taking a bite of her grilled cheese sandwich, Elm shook her head and said, "Yeah, I know, but I feel sorry for Daddy. His mother is a real monster. I mean, I knew she was tough and Mermie never liked her, but I just never realized how horrible she could be." She pushed her sandwich plate aside and added, "I don't know how Daddy puts up with her."

"Your father is a saint," said Snow, reaching for Elm's sandwich.

There was a commotion in the back of the room and Snow turned around. Two students were conversing with a teacher and pointing in Snow's direction. The teacher nodded and marched towards her.

"Uh oh," said Snow. "I think I'm about to get detention. Maybe you, too."

Elm didn't doubt it. And she was beginning to hate the people of Little Blessing and their gossipy ways.

But go ahead and threaten me with Bible verses. Pray for my soul and dunk me in the water until I'm almost drowned. Attack me any way you want, but you will never stop me from loving my Royce!

CHAPTER 11

*I*N ELM'S DREAM, SHE STOOD *in the center of a large office, watching hundreds of people push in like cattle. It was obvious there would soon be no room to breathe. Why hadn't they booked a gym or auditorium of some kind?*

She was in charge of the auditions, but she didn't know what the audition was for. She reached for a phone and called a department. The person she spoke to had no idea what the audition was about, either.

And yet the people continued to pour in, carrying their headshots and bios. Children. Adults. Seniors. They all pleaded for her attention, but she didn't know what to do with them. Should she give them numbers? Have them fill out forms? Who would go first? It was a madhouse and she had no idea what she was doing.

October arrived in Little Blessing with all its usual coppery bravado. One of Elm's favorite events was the Harvest Fair, held during Columbus Day weekend at the farm of her great-uncle Nicholas Abbott. She was looking forward to getting lost in the corn maze, eating caramel apples, and hanging out with Snow at the Moonwaters tribal booth.

It had been fun helping Snow make smudge sticks from the fresh sage, lavender, and sweetgrass that grew around the animal clinic. They had met at Snow's house the previous Saturday, where they assembled their wares outside on a picnic table. Elm was impressed by Snow's knowledge about Mother Earth and what ailed Her. Thanks to the Reiki II certification she had received from Kat, Snow could now infuse her herbal sprays and ointments with healing Reiki energy. Snow intended to become a Reiki Master and there was no doubt in Elm's mind that her friend was well on her way to becoming a great healer.

Snow also knew a lot about dreams and had promised to show Elm how to make a dreamcatcher some weekend. Being a Moonwater, Snow specialized in dreamcatchers with a water theme. She had already made twelve of them for the booth and they were all beautiful, varying in sizes and colors. Elm's favorite was the starfish dreamcatcher with white feathers, aqua beads, and cobalt ribbons.

"I've got a question," Elm said, wrapping organic cotton string around a bundle of dried sage leaves. "What does it mean when you dream about being in charge of an audition but you don't know what it's for?"

Snow frowned, annoyed that some of her lavender buds were falling out of her bundle. Normally, she would make her smudge sticks from fresh herbs but the fair was a week away and the herbs needed at least two weeks to dry. "An audition, huh? Like a play or dance or something?"

"I guess." Elm tightened the string, trimmed the ends and set her sage bundle next to the others.

"Well, did you look it up in that dream dictionary I gave you for your birthday?"

"Yeah, but it only talks about me auditioning, not leading it."

"Okay," said Snow, reaching for a handful of dried

lavender. "Well, it sounds like you're about to make a huge life change but you're freaking out about it because you don't think you're qualified to handle it. Like, maybe you don't think you're mature enough."

Elm thought about what Snow said. And then she thought about Royce, who had been emailing Elm once a week since August.

She longed to hear him profess his love for her but he never did. Alternatively, he wrote about his travels, regattas, and the drunken exploits of his crew mates. And when he did get personal, it was only to advise her on which websites and books would be of great benefit in her quest to becoming a powerful sea priestess.

Well, if I'm mature enough to have an older boyfriend who lives on the sea and can't be with me until next August, I think I'm mature enough to handle anything.

ON ANY NORMAL WEEKDAY AT 10:30 A.M., ELM WOULD have been daydreaming at her school desk, ignoring her English Literature teacher's tiresome lecture about the genius of Jane Austen or John Steinbeck.

Instead, she was two hours away in High City, sitting in an armless gray chair in the hospital waiting room and getting nauseous from the smell of rubbing alcohol.

"Mr. Sunday has early-onset Alzheimer's disease."

The doctor was very matter-of-fact about her diagnosis, as if it was as common as a cold or flu.

"What did you say?" Glorie's voice was quivering.

"He has Alzheimer's, Mermie."

Elm tried to remain composed, but her eyes filled with tears. It was bad enough for one parent to be losing their memory. Now she had two.

Glorie sighed, sinking down in one of the chairs and leaning her cane against the seat next to her. "Is this because he forgot to let the dogs out the other day?"

"That, and some other things we've been concerned about," said Dr. Rafael. "He's changing back into his street clothes and will join you soon. We've already told him what is happening."

Elm was thinking back to a few weeks ago when she was in the marina office and found Big Dave staring at the phone while it just rang and rang.

"But he's going to be okay, right?" she asked.

The doctor had already left and Glorie could not answer. Instead, she held onto Elm and wept while Elm worried. Her parents were both in their late forties and they both had neurological conditions. How much longer could they function? And who the heck would take care of her when they couldn't function any longer? She was still in high school, for Chrissakes.

It was a long drive home.

Elm sat in the passenger's seat, not feeling comfortable about her mother driving. Occasionally, she would look back at her father, who was sound asleep. He had always been her hero and it was difficult to imagine he was losing his mind and would never get better. In fact, it was often said that Little Blessing didn't need the internet because Big Dave was a walking, talking encyclopedia. Ask him a question about politics, nature, current affairs—even the love life of the most popular boy band—and he'd rattle off the answer without hesitation.

Eight years before, father and daughter had been sitting on the couch, watching a television documentary about a mariner's search for mermaids and sea serpents.

"Daddy, do you think mermaids really exist?"

"Definitely," Big Dave said, grabbing a handful of

popcorn from the metal bowl between them. "I know this is true because one of them is sound asleep in the bedroom."

Elm grimaced. "No, Daddy," she pressed. "I mean, for real."

"For real, huh?" he asked, not taking his eyes off the television. "Okay, then let me ask you this. What does your heart tell you?"

"My heart doesn't talk, Daddy."

"Doesn't it? Okay, then what does your intuition tell you?"

"Oh," she said, proud that she understood the word. "My *intuition* says it's probably true."

"So, there's your answer," he said, pointing to the television screen.

"Then why can't I see them?" Elm asked, disappointed that the investigative crew's mermaid looked like a sea elephant.

"Because they're in a different dimension, Sweetie."

Big Dave was knowledgeable about subjects that most men did not talk about. Besides mermaids, he also knew a lot about angels. He taught Elm about seven of the most well-known archangels—Michael, Raphael, Gabriel, Chamuel, Uriel, Jophiel, and Zadkiel.

Every night before she went to sleep, Elm would ask Archangel Michael to protect her, her parents, their dogs, Snow, Noah, Jason, and Grandmother Ruth. She also asked Michael to post angels at every doorway and window of their home, and watch over all the boats in the marina.

Elm asked Michael to protect her from nightmares, so she was surprised when her dreams became a bit darker as she grew older. She had never been afraid of the water, but she was often drowning in her dreams and this alarmed her.

Big Dave had an answer for this, too. "Send love to the water, Elm. Always love."

It was Glorie's decision to keep the diagnosis a secret as long as they could. This bothered Elm, but she agreed that her father's reputation as mayor, businessman, and model citizen was at stake. They debated on whether they should share the information with Ruth, but Big Dave said he didn't want to worry her and that was the end of that discussion.

Elm spent every night at at her computer, searching through Alzheimer's forums for a glimmer of hope. Unfortunately, none of the posters had anything positive to say. Patients never got better, they only got worse, and this information frightened the teenager. Living without the greatest, most loving person Elm had ever known was inconceivable.

The day of reckoning came when Ruth learned about Big Dave's condition. One evening at home, Elm overheard her mother in a heated telephone exchange. She could tell Glorie had reached her boiling point because she had her on speaker and was volleying with her strongest Southern sass.

"Well, thank y'all for calling," said Glorie.

"What are you doing, Gloria?"

"I'm tired and I'm hanging up," said Glorie. "You've told me how you feel, I heard you, and I'm done."

"Well, I'm not!" Ruth sputtered.

"My mistake," said Glorie. "I thought you had reached your daily quota for berating your daughter-in-law." Then she whistled "Onward, Christian Soldiers."

"Stop that!"

"Why?" Glorie asked innocently. "Aren't you marching off to war?"

Good one, Mermie!

"I should expect something like that from a Catholic," said Ruth.

"Thank you," Glorie retorted. "I aim to please."

"I'm glad to hear that because I'm not finished talking about David. You can't imagine how I felt when I heard from a *neighbor* that my only son is dying."

"Well, don't put him in the ground just yet," said Glorie. "Besides, it was Dave's decision not to tell you. I guess he didn't want to break his dear, sweet little mother's heart."

"That's because I raised a nice boy. It's unfortunate your mother didn't raise a nice girl."

Don't go there, Grandma.

"Well, bless your heart for saying so," Glorie replied, using her best Georgian twang.

"So I've hired a caregiver for David. He might not need one now, but he will someday and I like to be prepared. She'll be contacting you tomorrow. Now put my son on the phone."

"Sorry, no can do," said Glorie.

"Why not?" Ruth fumed.

"Because David is down yonder," Glorie replied. "He's busy doing his thing, so why don't you go and do yours? Oh, wait. This *is* your thing—harassing me!"

Score another point for Mermie!

"Hear me, you ungrateful woman!" Ruth roared, as if she was God commanding to Moses. "It's time you stepped up and pulled your weight in this family. Just admit the truth, Gloria. You don't have any such Lyme disease and you never did. What you *do* have is good old-fashioned laziness!"

"That's right, I don't do diddly squat around here. Never did. But I'll bet you think the sun comes up just to hear you crow!"

Yay, go get her, Mermie!

Ruth ignored the comment. "Were you expecting Mercy-Faith to take care of you both? The girl's nearly sixteen. Her only responsibilities should be to read The Bible, go to school, and obey her elders."

Oh, and don't forget about staying away from older black men, Grandma!

"That's pretty archaic, isn't it?" said Glorie, "And if Elm doesn't do what you want her to, will you hold me responsible for her choices? Will you call in your old biddies and dunk me in your blessed bathtub, too? I saw those bruises, Ruth. I wonder what The Bible has to say about torture?"

Daddy spoke to Grandma?

"I never make apologies for doing the Lord's work!" Ruth huffed.

"Well, you'd better pray to Jesus that I don't prosecute your ass!"

Ruth hung up and Glorie did, too. Elm ran into the living room, jumping and hollering like a cheerleader after a touchdown.

"Woo-hoo! Wow, Mermie, you really told Grandma off! It was so cool!"

Glorie sat in her wicker rocking chair and looked out at the water. "Thanks, and I would have told her to kiss my grits, too, if the old la—if your grandma hadn't hung up on me," she chuckled.

Elm suspected that her mother was still upset even if she was trying to be light-hearted. "Can I get you anything? I've finished my homework, so I still have some time before bed."

"Thanks, but I'm waiting for your father. He said he needed to do a few things in the office tonight."

"Okay," said Elm, turning to leave, then changed her mind. "Mermie, are you worried about Daddy?"

Glorie seemed surprised at the question, then unleashed a flood of tears. "Actually, I'm terrified," said Glorie.

Elm wrapped both arms around her mother's neck. "We'll get through this, Mermie. I know we will. With or without Grandma's ol' caregiver."

As she rocked in the chair, Glorie said, "Elm, I need you to promise me something."

"I'll try, Mermie."

"Promise me you won't ever let anybody hurt you again, do you hear me? And if anything ever happens, you have my permission to fight back—you're half Southerner, you know!"

CHAPTER 12

D*EAR MISS VI,*
     *Daddy has Alzheimer's disease and I'm really scared.
Mermie still has her good and bad days and I hope she gets better
soon because Daddy really needs her. But sometimes she has brain fog
or speaks gibberish, so she has her own problems. In fact, she hired
Cassie to manage the store on weekends and I'm going to work with
Cassie over the summer. I'm still not speaking to Grandmother Ruth
but she did come through for Daddy 'cause he's got a caregiver now.
But I'll tell you the truth, Miss Vi. I'm tired of my parents being sick
and I'm tired of worrying.*

     *I know it sounds like I'm doing a lot of complaining so let me tell
you about some good things. I'm going to be sixteen next month and
I'm hoping Mermie comes through with a Sweet Sixteen party. I also
hope I get a car because it would be a relief to get away sometimes.
And then, guess what happens in August? Royce comes back for the
regatta!*

     *I've been hanging out at some of the websites he wrote me about
and there sure is a lot to learn about becoming a sea priestess! You've
got to know how to work with the water, seashells, sea animals, moon
phases, all sorts of things.*

FYI—my username is Octopuppy. Snow says it's appropriate because I'll be following Royce around like a lost little puppy. She calls him "the guy with eight grabby hands." Well, I told Snow that she'd better not tell Noah where I'll be meeting Royce because he'll just blab to Sarah Lightfoot and then the whole town will be talking about it again. Yeah, Noah and "Cow Lips" are still together. He's stupid, right? Anyway, I love you and hope you still love me.

Your friend,
Elm

"SNOW, DO YOU KNOW IF THE MOONWATER TRIBE HAS ANY good water spells?"

It had been another busy day at the information booth and Elm was relieved the regatta was over. The girls were packing up their belongings and Elm figured Snow would have a few suggestions. After all, she was a Native American and future water carrier.

"What do you mean, like water blessings?"

"I don't know," said Elm, removing three empty boxes from under the table. "Something to say to make the water *do* stuff."

Snow slammed a stack of leftover maps into a box. "What the hell is your problem, Elm?"

"What do you mean?"

"Big Dave taught you to send *love* to the water, so why do you want to control it all of a sudden? What has water ever done to you?"

Elm tried to break the tension with a giggle. "You act like it has a mind."

"Well, you sure don't," her friend blasted. "And it sounds like something's happened to your heart, too. Like you deleted it from your body's hard drive."

"You're crazy," Elm retorted. "Maybe I'm just using my brain more."

"Yeah, right. You're spending too much time in those crazy chatrooms," accused Snow. "And this Royce guy is poison, a scam artist. If I had a gun, I'd blow up his stupid, octopus tattoo right off his stupid, scam artist arm!"

Elm placed her brochures on top of the maps and snorted. "Well, do you wanna know what I think, Snow? I think you're just mad because you don't have a boyfriend!"

Now shut up and leave me alone.

"That's right, and you don't either."

The two glared at each other for an awkward fifteen seconds, then Elm broke the connection and watched an ant on the ground. "It's not like I'm paying him or anything."

"Or he's paying you," Snow added. "So why do you think he's hanging with a sixteen-year-old virgin?"

Elm winced. Snow had said the word *virgin* much too loud and people were staring.

"Oh, I don't know. Maybe because I'm gifted? Look, Royce says it's his mission. He says I'm a natural born sea priestess but I forgot how to use my powers in this life, so he's gonna help me remember by teaching me everything he knows."

Elm could see that Snow was upset because she had quickly packed the rest of the brochures and was folding the long yellow tablecloth without Elm's help.

Finally, Snow said, "These sailors have a girl in every port. And did you ever consider that maybe this guy's only interested in you because he needs you?"

Aha, she gets it!

"I know he needs me, Snow. He says I'm special."

"You bet he needs you," said Snow. "He needs *special*

recruits for his Sea Whore School for Teenage Girls Without a Clue!"

THE LOCAL RADIO STATION REPORTED THAT *BERMUDA Breeze* had won two of the races that day and Elm was eager to ditch Snow so she could find Royce and celebrate their last night together.

Elm waited on the boat for over an hour, humming and singing and daydreaming about being with Royce, being his sea priestess and maybe his lover. She thought about his sexy mouth and his deep brown eyes, the way they sucked her in like a whirlpool. She imagined leaving Little Blessing and giving up her life for him. She even allowed herself to believe they could live together aboard the *Bermuda Breeze*, sailing the seas to regattas throughout the world.

Then she thought about Snow again. It wasn't Elm's fault that Snow didn't have any great powers, not unless you counted tree climbing or Reiki healing, which she didn't. They had been best friends forever but maybe it was time to get a new best friend. Maybe Royce was the only friend she really needed.

The coral pink sunset had just appeared over the horizon when Elm's phone rang and Glorie burst her romantic bubble.

"Elm, what are you doing on that boat?"

"Why?" Elm forgot her mother could see most of the marina from their second-floor balcony.

"Because I want you home," Glorie ordered. "That's why."

"I'm waiting for somebody."

"I don't care what you're doing, young lady. You come home right now."

Young lady?

Twenty minutes later, Elm shuffled through the door and was greeted by dogs *One, Two,* and *Seven.* She saw that Glorie was on the phone in the living room, so she went to the kitchen to grab a soda.

"I know they take up a lot of time, Mother Ruth, but Dave loves these dogs," said Glorie, stroking *One.* "Yes, they are expensive. No, I'm not getting any younger. Yes, I know Elm has a lot on her plate. So do I. Look, she's just walked in. I'll get back to you."

Glorie waited for Elm in the living room. It was a serene beach cottage confection of aqua cream, seafoam green love seats, rattan chairs, plump cushions, nautical throw pillows, and scattered area rugs. There were freshly cut lilacs in glass mason jars and hundreds of assorted seashells resting inside a wicker basket atop the aqua-painted coffee table. Generally, the room was comfortable and soothing, but Glorie looked like she was ready to erupt.

"Elm, I called you twenty minutes ago."

"I had to leave a note," Elm replied, attempting to retreat to her bedroom.

Glorie pointed with her cane to a loveseat. "Sit down, Elm."

Why is Mermie so mad? I'm the one she embarrassed!

The teenager sighed, then plopped both legs on the coffee table, rattling the seashells. She had never acted disrespectfully towards her mother before, but Glorie had never disrespected *her* before.

"So where's Daddy?"

"Get your legs off my table!" Glorie barked. "Your father had to deal with some boat emergency. But don't you worry about Daddy, little girl, because you're the one in big trouble."

Is that a spider crawling up the wall? What do you think of all this drama, Mr. Spider?

"You look at me, Elm Sunday, and I want the truth. Have you been hanging all over some man from the regatta?"

She knows. Elm patted *Seven*, avoiding her mother's eyes and saying nothing.

Glorie was in no mood to play games. She squeezed Elm's chin, forcing her to look at her. "A man. By the carousel. Have you?"

Royce was right. Nobody understands what we have.

"Did Noah tell you that?" Elm asked.

"It doesn't matter who told me, young lady," said Glorie, wobbling a bit. She sat in a chair and continued the interrogation. "Were you messing around with a strange man on the beach?"

Elm scowled. "He's not strange."

"Oh, he's not, huh? People have seen you with this man, Elm. I've seen you on his boat. What the *hell* were you thinking? Do you have any idea what this man was thinking? Tell me you didn't let him touch you—or kiss you!"

"Kissing doesn't cause babies."

"Is that right? Well, he could have some sort of mouth disease. And even if he doesn't, do you really think he's gonna stop at kissing? *There's* your babies, Elm!"

"I don't care," Elm protested. "I love him and I want to be with him!"

"You what?"

From the way Glorie grasped the handle of her mermaid cane, Elm thought she might be contemplating hitting her with it.

"I do," said Elm, standing and feeling a wave of

empowerment. "And I know that Daddy will understand, even if you don't—*Mother.*"

It was the first time Elm had called Glorie anything but Mermie. But this Mermie was nosy and nasty and Elm didn't want anything to do with her.

"Sit down!"

Reluctantly, Elm obeyed, wondering if she had pushed her mother too far.

"So I'll tell you what your father *will* understand, Little Missy," said Glorie, her Georgian accent whining like a mosquito. "He'll understand that his darling daughter has known this person for less than a month."

"I met him last year and we've been writing ever since, if it's any of your business!" Elm shouted.

"It sure as hell *is* my business, Elm Sunday! I'm telling you that this man is messing with you. And he sure as hell doesn't love you, no matter what he tells you."

"Oh yes, he does," Elm barked, continuing the tug-of-war. "He says I'm his sea priestess."

Glorie was so incensed that she was sputtering. "Are you kidding me?" she said, leaving the chair to face Elm. "Be for real, girl. Do you even know this man's name?"

"Royce."

"What kind of name is that?" her mother queried.

"His."

"And what's his last name?" Glorie tested.

"He didn't tell me."

And I don't want to answer any more of your stupid questions. I'm finished. Done.

"Right," said Glorie. "And maybe Royce isn't even his real first name. So while you were letting this Royce man paw all over you, did he just happen to mention that he is leaving in a day or two and you won't ever see him again?"

Seven jumped on Elm's lap but the girl was in no mood

to play and pushed her off. "He'll be back again next year —and maybe I'll sail away with him after I graduate!"

Glorie seemed intent on a showdown and leaned her cane on Elm's shoulder as intimidation. "Not if I can help it."

Elm accepted the challenge. "You can't stop me."

Her mother laughed. "Just watch me. I'll tell your great-uncle sheriff that your man's been sexually assaulting a minor," Glorie warned. "And you can be sure that will get him arrested."

"But it's not true!" Elm cried, throwing a loveseat pillow across the room.

"And how do I know that? Apparently, I can't even trust my own daughter. And Lord knows we raised you to be better than this, Elm. Much better!"

Elm stood in defiance. "You know what? I hate you!" she screamed, storming off to her bedroom.

"Oh yeah?" Glorie yelled. "Well, that's just too bad, Missy, because I love you and I'm telling you—as God is my witness—you are not seeing this man again! Do you hear me?"

Elm slammed her door. She grabbed an overnight bag from her closet, packed a toothbrush, and took all of her cash from the secret compartment in her jewelry box.

She's not keeping me from my Royce. Oh no, she isn't!

The door swung open and Elm felt Glorie's eyes boring an angry hole through her back.

"Where do you think you're going?" her mother snapped.

"None of your damn business!"

I'm starting to really like that word. I think I'll use it more often. Damn, damn, damn!

"No, you're gonna stay right here in your room until your father gets home," said Glorie.

"Oh no, I'm not," Elm retorted, zipping up her bag, "and you can't make me!"

She shoved Glorie aside and slammed the house front door behind her, running down the steps and into the night.

ELM RETURNED TO THE *BERMUDA BREEZE* BUT NO ONE WAS there. She thought Royce might be waiting for her at the carousel, so she rode her bike to Moonwater Beach.

It was a gorgeous night with a crescent moon and thousands of twinkling stars in the sky. Elm climbed into a mermaid chariot and waited, replaying all the horrid things she and Glorie had said to each other.

Royce never showed.

In the morning, the Smith family's house phone rang. Noah answered it, then knocked on his sister's door.

"Snowplow," he whispered. "Is Elm in there?"

The door opened and Snow stuck out her head. "Yeah, she got in early this morning. She's sleeping right now. I already called Mermie so she wouldn't worry. What do you want?"

"Someone's dead on the beach," he said. "Someone Elm knows."

Royce's body was found along the shore of Moonwater Beach, facedown in the water. A large piece of amber glass was found protruding out of the back of his head and the remaining fragments from a broken beer bottle were scattered on the ground.

"Does anybody know the name of this man?" Sheriff Josiah Sunday called out.

"I do," Elm said. She stepped through the onlookers as if in a slow-motion dream until she reached the stretcher.

Shaking, Elm took a deep breath and lifted the white sheet from the body.

"His name is Royce," she sobbed, wiping his bloody lip with her finger. "He's a member of the *Bermuda Breeze* crew and he's my boyfriend."

The crowd murmured but Elm didn't care. Through water-filled eyes, she saw something lying near her feet and reached for the familiar white box. Could it be more chocolate? *Her* chocolate?

"Don't touch anything, Elm," the sheriff warned. "We've got a homicide here."

CHAPTER 13

D*EAR MISS VI,*

I'm sorry I haven't visited lately. My boyfriend was killed and I've been very upset. Uncle Josiah said Royce got in a fight and was hit on the back of the head with a beer bottle. Lots of people were interrogated, but there have been no witnesses or clues.

Grandmother Ruth says it will always be an unsolved case because nobody cares about one dead black man in Little Blessing. Isn't she awful? She said black men aren't even supposed to be in Little Blessing and haven't been here since we had slaves, so he got what was coming to him. I can't understand how she can talk like that, being a reverend's wife and all.

Of course, I'm sure Mother is thrilled about all this because she said she would stop him from seeing me. I wouldn't put it past her if she had him killed.

Did I tell you that she had Jason pick up all our dogs and take them away? It happened just after I heard about Royce. Mother tripped over a dog and smashed into a ceramic vase and that was it. I miss the dogs so much and I know Daddy does, too. I told him I wasn't going to speak to Mother until I've graduated and moved out of the house and probably not after that, either. Daddy doesn't seem to

*have an opinion about Royce. He just pats me on the head and tells
me he loves me. Sometimes I think he thinks I'm one of the dogs.*

*Anyway, I decided to get rid of all the little girl things I've
collected and all those stupid mermaids that remind me of my awful
mother. And I don't want to look like her anymore, either, so Snow is
going to help me with that. You know, you're lucky you don't have to
deal with mothers. But even though I am mad as hell and very sad
because I never got to say goodbye to Royce, I will always love you
and hope you still love me.*

Your friend,

Elm

AS RUTH PREDICTED, ROYCE'S KILLER WAS NEVER CAUGHT.
His crewmates told the sheriff that the last time they had
seen him was when he joined them for victory beers at
Gluttony Tavern. Someone at the bar made a racial slur
and a fight broke out, one of those crazy cowboy movie
brawls that seem to go on forever. The official report stated
that Royce was alone when he left and no one knew where
he was heading.

Elm mourned for months, making it crystal clear that
she blamed Glorie for cursing "the only man I will ever
love."

One of Elm's first acts of revolt was to redecorate her
bedroom, which she liked to think as "The Great Demoli-
tion." She stripped the room of its pretty beachy hues and
replaced them with maudlin blacks and deep purples. Her
horde of water globes, mermaids, and stuffed dolphins had
been boxed away and the aquarium became a gruesome,
green water sludge for her new octopus figurine collection.

The war between mother and daughter had been
declared and Glorie was determined to win it. Every day
she would stand outside Elm's bedroom door, ranting a list

of complaints. When that didn't work, she decided to try a new strategy: bribery.

Trying to sound upbeat, Glorie said, "Elm, I know you're in twelfth grade now and I don't have a problem with you redecorating your room, but purple and black are too depressing. Let's go out, have some lunch, and then stop at the fabric store to get something cheerier, something in pink and yellow. What do you think?"

What Elm thought was she didn't do cheery anymore. In fact, the notion of waking up to a roomful of smiley faces and sunshine and lollipops made her want to barf. Her bedroom was *her* domain—not her mother's—and she was old enough to decorate it any damn way she wanted! And what Elm wanted was a dark fantasy cave filled with magic books and mirrors and crystals, a sacred space where she could study and practice to become the great sea priestess she was meant to be. Royce said it was her destiny and this was the way she would honor his memory. Her mother would just have to get used to it.

"Elm, when are you going to clean this place up?" Glorie asked one day, exasperated.

"Don't worry about it." Elm was painting her middle fingernail with a sleek black polish.

"And what happened to your goldfish?" her mother asked.

"They died," said Elm. "I'm replacing them with a baby octopus."

"An octopus?!"

Elm blew on her nail before answering. "Yeah. They're very cute. The hatchlings are only about a half inch long."

Glorie wasn't allowing it.

"I don't care how cute and little they are as babies. They're gonna grow up big and ugly and I won't have an octopus in my house!"

"That's unfair!" Elm cried. "It's my house, too!"

She threw her nail polish bottle across the room. "You never let me have anything I want! I wanted Royce and you put a curse on him! I know you did, Mother, don't lie! You killed my Royce, and I will never forgive you!"

~

LATER THAT DAY, ELM RETURNED TO THE CAVE WHERE SHE had first spied the black seal.

Why did Royce appear to me as a seal? Why did he have to die? Why am I stuck with such a hateful mother?

Elm tried to make sense of it all, but she had never loved and lost anyone before.

She comforted herself by throwing rocks into the little cave pool as if they were exploding grenades on her thought bubbles. When tiny seashells were tossed back at her, followed by a stream of giggles, Elm knew she was not alone and was grateful for the company.

The first time Elm realized there were mermaids in Little Blessing was when she was nine. Snow told her she was crazy but Elm knew they were there. She had seen them, conversed with them. The mermaids had become her friends, especially the youngest one, Nee-nah.

"Would you like to have more power than she?"

Nee-nah was leaning against the edge of the pool, her silvery green curls hiding her small breasts.

"Who?" asked Elm.

"Your human mother."

"Oh. *Her.*"

Elm visualized Glorie's face and threw a rock in the middle of it.

Bullseye!

"She killed your boyfriend," said Nee-nah. "Isn't that what you believe?"

"I guess."

Elm didn't want to think about Royce because it hurt too much. *Except I'm always thinking of him.*

Nee-nah pulled herself out of the water to sit next to Elm, allowing two feet of her tail to soak in the pool. "Do you not know that negative thoughts can cause as much harm as if one was cutting the flesh with a blade?"

Elm was confused. "I thought that sticks and stones can break my bones but—"

"—oh, yes, words *can* hurt you," Nee-nah interrupted.

In the distance, Elm saw a black seal. She perked up, excited at the possibility of Royce returning from his grave to be with her. Unfortunately, it was just her imagination.

"You know what, Nee-nah? I'm tired of Mother bossing me around. I know she hated Royce and I hate her for hating him."

The mermaid giggled. "Of course you are upset, Elm. And the first thing you need to do—in my humble opinion, of course—is to show your independence. Mothers don't like that."

ELM WAS READY FOR HER RITE OF PASSAGE. SHE WAS SO excited that she called Snow again to confirm their plans. Yes, everything was all set.

"What's all set? Who were you talking to?"

A bare-chested Noah was standing in the doorway of his sister's bedroom. He was wearing khaki shorts and a wet towel draped around his neck.

"I hope you cleaned up the bathroom this time," Snow warned.

"I never do," he said, towel-drying his ears. "Not when I've got my Snow Maid around!"

Snow frowned.

"Hey, you didn't answer me. Was it Elm?"

"Was it Elm? Was it Elm?" Snow mocked. "Jeez, why don't you just call her and ask her yourself, Snoopy?"

She shoved past him, heading for the kitchen.

Noah followed her. "Now why would I call her when I have you for a sister, Little Big Mouth?"

"You're disgusting," said Snow.

"Thank you," he said. "And speaking of disgusting, I can't believe you're still hanging out with Elm."

"So?" Snow was getting out a plate, a knife, and a loaf of bread. "What do you care?"

"I feel sorry for her. She's changed, and nobody wants to be around her anymore. And it's not just about that murdered guy, either. Elm's attitude really sucks. She acts like she's got some sort of super power, like she's better than everyone."

"Wow, I'm surprised you even noticed," said Snow, reaching inside the refrigerator for a bottle of mustard, cheese, and ham slices. "I mean, considering your tongue is always down Sarah Lightfoot's throat."

He snapped his towel at her. "Yeah, I've been kinda busy. So why don't you talk to her about it? You're supposed to be her best friend."

Snow quickly assembled her sandwich and said, "I *am* her best friend, but Elm is doing her own thing right now. And she sure as hell isn't listening to me!"

CHAPTER 14

A S THE DAYS WENT BY, Elm practiced her sea priestess lessons with Nee-nah.

Her training included keeping a meditation journal about crystals and gemstones, which she created from a black hardcover sketchbook, decorating it with ribbon, feathers, and rhinestones.

Elm spent her *Vitamin Sea by E* profits on crystals and gemstones, often meditating with them to see what mysteries they revealed.

"Honey, can I come in?"

"Sure, Daddy."

Elm had no issue with her father entering her bedroom because he was always supportive, even when the entire town of Little Blessing seemed against her.

Big Dave found Elm lying on top of her satiny, deep purple bed with a clear quartz crystal taped to her forehead. "Getting any good signals?" he laughed.

"Funny." She ripped the tape off and sat up. "I'm meditating with my crystals."

"I heard that turquoise is good for clairvoyance."

"How did you know that?" she asked, thrilled that he could remember.

Big Dave smiled. "Oh, just something I read somewhere." Then he removed an item from his pocket. "Here, I want to give you something." He sat on the edge of her bed and placed a small tied herb bundle in her hand.

"A smudge stick?"

"Yeah. A tiny one. It's a combination of sage and lavender. I thought you could use it for your healing work."

"Thanks, but Mother will probably think I'm smoking pot in here if I burn it. Have you ever smoked pot, Daddy?"

Big Dave laughed. "Probably. I don't know. Maybe. I forget. Oh, and that's not all I've got for you." He handed her an odd-looking pencil. "It's made from a twig. I thought you could use it for your tree mail."

She gave him a quick hug. "It's so cool! Thanks, Daddy."

"So—guess what happened at the pow-wow today?"

"What?" Elm was scribbling on a notepad with her new pencil.

"Your brother Noah became a full-fledged pipe carrier."

Elm stopped writing. "First of all, he's not my brother and I hate his stupid guts. Anyway, I thought those ceremonies were supposed to be secret. Are you gonna get kicked out for telling me?"

"I don't think so," he said. "Besides, I thought you'd want to know because Noah received a great honor. And because we both know you have a crush on him."

"Eww, gross!" Elm exclaimed.

Had she really been so obvious? Well, who could resist those eyes, that hair, and that sexy smirk?

"Okay," she admitted. "Maybe when I was younger. But not anymore. He's way too bossy for me."

Big Dave picked up an amethyst crystal and placed it on his head. "Is this where it goes?"

Elm was amazed that her father knew the color violet corresponded with the crown chakra and the amethyst was definitely violet. "Yes, but how did you know?"

He placed the amethyst on her dresser. "Oh, just another thing I read somewhere. Luckily, I didn't forget it. Listen, Honey, I want you to do me a favor. A *big* favor."

"I'm listening," she said, hoping it had nothing to do with her mother.

He took her hand in his and rubbed it. "Give Mermie a break. She had nothing to do with your friend's death and I know she feels bad for you. So I hope you will forgive her for whatever she said to upset you. Otherwise, the anger is going to destroy you."

Destroy?

"I'll think about it, Daddy." But she knew she wouldn't.

After Big Dave left, Elm switched on her computer. When she wasn't at school, she spent most of her time sitting in front of it, stimulated by websites with darkened backgrounds and flashing neon green text that spewed words of hate, like a dragon whose destructive flame could never be extinguished.

Dark thoughts empowered her and she joined others to help increase their energies and psychically attack internationally-known spiritual teachers and New Agers. Once known as sweet and compassionate, Elm had transformed into a venomous being, intent on a search-and-destroy mission to rid the planet of anyone practicing "fluffy-bunny-light" philosophy.

Scrolling through the discussions in the secret forum, she paused at the "Starting Your Own Circle" and "What is a Sea Witch?" topic, then continued down the screen until she found the one comment thread she had visited most.

Her forum "friends" had warned her that Glorie was an evil sea goddess who had incarnated to destroy Elm, who was actually her earthbound sister. They gave explicit instructions on how to send Glorie straight back to the ocean, assuring there would be no repercussions.

While Elm wasn't ready to exterminate her mother, it was good to know that she had the power—and support—to do so.

ONE SATURDAY AFTERNOON A SMALL GROUP OF MOTHERS and daughters assembled around the stage at Sea Angels. They were there to hear Yemanja Sol read from her latest children's book, *Phony Abalone*.

The author sat on the pink and gold throne with the picture book spread open in her lap, her young audience enthralled by the rhyming story about a lowly clamshell that wanted to feel important.

Feeling better that day, Glorie decided to help Cassie at the store. She was pleased with the attendance and watched the book reading from the sales counter, calculating potential book sales in her mind.

"It tried to convince all the other clamshells that it was actually a beautiful abalone," Yemanja read, "even though it was obvious to all the other clamshells that the phony abalone was one of them."

After the reading, a line formed as Yemanja signed her books. When the last customer had left, Yemanja beckoned Glorie to join her.

"You think it went well?"

Glorie smiled, captivated by the author's bright turquoise-magenta dress and shiny gold turban. Yemanja had been visiting some friends on the East Coast and it was fortunate that Glorie knew someone (who knew someone) who helped bring the Caribbean writer to Little Blessing.

"Definitely," said Glorie. "We sold fifteen books today. And you were amazing, of course, so thank you very much for coming."

Then Yemanja took Glorie's hand.

"And now, My Dear," she said in a mysterious tone, "I have a gift for you."

"Oh?"

"You may ask me anything," said Yemanja. "Give me any question about your life and my shells will answer."

Glorie didn't believe in psychic readings but Yemanja looked so regal and sincere that she couldn't decline.

"Okay. Let me think."

Outside, it was beginning to rain and she watched the Saturday shoppers raise their umbrellas for protection. For some reason, this made her think of Elm.

"Why does my daughter hate me so much?"

Yemanja smiled, turning over Glorie's hand. She reached inside a small pouch tied to her dress, withdrew a fang-like shell and placed it on Glorie's palm.

"This is a tusk shell, My Dear. It means your daughter walks in darkness with no heart."

"No heart?" Glorie was stunned, letting the shell drop to the floor.

Yemanja nodded. "Sadly, she will despise you until the day she dies."

❧

IT FELT ODD TO BE TAKING AN AFTERNOON NAP BUT ELM anticipated a late night and wanted to be well-rested when she got to Snow's place.

To her dismay, she had a strange dream about being on an octopus ride at an amusement park. There were others on the ride, too, and they were screaming, enjoying the exhilaration. When the ride ended, Elm was frightened because she was the only one not allowed to leave. Would she be strapped in that ride forever?

Later at Snow's house, Elm sat on the closed toilet seat, watching Snow line up all the hair dye and makeup products on the bathroom counter. Overall, it took two hours for the transformation to be complete.

"Oh, jeez, Snow. You look like you're ready to cry."

Snow stared at Elm's new raven-dyed hair. "Oh god, Elm."

"What?"

"Your mom's gonna kill you. Seriously."

Elm shrugged her shoulders. "She can try."

She looked in the mirror and smiled, admiring her new reflection. Without her trademark strawberry gold locks, she figured she looked more mature, probably around twenty.

Excellent.

"Maybe we should have just used a temporary rinse," said Snow.

"No, it had to be permanent," Elm said. "That's the only way people will take me seriously."

She rummaged through her makeup bag on the counter, removing a deep blue eye pencil and a spray can.

"Okay, let's get this blue stuff around my eyes and then you can dry my hair and spray some purple on the ends."

Snow shook her head. "Yeah, your mom's gonna seriously kill you. And your grandmother will probably have a heart attack."

And it's my hair and my eyes, dammit, and I'll do whatever the hell I want!

CHAPTER 15

W HILE ELM SPENT THE WEEKEND with Snow, Glorie took the opportunity to snoop in her daughter's bedroom.

She rarely visited the harborfront room because they always argued when she did and it was disheartening to be there. Elm had sucked out all the sweetness and light to create a creepy cavern of hideous, frightening images of bats and vampires, decorating with lots of blacks, deep purples, and blood reds.

There was a scrapbook on the top shelf of the bookcase. As Glorie turned its pages, she noticed there were no pictures of her anywhere. The last page had no pictures at all, but there were some folded papers that Glorie was curious about.

She recognized Elm's frantic handwriting and began reading a short story, entitled "The Hottest Summer":

It was hot and steamy and the cheap fan from Woolworth's did not help much, blowing the stale, dry air across her reclining frame and disturbing the dust within the rotting sofa. The shades were down but the sun was ruthless and baked the little room to exhaustion, stripping the paint from its fractured walls.

"Thank God it's almost time," Becca sighed, as she brushed the flies from her naked face.

She looked up at the ceiling peeling above her, at the pattern of congregating flies, and the webs in the corners, and felt so angry that she wanted to scream. She was tired of waiting on her back, day in and day out, and damn tired of bathing in sweat on that dirty old sofa. And she was tired of being hot and dizzy and so damn weak that she could barely stand without falling.

Her throat was dust-clogged and scratchy and she needed a drink. A nice cold one. But the refrigerator seemed miles away.

"Whatcha doin' in here?" Big Dave asked. He was yawning and on his way to bed.

"Oh, just reading something depressing."

Big Dave sat on the bed next to her, pushing her gently until they were both horizontal, staring up at the starry, glow-in-the-dark ceiling. He reached for her hand and she squeezed. "Are you having problems again with your memory?"

It was an interesting question, coming from a man who had Alzheimer's.

Glorie sighed. "Yes, I'm just trying to remember when Elm decided she didn't love me."

"But she does love you, Mermie. Why do you think she doesn't?"

"Oh, I don't know," she pondered. "Maybe because there are no pictures of me anywhere in this room."

Big Dave never thought the worst of anybody. "She's just going through a phase," he assured her. "I think the kids call it role-playing. Look, you two definitely have your differences, but don't let it worry you. It's probably your typical mother-daughter stuff. Look at my own mother. You're like a daughter to her and you two butt heads all the time."

Frowning, Glorie said, "Sorry to burst your bubble, but your mother has never thought of me as a daughter. I'm the Southern slut her precious son was tricked into marrying, remember?"

He chuckled. "I admit that Mom has never been the cheeriest of people. But look at Elm—she's so full of life!"

"She's full of something all right, Dave," Glorie said, sitting up. "I know things are changing for you, but have you not noticed how much *she's* changed? She's angry all the time. It's like she got a personality transplant. The next thing you know she'll be marking up her body with weird tattoos."

"Well, it is her body, I guess." He was sitting up, too, taking in the rest of the room.

"Tattoos are disgusting," Glorie continued. "And did Elm tell you she wants a *real* baby octopus for her fish tank?"

"That's funny," he replied. "There's no room in our house for an octopus. So what did you tell her?"

Glorie stood up and looked out the window. Somehow the full moon appeared larger than normal, like it was crashing towards Earth.

"I told her it's not gonna happen. They're ugly and dangerous and I don't want one in my house. And then she screamed at me and said I never, ever let her have anything she wants, that I put a curse on that boyfriend of hers and it killed him. And then she said she was gonna talk to you about it."

For a second, Big Dave's pleasant face looked grim.

"Well, she's probably still grieving, Mermie." He went over to his wife and wrapped his arm around her.

"But he was a man, Dave. A *man*." Glorie tried to wriggle away from her husband but he held on. "I can't believe you're so calm about this."

"Because I know Elm didn't do anything inappropriate," he said with certainty, stroking Glorie's hair. "Honey, maybe this extreme behavioral change means we need to send her to a therapist. What do you think?"

"Yeah, that's a laugh," she snickered. "You know Little Blessing doesn't have therapists. Your mother wouldn't have it. She'd say it would give a bad impression about our community. The closest we've got is Kat and I'm surprised Ruth hasn't run *her* out of town."

Staring out at the moon's reflection on the water, they were silent for a while, taking in the beauty of the night.

"So what about Kat?" Big Dave asked. "She may not be a traditional therapist but maybe that crystal machine she put you on will help Elm, too."

"Maybe," said Glorie. "But who's gonna make Elm go? She won't listen to me anymore."

"I'll see what I can do," said her husband. After a pause, he laughed. "So no octopus, then?"

"She already asked you, didn't she?"

"Yesterday," he admitted. "She said it would make an interesting science project and that she would get an 'A' and I would be proud of her."

"Tell me you didn't fall for that line, Dave. Please tell me you didn't."

"Well—I did tell her there's nothing I wouldn't do for her. But in this case, the octopus would grow too big for her aquarium and it's not fair to remove them from the ocean."

"Bravo," Glorie cheered, clapping like a seal. Big Dave tickled her and she yelped.

He leaned over to study her face, knowing that she was hurting, both physically and emotionally. "You know what, Mermie? You need some fun and I'm gonna give it to you. How about we continue this conversation in my very pleasant bedroom?"

"Okay, but be warned," she teased. "Mermaids have been known to have their way with sailors."

ELM AND SNOW WERE JUST APPROACHING THE BANDSTAND at Moonwater Beach. The moon was deliciously full, casting its golden light across the indigo ocean. Elm was carrying a 5" x 7" drawstring bag and a recording device.

"What's that for?" Snow asked.

Elm rolled her eyes. "To record the spirits of the sea," she snapped. "What else?"

They walked in silence to the shore and waited for their ride. A light flashed several times over the waves and soon a dinghy appeared, driven by Cassie Hamilton. Elm took it as a personal victory when she recruited her mother's do-gooder store manager for her secret group. As part of her initiation, Cassie had to volunteer her own forty-five-foot sailboat as their meeting place.

When they reached *Free Spirit*, Elm glanced back to make sure they were far away from Little Blessing's prying eyes. Cassie turned off the motor and the three girls boarded the sailboat, going below deck to where four more girls waited in giggly anticipation.

Then there was silence.

By the shock on their faces, Elm's hair color change

and garish makeup received the dramatic reception she had expected.

"Welcome to the first meeting of the Secret School of Sea Gypsies," Elm said. "I am your sea priestess and the first thing you people need to know is I am in charge."

The girls were still staring at her so she knew she had their attention. Or was it fear? Even so, fear wasn't necessarily a bad thing. Didn't preachers use fear to keep their flock in line? Why should she be any different?

Elm waited for applause or some other positive reaction, but none were forthcoming. Even Snow was silent.

Finally, Clemency Wheelwright made a motion. "I move that the first meeting of the Secret School of Sea Gypsies be our last."

A vote was taken and the motion was carried.

"Now let's get the hell out of here!" Clemency cried.

CHAPTER 16

ELM WAS STILL SMARTING FROM the Sea Gypsies fiasco when she walked through the door on Sunday evening. She didn't need any hassles at home, too.

Glorie was right there to greet her. But when she saw her daughter's macabre makeover, she was not amused. In fact, she screamed.

"What have you done to yourself?! Are you trying to give me a heart attack? Dave, look what your daughter's done!"

But Big Dave did nothing except to laugh and praise Elm for showing her creative side.

"Are you kidding me?" Glorie cried. "Look at her! She's destroyed her beautiful hair!"

Big Dave wrapped one of his beefy arms around Elm and said, "Aww, Mermie. She's still our little girl."

Thank you, Daddy. Now get away from me, Mother. I've had a rough weekend and I don't need you in my face!

~

It wasn't long before Ruth learned about Elm's new look and decided to make an "emergency visit" to Sunday's Marina.

Glorie dragged herself out of bed to answer the door. She had been suffering a difficult herxheimer reaction to a new Lyme treatment and hadn't bothered to wash her face or brush her hair.

"It took you long enough!" Ruth huffed, pushing past Glorie to take a seat in the living room. "Do you always answer the door like that?"

Glorie was dizzy and just wanted to return to bed. "I didn't know you were coming," she said in a hoarse whisper.

"Nevertheless, that's no excuse to look the way you do," scolded Ruth, who was fidgeting in her chair. "I won't be here long anyway."

Glorie nodded and lay on the couch.

"What are you doing?!" Ruth shrieked.

"I'm lying down," Glorie said, covering her eyes with one of the accent pillows.

"Well, it's very rude," Ruth sputtered. "You don't set a very good example for your daughter, seeing you lying around the place, looking like death warmed over."

"You know I have Lyme disease, right?" Glorie asked.

"And I've told you a hundred times that's nonsense," said Ruth. "My physician says it's all in your head." She left the room for a minute and came back in a huff. "Mercy-Faith's bedroom looks like a dungeon. I thought a bat might fly out and bite me."

"One can only hope," Glorie mumbled.

"What?"

"I said she likes it that way."

"I don't care if you are sick, Gloria. You should look at me when I am speaking to you!" Ruth demanded.

Glorie groaned, moving the pillow away from her face.

"I'm here to discuss Mercy-Faith," Ruth began. "I don't like that ugly black hair and that dark eye makeup she's been wearing lately. She looks like a witch from hell and we don't have witches in Little Blessing and we certainly do not have them in the Sunday family. And you're the problem, Gloria."

"Of course I am."

"I'm glad you see that, too, because you've never laid down the law with that girl. I'll tell you what she needs—she needs to go to church. And I'm not talking about one of your ridiculous Catholic churches with all that sinful incense, but an honest, God-fearing Protestant congregation. You tell her I said so. I'm her grandmother and I know what's good for that girl."

Glorie rolled her eyes.

"Did you hear what I said?"

"Yes. Something about church."

"What is wrong with you, woman?" asked Ruth. "Are you intoxicated?"

Glorie laughed. "Don't I wish."

Exasperated, Ruth rose from her chair. "I repeat—are you going to make Mercy-Faith go to church?"

"The first chance I get," replied Glorie. "Right after you save the world from Armageddon."

Ruth's eyes narrowed. "I never spoke to my mother-in-law like that."

"I'm not surprised," Glorie countered. "Wasn't she dead when you got married?"

WHILE GLORIE DEALT WITH RUTH, ELM WAS PRACTICING A little magic in the treehouse.

Snow never joined her anymore, telling Elm she was too busy working at her father's clinic. Elm sensed she was avoiding her but it didn't matter. She still hadn't forgiven Snow for not speaking up at the Sea Gypsies meeting.

Staring into the flame of a flickering candle, Elm waited for inspiration to come.

I am strong. I am powerful.

Suddenly, Miss Vi's leaves were shaking and Noah bounded up the ladder. "Hey!" he said, catching his breath and sitting next to her.

Elm covered the flame with her hand. "Watch it, you jerk! Can't you see I'm burning a candle?"

He moved her hand to take a peek. "Yeah, I see it. But where's the fire extinguisher? You wanna burn the place down? I don't think Miss Vi would like that."

Elm removed a small red canister from her bag and poked Noah with it. "Right here, Mister Nosey."

"Well, at least you're showing *some* responsibility," he said, scrunching his face. "God, Elm, why are you so mad all the time? And when did you get so gross? I can barely stand to look at you with all that makeup."

"So don't look at me, then," she snapped, pushing him away. "And give me some room to breathe, will ya?" She closed her eyes, trying to shut out his presence.

But Noah would not be ignored. He pulled out a handkerchief from his pocket and wiped the makeup from her face.

"Don't you touch me!" Elm screamed. She grabbed the handkerchief and tossed it out the window.

"Hey, my dad gave me that!" he cried. Then he grabbed a hank of her hair and threatened to pull it. "Jeez, your hair looks like shoe polish." He leaned over and sniffed. "Yuck. It smells like a barrel of dead fish at low tide."

She wriggled away. "So don't smell it then. And stop touching it, too." She took a mirror from her bag and fussed with her makeup. "So why are you here, Noah Skyfeather? I know I didn't invite you."

"I haven't seen you in a while, Smelly Girl."

As part of her rebellion, Elm rarely showered and masked her body odor with bottles of patchouli oil.

"So? Maybe I like it that way."

God, he's hot. Why does he always look so hot?

Noah looked deep into her soul, searching for traces of the old Elm, the sweet and naive girl he had fallen in love with. "You like it that way? Are you sure about that?"

It was a moment that Elm had dreamed about, the scene that had played in her pre-teen mind over and over, long before she had ever met the mysterious Royce.

Could it be that Noah was actually aroused by her new image?

And so it shall be!

To Noah's surprise, Elm blew out the candle and body-slammed him to the floor, covering him with smelly kisses.

CHAPTER 17

Dear Miss Vi,

I think I told you that Daddy has Alzheimer's, right? Well, it wasn't too bad at first but now he's doing all this weird stuff like forgetting how to dress and how to turn off the shower. Mother says she's worried about him going out in public, so she told Noah and Jason to keep an eye on him.

Mother is useless, of course. She says her Lyme disease has gotten worse and I have noticed her stammering and slurring her words a lot but I thought that might be because she's drinking. She doesn't think I know but I've seen the empty wine cooler bottles in the trash. And whenever I'm home, I see her stuffing her face with cake and cookies and ice cream, even though her doctor told her to cut out the sugar because it feeds the Lyme. No wonder she's having trouble walking—she's so damn fat!

Anyway, I don't care about her stupid Lyme but I do care about Daddy. His condition is supposed to be a big secret, but I'm sure it's okay to tell you. I don't think it will be a secret for long because Daddy is not going to get any better, even though I keep praying that he will. You know what? I'm going to stop praying. It doesn't work and I don't think anyone's listening anyway. If they were, Royce wouldn't be dead.

As always, thanks for listening. Even though my life really sucks these days, I love you and hope you still love me.

    Your friend,

    Elm

P.S. I hope those stupid tourists "leaf" you alone. Get it?

                    ~

Tweeeeeet! Tweet! Tweet! Tweeeeeet!

    The drum major blew his brass whistle, twirling his red, white and blue baton. The cymbals crashed behind him as the George Sunday High School Band marched down Charity Street, playing "God Bless America."

Glorie was adjusting Big Dave's patriotic necktie. She had too many things to do in preparation for the Fourth of July arts festival so she would not be joining him in the mayor's car this year, but she wanted him to look perfect.

"Wish me luck, Mermie!" he said. He gave her a quick peck on the lips and stepped into the red convertible with the "Mayor David Sunday" banner.

Glorie waved and the driver pulled away.

"Are you ready?"

Glorie nodded to Ruth and the two pushed through the crowd. As soon as they had reached the boardwalk, Ruth began clipping at her usual pace, while Glorie hobbled behind with her cane.

Due to her limited mobility, it had been decided that Glorie would oversee the musical activities and small arts display at the bandstand location. She had recruited Kat to take over her regular duties at Faith Camp Meeting

Grounds and there were nearly twenty volunteers to assist her.

Elm and Snow were watching the parade from a third-floor open window in Hallelujah House.

"There goes Daddy," Elm said, pointing at her father. Big Dave was dressed in a business suit and a funny Uncle Sam top hat, waving to the crowd as his car crawled along the parade route until it was no longer in her sight. Elm held out her hand to Snow. "Give it to me."

Snow was hesitant. "Not yet, Elm. Let's wait 'til the horses go by. We don't want to spook them."

"You're kidding, right?"

Elm couldn't remember Snow being this goody-goody. She grabbed a firecracker, lit it, and tossed it down to the street.

Bang!

"Damn, it sounds like a gun went off," Snow said.

"Yeah," Elm giggled. "Give me another one."

Bang!

The parade stopped and everyone looked up, but the girls had disappeared.

After the parade, the crowd dispersed into different directions. A full schedule of band concerts had been planned, featuring a town barbecue, sack races, evening fireworks and, of course, the annual arts festival. Umbrellas and blankets had already claimed prime beach spots for the windsurfing competition at Moonwater Beach.

At the bandstand, *The Beach Bums* were tuning up their instruments while Glorie sat in a front row seat, serving as troubleshooter. She loved the band's repertoire of surf music but was surprised that Ruth approved them. To appease her mother-in-law, another band had been booked for that evening; a much older group who would play "God

Bless America" and the traditional John Philip Sousa marching songs, including the show-stopping "The Stars and Stripes Forever."

Big Dave joined Glorie, just when the band began to play "Wipeout." He had changed into a crisp white Sunday's Marina shirt and khaki shorts, accessorizing his outfit with a small U.S. flag pin. When he put his arm around Glorie, the pin scratched her neck and she winced.

"Hi," he said. "Everything okay?"

"For now," she said, rubbing her neck. "I've still got a whole afternoon of arts festival with your mother."

"I've got faith in you," he assured her. "Well, I'm next for barbecuing duty."

Glorie shook her head. "I don't know how you can do it, Dave, being a vegetarian and all. Can't they get someone else?"

His eyes glazed over; he seemed a million miles away. "What did you say, Miss?"

No one was hurt in the fire.

According to the article in the *Little Blessing Observer*, Big Dave had accidentally set the blaze when he dumped a lit chunk of charcoal onto Sheriff Sunday's paper plate instead of a burger. The lawman yelped while Big Dave calmly stood there, watching the flames and cheering. Jason rushed to his side and escorted him home, staying with him until Glorie arrived.

So the word was out: something was seriously wrong with the mayor of Little Blessing. This discovery was fodder for the rumor mills and the public embarrassment forced Glorie to cancel her plans for Elm's Sweet Sixteen party.

It didn't matter much to Elm because all she wanted was a new car to "get the heck out of Dodge" and leave Little Blessing in the dust. Fortunately, Ruth's generous birthday check granted that wish and Elm didn't even care if it was a peace offering.

After that dunking she pulled with her friends, the old lady owes it to me.

CHAPTER 18

B Y THE FIRST WEEK OF August, a caregiver named Kathleen moved in to take care of Big Dave. The large red-cheeked woman from High City was hanging up her clothes in the guest room when Elm appeared in the doorway.

"Who are you?" Elm asked.

"I'm Kathleen, from The Caregiver Agency. Are you Elm?"

"That's what they tell me."

Kathleen invited her to sit down. "I'm glad to meet you, Elm. I've already discussed with your mother what's going to happen here but you need to know these things, too."

"What *things*?" It sounded like the seventeen-year-old was about to get dumped with a whole laundry list of chores.

"Well," Kathleen explained, "your father has Alzheimer's—"

"I know that," Elm snorted. "We all know that."

"—so he needs special care," Kathleen continued. "That's why I'm here."

"So what do you need me for?"

Elm wasn't thrilled to have a stranger living in their home and was desperate to get outside. Kathleen had closed the windows in the guest room and Elm was longing to feel the salty breeze on her cheeks.

"Because your father needs his family to be support-ive," Kathleen replied. "It's important for you to spend time with him, Elm. Just sit down and have a chat. Hold his hand. Be loving. And remember not to take it person-ally if he doesn't remember you. He'll have his good days and his bad days, but mostly not good."

"Uh huh."

"Here's something I'd like you to read," said the care-giver, handing Elm a brochure. "I'll be here, of course, if you have any questions. But this brochure gives you an idea of what to expect, like hallucinations, wandering, and violent outbursts."

"Great." Elm flipped through the document, feeling like a dark cloud ready to burst into rain.

Whoever's listening to this, please don't let my Daddy die.

But she knew that he would. Everybody died. Royce died, Snow's mother had died. Elm, too, would die some-day. But Big Dave would die long before his physical body expired and it wasn't fair that she had to watch.

The next day, Elm was on a Harley with a guy she had met on the internet.

They roared up and down the pier at Sunday's Marina, passing Noah where he was cleaning one of the dock pedestals.

"No riding on the pier!" he yelled.

Elm scowled. "You can't tell me what to do!"

She gave him the finger and rode off.

"Hey, was that Elm?" Snow asked, carrying a takeout lunch and a soda.

"Yeah, with that jerky virtual boyfriend of hers," he huffed.

"Jealous much?"

"You wish!" Noah followed Snow to one of the tables under the picnic gazebo. "I'm the assistant dockmaster now and it's my job to make sure all marina rules are observed."

Snow snorted and said, "I thought your job was to clean up the docks and pump out the sewage!"

"Knock it off," he warned, pretending to throw a punch.

"Well, cheer up, Loser," she said, setting the lunch bag and soda on the table. "You won't have to worry about Elm for a while. Or me, either, 'cause we're flying off to Merry Olde England this weekend—woo hoo!"

"Yeah, you've told me that, like, a thousand times," Noah said. He opened the bag and grabbed his triple-decker Turkey Club on Wheat with Extra Bacon. "It's too bad you're gonna miss the regatta this year. But what I'd like to know is how the heck you convinced Dad to let you go."

"No problemo, O-ah-nay," she said, speaking Pig Latin. "Since we're both minors, Kat's gonna be our chaperone and you know Dad trusts her. Actually, I think he likes her a lot. A *real* lot, if you know what I mean."

"Nobody *ever* knows what you mean," he snickered, stuffing his mouth with sandwich.

"Anyway, Elm avoids Kat like the plague, probably 'cause Kat can read her energy and Elm doesn't like that." Snow twirled her dreamcatcher windchimes keychain to make it tinkle. "But Kat's the only reason we get to go in the first place so Elm's just gonna have to get over it. Of course, Mermie trusts Kat because she's helped her with the Lyme. And nobody mentioned it to Big Dave because he's not even sure who we are half the time."

Noah took a gulp of his soda and said, "Yeah, tell me about it."

Snow looked up and saw Glorie standing on the balcony, waving at her.

"I gotta go," she said, her hand open. "You owe me twenty dollars."

"What? My food cost five."

"Wrong. It was a *triple*-decker with extra bacon, so that's ten. And your drink was a couple of dollars. And then there's my standard delivery fee."

Noah slapped the money in her hand. "Thief."

"Sucker!" She laughed like an evil genius and bolted before he could punch her for real.

"Ah, my *other* daughter!" Glorie said as Snow walked into her kitchen. "Grab a seat and help me eat this luscious-looking cake!"

They sat at the table, discussing the girls' plans for their upcoming trip to England while eating platefuls of moist carrot cake with walnuts and raisins and gooey cream cheese frosting.

ELM KNELT ON THE BEACH SAND AT SUNSET, HER SEA DRUM held tight between her hands. For each wave that came in, she answered it with her drum, letting the metal beads mimic the wave.

"To change the weather, you must first use the beat of your drum to connect with the elements," said Nee-nah's musical voice from the water.

Elm nodded, playing the requested rhythms with her bare hand.

A circle swish for Air. A full hand stroke for Water.

"Good," said Nee-nah, still out of sight. "Now concentrate on the ocean waves. Study their crests. Become one with the water."

Elm stopped drumming to study the waves, but nothing magical happened. "Dammit."

Nee-nah's laughter crested with the waves. "As the daughter of a mermaid, this should be easy for you."

"You know she's not a real mermaid," Elm said in frustration. "She's just some stupid showgirl. *Ex*-showgirl. Where are you, Nee-nah?"

"Here I am!" Nee-nah called out, her head bobbing near a boulder. "Please try to remember to communicate through your thoughts."

Sorry. I forgot that human voices give you a headache.

"In this lifetime, your mother is nothing special," the mermaid explained. "In this world, your mother cannot even control her own body. But she came from the water—as you do—although she does not remember how to *be* the water. Do you understand? You must remember, Elm. Now try again."

And so Elm tried repeatedly to become one with the water and repeatedly failed. Two hours later, she picked up an abandoned shell and threw it in the water.

I can't do this, Nee-nah. I'm hopeless.

"Go to the water," the mermaid insisted.

No, I'm tired.

"Go to the water!"

Elm set the drum down next to her backpack and walked to the water's edge.

Now what?

"Dive in."

But I have my clothes on.

"Take them off then."

Elm glanced behind for onlookers.

Do I have to? I've never been naked outdoors before.

"Then this will be a new experience," said Nee-nah, sounding bored.

Well, okay, but don't look.

When Elm was satisfied they were alone, she removed her T-shirt, shorts, and underwear. Then she waded, feeling the cold assault of wetness envelop her body.

"What were you worried I might see—your funny legs?" Nee-nah giggled. "You need to stop worrying about what others think. Do what you wish, the others will follow. Or not. Claim your power."

Claim my power.

"Now tell me how you feel."

Cold. Very cold.

"You will get over that," said Nee-nah. "Just don't think about it. The less you feel, the more powerful you become."

After her lesson, Elm wasn't ready to go home so she decided to stop at Holy Cow Sundaes. She thought about Nee-nah's advice. The mermaid's instructions were simple, but could she really train herself not to feel?

Reading from the multicolored menu hanging from a cloud-shaped sign behind the ice cream counter, Elm couldn't decide if she preferred Mango White Chocolate over Truffle Temptation. Then she saw the weekly special and wished she hadn't.

> ***Noah's Chocolate Ark***, a classic French vanilla bean and rainbow sherbet, cradled inside a molded, chocolate ark stuffed with white chocolate-dipped animal crackers.

Elm heard Sarah Lightfoot's braying laugh and spun around to see her sitting with Noah in one of the red vinyl booths, eating ice cream sundaes.

God, he looks great.

The line was moving, but Elm barely noticed because she couldn't stop staring at Noah. And then he did something that grossed her out. He dipped his finger into the whipped cream and painted Sarah's mouth.

It's not like she's pretty or anything. All she's got are big—wow, he's not even trying to hide it!

The attraction was abundantly clear because Noah's eyes kept lowering to Sarah's huge rack of breasts that hung suggestively over their table like a second dessert.

"They're such a cute couple, aren't they?" chirped Mrs. Lightfoot, her ice cream scoop at the ready. "Well, what can I get for you today, Elm?"

That stupid Noah. Why is he torturing me?

She knew why, of course. She had mistreated Noah for over a year, so now he was getting his milk—and his ice cream—from that laughing, toothy cow for free. And Noah knew Elm would hear about it.

The less I feel, the more powerful I become. The less I feel, the more powerful I become.

A customer tapped her on the shoulder. "Excuse me, Miss, but it's your turn."

"Huh?"

Elm dashed from the shop, seething from the image of Sarah Lightfoot feeding Noah a maraschino cherry from her sundae.

She was well-acquainted with the power of cherries.

CHAPTER 19

T HE DAY BEFORE HER TRIP, Elm returned to Nee-nah's cove with her Book of Water.

She had worked on it all summer, beginning with a brand new black leather journal with blank pages. She decorated the cover with a drawing of a full moon over the ocean, then framed it with tiny shells and glitter. Inside were collected water legends, pictures of water goddesses and seashells, gem elixir recipes, magical incantations, moon rituals, and tide notations that she had documented in silver ink.

"Today you will summon a tidal wave," Nee-nah told her. "Ready? Now!"

Whoa!

Elm's breath felt like it had just slammed on the brakes.

Wait, how do I do that? I mean, shouldn't I say my magic word first?

"Like an incantation?"

I've got some of those in my Book of Water, but I was thinking about using only one word to start off with. I've got a cool water word that's Latin.

"It is clarity and intention that makes the magic work," said Nee-nah. "You are the sea priestess. Say one word, many words or no words—it is your choice. Now where is your altar?"

The small tin box was inside Elm's backpack on the blanket. It contained one white tealight candle, one tiny seashell, a matchbook, one vial of rose essential oil, and a second vial filled with tiny rose quartz and clear quartz crystal gemstone chips.

Here it is. Should I light the candle now?

"Proceed."

Elm removed the lid, propping it against the box like a lean-to, then packed clumps of moist sand behind it to ensure her valuables would be protected from the wind.

Standing barefoot, Elm felt the electricity in the sand. She took a deep breath, then lifted her arms to address the water, focusing on a wave in the center of her view.

Aquaortum!

Incredibly, the wave rose higher and higher until it was nearly thirty feet tall. It rolled towards Elm at a quickening pace until it crashed onshore and she fell over backward.

"Wow!" she cried. "I did it!"

But as delighted as she was, Elm's training was far from complete. She still had to learn how to communicate with the sea spirits and the dolphins, and how to change the weather from calm to stormy to calm again.

Nee-nah had also promised to teach her the language of the seashells, although Elm wasn't sure how that would help her increase her magical powers. She knew she wanted to make a good impression when she met up with "AvalonGirl," "FireDragon," "GoddessKnows," and her other cyber friends at the Goddess Temple in Glastonbury. She didn't want them to think she was just some silly nobody practicing pretend magic with seashells.

But how am I gonna learn everything before I leave for England tomorrow?

"What's your hurry, Sea Priestess? It will take you centuries to know what I know," the mermaid declared. "And maybe not even then. Class is over. Payment now, please."

I hope you like it.

Elm removed an ornate hand mirror from her backpack. Adorned with sparkling rhinestones, the mirror had once belonged to Glorie's grandmother, which Elm had casually taken from its usual place on her mother's bedroom dresser.

She felt no remorse for the deed—but why should she? Did Glorie feel bad about Royce being murdered or when she got rid of the dogs?

Besides, one stolen mirror was small payment for the ancient knowledge that Nee-nah provided.

SEVEN HOURS.

Elm had never flown before and wasn't enjoying the experience.

A young boy had been kicking the back of her seat for most of the trip and her legs were cramped. She was also tired of reading celebrity magazines, tired of her head buzzing from the altitude, tired of the constant drone of the engines. And she was most certainly tired of the prattle of multitude conversations:

> "Well, you know I wasn't gonna just let her
> get away with that so I told her she
> could kiss my—"

"Mama, Joey said there aren't any clowns at
    Piccadilly Circus. He's lying, isn't he?"
"I can't believe we're married. Me—Mrs.
    Anthony James Sardello…"
"Are you sure we didn't leave the garage
    door open? What about the back door?"
"Logan, get your finger out of your nose
    and give that doll back to your sister!"
"Excuse me, but that's my seat."
"Mommy, when are we gonna get there?
    I'm tired of sitting!"
"Hey, it was your mother's idea. I didn't
    want to come on this trip in the first
    place."
"Yes, it's all free, like in the hotel. Just stuff it
    in my bag and keep your mouth shut!"

Snow sat next to Elm, looking out the window,
humming and happy. It was her first time on a plane, too,
but nothing seemed to bother her, not even the odor of
gaseous babies and sour milk. She wore earphones and her
head was bobbing, so Elm supposed she had tuned out the
real world.

Good for her. Now it's my turn.

Elm had been practicing a visualization technique
called Dimension Hopping. After watching a few how-to
videos online, she had successfully hopped over to ancient
Avalon for a magical conference for priestesses.

Sitting in an airplane wasn't the ideal hopping situation
but Elm was determined to try. Curious about her life as an
adult, she was eager to get into the alpha state to meet one
of her multiple doppelgangers in other dimensions.

After inserting her earphones, Elm turned to a New

Age music station and settled back in her seat. *Ten. Nine. Eight. Seven…*

She reached alpha state.

Elm visualized she was walking down a long corridor inside George Sunday High School. At the end of the corridor was a single metal locker, *her* locker. There was no combination lock, so she lifted the latch and walked in.

Waiting for Elm on the other side was an older, very pregnant version of herself.

"God bless you, younger Elm," gushed the hostess, her strawberry blond curls pulled back into a bouncy ponytail. "Welcome to our humble home."

Hi, Elm. I'm sorry to bother you but I'm on a plane to England and I'm bored out of my mind so I thought it would be cool to see what my life is like in another dimension.

"No problem. Let's go into the parlor," said her waddling doppelganger. "Actually, I'm not surprised by your visit. In fact, if you hadn't arrived, I would have come to see you."

The house seemed familiar and it should. The giveaway was the huge wooden cross hanging on the wall.

You live in Ruth's house?

"Well, it hasn't been Grandma's for a long time. She decided to become an artist and moved to a cottage at Faith Camp Meeting Grounds. She sells her paintings to the tourists. They're very good. Colorful and cheery, like her, you know?"

You're kidding.

"I'm guessing Grandma is nothing like that in your dimension," laughed The Other Elm.

No, mine is completely different.

The two Elms stared at each other. Laughing, The Other Elm said, "I'm sorry to stare, but this is so unusual, isn't it?"

I'll say. And it seems like you knew I'd be visiting.

"I did," said The Other Elm. "I knew it was just a matter of time, even though time doesn't really exist. In truth, everything exists simultaneously and that is why there are parallel dimensions. So how old are you now, Elm?"

Sixteen.

"That was a fun age. It was important to me because that's when I received 'the calling.' Well, you're welcome to stay here and observe. My best friend is hosting a baby shower for me in the backyard. I've been trying not to peek out the window while she's decorating it. Did you know that Grandma put in a pool? We thought it was strange, considering what happened to Daddy's brother. Anyway, the shower's supposed to be a surprise, but I've known about it for weeks."

Congratulations.

"Thanks. We're having twins."

Elm spied a framed wedding photo, depicting Snow dressed in a violet-colored bridesmaid gown.

So how is good ol' Snow?

"Snow Whitedove? She's fine. Busy teaching at the high school, of course. She's my sister-in-law."

Sister-in-law? Then who's your best friend?

"Oh, that's Sarah. Sarah Lightfoot. We grew up together. Do you know her?"

Yes, Elm did, but Noah knew her better.

I used to babysit for Sarah's mother. I love Holy Cow ice cream.

The Other Elm was puzzled. "Ice cream? So you're not lactose intolerant? I can't even go near the stuff without gassing up!"

There was a commotion as people were arriving through the front and back doors.

"Elm! Where are you?"

"In here, Noah!" said The Other Elm. She looked at Elm and whispered, "It's probably best that I don't speak to you for a while. But you're welcome to stay and watch me eat cake. Just follow me to the pool. No one else will see you except me. It will be our little secret, Elm."

The backyard looked like a Noah's Ark convention. There were rainbow balloons and streamers everywhere and the yard was crowded with family members, friends, and half the congregation of Grace Church, all wearing animal hats.

A "Two By Two" double rainbow sign hung over a long, turquoise-covered table where towers of colorfully-wrapped gifts had been stacked. Another table displayed an assortment of appetizers and a giant rainbow cake with a chocolate ark.

Sporting a fuzzy brown bear cap, Big Dave was juggling two large presents when he found his daughter.

"Happy Shower Day, Babycakes!" he said, kissing her on the cheek and nearly spilling his cargo.

"Here, let me help you with that," said Glorie, taking one of the gifts and placing it on the table. She was the picture of health and wore an identical bear hat to Big Dave's.

"Thanks, Hun," said her husband, handing the second gift to Glorie. "So, Reverend Smith, what do you think of that dimension-hopping book I gave you to read?"

The Other Elm laughed, holding her abundant belly. "Oh, Daddy, you know I love it. In fact, Noah's been doing some hopping himself. And thanks to *If You Want to Remember Who You Are, You'd Better Start Dimension Hopping*, I learned a lot about me. For instance, I thought it was rough carrying twins and writing church sermons every week, but my life could have turned out so, so different!"

"Like how?" Noah asked. He was wearing a rabbit hat.

"Like, what if I had made different choices? What if I had skipped college and not become a minister? Can you imagine if you had married someone else or if I became a sea priestess?"

"A what?"

"A sea priestess," said The Other Elm, tossing her golden red curls. "Apparently I wanted to have power over everything and everybody, including the water. And in this particular alternate experience, Mermie was sick and Daddy drowned."

"Gee, thanks a lot," said Big Dave. "I hope I had a big, juicy steak before I was offed."

"Sorry, you were a vegetarian in the other dimension, can you believe it? And you weren't a neurologist, either. You actually owned the marina."

"You're kidding," said Noah. "The Moonwaters have owned the marina, the beach, and Purity Park before the first colony was even founded by the Puritans. I don't think I'm liking this parallel world of yours very much, Elm."

"Oh, don't worry, Honey," his wife assured him. "Daddy let you work for him!"

The Other Elm also explained that her doppelganger kept having a disturbing dream about an audition. "Maybe *that* Elm didn't know what it was about, but I think I do. Remember the first time I tried to organize a youth choir? I think every child in Little Blessing lined up for those auditions—and I just didn't have the heart to reject any of them!"

"But eventually you did," said Snow, wearing an elephant cap. "My poor little Bobby didn't make the cut."

Noah draped his arm around his sister. "No, he didn't, Sis, 'cause let's face it, poor little Bobby can't sing."

"But have you seen his drawings of tree houses?" his

wife interjected. "Some of them are very good. So maybe his gift is creativity."

"That's true," Snow agreed. "I think he's going to be an architect someday. But this topic of parallel lives is real interesting. I mean, you sure don't preach these things at church, Elm."

"That's for sure," The Other Elm agreed. "Anyway, the book says we all have numerous versions of ourselves so that we can have a variety of experiences. So you might be poor in one life and rich in the other. Or you might be married in one life and single in another. That kind of thing."

Noah winked at Big Dave. "Hmm. I wonder what my single life is like."

"Don't even think about it, Noah," The Other Elm warned, "or you just might find yourself doing a solo at church next Sunday."

"And that's punishment for everybody," Snow groaned. "Bobby may not be able to carry a tune, but even God covers his ears when Noah is singing!"

The Other Elm sidled up to Big Dave and gave him a hug. "You know, one of the most curious things about my other life was that I discovered you've been keeping a little secret, Daddy."

All eyes were on Big Dave.

"Who, me?" he said.

"Yes. But maybe it wasn't real. I might have dreamt it."

Jason overheard the remark and tipped his eagle hat at his boyhood friend. "A secret, huh? And you didn't tell your best friend?"

Ruth joined them, her giraffe hat wobbling. "Well, Lord knows I love my son but I've watched him all his life and I can tell you in all certainty that David is an open book. The child never could keep a secret. Am I right, Mermie?"

"Boy, are you ever, Ruthie!" said Glorie.

Big Dave blushed. "Okay, I'm officially embarrassed now. Let's change the subject. Who'd like a swim?"

"You don't have to ask me twice!" Glorie said, racing her husband to the pool.

Tired, The Other Elm waddled to a chair by the pool to watch her parents.

"Hey there, Elm," said Snow, sitting next to her. "You forgot your hat!" Chuckling, she pulled the rabbit hat over The Other Elm's head.

"Thanks a lot."

"No problem," said Snow. "So, Noah said the boy's name is 'Fisher Moonwater,' but he won't tell me the girl's name. He says it's a secret."

"Ha! He means it's a secret from *him*. Okay, Snow, I'll tell you but you've got to keep it to yourself for now, okay?"

"Come on, Elm. When have I ever blabbed? Seriously, what's the name of my new niece-to-be?"

"Silver," said The Other Elm. "Silver Violet Light-mover Smith."

TURBULENCE AND SNOW'S FINGERNAILS DIGGING INTO Elm's wrist jolted her subconscious mind back to the Third Dimension.

"Well, that was exciting," said Kat, retrieving her book from the floor. "Oh, good. No harm done. Elm, have you ever heard of Mary Magdalene?"

Elm sighed. Kat had been reading a book about the saint for the past few hours and now she wanted to talk about it. She would have much preferred to stay with The

Other Elm to learn how Glorie and "Ruthie" had become such great friends.

"Yeah, she was that prostitute from the Bible."

Kat brightened. "Actually, she wasn't. It all began with a mix-up with too many Mary's in the New Testament and then Pope Gregory the Great proclaimed her to be a prostitute, but she wasn't. So after thousands of years, the Catholic Church cleared her reputation by making Mary Magdalene a saint. Many people think she was one of Christ's apostles and probably his wife. Her feast day was July 22, did you know that?"

Elm stared blankly. Why *would* she know that? She hadn't been raised Catholic. And who was this Mary person to her? Was she a sea priestess?

"No, I didn't," Elm mumbled, hoping that was the end of Kat's questions for the day. The woman always seemed to be staring at her, as if she was scrutinizing her soul, searching for the faintest hope of light.

Whatever.

Elm removed the eye mask from her complimentary in-flight kit, placed it over her eyes, and thought of England.

CHAPTER 20

A S THEIR JET LANDED AT the airport in London, Elm and her companions were unaware that an emergency meeting of the Little Blessing town council was in session.

The six council members looked grim as they sat around a long oak table, carved in 1706 by the famed local carpenter Marcus Sunday.

Terence Sharpe sat at the head, clearing his throat and pushing his glasses to the top of his long, straight nose.

"Let's make this meeting as brief as possible because we all want to get back to our homes before the storm. According to the National Weather Service, Hurricane Jonas will hit within thirty-six hours. The regatta's been canceled, which is a shame because it's always good for business. But I don't want to dwell on that now. I'm glad to see that most of the shops and businesses have already been boarded. Jason, what is the situation with the animals?"

Jason glanced at his notes. "Autumn has called all the residents to tell them they need to get their animals indoors. When I leave here today, I'll patrol the town to make sure there aren't any pets left outside. We can take maybe twelve more animals at the shelter if we need to. Other than that, Autumn's told everyone how to create an emergency pet disaster kit. We want to make sure people remember to include their animals' medical records, leashes, collars, food, and water—that kind of thing."

"Excellent," said Terence. "Virginia, how are we doing with the emergency shelter?"

Virginia Chamberlain, the town's gap-toothed librarian, nodded. "It's nearly ready. We've got food and water and about fifty beds and blankets set up in the high school gymnasium. There's a first aid station, too, and a backup generator if we lose electricity."

"Sounds good," said Terence. "I hope we won't need it but we must be prepared because some people may have to be evacuated. And the ferry's not running, which means that all the tourists are pretty much stuck here until the storm passes over. So the rest is in God's hands." He paused, wiping the sweat from his forehead. "Now the next order of business is to discuss the matter of His Honor."

There were a few nods and one "That's right" and Terence continued. "Sad to say, it looks like Alzheimer's has taken full possession of our mayor."

Robert Small, an ironically small man with bulging eyes under his red fishing cap, agreed. "I'll say. Last month I found him here in the chambers, just staring at a page in the bylaws. For probably five minutes, like he was memorizing it. And when I asked him what he was doing, he said, 'Who are you?' Very sad."

Waving her jangly charm bracelet, Mary Elizabeth Carpenter, the young stringy-haired recording secretary, broke in.

"Yes, and don't forget what happened at the barbecue.

Thank goodness our fire chief was already there to control the flames. Otherwise, Lord knows that Purity Park would have been burned to the ground."

There were more "uh huh's" and one "That's right" and Terence continued.

"Okay, let's be honest here, Folks. Big Dave's done a great job as mayor for many years and everyone respects him but we need to find a replacement. Otherwise, it's only a matter of time before he's completely catatonic."

Mabel Sunday Black, who was Big Dave's roly-poly second cousin, put away her silver nail file before she spoke. "Look, that incident at the barbecue is completely overblown. It was just a little fire on a paper plate and it got taken care of immediately and not by the fire chief. Obviously, I've known my cousin my entire life. He's a good man and I love him. Having said that, it breaks my heart to agree with the rest of you. We can't have a mayor who's an embarrassment to the town."

Jason cleared his throat. "Ruth Sunday hired a live-in caregiver, so he's got someone watching over him now."

"Oh, I can just see his caregiver attending council meetings," Mary Elizabeth huffed. "Look, Jason. We know he can't control his illness and it's a real shame and I feel sorry for him and his family. But we have to replace him. There's no getting around that."

After twenty seconds, Virginia broke the collective silence. "What about Glorie?"

"Oh, I'd take Glorie out of the equation," said Jason. "She doesn't have the energy nor the brain power to do the job, and she wouldn't accept the position even if we asked her. I checked our bylaws and it says the spouse only takes over as mayor if he or she is capable."

Robert drummed his fingers on the table. "So Glorie's out. But we have to put it to a vote right now. Today.

There's a hurricane coming and we need a capable mayor to lead us, especially if we have any emergency situations, God forbid."

As the presiding officer, Terence made the motion everyone had dreaded. The hands went up and the decision was unanimous. Big Dave was no longer the mayor of Little Blessing.

Another vote was taken and his best friend, Jason Moontree Smith, was appointed his successor, effective immediately.

"So that's it," said Terence. "Mr. Mayor, do you have anything to say before we get back to our families?"

Jason glanced at each of the concerned faces around the table. "Yes, I do. God bless Big Dave and his family. And may God protect Little Blessing."

"Amen!"

ELM SLEPT FOR NINE HOURS IN A CHEERY YELLOW AND pewter gray canopied bed inside a stately manor. According to the brochure lying on the end table next to her, the inn had an excellent rating, a charming hostess, and was conveniently located near Bath.

After a delicious breakfast of fried eggs, bacon, sausage, and grilled tomato (Elm decided that real sea priestesses really do eat meat), the threesome waited for a taxi to take them to Bath. From there, they bought tickets for a sightseeing tour aboard a double-decker bus that drove around the historical city.

Kat and Snow were literary buffs and wanted to walk in the steps of Jane Austen, which was not Elm's idea of fun. She never understood the appeal of *Pride and Prejudice* or *Emma* nor the rest of Austen's books. And she sure as heck didn't want to know more about the incredibly uptight Mr. Darcy. But she had read about The Great Bath, the centerpiece of the ancient Roman community spa, and felt drawn to it.

"Listen, Kat," said Elm. "I'm gonna go nuts if you drag me through that Jane Austen stuff. What if I just go on to the Roman baths and we can meet up later?"

And I'll get a few hours to myself when I don't feel like I'm on a leash.

"Sorry, Elm," Kat said. "I'm responsible for your safety and I don't feel comfortable letting you run off somewhere, especially since you've never been there before."

Seeing the frown on Elm's face, Snow added: "Oh, cheer up, Gloomy Gus. We'll go there after lunch at the Jane Austen tea room. Seriously, it won't kill you to learn something about great literature."

"It just might," Elm huffed, dreading a full morning of droning audio history and prissy costumes.

IT WAS SUMMER, SO THE LINE TO GET INTO THE BATHS WAS frustratingly long. But Elm had a feeling that something important was going to happen there so she continued through the archways and terraces, pushing in and out of the crowded rooms, and getting nauseous from inhaling too much limestone dust and sulfurous steam.

They finally reached the Circular Bath, intriguing with its green water and shiny floor of copper and silver coins.

This is the place. I know it is.

She decided to linger, managing to lose Snow and Kat in the process, which had been her intention all along.

When she thought no one was looking, Elm stretched her right hand over the water. Concentrating hard, she visualized that she was raising her arms, just as she had learned from Nee-nah.

Aquaortum!

Even though she had been successful back home, she was surprised to see the bath water actually rise a few inches.

Excellent! So I can do this in England, too. I wonder if I can get it to go higher.

What occurred next was unexpected. And frightening.

Lying on his back and levitating twelve feet above the pool was Big Dave. Elm had never experienced a vision before and as her father floated towards her, she froze, afraid of the message she was receiving.

"Honey, look!" said a middle-aged American tourist behind Elm. The woman was dressed in a horizontal turquoise-and-white striped shirt, red pants, and a red visor cap. "Look at what that young girl's doing!"

Her husband, wearing a black baseball cap, turquoise Bermuda shorts, white socks, and a white I ♥ NY T-shirt, bent over the pool and shrugged. "So the water's rising. So what?"

"Do you think she's part of the show?"

The man stood next to Elm to get a closer look. "Probably," he guessed. "I'll bet they've got a computer hidden somewhere and she's pressing a button to activate the water."

His wife was unimpressed. "Well, our water shows are much better in the States. And they're not in stinky old bathtubs, either!"

Snapping out of her trance, Elm glared at the couple leaving through the stone archway.

Stupid, stupid Americans. Don't they care that I can hear them?

She shook her head and continued through the chambers to The Great Bath.

CHAPTER 21

NOAH WAS IN THE MARINA office, listening to the radio and calculating in his mind all the things he needed to do before Hurricane Jonas hit Little Blessing.

It was predicted to be the largest storm to strike the East Coast in forty years and most of the town's residents were either busy nailing boards to their windows or moving bicycles and garbage cans away from their homes.

He pressed the button on his phone. "Hey, Martin." Martin was the new marina manager.

"Hey. How's it looking out there?"

"Uh, calm right now," said Noah. "Should be here by sunrise tomorrow."

"Okay, I just left the hardware store," Martin said. "Can you get the dockhands to put away the picnic tables and the barbecue grills? After that, have them get the chairs and tables from the pool area and lock them up in the storage room."

Noah left the office and walked towards the swimming pool. "Roger," he answered. "And should we drain the pool?"

"Negative," said Martin. "Just pour more chlorine and make sure you unplug the pump motor and anything else electrical."

"Roger."

"And Noah? Don't forget to tell all the boat owners about Jonas, just in case they haven't been listening to their radios. They probably are, but you never know. And tell them about the emergency shelter at the high school. Some will probably stay on their boats, but they need to know they have an option."

THE TEMPERATURE IN LITTLE BLESSING WAS ALREADY steamy hot at quarter past nine. Bored with chilling upstairs in their living quarters with the air conditioning blasting, Glorie needed the pool. She needed to feel the cool, soothing water on her sore body. She needed the healing.

Getting into the pool was always tricky, especially without Big Dave to spot her. She glanced at the man she married, sitting in front of the television set with no idea what he was watching. Sadly, the man she married did not even remember he had a wife.

Since she had gained so much weight (no doubt due to inactivity and her craving for carbs and Holy Cow sundaes), Glorie was unable to find a bathing suit that was flattering. Shaving her legs was difficult, too, but she was determined to be in the water and maybe stay there until noon.

"I'm going to the pool now, Kathleen!" she called out.

The caregiver was a godsend. Not only did she cook and clean, but she proved to be a terrific companion for Big Dave.

"Okay, Ma'am!" said the female in the living room.

Glorie was already wearing her shorts and tank top, so she grabbed her cane and a towel from the bathroom and walked out into the brilliant sunshine.

She could see the pool from the top of the stairs. It looked so clear and inviting that Glorie couldn't wait to merge with the water. She grabbed the railing and shuffled down the ramp to the pier. From there, it was another thirty yards to the pool.

Glorie tightened her towel around her, then opened the white picket gate. Two women were sitting at a table. Adorned with gold chains and bracelets, the tanned travelers were laughing and chatting about their latest adventure at sea with their yacht captain husbands.

There was a hushed silence as Glorie waddled down the step tiles at the shallow end of the pool.

Once her body's water connected with the water in the pool, Glorie felt miraculously whole again. Soon she was on her back, floating towards the center as the sun's golden rays cleansed her body, mind, and soul.

"Good morning, Mermie."

Glorie looked up and paddled herself upright until her toes were touching the bottom of the pool. "Good morning, Noah."

"I hate to interrupt your swim," he said, holding a container of chlorine, "but there's a hurricane coming and I need to make sure you and Big Dave and Kathleen are safe. My dad will be over later to check on you. Hopefully, you won't have to evacuate but I'll let you know."

"I guess that means we'd better go find the guys," said one of the women. They grabbed their towels and left.

"Thank you, Noah," Glorie said, making her way to the edge of the pool. "I didn't think it would be here for a while yet. Would you help me out, please?"

"Sure," he said, reaching for her hand. "It's a good thing Elm's away in England, right? I mean, you won't have to worry about her."

Had they shared their thoughts, they would have realized that neither could ever stop worrying about Elm.

AFTER A LIGHT BREAKFAST BEFORE DAWN, ELM FOUND herself huffing uphill with Snow and Kat for nearly an hour, hiking along the legendary labyrinth until they reached the top of Glastonbury Tor. It was their first point of interest on what Elm had secretly dubbed The Oh-My-Goddess Tour. Avalon, mystics, fairies, ley lines, enlightenment, The Goddess—all the ancient wisdom was there in that one sacred spot and Kat raised her arms to accept it.

"Let's say a prayer of thanks," she said, closing her eyes.

Winded, Snow collapsed on the ground at the foot of the archway. "Amen!" she puffed, wiping her sweaty forehead with her sleeve. "Thank you for getting me to the top of this hill!"

Elm remained standing. She removed a small pouch from under her cloak and took out a small, handmade prayer book from the turquoise lining.

"Dear Mother Goddess," she began, attempting to sound serious and powerful. "We thank you for guiding us and for giving us the courage and freedom to reach new heights as we continue our magical journey. Please continue to light up our path with blessings and keep us safe. We love you and shall always remain your faithful servants."

Kat and Snow exchanged glances. "That's a nice

prayer, Elm," said Kat. "You seem to be in your element here."

Yes, I am. But I can't believe I'm standing in one of the most sacred places on earth with this stupid Fluffy-Bunny-Lighter.

Elm had hoped for a stronger reaction from Kat when she emerged from her room that morning. She was wearing a long, forest green cloak with a hood, several strands of crystals and amethyst pendants, and extreme eye makeup. But Kat didn't react. The woman maintained her serene temperament, even when her luggage was temporarily lost at the airport.

Elm explored St. Michael's Tower and rested on the grass for a while. Afterwards, the trio joined the meandering line of curiosity seekers, "New Age Travellers," and purple-robed pagans to make the downhill trek, past beautiful green fields dotted with sheep.

Back in the medieval town, Elm quickly understood why the legendary Isle of Avalon was considered one of the most powerful, magical centers on earth. Nearly every proprietor catered to the magic folk, selling mystical wares like runes, tarot cards, amulets, and crystals.

It had begun to rain so they hurried inside an old bookstore, a musty jumble that reminded Elm of a shop she had seen in a Harry Potter movie. Despite the weather, Elm could have happily stayed in Glastonbury all day. But since they were on a bus tour with a tight schedule, Kat said they had to browse quickly.

Jeez. What's the fun in browsing fast?

Despite her doubts, Elm managed to find and purchase three books during their allotted time. She went to look for Snow, who had two books tucked under her arm and was still browsing through the higgledy-piggledy mess.

"You'd better hurry," Elm whispered. "The Kat Lady has her claws out. So what books are you getting?"

Snow looked surprised to be asked. "I've got a book on crop circles and one on The Holy Grail. That was the chalice with the blood of Christ that some people think was buried under Glastonbury Tor by Joseph of Arimathea. Apparently, he came here, stuck his staff in the ground and that's where a red spring appeared. They say that if you drink the water you will have eternal youth."

"And Chalice Well is where we're heading after lunch," added Kat, placing *Reiki in Avalon* on the sales counter.

"Where are you ladies from in America?"

The salesperson reeked of patchouli and wore a dark blue robe. He was tall with straggly brown hair, a thin nose, green eyes, and spacey teeth that resembled cashews.

"Little Blessing," said Kat, handing the man her credit card. "It's in New England. But how did you know we were from the States?"

The man laughed, but offered no explanation.

After leaving the bookstore, Kat led them to a noisy pub where they ate tasteless *chips* and *pasties*. Pouting, Elm left most of hers on her plate. She had hoped for lunch at a little cafe they had passed while shopping at The Glastonbury Experience. The scent of buttery, fresh-baked bread was heavenly and there was a folk duo playing their guitars in the courtyard.

Why can't I listen to the songs of Avalon? Why do we have to go where Kat wants to go? Why do we have to be on a stupid schedule?

"Don't sulk," Snow whispered in Elm's ear. "The cafe you wanted to go to was crowded and nobody wanted to wait in the rain for an hour."

Elm grew even grumpier when Kat told her they didn't have time to visit the world-renowned Goddess Temple.

"That's just great," Elm huffed.

Now my friends will think I lied about going to meet them at the temple. I'll never be able to show my face in chatrooms again!

As Elm noticeably stewed, Kat went into a quick meditation for guidance.

"Okay," the chaperone announced in her cheeriest voice. "Let's all breathe in the color yellow to invite the sunshine into our hearts."

Scowling, Elm doubted Kat had the power to make her feel good about anything.

CHAPTER 22

T HE SOUND OF A HURRICANE is sometimes described as a constant *whoosh*, a deafening thunder or a howling freight train. To Glorie Sunday, already tormented by a long list of Lyme-activated fears, Hurricane Jonas would forever haunt her dreams as one day-long scream.

Since their apartment windows had been boarded and Glorie was feeling confined and eager to see the sky, she chose to have her morning coffee and danish on their balcony. Big Dave was watching cartoons in the living room while Kathleen made his steel cut oatmeal. Fortunately, he still remembered how to swallow but he had lost his appetite and was thin and frail.

The wind was getting stronger. It blew Glorie's newspaper right off the cafe table and she watched it fly over the marina like a runaway kite. Her stomach was queasy as she sat and watched the rising waves and foreboding gray sky. Two of the transients were tying new lines to their boats and she wondered if they were staying with their vessels or heading later for the emergency shelter.

She was startled when the phone rang on the table.

"Glorie? It's Jason. Look, I'm coming by with the van in an hour. Noah is coming, too. He'll help you pack what you need and then I'll come back to get all of you to take you to Ruth Sunday's house until the storm has passed."

"How bad is it going to be, Jason?"

"It looks like a Category Four," Jason replied. "So we're expecting winds up to 140 miles per hour. The storm surge might get as high as twenty feet so the marina's going to get flooded for sure. That's why we need to get you all away from the water and safely to higher ground."

There was no person in Little Blessing who flaunted her moral high ground more than Ruth Abbott Sunday, so it was no surprise that her house was situated on higher ground than her neighbors. Had Glorie just witnessed a miracle? What other reason would urge Ruth to open her big black-hearted door?

She finished her coffee and rose from her seat, wondering which was more unsettling—the approaching hurricane or living with her destructive mother-in-law.

ANOTHER DAMN ROUNDABOUT.

The tour bus was heading in the direction of Loch Ness. They hadn't planned on going to Scotland, but the site of the mythological Nessie monster was only eight hours away from where they spent their previous night in York, so they decided the diversion might be fun. Kat couldn't get Glorie on the phone to tell her about the itinerary change, so she left a message on her voice mail.

Elm's impression of their trip thus far was underwhelming, although she did enjoy the sweeping countryside of Yorkshire, the medieval city of York, the Lake District, Bath, Glastonbury, and parts of London. But she disliked the hordes of summer tourists, hated the biting "midges," longed for a soda with more than one ice cube, and would *kill* for a salad that offered more than a small wedge of lettuce and a tomato. With the exception of Stonehenge (whose genuine stone height was a huge disappointment), Elm was most disillusioned with Chalice Well.

Not that the gardens weren't as lovely as the guidebooks described. But Elm had expected the *wow* factor at the well. What she got was an hour's worth of beauty but nothing particularly exciting, unless you count the fact that she almost tripped over a stray cat on her way to the sacred waters.

Elm had sat on a meditation bench and closed her eyes but no visions occurred. She stood over the Chalice Well head and no friendly spirits materialized to support her. She raised her hand over the trickling red water and the water level did not change. Unlike the euphoria she felt in Bath and at the top of Glastonbury Tor, Elm was powerless at Chalice Well and she didn't like it.

On the other hand, Kat felt the Divine Feminine everywhere she walked and reported all kinds of miracles. She had dipped her hand in the red spring and healed a hangnail. She had prayed for guidance and received a special message of peace from The White Lady. She saw orbs, too, and told the girls that she had been gifted with a clearer understanding of the union between male and female, as well as light and dark.

As peeved as she was about Kat being the one having revelations, Elm did manage to revive her tired feet in the spring and sip some of the iron water. It tasted bloody and vile, but Elm did feel more energetic, so she bought a glass bottle and filled it with water spewing from the Lion's Head fountain.

~

THEY HAD REACHED LOCH NESS. HUDDLING UNDER A large black umbrella, Elm stood shivering in the summer rain on a loading platform at Urquhart Bay Harbour, her bones invaded by an aching chill.

They were boarding a twelve-passenger tour boat, despite the fact that Kat had left her seasickness pills in her Loch Ness hotel room. She tried to laugh it off, saying: "I guess this is the Universe's way of telling me that I need to take more risks."

The day was dreary with a heavy mist hanging over the cold dark water. Kat found a seat on the aft deck and the girls sat beside her as they watched the rest of the tourists pile on, eager to begin their great hour-long Loch Ness adventure.

Apart from the rain, the cruise was pleasant, motoring past Urquhart Castle, Cherry Island, and Fort Augustus Abbey. The skipper gave historical highlights over the loud-speaker but Elm tuned him out because his strong accent made his words sound like gibberish.

"Wow. Can you understand this guy?" she asked Snow, who was snapping pictures of the passing vista.

"Not really," Snow replied. "I'm not even sure he's speaking English."

Elm stared out at the water, thinking about something she had read about "selkies." According to the ancient legends, they were shapeshifters that could appear as seals or humans. This, of course, made her think of Royce.

"Water, water
Cleanse my spirit
Flood my life with
Magic song."

Snow tapped her on the arm, yelling in the wind. "What did you say?"

Elm shook her head. "What? I didn't say anything."

She glanced around. A boy wearing a silly frog cap was searching through his mother's purse for a juice box. Kat hung her head over the side in misery. No one was staring at her except for Snow.

> "*Water, water*
> *Cleanse my spirit*
> *Flood my life with*
> *Magic song.*"

"You did it again, Elm—you're chanting something!" Snow cried.

"I am?"

Snow gave her a funny look, then went back to taking pictures. Bored, Elm stretched out her hand over the water and waited. Nothing happened. She tried again and the result was the same. Was this to be a repeat of her failed experiment at Chalice Well?

But I'm a sea priestess. I'm supposed to control the water.

"You do not control *me*."

What? Who said that?

"Look into the water, 3-D."

Elm obeyed but saw nothing but a murky lake with ripples.

"Not with your physical eyes, 3-D. See me with your Third Eye."

Elm closed her eyes and "looked" upwards between her eyebrows. In her mind's eye, she saw all the water in the loch disappearing, as if it had been resting in a huge sink and flushing quickly down a drain. When the last drop of water was gone, she saw only an empty lake with a rocky bottom littered with fish skeletons.

Where are you?

The water refilled and the loch returned to normal.

"Look again."

She did and that's when she found herself staring at a creature that looked amazingly like the Loch Ness Monster photos she had seen in the brochures. It rose to an intimidating height, stretching its long neck toward the boat until they were eye-to-eye.

Before she could blink, Elm was dragged under by the great mythological beast!

CHAPTER 23

ELM LANDED ON A SOFT grassy spot on the banks of the loch. The rain had stopped and a double rainbow hung like a painting in the crystal blue sky. Their colors tasted like tropical fruit salad.

"Welcome to my home," the voice said.

Elm sat upright to face a huge dinosaur, grazing on emerald green grass.

Wow. You're big. You look like a brontosaurus. Well, sort of. Are you Nessie?

"If you wish, 3-D."

And you can read my thoughts, too.

Elm wondered why she wasn't afraid. After all, this was the legendary Loch Ness Monster. She decided to take advantage of the opportunity to practice her telepathy.

Why aren't you in the water?

"The water is a portal to the last dimension."

So you just sort of visit us every now and then?

"Exactly, 3-D."

Why do you call me "3-D"?

"It's short for Third Dimension. That's where you come from."

I guess so, but where am I now?

It looked like the same Loch Ness landscape from the postcards except there were no boats, no roads, no buses, no people, no castle, no abbey, no buildings of any kind.

Suddenly, there was a swarm of voices buzzing about her:

"Is she the one?"
"Yes, I think so."
"Where are her wings?"
"I don't think she has any."
"What a pity."
"Maybe they come out at night."
"Do you think she'll stay?"
"How could she?"
"Hush—all of you!"

A small being with illuminated wings materialized, handing Elm a leaf from an alder tree.

"Tree mail!" she giggled.

Elm sniffed the spicy leaf and read the engraved words that magically appeared in liquid gold light:

Miss Elm Sunday of Little Blessing, Planet Earth
is cordially invited to attend a Once-in-a-Lifetime,
Magical, Enchanting, Unbelievably Fantastic
Come-as-you-think-you-are Party.

Elm stared at the invitation in her hand. *A Come-as-you-think-you-are Party. What is that?*

The fairy's wings flapped with excitement. "Did you think? Did you think?"

Elm could barely think at all because the fairy was pointing a crystal wand at her, causing her to twirl about like a ballerina in a music box.

Did I think what?

"Who you think you are," Nessie offered. "It should be the first thing that comes to mind."

Seriously, it's hard to think when you're spinning around. Okay, I'm a sea priestess. Is that what you mean?

"No. Think again," Nessie said.

But that's it. That's who I am. I'm a sea priestess!

"Are you sure?" a new voice whispered.

Elm was tired of playing games and the fairy must have gotten the message because Elm's body stopped spinning.

Okay, where am I and what am I doing here?

Elm found herself leaning against the trunk of an alder tree, overlooking the water. There were hundreds of butterflies of all colors and sizes resting on its white trunk and branches.

"Hello, Elm."

Hello?

"Do you not recognize me, Dear One?"

The tree shook, causing some of the butterflies to scatter. Then a violet ray detached from one of the rainbows and encircled the alder.

"Miss Vi?"

"Yes, it is I," said the tree.

Elm was so overjoyed that she gave the tree a big hug. "But you look so different," Elm said. "I mean, you're not a pine. And you're in Scotland. Or at least I think this is Scotland. How did you get here?"

"The same way you arrived, Dear One. Magical thinking."

As if on cue, a parade of Elm Sundays pranced before

them on the grassy runway, all modeling different Elms from different periods of her life. There was the sweet, strawberry-haired toddler, the little mermaid, the Girl Scout, the homeschooler, the babysitter, the jewelry designer, the sea drummer.

But where is Elm, the sea priestess?

Her thought whisked her away to an ocean cave reeking of seaweed and dead fish. She was dressed in a long sea-green robe with pale blue crystals sparkling from her neck and earlobes. Reciting incantations to control the water, she was unsuccessful, cold, wet, and very much alone.

Seconds later, Elm transformed into an alder tree in the same grove as Miss Vi. She marveled at her new roots shooting deep into the soil and the butterflies tickling her arm-like branches.

"Like me, you are an alder tree," Miss Vi said in her airy whisper. "We are ancient and magical. Now tell me what you see, Dear One."

From her new vantage point, Elm could see Loch Ness and the surrounding villages, the House of Parliament in London, the Eiffel Tower in Paris, even the White House in Washington. But when she began witnessing blood-soaked battlefields, polluted waters, abandoned babes crying for their mothers, flag burnings, angry crowds and shouting politicians, she stopped looking.

Depressing. Like watching television.

"I agree," said Miss Vi, sighing. "Unfortunately, it is what we have come to expect of the Third Dimension."

Elm was about to agree when she felt a sudden movement in her roots, leaves, and branches. When her consciousness returned to its human form, she looked up at the ancient alder and said, "Whew. You can really see a lot when you're a tree."

Feeling a bit embarrassed, she wondered if Miss Vi recalled a certain day when Elm had spent some serious make-out time with a certain Noah Skyfeather Smith.

Miss Vi chuckled. "Your secret is safe with me. But I have been saddened by your recent tree mail."

"Oh. Bad grammar, huh?"

Or maybe it's my penmanship? I think that last letter I sent you wasn't very pretty.

"None of that, Dear One," the tree replied. "The major issue, sad to say, is that you have attached to the energy of fear. This is why you are angry much of the time. And because of that anger, you have sworn to use magic with the intent of demonstrating power and control. You no longer exhibit traits of compassion for your fellow human beings and you are caustic and judgmental. Can you not move into a state of loving everything as equals?"

Everything?

"I don't think so, Miss Vi," said Elm, entranced by all the different Elms posing before them. "But I do love Royce, and my daddy and our dogs, but they're gone now. And I guess I still love my friend Snow, although she can be a real pain. And maybe Noah."

She thought of Noah playing whipped cream artist with Sarah Lightfoot's lips. "No, definitely forget Noah."

"And your mother?"

"Cross her off the list, too." The woman formerly known as Mermie was a traitor and a poor excuse for a parent. She didn't deserve Elm's love.

Suddenly, the procession of Elms formed a sacred circle around their guest. They spun into a carousel of lightbodies, forming a dancing kaleidoscope of red, orange, yellow, green, blue, indigo, and violet. Then the lightbodies changed into a group of Glories, then back into lightbodies, then switched into a circle of Elms again and disappeared.

Elm was not alone. Standing before her was a congregation of mythological creatures—fairies, leprechauns, elves, brownies, gnomes. Even Nessie and a unicorn were among them.

"Like you, we are all one being, all light and all connected," Miss Vi explained. "And we are all creators, Elm. That is the real magic. So I ask you to reconsider your choices very carefully. Be mindful of what you create or there may be dire consequences which you are not equipped to handle."

A horn sounded, indicating that Elm's time with Miss Vi had ended. Like a missing puzzle piece that was finally connected to make a complete picture, the violet ray returned to its place on the rainbow, now flashing in neon colors. The *Come-as-you-think-you-are Party* had officially begun!

Elm laughed as the butterflies blew up into all hues of balloons and streamers. One settled in her hand and wrapped itself around her wrist as it led her through an energizing rainbow waterfall.

"But wait!" Elm had stopped so abruptly that the butterfly detached itself and settled into the nearest tree. "I didn't bring my sea priestess costume."

"What does it look like?" asked Nessie, winking at the fairies who were giggling in the bushes.

"I'm not even sure," Elm admitted. "Sort of like a mermaid but without the tail. Mystical-looking, powerful. Lots of amulets, seashells in the hair. Carrying a crystal wand—that kind of thing."

Elm had no sooner spoken than a fairy presented her with a beautiful sea priestess gown, robe, jewelry, hairpiece, and wand. The entire wardrobe not only sparkled, it changed colors every few seconds.

She sat on a stone bench, feeling very regal in her costume as the fairies served her a trayful of rainbow cupcakes and sunbeam lemonade. Every color tasted delicious!

Besides the food, there was colorful entertainment. The elementals opened with their extraordinary manifesting and flying abilities. The next act showcased Nessie tossing rainbow rings on the unicorn's horn. There were many more performances, but Elm especially enjoyed The Heathers, a trio of purple-haired botanicals who sang a swinging rendition of "The Bluebells of Scotland."

Overall, it was a fantastic party, one that Elm would remember for the rest of her life. She almost felt sorry for Snow and Kat, who were far, far away in rainy 3-D land.

BACK IN LITTLE BLESSING, THE WIND WAS HOWLING AND the trees surrounding the Sunday's Marina property were bowing to the air.

Glorie peered inside the living room, where Kathleen and Big Dave waited on the couch, the latter wearing his white Sunday's Marina cap and teal sailing jacket. Their packed suitcases were next to the front door and Glorie had an intense suspicion that she had forgotten something.

Never in a million years would she have guessed that they would be evacuated from their home, and now she had to decide what she could not live without.

She found a recycled shopping bag in the kitchen, filling it with objects that were important or sentimental and could never be replaced. In went her wedding album, marriage license, a framed photo of Big Dave in his Navy uniform, and Elm's baby book containing a lock of strawberry gold hair from her first haircut. She also managed to squeeze in a bulging file folder containing their most important household and medical documents.

When the bag was full, Glorie set it next to the suitcases and continued to hobble through the rooms, judging what was expendable and what was not. She retrieved a mermaid backpack from Elm's bedroom closet and grabbed whatever she could from her daughter's room.

Her last stop was her own bedroom. She searched through her jewelry box to locate the most precious pieces and scooped them into a white organza bag. That's when she noticed that something precious was missing from the dresser top, an heirloom that could never be replaced.

Jason and Noah were walking through the front door, dressed in hurricane jackets.

"Is everybody ready?" asked Jason. "Noah will be back to pick up your computers and turn off all the electrical appliances."

Glorie panicked. "Jason, I can't find my mirror. It's always on my dresser but it's not there now and it belonged to my grandmother and it's an antique and—"

Exchanging worried glances with his father, Noah said: "I'm sorry, Mermie, but we really need to leave now. The wind picked up so fast and it looks like the marina's gonna get clobbered. Wait here for a second and I'll come back to help you."

Glorie burst into tears, watching as Jason and Kathleen led Big Dave carefully out the door and down the ramp to the marina parking lot. Noah left with a suitcase under each arm and followed them.

Grabbing one of her ridiculous-looking floppy pink starfish hats, she pulled it over her head and walked out to the balcony to wait for Noah.

Looking out at the crashing waves and listening to the sounds of halyards clanging and the docks shrieking, Glorie's senses were on overload. Feeling dizzy, she grabbed the railing but the wind was too great and she fell to the floor.

"My hat!" she screamed, as it rolled off the balcony and merged with the storm.

Down below, Jason had just helped Kathleen get into the van. She was extending her hand to Big Dave when they heard Glorie scream.

Then the former mayor did something unexpected, if not miraculous.

As if a floodlight had switched on in his muddled brain, Big Dave suddenly stood at attention. He looked up at Glorie on the balcony and cried, "I hear you, Mermie! Don't worry, I'll save your hat!"

With near superhero strength, Big Dave pushed free from Jason's hold and ran through the hurricane winds, chasing the rolling hat as it traveled the pier. Jason fought to go after him but a board broke off an upstairs window and flew in front of him, striking his arm and hitting the van.

Glorie was horrified. She watched helplessly from the balcony, screaming "Dave! Dave!" but he kept chasing the hat through the flying debris, the wind taunting and pushing his prize further away from his grasp.

The last thing Glorie remembered seeing was a giant column of waves and Big Dave running off the pier into the hungry ocean.

CHAPTER 24

I T TOOK A FEW MOMENTS before Elm snapped back into her body and realized that she was on the boat and the cruise was over.

"Wow," said Snow, laughing. "You were really out of it."

Kat nodded. As seasick as she was, she scanned the girl's energy with her hands. "Your Third Eye is wide open but the rest of you is seriously out of balance, Elm. We've got to get back on the bus now but I want to give you some Reiki when we're at the hotel."

"No thanks," said Elm, feeling triumphant. She was certain that being the guest of honor at a *Come-as-you-think-you-are Party*, attended by Nessie, Miss Vi and an assortment of mythical creatures, completely eclipsed Kat's trivial experiences at Chalice Well.

You're the one who's seasick. Go balance yourself.

"Well, if you change your mind—" Kat said, heading for the bus.

"I won't."

Before boarding, the trio stopped for a quick peek at

the information center's museum and souvenir shop, where Elm bought a stuffed Nessie toy.

"Well, I guess that was a total bust," said Snow, when they were on the bus, looking out at the rainy countryside.

"Not really," said Elm, stroking Nessie's plush fur and thinking about her adventure.

"You're kidding, right? I'm talking about that damn Nessie not showing up! The closest anyone got to that thing was that stupid toy you're holding."

Elm shoved the little Nessie in Snow's face. "Don't you call me *stupid*," she said in a squeaky mouse voice, although she knew the real Nessie's voice was much deeper.

"Oh, give me that thing!" said Snow, grabbing Nessie and using it as a headrest.

Elm pinched Snow, who returned the toy immediately.

"So where the hell were *you*, Elm?" Snow asked. "When you zoned out on the boat?"

"At a party," Elm replied, still holding the alder leaf. The gold script was no longer visible, but it was the only keepsake she had from her multi-dimensional experience.

When they returned to their country lodge hotel that evening, Elm wished she had stayed with her magical friends because the message from Noah was a real downer:

Emergency! Please come home.

GETTING BACK TO LITTLE BLESSING WAS EXASPERATING. Neither the summer ferry nor the year-round daily ferry was running, forcing the group of weary travelers to stay in a hotel in Boston for five days. Thanks to Jonas, the city sidewalks were a mess so they spent most of their time in their rooms, reading and talking but anxious to return home.

With the power lines down in Little Blessing, Noah was unable to keep in touch for their first four days. When he and Elm finally connected, his words were like a punch to her heart:

Big Dave is dead. It was an accident. I'm so sorry.

Instead of crying, Elm remembered a time when her goldfish had died. To comfort her, Big Dave took her aboard the *Sea Angel*. He had attached a purple kite to the sloop's hull and they watched it bobbing through the wind as he told a story about a little girl (just like her) who was sad about losing her goldfish.

"It's okay to be sad when you lose someone you love," he had assured her. "Thankfully, the Creator gave us the color violet and all its hues to help us through the grief."

And now Daddy is dead.

Noah picked them up from the ferry landing, driving through Little Blessing in silence. Not since The Great Hurricane of 1938 had the town suffered such devastating loss and destruction.

Hundreds of trees had downed and much of the community was still without power. Elm was sad to see that the carousel was overturned and the mermaid chariot and several plaster dolphins and seahorses were strewn across the beach.

"Oh, thank God," Kat muttered, as they passed Hallelujah House, still boarded.

It looked like Holy Cow Sundaes, the tea house, and all the other shops on the ground floor had suffered little damage. As they approached the corner, Elm held her breath. Even though she was mad at Glorie, she still had fond memories of playing and working at the mermaid store.

"Look, Elm," said Snow, excitedly. "Sea Angels made it!"

Yeah, but Daddy didn't.

DAYS LATER WHEN IT WAS SAFE TO GO MUCKING ABOUT, Jason and Noah surveyed the damage at the marina.

The Sundays' apartment got the worst of it. The upper floors of the building were completely destroyed. Amidst the rubble of books, broken china, glass, furniture, and clothing, Noah spotted Elm's starfish pillow and tucked it inside his jacket.

"Well, everybody who stayed here with their boats is safe, thank God," Jason told Noah. "But it looks like there's a year's worth of repairs needed. Now that I'm mayor, I'll make sure the marina is a town priority. Big Dave deserves that."

They headed up the pier, talking to boat owners and to Martin, the marina manager, who had survived "the perfect storm" aboard his fishing boat, *The Reel Deal*.

Noah glanced up at the clear blue sky, then down to the top deck of *My Retirement Plan*. The owner had not returned to his boat since before the storm. The water and wind were calm now, yet the deck chair was shaking.

"What's going on here?" Noah muttered as he went onboard to investigate.

Perched on the seat was a squawking young seagull hiding under a floppy pink hat. Next to it was a dirty Sunday's Marina cap.

"It is a sign from Big Dave," Jason said. "He is back in the heavens now. Go in peace, my brother."

Look at all these stupid Easter lilies. What do they think is going to happen, that Daddy will rise again like Jesus?

Maudlin organ music played as mourners paid their last respects at the Grace Church of the Ascension. While the choir sang "Rock of Ages," Elm sat with her head bowed in a front pew between Snow and Noah, recalling a father-daughter nature hike through Purity Park.

"Do you see this?" Big Dave had asked the eight-year-old, pointing at an odd-shaped tree. "It's a tree marker. It was bent that way by the Native Americans when the tree was a little sapling."

Elm had reached out to touch the tree and exclaimed, "My hand is buzzing, Daddy!"

"That's good," said her father. "Now send it love. Remember that everything is connected, Elm. So as you send the tree love, it will love you right back."

She touched the tree again and whispered: "I love you, Tree!" A few moments later, she was elated. "I feel it, Daddy! I feel the love!"

It was a good memory.

Now she was raging inside, trying to make sense of a senseless situation.

Why did her father have to die? Where was Kathleen when he was running all over the place? Wasn't she supposed to be watching him? And what about Glorie? Where was she at the time?

I'm sending you love, Daddy. Please come back! I'm sending you love!

Months after the memorial service, the town

honored its favorite son with an engraved plaque, mounted on a boulder in front of the Little Blessing Town Hall & Post Office.

Jason renamed his animal shelter "The David Sunday Shelter for Lost Animals" and launched an animal parade to help promote adoptions.

The most unusual tribute was a new sandwich created by The Good Book Tea Room:

> *Big Dave's Compassionate Thanksgiving*, a generous portion of roasted vegan turkey, native cornbread stuffing, mashed butternut squash, and tangy orange-cranberry sauce stuffed inside a golden, heart-shaped bun.

Like the man himself, it quickly became a hometown favorite.

CHAPTER 25

T HE DAY THAT NOAH DELIVERED Elm's bike to Ruth's house could not have come sooner for the antsy girl. She had barely thanked Noah before she made her escape, peddling furiously to Purity Park.

Elm hadn't visited Miss Vi since before she left for England. She was relieved to find that the tree had lost only a few branches during the hurricane, although she had to be extra careful while climbing the ladder because two steps were missing. Once inside, she found the tree-house in total disarray.

While clearing away some of the mess, Elm happened upon a yellowed letter trapped in a floorboard. She settled back against a damp pillow to read the faded writing.

Dear Miss Violet:

I am running away from home. I don't want to but Mother is being very unreasonable. She won't let me go swimming. In fact, she ordered me to stay away from the water completely.

But how can I get my Boy Scout merit badge without going in the water? I told her that I love the water and that I would be extra careful but she screamed and screamed and said George died in our baby pool and did I want to kill her, too? She said she would have a heart attack if I disobeyed her and then she made me stay in my room all weekend to read the Bible. I couldn't go out to play at all.

You know I can't talk to Father about this because he is usually at the church or visiting a congregation member and is rarely at home. And when he is home, he lets Mother run the house, and does she ever!

Curious about the author of the letter, Elm scrolled down to locate the signature. *David.* The only David she knew was her father. It was strange to think of her father as a boy, to discover that he had had problems with his mother, too! This surprised Elm because they usually got along so well.

I miss my brother, even though I see him every day. Jason says there is a special bond between twins and that is why George's spirit visits me. I probably shouldn't have mentioned this to Mother because she said the devil is making me see George and it's not really George but another demon and that I am going straight to hell for believing in ghosts. I told her I am not going to hell, that I am a good boy and I get good grades and I do all my chores and I love God. But Mother says she doesn't want to discuss it anymore and that she has decided I must quit Boy Scouts altogether.

Elm was stunned to learn that her father was a twin. If George had lived, would they have taken turns being mayor? Had Big Dave felt guilty for the death of his brother?

This reminded her of a story Glorie had shared about the famous singer Elvis Presley and his deep attachment to his deceased twin, Jesse. According to her mother (a self-professed Elvis fan), "The King of Rock 'n' Roll" felt guilty about being the living twin. She didn't know if her father felt the same way but there was a similarity between Big Dave and Elvis. They were both men of great faith.

So this is why I am running away. I don't want to quit the Scouts. I don't want to stay out of the water. I don't want Mother to boss me around anymore. I am 11 1/2 years old and almost a man. I think I might join the Navy someday. Maybe I'll come back to Little Blessing and tell you about my big adventures. I hope you are well.

Love,
David

The more Elm mulled over the letter, the more she was convinced that Water had betrayed her family. She had no intention of ever sending it love again.

CHAPTER 26

Oⁿ Elm's ꜱᴇᴄᴏɴᴅ ᴅᴀʏ ᴏꜰ her senior year, she was suspended.

The assistant principal called her into his office after lunch. Mr. Langmore did not conceal his disapproval as Elm shuffled in, wearing a long black dress and a dozen strands of Celtic and Egyptian paraphernalia. Her exaggerated eyeliner was thick and winglike and her jet black hair hung loosely in a dry, scrunchy mess.

"Take a seat," he ordered, pointing to a chair.

"If you say so."

"Do you know why you are here?"

Okay, I'll play his game.

"Do I know why I am *where*?" Elm countered.

Mr. Langmore was a nervous, balding man with no patience for smart alecks. "Do you know why you are sitting in my office?"

"Because you won't let me stand?"

"I don't like jokers, Miss Sunday," he said. "Here at George Sunday High School, we have rules. And one of those rules is we never strike a teacher."

But she struck me first.

"Oh, is that all? Well, that crazy Mrs. Winslow assaulted me first. She grabbed my arm and wiped my face with a tissue."

"We have witnesses who say you pushed her and that's how she fell on the floor."

Elm picked up a pencil from Mr. Langmore's desk, drumming on her knee.

"Well, would *you* let some old biddy touch *your* face?"

He held out his hand for the pencil. Elm shrugged and dropped it in his palm.

"I have personally seen the bruises," he continued, "and you had better hope she won't be pressing any charges."

"Hey, what about *my* bruises where she pulled my arm and practically tore my face off?" Elm rolled up her sleeve to reveal a large purple mark.

The man was not impressed. "How do I know that wasn't self-inflicted, Mercy-Faith? I interviewed several of your classmates and from what they told me, Mrs. Winslow was merely demonstrating how you were abusing our school's dress code."

They're trying to change me. They're trying to change who I am, and it's not fair. I won't let them.

Elm stood up with such force that the chair fell over.

"Yeah, in front of the whole class, so she was abusing *me*, Mister."

In truth, English Lit had been one big yawn and a giant waste of time because Elm was a million light years ahead of her fellow students. Or so she believed.

"Sit down," Mr. Langmore commanded.

"I don't like your chair," Elm said.

She continued to stand as the assistant principal

removed a thick, spiral-bound document from his desk drawer and handed it to Elm.

"Here is a copy of our official school handbook. I have taken the liberty of highlighting some of the rules you have already broken during this first week of the new school year."

Elm grabbed the book and read aloud in her snootiest voice:

"All students of George Sunday High School are expected to treat their peers, faculty members, and administrative staff with nothing less than the utmost respect. All acts of defiance, bullying, and violence shall not be tolerated and may result in suspension."

She let out an exaggerated snort and threw the book across the room, barely missing the assistant principal's head.

～

Dear Miss Vi,

This tree mail is going to be longer than normal because I'm running away from home and I have a lot to tell you. Actually, I don't really have a home because Hurricane Jonas completely destroyed it and most of my stuff is gone.

Anyway, I was staying with my grandmother but I had to get out of there after I got suspended from school because she was driving me crazy. Would you believe she ordered me to change my hair back to its natural color and take off all my makeup? I'm surprised she didn't have me dunked in the bathtub again.

Anyway, I told her where to go (yes, really!) and I packed up my suitcase and just left. Mother's still there, of course, and they're prob-ably yelling at each other right now about who's supposed to be taking

*care of me and how will I survive in the big bad city without a job or
a diploma and should they call the police. Mother threatened to leave,
too, but Grandma told her she's got nowhere to go and then they both
started bickering again about what Daddy would have wanted and
I'm so tired of it. Unfortunately, I don't have any real friends I can
trust. As you know, Snow and Noah are super snitches.*

*Did I ever tell you about Garrett? He's the guy I met online, the
one with the motorcycle. Noah hates him. Anyway, Garrett lives in a
trailer in Ashland with his two cats and I'm going to stay with him
for a while. (In case you don't have your higher dimensional gifts yet,
Ashland's about two hours from Little Blessing.) Garrett says I have
to help pay for his rent, which won't be easy because I won't have a
job at first. Until I find one, he says I'm going to have to sell my car.
Won't that make Grandma mad!*

*Between you and me, I don't love Garrett but that's okay because
I know he doesn't love me, either. He says I'm jailbait, but we have
fooled around a little. I know what you're thinking, Miss Vi, but
don't worry. I'm still a virgin and I plan to stay that way. Sometimes
I wish I could talk to Mother about all this boy/girl stuff but I still
hate her for getting rid of our dogs and for what happened to Royce.
And now I TRIPLE hate her because I heard that Daddy died trying
to save her stupid hut. It makes me so mad when I think about it.
Snow says I'm always mad these days, but so what?*

*Sometimes I think that Daddy will come back. He'll be walking
along the marina pier and somebody will stop him—probably Noah
—and we'll find out that he didn't really drown because he's been
living on an uninhabited island somewhere with amnesia. Wouldn't
that be cool?*

*Actually, I had a weird dream about Daddy. He was swimming
in the ocean and he kept telling me to send love to the water before it
was too late. Too late for what? I don't get it. Anyway, I still love you
and hope you still love me.*

Your friend,

Elm

P.S. I don't want you to think that Mother had our dogs killed or anything. She had Jason pick them up and Snow says that they were all adopted. So that's good, I guess. But I'm still mad. Do you ever get mad? Like when somebody pulls your branches or a bird pees on you? Ha ha.

OVER A YEAR HAD PASSED SINCE BIG DAVE'S DEMISE AND now it was Christmastime. Glorie was watching television in her room at Ruth's house when her phone rang. The television was a gift from Jason, who had convinced Ruth that her daughter-in-law needed some form of entertainment.

The phone rang again and Glorie answered it. "Hello?"

"Mother?"

"Hello? I can't hear you. Just a minute."

Glorie muted *I've Got Your Number* and said, "Who is this? Have you found my husband?"

"Mother, it's me. Elm."

There was silence.

"Are you there?"

Glorie paused a few beats before answering flatly. "Daddy's *gone.*"

She hung up and unmuted the television.

Elm stared at her phone in disbelief. It never occurred to her that Glorie would be angry at *her.*

As if a brass gong had sounded, Garrett's two cats, Mini and Me-Me, stood upright from their perches at opposite sides of the bedroom. Their ears twitched, listening for the scraping of food into their metal bowls. They bolted, and Elm laughed at the sight of little white Mini bunny-hopping over her younger, darker sister.

Garrett was up. She knew this because he had blown his nose so hard that the sound echoed like an elephant trumpeting. At least he had fed the cats. Now she had some time to think about her next plan of action.

"Did you get your grandmother?" Garrett asked. He was naked and leaning on the bathroom door.

"No."

Garrett's face reddened, which it always did when he was perturbed. "What do you mean *no?*"

"She wasn't home."

Elm sprawled across the bed, pretending to read a crumpled tabloid magazine about government conspiracies.

"Dammit, Tree Bark," he said, throwing his wallet at her. "What's it gonna take for you to fill this baby up?"

"Well, you could always get a job yourself," she replied matter-of-factly, "instead of sitting around smoking pot all day and collecting unemployment."

Whack!

Elm covered her eye with her hand, stinging from the punch. Garrett had been hitting her a lot lately, but she refused to cry. The jerk didn't deserve her tears.

"You made me do that, Elm," he said. "Now get back on that phone and tell your sweet little old grandmother or her maid or her answering machine that we're coming for a visit."

He grabbed a towel from the linen closet and slammed the bathroom door behind him.

Elm stared at the door, listening for the shower running. She grabbed her patchwork gypsy bag from under the bed, searching for money but finding only a few dollars. Then she saw Garrett's wallet on the bed. Without hesitation, she took it and counted out eight $100 bills.

Where the heck did he get this kind of money?

She stuffed the cash in her jeans pocket, grabbed her purse and shoes and tip-toed to the tiny kitchen. It was a disaster with dilapidated cabinets, a graffitied refrigerator, sink full of dirty dishes, and the garbage overflowed with empty beer bottles.

She paused to check her sore eye in the small car mirror by the door. *I'll buy some makeup to cover it later.*

Garrett was singing now and since his showers were brief, Elm had no time to pack any clothes. With her bag hanging from her shoulder, she turned the doorknob and left the trailer. Mini and Me-Me had their faces stuck in their food bowls and never noticed she had gone. She wondered if they would miss her. Probably not. Cats weren't as needy as dogs.

THE HIGH CITY EXPRESS WAS FULL OF HOLIDAY PASSENGERS, so Elm felt fortunate to find a seat next to the window. She wished she still had her car, but she'd rather be a pedestrian for the rest of her life than have to deal with Garrett again. Why did she ever get involved with that guy? She was smarter than that!

As the train jerked forward, Elm couldn't believe she had to spend the next few hours sitting next to a heavily-perfumed woman wearing jingle-bell jewelry, singing Christmas carols with her friends across the aisle.

Elm used to love Christmas. She had fond memories of the Christmas Parade of Sail and the Moonwaters' annual Christmas Eve dance. She even missed her mother's Southern Pralines and her pink and turquoise "Under the Sea" tree lights.

Looking out her window at trees, houses, farms, people, cows, horses, city buildings, garbage, dogs, and cats, Elm felt a twinge of guilt for leaving the cats in the care of a twenty-five-year-old degenerate.

Lucky for them they have eight more lives.

"Next stop…High City!" the conductor cried.

Elm grabbed her bag and made her way to the front of the car. She had no idea what to expect from the big city, but she was confident that a powerful sea priestess could handle anything.

Even a year without Christmas.

CHAPTER 27

E LM SAT AT AN OUTDOOR table at *The Stone's Throw Cafe* in High City with her spiral notebook opened. She was doodling circles while watching school children pour through the doors of the high school across the street.

I can't believe it's September already.

As she watched a giggly cheerleader throwing her pompoms around her boyfriend's neck and kissing him, Elm thought about Noah. Did he ever think about her?

Surviving in the big city had not been easy. One of the skills Elm had to learn was the fine art of lying. When asked her name, she told people that she was Snow Moon-water, a twenty-one-year-old Native American from Alaska. Elm thought the black hair made her look more mature, so she used a black marker to mask her strawberry blond roots. It was a cheaper solution than hair dye.

Without a job, money was scarce. When the cash she had stolen from Garrett was spent, she contacted Snow, who was upset but willing to send her a money order. Snow's money kept her eating for a few days but it wasn't security, so Elm was forced to stay for a week at a women's shelter in the grungiest part of town. It wasn't too bad because they gave her a bed and three meals a day, in exchange for washing dishes and mopping floors.

When her week was up, Elm slept in an alley next to a dumpster. For cash, she cleaned out toilets at night in an office building with a woman she had met at the shelter. But overall, Elm never knew when her next meal would be and often her dinner consisted of a bag of chips and a candy bar from a vending machine. The few dollars she had saved were tucked away in her gypsy bag, now hidden beneath the cafe table.

She nearly jumped when her phone rang, identifying the caller as Noah.

"How did you get this number?"

She knew the answer, of course. Blabbermouth Snow had told him. She half-listened to what became one long rant about her not being there for Glorie and what did she hope to accomplish on her own when she didn't even know how to take care of herself.

Yeah? Well, thanks for reminding me that you're nothing but a big ol' pain and you always will be. And to think I was actually missing you.

"Did you know that your grandmother had the assistant principal call in a bunch of kids—including my sister—to see if she could get them to tell her where you are?"

"So?" Elm felt sorry for the girl who got stuck with Noah, and then she remembered that The Other Elm had married him. *Poor woman.*

"And on top of all that," a frustrated Noah continued, "your grandmother hired a detective to find you and Snow Queen's about to crack under the pressure."

It figures.

"Look, Noah," she said, lowering her voice and trying

not to sound concerned, although she was suddenly suspicious of every person reading a newspaper. "I can take care of myself. I've got friends here. Friends that don't judge, you know? So this is goodbye, Noah. Don't ever call me again—unless you want to send me money!"

She pressed *End* on the phone and angrily sipped her cold coffee.

Noah called back. "By the way, Mercy-Faith, Happy Belated Birthday!"

This time, Noah hung up first.

Damn!

Why did Noah have to call? Hearing his voice on the phone made her feel homesick and she didn't want to feel anything anymore. She was eighteen now with new friends and a new life. She had moved on.

Elm had met her new roommates through Willow, a scrawny twenty-two-year-old, bespectacled tarot reader whom she had met at the Flying High Psychic Faire. Elm had seen the event flyer on a bulletin board in the convenience store where she had applied for a job as a cashier. They didn't have any openings but she continued to shop there because corn chips and beef jerky were a cheap meal.

Willow introduced her to The Nine, a group of self-employed independents who always wore black, cast spells on people they didn't like, and maintained a magickal website for teenagers, even though most of The Nine appeared to be in their twenties.

They lived in a drab, basement apartment and allowed Elm to sleep on their flea-infested couch and share an occasional meal, in exchange for her cleaning skills, which were sorely needed. But even though they treated her like their token Cinderella, at least Elm had a safe place to sleep and learn about magick. They taught her how to use protection shields, how to work with the moon phases, and which herbs were the most poisonous. They also insisted that nothing was *true* magic unless the word ended with a "k".

Unfortunately for Elm, The Nine didn't believe she was a sea priestess and frequently made fun of her, saying she was way too young to have that kind of power. And despite assuring them she was a good writer, they refused to let her post a sea magick article on their blog.

Well, why do they even bother hosting a website for teenagers when they won't even let a real teenager write for them?

The Nine also doubted that she had met the Loch Ness Monster or knew any real mermaids. It was a frustrating situation because nothing Elm did or said impressed them and she desperately wanted their acceptance.

Sometimes I wish I could just go back to Little Blessing, practice my sea magick with Nee-nah, and eat a humongous fried shrimp dinner at The Good Book Tea Room.

"Hello," hissed a voice in Elm's ear. "I've been watching you from across the street."

"Uh huh."

She sized the man up, immediately.

Scratchy voice. Fuzzy hair. Missing front tooth. Old guy, probably about thirty. Wearing a torn black T-shirt. Smells like cigarettes.

Her stomach tightened. Could this stranger be working for her grandmother?

"I own the used bookstore. My name is Ronan."

The man extended his hand but she did not shake it. He had dirty fingernails, which Elm figured were from handling a lot of dusty books, ink pens, and probably some cobwebs.

And he might be evil.

She quickly imagined a triple-thick mirror covering her

body like a protective shield, just the way The Nine had taught her.

Now I'm safe. Wow, that was a close one.

"That's nice," Elm replied, keeping her head down and concentrating on her doodling.

"It seems we have a mutual friend," he continued.

"Oh yeah?"

Ronan sat in a chair next to her and leaned over. "Hello, Elm," he whispered, squeezing her arm. "I have a message from Garrett. He wants his money."

CHAPTER 28

THERE WAS NO USED BOOKSTORE across the street. There was a dingy back alley behind the cafe and that is where Ronan was taking Elm.

"Just smile," he said, showing the tip of his switchblade. "And you'd better not scream or I'll have to use this."

Damn, the shield didn't work!

Elm had to think fast. "Look, Mister, I don't know who you think I am but my name is Snow—Snow Moonwater —and I'm from a small town in Alaska and—"

"Shut up, punk!"

The cafe was on a well-traveled street, so there were hundreds of passersby who could have seen the situation. But they all had busy lives and took no notice of one teenage girl and an older man yelling at her. For all Elm knew, they probably thought Ronan was her pimp.

Garrett was waiting for them in the alley, leaning against a wall and drinking beer. As soon as he saw Elm, he chugged the beer and threw the empty bottle on the ground. "So, if it isn't my old friend Elm," he sneered.

Maybe I can pretend to have amnesia.

"Who are you?"

"Who am I?" said Garrett, kicking the broken beer glass with his boot. "I'm just the poor guy you screwed over, Elm Sunday. And guess what? I'm here to collect!"

Elm clutched her bag, wondering if she could use it as a weapon. "Look, I don't know who this Elm person is but—"

Ronan laughed, pushing Elm toward Garrett. "The kid says her name is Snow White. Can you believe it?"

"Oh, she's white all right," said Garrett. He grabbed Elm and kissed her hard on the lips. She tried pushing him away but he was stronger, even though he was clearly intoxicated.

"You can fight me all you want, Tree Bark, but I'm gonna get my money, one way or another. Hold her, Ronan!"

Ronan moved in behind Elm and covered her mouth. He held his knife to her throat with his other tobacco-stenched hand while Garrett fumbled with the zipper of her jeans.

Daddy Lighthouse, help me!

Big Dave had been a peaceable man but he did teach her how to defend herself, at Glorie's insistence. Elm pulled two of Ronan's fingers in opposite directions, then made a hitchhiker's thumb and swung it back to connect with Ronan's face.

It stabbed him square in the eye.

"You stupid bitch!" he wailed, dropping the knife to rub his sore eye.

With no time to lose, Elm turned her attention to Garrett and swung her bag at him. When that failed to stop him, she took aim and kicked hard. It was a direct hit to the testicles as she watched the man she had once "played house with" collapse to the ground in agony.

Elm turned and ran until she reached a subway stop, tearing down the stairs, breathless, knocking into a few people along the way. "Excuse me! Excuse me! Sorry! Excuse me!"

Within seconds, Elm was through the turnstile and jumping aboard a waiting train, heading outbound. She searched in vain for an empty seat but the train was packed, so she was forced to stand between an overweight nurse eating a granola bar and a surly business man with his nose pushed against her breast.

Well, at least I'm still standing.

WHEN ELM FINALLY REACHED THE APARTMENT, SHE FLUNG herself on the couch and cried. Her altercation with Garrett was one of the few times she had ever experienced intense fear.

Finally, she stopped sobbing and sat up, considering the gravity of the situation. She had to tell one of The Nine about Garrett and Ronan, just in case her unidentified dead body ended up in the Crime section of the *High City Times*.

Since all of her roommates had some type of employment outside of their website venture, she turned on the television and waited.

Jade, a spike-haired fast food cashier, was the first to arrive. At nineteen years, she was closest to Elm in age and she didn't treat her with disdain like the rest of The Nine. "Hey, Baby Snow," Jade said, plopping herself down on the couch next to Elm. "What's wrong?"

Elm wondered how much she should confess. "I ran into my old man and he wants money. He threatened to kill me if I don't come up with it."

Jade laughed. "Oh, is that all?"

Is that all?

Elm was disappointed. Out of everyone in the apartment, she thought Jade would be the most understanding.

"Don't you think that's *enough*?" she sniffed, perhaps a little too dramatically.

"Snow, you've got to learn to stand up for yourself," said Jade. "Otherwise, people will stomp all over you. Look, go clean your face and meet me in my room. We're gonna freeze that creep and you won't even need a lock of his hair to do it."

Jade's tiny room was depressing. She slept on a thin mattress on the concrete floor, next to the building's noisy furnace. The only other furniture in the room was a wobbly coffee table with a large rainbow-dripped candle resting on a black ceramic plate. For art, she had thumb-tacked hundreds of autumn leaves on one of the cracked walls.

"So what's the guy's name?" Jade asked, motioning for Elm to sit next to her on the mattress. There was a sealable clear bag of ice on the table, along with a notepad and permanent marker.

"You mean the guy who wants to kill me?" Elm asked. "Or the guy he sent to do it for him?"

Jade removed the cap from the marker and handed it to Elm. "You know what? Let's get both of them."

Elm wrote *Garrett and Ronan* and placed the note inside the plastic bag.

"Now go to the kitchen," Jade instructed. "Fill the bag with more water—maybe leave an inch of space—seal it, and stick it in the freezer with all the other bags."

ELM NEVER SAW GARRETT NOR RONAN AGAIN. SHE supposed the reprieve had something to do with the freezer spell she had learned from her mentor.

She was happy to have made a new friend. Jade taught her spells, helped with her makeup, and even found Elm a part-time crew position at a local fast food place, although Elm hated it. The Sea Priestess had been reduced to sliding on greasy kitchen floors, wiping spilled ketchup from sticky tabletops, and dodging groping hands from drunks who came to sit for hours with one cup of stale coffee.

Now that she was bringing in some regular cash, The Nine expected Elm to pay rent and continue to clean up after them, even though she still had no privacy.

"I don't see why I should have to pay as much as everybody else," Elm complained one night, while The Nine were putting their new web magazine "to bed". They allowed her to observe but the rule was she had to keep her juvenile opinions to herself.

"Look, I sleep on the couch," Elm continued. "It's not like I have my own room or even my own bathroom shelf and I think it's very unfair."

Jeez, I really do sound like a kid.

Storm Sage cackled and threw a half-eaten apple across the room, barely missing Elm's head. The huge woman with the beaked nose and straggly gray-brown hair was the unofficial leader of the group, probably because she was the eldest and in her forties.

Storm Sage was prickly on her best days, so Elm was warned not to mess with her because she excelled at death charms and potions. Indeed, Storm Sage's personal philosophy was "Do unto others *before* they do unto you". Elm didn't want to keep "poking the bear," but she also didn't want to be bullied. She was a sea priestess, for Chrissakes! Had The Nine ever been to Glastonbury or Bath or Loch

Ness? Had *they* ever partied with talking trees and dinosaurs?

She needed a plan. Checking the dates on the dragon calendar that hung on the grimy kitchen wall, Elm couldn't believe she had lived with The Nine for over a year. When she had first moved in, her sole focus was to survive, but she was determined to make a better life for herself, one that didn't include a freezer full of spells instead of food.

It was time to take back her own power and to reconnect with the source of that power—Water.

Elm flipped the calendar to "October" and saw that Halloween was circled in red, with one added note:

Blue Moon Cruise

CHAPTER 29

THE SUPERMOON WAS SO FULL that it looked like it was going to collide with Earth, which was eerily appropriate because it was the night of ghouls and goblins.

High City went all out for Halloween with its month-long spooktacular of seances, ghost tours, haunted hayrides, animal costume parades, jack o'lantern carvings, and a public Halloween ball held in a gothic-inspired castle. For Elm, Halloween was an entirely new experience.

As a little girl, she corresponded with a girl from Texas who wrote her about the blue fairy costume she would be wearing on October 31. Quite innocently, Elm asked Ruth why there were no costume parties or trick-or-treating in Little Blessing.

"Halloween is the devil's holiday!" Ruth had chided. "And you are a very wicked girl for bringing it up."

Elm's penance was to attend a weeknight church service to pray for her little lost soul. As she sat in the pew staring up at the pulpit and trying her best to repent, she wondered if God was really furious at people who were out begging for sweets in their fairy costumes. Surely, He had better things to worry about. After all, it was just one night of the year and the rest of the country seemed to be doing it, so how bad could Halloween be?

Back in the present, Elm's Halloween began with a Blue Moon ceremony in the city park. Dressed in black, Elm, The Nine and six others cast their circle and shared their intentions, followed by a half hour of drumming and dancing. By the time they were due to board the boat, everyone was giddy and high, confident their highest hopes and dreams were magickally manifesting.

Elm was high, too, but for an entirely different reason, thanks to Jade, who had presented her with a little Halloween gift on paper. It took over an hour for Elm to swallow the tab of acid. (Or did it only seem that long?) The paper was dry and scratchy against her throat and even a full bottle of beer didn't clear the blockage. She tried coughing, but that didn't help, either.

Oh, jeez. What if the paper is stuck in my throat and I choke to death?

Jade gave her another two swigs of beer, which finally dislodged the paper.

They boarded the forty-five-foot sailboat, *Soul Destruction*, with her fellow "Halloweenies," who resembled a slithering black snake as they claimed the deck, attacking huge coolers containing ice and ales, and devouring platters of "horror" d'oeuvres in neon colors of orange, purple, and slime green.

Dressed as a zombie sailor, the captain motored out of the boat slip and everybody whooped and hollered because the cruise had begun.

It was cold on the water. Elm clutched her black cloak tightly, looking back at the High City skyline. The buildings were shooting up and down in various electric rhythms and her body responded in near-orgasmic ecstasy.

When they had reached the middle of the bay, the captain turned off the engine. Elm laughed hysterically because his head had blown up into a huge, fleshy balloon, with hair follicles growing like weeds beneath his sailor's cap.

Except for cough medicine prescribed by her doctor when she was little, Elm had never taken a drug before, so it was fascinating to watch the circus of mammoth clown heads quickly surround her, stuffing their abundant faces with booze and appetizers. Additionally, the moon had become so large that it was now bouncing along the water before them, breathing in and out, in and out through its huge "blue" heart.

Wow.

Not only were shapes expanding in size, but sounds had amplified, too. In fact, the conversations of the passengers had become so deafening that Elm was dizzy from listening:

"Hey, what's happening?"
"We're not moving!"
"Captain, Oh Captain!"
"Let's go, Man!"
"Yeah, we want our cruise!"
"I hereby command all the elements in the Universe to make us move!"
"Hey, where's that teeny bopper sea priestess chick?"
"Snow! Snow Moonwater! Where's that kid?"
"Here she is—I found her!"
"Let's get this tub moving, Sea Girl!"

And then Elm felt her body being lifted up and forced to stand on the feet she did not remember she had.

"Blow, Snow, blow!" the voices chanted. "Blow, Snow, blow!"

The world was spinning and Elm was laughing as the moon completely took over the vessel, enveloping her body until its huge moon heart was her heart.

And then she saw Royce and burst into tears of joy.

He was perched on the top of the moon, his smile huge and hypnotic. Then he metamorphosed into a gigantic octopus, stretching his long tentacles towards her.

"Go ahead, Sea Priestess," Royce commanded. "Show these clueless people how you can make a tidal wave."

Elm wiped her tears and clapped with delight as Royce transformed from an octopus to a sea snake to a black seal, then back to the man she loved.

I'm here, Royce—I'm your sea priestess!

"Then show me your anger, Elm," said Royce. "Feel all the hatred you have ever had for your mother and for Garrett and all these know-nothing posers on the boat— and make the water rise!"

I'll do it, Royce. I'll do it for you!

Elm raised her arms and the water rose higher. Her body filled from root to crown with the energy of complete power as she made the tidal wave appear.

The Halloween party was in complete chaos, a sick kaleidoscope of black robes, orange pumpkins, and slime green punch. Passengers were sliding across the deck and into the water and with every desperate scream, Elm laughed with maniacal glee, so proud of her magickal handiwork.

The water completely flooded the boat and the last thing Elm remembered seeing was Royce straddling the moon above her as it floated higher and higher into the sky. He smiled that great white smile of his and tossed a confetti of chocolate-covered cherries. Elm caught one and popped it in her mouth, watching Royce reclaim his octopus persona and squirting massive amounts of black ink until the entire world went dark.

I<small>T WAS OVER A WEEK LATER BEFORE PEOPLE BEGAN TO</small> realize that Mercy-Faith "Elm" Sunday had disappeared. Garrett was at the High City police department filing a missing person's report, confirming that eighteen-year-old Mercy-Faith "Elm" Sunday (also known as Snow Moonwater) was last seen attending a Halloween party aboard a forty-five-foot yacht called *Soul Destruction*. The captain had motored the boat from Green Wharf to the middle of the bay and they partied that night under the light of the Supermoon.

Sergeant Tinker, a large man with a bulbous nose and buzzed haircut, was taking Garrett's report. "Is it possible your girlfriend—"

"*Ex*-girlfriend."

"Okay, is it possible your ex-girlfriend did not get on that boat?" Tinker queried. "There were nine survivors plus the captain and one of the passengers has amnesia, but he's a twenty-eight-year-old male."

"Yeah, I read that in the newspaper," said Garrett. "Elm was there all right. I know because I had a friend keeping an eye on her. He said she was wearing some long cloak with a hood, which she probably paid for with my money. The bitch stole five thousand dollars from me before she left, so how do I collect that?"

The sergeant frowned. "So you're not worried that your girlfriend's missing?"

"No, and I said she's my ex. If she's gone, she's gone.

But I really need that money, Man. I've got bills, you know?"

"Damn!" said the sergeant, slamming his hand on his keyboard. He pushed a button on his phone and said, "Mike? Yeah, Joe. Look, the damn computer froze on me again. Get me something that works, will ya?" He hung up and took out a notepad and pen from his desk drawer.

Garrett was getting impatient. "So what about my money, Sarge?"

Sergeant Tinker eyed him suspiciously. "The investigation is still ongoing, Mr. Waite." He pulled out a form from his desk drawer. "Fill out this form and we'll see what we can do."

"But when am I—"

The desk phone rang and Garrett stewed, barely listening to the sergeant's conversation about how he might resolve his driver issue after he cleared his computer cache.

CHAPTER 30

"**S**unday's Marina. Noah speaking."

"Uh, yeah. This is Garrett Waite. I'm calling about Elm Sunday—do you know her?"

He told Noah that Elm had been on a Blue Moon cruise in High City, the boat capsized, broke into pieces, and Elm was missing, so there was no body found and the cops were still looking.

After a long pause, Noah said, "I know who you are. Okay, tell me how to get there. I'm bringing her mother."

It was a long trip to High City. After their briefing at the police department, Glorie and Noah went to Green Wharf to meet with the boat captain. Unfortunately, he was more distraught about losing his vessel and gave them little hope of finding Elm.

Weary, they sat together on a bench overlooking the harbor to contemplate what they had learned.

"I just don't believe it," Glorie whispered, reaching inside her purse for a clean tissue. "First Dave, now Elm. I can't deal with this."

Noah's heart was breaking for the woman who was like

a second mother to him. "Look, we don't know for sure that she drowned. So what do you want to do now?"

"I want to go back to Little Blessing," she said, wiping her eyes. "I want to be there when Elm comes home."

"You're a liar!" Snow cried, after Noah told her the news. "Elm Sunday is not dead! She wouldn't dare die without telling me!"

Snow ran into her bedroom, where she remained for two days.

The best friends had not spoken in many months, so Snow had no idea about Elm's altercation with Garrett nor did she know anything about the Halloween boat party.

When Snow finally emerged from her bedroom, there was no one at home. In the kitchen, she poured a glass of ginger ale and ate a few saltine crackers. That's when she got a great idea. But first, she had to see Mermie.

Glorie's life since the hurricane had been dreary, so once a month Snow took Glorie to get her hair done at Vanity Hair Salon, then for lunch at The Good Book Tea Room. She listened to Glorie's troubles about being "homeless" and having to live with her mother-in-law, about closing Sea Angels, and about Big Dave and how she knew he would return to her someday. But in all their conversations she never mentioned Elm. Of course, the stress had exacerbated her Lyme disease issues and some-times Glorie's speech was inaudible. Still, it broke Snow's heart to see her surrogate mother in such distress and she wished she could do more to help her.

While Noah waited in the car, Snow rang the doorbell of the old sea captain's house. A dog howled from inside. The door opened and standing there was "The Pray Lady" herself. It was Snow and Elm's nickname for the woman who was forever preaching and predicting impending doom for all sinners.

"Yes?" Ruth said, intimidatingly.

From her red brick and black-shuttered Federal-style house on the hill, Ruth Abbott Sunday had one of the best views of the harbor, which she didn't like sharing with anyone except her dog, Silence.

"Snow Whitedove, Ma'am. I'm here every month."

And every month Ruth treated Snow with the same indifference.

"Do we have an appointment?"

"No, but I'd like to see how Mermie—uh, *Glorie's* doing. I can't get her on the phone."

Ruth peered over Snow's head. "Who's that in the car?"

"My brother, Noah."

"Well, follow me," Ruth huffed, "but don't touch anything."

There wasn't much to touch. The house was sparsely furnished with no knick knacks or family photos displayed.

Snow knocked on Glorie's door. "Mermie?"

Glorie was sitting in a rocking chair, wrapped in a dowdy gray shawl and staring at the television. It was one of the few times Snow had ever seen her hatless and she noticed that her white roots had grown about an inch and a half.

"Hi, Mermie!" Snow sang out, trying to sound cheery. She hugged her friend but Glorie didn't flinch. "Mermie?"

Glorie moaned, unable to speak. The left side of her face was paralyzed and her eyes were glazed.

Snow called out. "Mrs. Sunday? Mrs. Sunday!"

Ruth was not happy to be summoned like a common servant. "What is it, girl?"

"Mrs. Sunday, something's wrong with Mermie. She can't speak. Do you know how long she's been like this?"

Ruth barely glanced at Glorie. "I have no idea."

"Well, I'm calling her doctor."

Snow removed her phone from her jacket and searched for the number.

Ruth Abbott Sunday's lips pursed as she watched Dr. Matthews and his ambulance team remove Glorie on a stretcher. From her sordid facial expressions, it was apparent that Ruth did not appreciate surprise visitors nor being grilled with questions like "When was the last time you looked in on her?", "What kinds of medication was she taking?" or "What was she doing before this happened?"

The doctor assessed that Glorie had suffered a stroke and should be transported to High City Hospital.

"Am I expected to pay for my daughter-in-law's medical expenses, considering the fact that I've been giving that woman free room and board for the past two years?"

Snow answered for the doctor. "You know what, Mrs. Sunday? You don't need to do anything—not one damn thing!"

In the car, Snow quickly told Noah what had happened and called Jason.

"They're taking her to the hospital now but Mermie can't go back to Mrs. Sunday's house, Dad, the old lady is crazy. Any chance you can take up a collection or something to get Mermie into her own house—maybe hire a full-time caregiver until she gets better?"

Mayor Jason came through. When Glorie returned from the hospital, she was moved into a cute, standalone gingerbread cottage at Faith Camp Meeting Grounds.

With Glorie finally settled, Snow and Noah met the following Sunday for a private memorial in Purity Park. First, they hung framed pictures of Elm on Miss Vi's wide trunk and fastened glass mason jars to the tree limbs, filling the jars with water and fresh flowers. Then the siblings performed their version of a Moonwater tribe mourning ceremony.

Noah was on the ground with his drum in his lap while his sister swung her hips to the beat, shaking her colored rattles and chanting: "Ah-hey anah, ah-hey anah, ah-hey anah, ah-hey oh!"

When they had finished, they held hands and admired their tribute.

"She would have loved it," said Noah.

He was gathering their ceremonial tools when he noticed his sister holding a metal box. With trembling fingers, she passed it to Noah.

"Read them," Snow urged, sitting on the ground. "Out loud."

Noah nodded, withdrawing the packet of letters from the box while his sister rocked herself and cried.

Dear Miss Vi,

Can you believe it's almost Christmas again? I'll take the candy canes and the presents, of course, but I plan on celebrating my first Yule with Snow in the treehouse if the weather isn't bad. Wow, wouldn't that send The Pray Lady into a tailspin? Or Mother? Hope there isn't too much ice this month. Do you ever get cold? Anyway, Merry Christmas and I hope you enjoy the orange slices and cloves ornaments I left you. I love you and hope you still love me.

Your friend,
Elm

Dear Miss Vi,

    I went with Daddy to the pow-wow today. He looked so happy. Mother wasn't there, of course. She said she was having a bad Lyme day and couldn't walk and for me to take pictures to show her later. Yeah, right. I'm so tired of her excuses. It was just a little bug, Mother, get over it! I think Grandmother Ruth is right about Mother imagining her symptoms just to get more attention from Daddy, seeing how she's not his pretty "little" mermaid anymore. More like a sea COW. Yeah, I'm still mad at her because Royce is dead. I'll never call her "Mermie" again and I will never let myself get fat like her. And I won't let a tick bite me, either. If I see one, I'll kill it. Anyway, I love you and hope you still love me.

    Your friend,

    Elm

Dear Miss Vi,

    Daddy is dead. I am dead. The world is dead, so this will probably be the last time you hear from me because I'm running away from home.

    I hate it at Grandmother Ruth's house. There's nothing to do there except read her damn Bible and she still doesn't have a television. And she's always nagging me about my clothes and my hair and my makeup. Mother can stay there if she wants, but not me.

    I'm sorry that I won't be graduating high school with Snow but life really sucks so I've gotta do what I gotta do. If I never see you again I do hope you grow for a thousand more years. Remember when I saw you at Loch Ness? That was a fun time.

    Anyway, no matter what happens, just remember that I still love you and hope you still love me.

    Your friend,

    Elm

CHAPTER 31

A WISE PERSON ONCE SAID *that you don't drown by falling in the water, you drown by staying there.*

It's a strange thing to think about when you're actually drowning, but I guess you could say that this is a strange situation. Here I am in the middle of High City Bay, my chest exploding, my air decreasing, sinking down to the deep and watery bowels of my painful and pitiful existence; sinking down into the blackness, the abyss, the hellish absence of love and hope.

So this is how Elm Sunday will end. The big finish. The big sleep. Dead in the water. All those awful death cliches stop right here and I don't have to worry about living or breathing or seeing Little Blessing ever again. I guess this is my last acid trip, too. Well, it wasn't that great anyway.

SERAPHINA STOPPED ROWING, TAKING A DEEP BREATH before she plunged into the turquoise waters. Through the vibrant coral and tropical fish, she saw Elm's body and reached to pull her by her bra strap. The two swam up to the surface until they had reached the small boat. Elm hung on to the side, sputtering from the inhalation of the fresh, salty air. And then the agile old woman pushed the girl into the vessel.

Exhausted, Elm fell asleep.

Looking across at her passenger, Seraphina smiled, knowing there would be many souls excited to see the teenager, especially one little boy. She decided to rush their arrival.

"Well, why not?" she giggled.

Seraphina transformed herself into a pod of white dolphins, leading the illuminated boat safely to shore.

She had taken Elm to the lighthouse. Bending over her sheet-covered body was a group of tall, faceless beings in translucent robes. Sweet music emanated from them and they vibrated with all the colors that existed. The rays were so intense that Elm closed her eyes tight, wondering where the heck she was but feeling surprisingly calm, considering she didn't know if she was alive or dead.

In the blink of an eye, Elm was sitting in a chair inside an all-white kitchen. A young Latin-looking man was dancing to Samba music while simultaneously reading a book and removing a whistling red teakettle from the stove.

Without missing a beat (or a book passage), he poured the boiling water into a shiny orange mug, the fragrance of spearmint and chamomile permeating the room. The man let the tea steep a few minutes before removing the herbs, adding honey, and squeezing a fresh lemon. He placed it on a tray and reached for a glass of clear water from the kitchen counter, which he also set on the tray. Then he placed his hands lightly over each beverage, closing his eyes until the positive energy had transferred.

"How are you feeling, Sister?" he asked in his thick accent. "I have some nice tea for you."

Elm studied the man. He had shiny black hair, deep brown eyes, and was wearing a white Guayabera shirt.

Who is this guy? Have I been kidnapped? Is he a doctor? A ghost? An alien? If he's an alien, is this the mother ship?

"No aliens here, Sister. Is that something you saw in a movie? Which one? I love movies. Have you ever seen *E.T.*? He was an alien, yes? Very cute."

That's weird. I didn't say anything. And the guy's still dancing, so where's that music coming from?

The man chuckled. "Oh, it's just one of our many fascinations, but I've turned off the music for now. Are you cold? Are you hot? I brought you some tea and a glass of water, just in case. You've been through a terrible *accidente*, but you are safe now, Sister."

"What happened?" Elm's voice was raspy.

"You drowned," he answered, still dancing.

"I don't remember," she said, wondering if she should drink the tea.

"Of course, you should," he urged. "It is good tea. Very divine, actually."

Did you just read my mind?

Elm thought there must have been something in the tea leaves because the man was gyrating like crazy, even without the music. He danced around the room and plopped himself in the chair across from Elm, smiling at her. The man's huge teeth reminded Elm of her toy piano. She sipped her tea, which was surprisingly good.

"You said I was back. Back where?"

The man's energy was incredible. He jumped out of the chair and juggled a stack of ceramic plates into a flurry of red, orange and yellow. "Back to Inn Lak'ech, of course!"

"Never heard of it."

The man had become twins and was tossing the plates to his doppelgänger.

"So how did I get here?" Elm asked, fascinated by the performance.

"I brought you, Sister."

Within seconds, the twins had transformed into one elderly woman. She was a skinny old thing with chin-length, curly white hair, a pink bow-shaped mouth, thin arms, big biceps, and a melodic voice. Elm thought she had the pinkest skin she had ever seen, like pretty pink porcelain. And the woman sang her words!

Wait a minute. You brought me? Aren't you, like, eighty or something?

Again Seraphina read her mind. "I had my faithful rowboat," she sang. "I rowed out and swam until I reached you. Then I pulled you up to the surface, into the boat, and here you are!"

Elm found it hard to believe that the oldster was her sole rescuer. "I think I remember seeing a lot of colors."

"That's my little Kroma," Seraphina replied. "She looks like a boat but she's actually a floating crystal healing bed with a seven-ray illumination motor. I had her custom made for balancing and 7-D."

Elm didn't know how to respond. It all sounded completely foreign, although she thought she might know something about a crystal healing bed.

"So—in answer to the question you did not ask—'7-D' means the Seventh Dimension."

"Uh, okay."

Elm was still groggy and wanted to close her eyes again but she didn't dare. Who knew where she'd be afterward?

She noticed a large bookcase arched over the doorway, overstuffed with a variety of religious texts. There was also a shelf dedicated to angel books and another for afterlife topics, including *Can't Wait to Get to Heaven* by Fannie Flagg.

"Have you read it?" Seraphina asked, excitedly. "I just love reading her books, don't you? Great characters. Of course, I have plenty of favorite authors and every book that was ever written. There's a lot of good writing out there, don't you think? If only everybody was brave enough to tell their stories."

Elm sipped her tea again, which was still hot. "So, who are you again?" she asked, wondering why the old lady kept singing her words. It was annoying.

"Oh, you'll get used to the singing," her hostess assured her. "It's my trademark. My name is Seraphina. I run the inn."

"This is an inn?"

"No, this is the lighthouse," Seraphina corrected.

"A *lighthouse*," Elm repeated, thrilled she could remember the word. "That's a building with a search light that helps boats find their way, right?"

"Bingo!"

Yes, you look like you should be playing bingo. "But what happened to the guy who was here? The one who gave me the tea?"

Seraphina grinned, transforming into the young man with the keyboard smile and back to her elderly self again.

"You're a shapeshifter!" Elm exclaimed. *And yet another word remembered.*

"Yes, in a way," Seraphina chuckled. "Are you hungry, Sister?"

Elm hadn't thought about food until it was suggested. "Maybe."

A plate of black beans and rice magically appeared before her, along with a glass of orange juice.

"Something wrong, Sister?"

"What is this?"

To Elm, the meal appeared suspicious, as if it was hiding a dead rat.

"The natives call it 'Arroz Moro'," said Seraphina. "It's Cuban for rice and black beans."

"For breakfast?"

Actually, I don't know what time it is. I just assumed it was breakfast because of the orange juice.

Seraphina laughed. "If you say it is breakfast, it is breakfast. There is no time here, so ask and you shall receive is our motto! We're into muy manifesting!"

With that pronouncement, dozens of plates full of rice and beans floated around Elm's head. Then Seraphina twirled toward the ceiling as a miniature cyclone and then back again to her original form, landing in her chair in a headstand. "Now *that* was fun!"

Wow. This is like one big floor show.

"I don't think I've ever tasted Cuban before," Elm said, trying to keep up her end of the conversation but scanning the room for a quick exit.

"Perhaps not," Seraphina said. "But since we are so close to Cuba, I thought it would be fun for you to try. You're vegetarian, yes?"

"I don't know," Elm said. "It sounds familiar, but I don't remember if I am or not."

"Well, you won't remember much for a while. But as long as you desire food, you will be a vegetarian here."

What does she mean 'as long as you desire food'?

Elm dared to taste the first forkful. "It's good," she said, surprised at how hungry she was. "Spicy."

Seraphina was delighted. "That's the peppers and cumin. And how's your orange juice?"

Elm took a sip. "Orange-y."

Then something odd happened. Elm's hands turned bright orange!

"You must need more of the orange ray," Seraphina explained. "It helps you become more friendly, more creative."

Elm wasn't sure she liked having orange hands, but she was positive her glass kept refilling with juice by itself. Was this some kind of voodoo place? Had she been drugged with mysterious orange elixir and was being held captive against her will?

Seraphina shook her head. "No drugs here, Sister—nor captives, either. It was our joy to clear the hallucinogens from your system. But no judgment. We never judge. That was your choice. It has always been your choice."

Elm had a great many questions and was eager to change the subject. "You said we were close to Cuba."

In response, more beans and rice appeared on Elm's plate. She glanced at the stove. There were no signs of pots or frying pans. Absolutely nothing was cooking.

"How did you do that?" she asked.

Seraphina laughed, singing her words in a sweet soprano. "By thinking, Sister. Always thinking."

Apparently, Elm had been thinking she needed to leave the lighthouse and go sleuthing because she was now standing in front of the *Concierge* counter.

"Welcome to Inn Lak'ech," greeted a young teenage girl with a lovely pink aura. "We help you remember who you are."

So even the afterlife has a slogan.

Still a bit unsteady, Elm clung to the wooden counter

which felt solid but appeared transparent. "And who are you?" she queried.

The girl beamed. "Oh, thank you for asking, Sister. I have just progressed to pink, so you may call me Love."

And I shall dub thee Pink Girl!

"I beg your pardon?"

"Oh, nothing," Elm answered.

I guess all the employees read minds.

"So, tell me about this place," Elm continued. "What did you call it? Inn *what?*"

"Inn Lak'ech. It means 'I am another yourself.' We are a healing retreat situated in the ethereal realm of Archangel Zadkiel," she said, taking a deep pink breath. "Our angelic amenities include Steam Caves, a Singing Garden, Complimentary Guardian Element, and a Full Menu of Soul Spa Treatments. We offer luxury accommodations with 144 beautifully-appointed rooms, Eternal Housekeeping, In-Room Movies, Private Reflection Pool, and unlimited Di-Fi."

The girl paused for effect.

"Di-Fi? What's that?"

"Our wireless network to the Divine."

There was a lot to take in. Having noticed no other guests walking around, Elm said, "I guess this is your slow season, huh?"

"No, we're always full."

"Okay," said Elm, convinced she was in The Twilight Zone. "So now what?"

"Thank you for asking," Pink Girl replied. "We have Suite Number 8 all ready for you. Of course, it has a breathtaking view of the water. There is always water, inside and out. Would you like to register now?"

"Sure."

I might as well. Until I find out how to get out of here. Or who I am. I'm just wondering how I'm gonna pay my bill.

A transparent flatscreen monitor floated in front of Pink Girl. "May I have your name, please?"

Don't you know?

"Um, just call me Snow," Elm stammered. "Snow Moonwater. From the Sockitoomie Tribe."

And I have no idea where that came from.

Pink Girl was excited. "Ah, one of the indigenous people. Sometimes called Native American. Yes, I see it— the long brown hair, dark brown eyes, bronze complexion. Just lovely."

In her mind, Elm saw a quick vision of a young girl with strawberry blond hair and freckles. She strained to see her reflection in the monitor for confirmation but saw nothing. In fact, the monitor was totally blank.

"Would you like to be transported to your room now, Miss Moonwater?"

Elm was reluctant but didn't think she had a choice. She had no real identity nor recollection of her past.

If this is what death feels like, I might as well get comfortable with the idea.

CHAPTER 32

ELM AWOKE TO THE PERFUME of lavender. She rubbed her eyes and stretched her limbs like a cat, lounging on the king-sized bed until she felt ready to explore her luxury accommodations.

A white grotto with two chamber rooms, all of the furnishings in Suite 8 were translucent, including Elm's bed which was tucked inside a curved nook in the sleeping chamber. The transparent color scheme continued in the second chamber, a room with two plush chairs and sofa.

Besides the clear, plastic-looking flowers and candles Elm discovered in little nooks in the cave walls, the only decorative accent was a trio of cute angel figurines situated on the fireplace mantel. She laughed at their amusing "see no evil, hear no evil, speak no evil" poses.

Overall, Elm's new lodging was larger than her grand-mother's sitting room, so she didn't feel claustrophobic, thanks in part to the wide balcony overlooking a spectac-ular view of the ocean. It was a pretty suite with arched doorways connecting the chambers and a door that opened to the inn's corridor.

So the balcony is the only exit. Does that mean I'm a prisoner?

Splash.

Her attention focused on the reflection pool, a water feature that ran along the walls of the entire suite.

"Oh, no," she groaned. "More water."

Splash.

Suddenly, Elm was floating on her back in the pool, staring up at the white-domed ceiling. A ticker-tape marquee appeared:

Got a question? Ask Flo!

The pool water bubbled and crested, then a voice trembled from its depths. "I am Flo. Let it go."

Elm had just been introduced to her guardian element.

"Let *what* go?" the teen asked, wondering if she was about to drown again.

"Think about it, Suite 8."

Another splash.

Elm crawled out from a huge marble fountain with water pouring through the mouths of seven angel heads. Amazingly, she was not wet but she was curious about how she had arrived in the strange garden.

"Through water," said Flo from her fountain view. "My water, your water. We communicate through water."

"I think I've heard that before," said Elm.

"Yes, you have, and now you have another opportunity to listen," Flo offered. "Go listen to the garden, Suite 8."

Elm had walked a few steps before she realized she was barefoot. "Wait! I need my shoes!" she cried.

"No shoes necessary," Flo gurgled.

The garden was gorgeous and Elm's senses were in overload, surrounded by brilliant emeralds, pinks, yellows, vermillions, and purples. Heady from the sweet floral and woodsy fragrances, she heard a Bach concerto playing from an invisible orchestra.

"What you hear is the music of the plants," said Flo, from the fountain.

Hmm. I guess that's pretty cool.

But cool or not, Elm was still wary. For all she knew, she was heading on the pathway straight to hell!

Walking down the grassy lane, Elm was joined by a spectrum of butterflies and bluebirds. As she wandered past every flower and tree imaginable, she did not realize she was being watched.

A dark-skinned little boy with a bright green aura peered from behind a patch of orange tiger lilies. His face broke out into a hundred smiles.

"Bapu, you're here!" he cried, running to her. "I had hoped you would be here one day!" The child was ecstatic and wrapped his arms around her leg, sobbing and chanting *Bapu* over and over again.

The veil of amnesia must have cleared a little because Elm recognized the child as her own son, Prabhakar, which meant "lightmaker."

She was his father, Sankhar, a wealthy grocer who lived in New Delhi with a brood of seven children of varying ages.

It was good to see her youngest son again.

They sat on a garden bench near another fountain, where Flo gurgled with interest. "What happened to your leg?" Elm asked, having a vision of the little boy losing his leg to a crocodile.

"Oh, I had forgotten," said the boy. "I have evolved to Green Level now, so I have healed myself emotionally and physically. You will, too, Bapu. I know you will."

Elm loved Prabhakar's enthusiasm but had no idea

what he was talking about. "Tell me about Inn Lak'ech," she said. "Is it heaven? Is it hell? What is it, exactly?"

Prabhakar lovingly stroked Elm's face, tracing the area above her lip with his finger. "I am so glad you did not shave off your mustache, Bapu. You are so handsome."

Elm touched the area and was relieved to find that it was completely hair free.

Interesting.

The boy squeezed her arm and kissed her cheek. "I love you, Bapu, and I am so glad you are here! So I will tell you what I know, yes?"

Inn Lak'ech was one big fantastical playground where Prabhakar could swim whenever he wished and take nature walks where the plants would sing and speak to him. He rode on rainbows and talked with the animals and the elementals and they would talk back. There was no evil, no illness, and the sun was always shining.

"That's all nice, but we're still prisoners, right?" Elm queried.

Prabhakar did not lose his smile while answering. "Prisoners? Oh, no, Bapu. We are *guests*. We are here to heal and to remember who we are."

Elm nodded, although she still did not understand. Heal what? Remember what? She was also wondering about the green aura around her son.

"Ah, that is an easy question," he said. "The color indicates the level of spirituality my soul has achieved. There are seven different color levels—pink, blue, gold, green, yellow, white, and violet. As we master these levels, we are rewarded with that particular color aura. Understand? You will also see the colors change in your suite whenever you advance."

That's good 'cause it looks like the decorator went crazy with all that clear plastic.

"Oh, that will change when you have earned your pink aura."

Hmm. Does everyone read minds around here?

"Yes, and you will, too," Prabhakar assured her.

"But what if I want to keep something to myself, like *private*? I don't want everybody knowing my business."

The boy chuckled. "There is no cause for secrecy, Bapu. But why would you wish to have private thoughts? We are all One here. Transparency, you see? Extremely important for advancement!"

It was a lot for Elm to absorb, including why she was unable to taste all the different colors of the flowers when she had always had synesthesia.

"Ah, another simple answer. All gifts from before are gone. Erased."

"Even my intuition? My sea priestess magick?"

"Yes, isn't it wonderful?"

Elm wasn't sure it was wonderful, but Prabhakar certainly was excited about it. Actually, he seemed to be excited about everything.

But does he remember?

As Elm looked down at her sweet son, she wondered if he had forgiven her for being so cruel and cowardly.

"Oh, yes, I remember. But my leg is fine now, Bapu. Let me demonstrate."

Two rainbows suddenly appeared in the distance and Prabhakar ran and hopped aboard one of them. "Now, *you*!" he urged.

Elm had a sudden fear of heights. "I can't just jump on top of that thing—"

"Yes, you can, Bapu. Just try. Just *think*. Think 'I am on top of the rainbow'!"

Okay, I'll humor you, kid. I am on top of the rainbow.

In an instant, Elm was giggling and sliding from one

rainbow to the next. After awhile, she stopped to catch her breath. "How long have we been doing this?" she asked.

"Time does not exist at Inn Lak'ech," said her happy son, "but I sense you would like to rest. Would you like to stop now and watch your movie, Bapu?"

"What movie?" Elm asked.

"The last one you made, of course. I looked up your credits in the Akashic Records and it's going to be a—how you say? It's going to be a *doozy*!"

CHAPTER 33

T*A DA!* TRUMPETS HERALDED AS the movie theater
curtains opened for the feature presentation.

My Life in Little Blessing
a Third Dimensional Saga
starring Miss Mercy-Faith "Elm" Sunday

Prabhakar clapped. He leaned back in his seat with a
huge bowl of hot-buttered "thought" popcorn on his lap.

"Take some, Bapu. We will share."

Elm had never tasted popcorn that was so buttery,
sweet and heavily sprinkled with a rainbow of spices. It
was deliciously addictive.

The movie opened with a young Glorie and Big Dave
pushing a baby stroller. As they drew closer to the camera,
Elm recognized the squirming, red-faced passenger in the
frilly pink dress and matching bonnet.

Uggh. Pink. My least favorite color.

"Who are they?" the boy asked, pointing to the
screen.

It was difficult for Elm to look. "My parents," she mumbled.

"Very nice. And you are the child?"

"Yeah." Elm's eyes welled up.

The boy was fascinated. "No brothers or sisters?"

"No." A tear flowed down Elm's cheek.

"And what is that contraption?"

Wiping her eyes, Elm glanced at the screen. "My baby stroller."

"You are not looking too happy there, Bapu."

"I guess not," she replied. "But would you? Look at the outfit they made me wear."

And I probably wanted to get out of that stroller, too.

As a toddler, Elm was called "our little escape artist" because there was no crib that could contain her. Soon after she was put in bed for the night, baby Elm would flex her diminutive body into all sorts of contortions until she was over the railing and out. Then she would toddle off to her parents' room, laughing at her success.

"Pink is a charming color, very special," Prabhakar said. "You may think you appear silly here, Bapu, but surely you must be grateful that you had two parents when you were my age, yes?"

Elm sank deep into her chair, trying to hide her shame. In her seventy-eight-year life as Sankhar, he had been fortunate to enjoy many possessions, none of which brought him more joy and misery than his wife, Archana, and his much younger mistress, Bala. Sankhar enjoyed the attention of both women and often encouraged them to compete for his affections for sport, whether it was cooking his favorite curry or sewing a beautiful new shirt.

Besides drinking to excess, bullying "my women" was Sankhar's favorite pastime and destined to end badly. One day he enraged Archana so much that she bashed Bala's head with a large rock, then dragged the unconscious teenager to the edge of the Yamuna River.

Seeing his mother's body float away from the shore, little Prabhakar jumped into the black water to save her. Unfortunately, two hungry crocodiles were lurking. One feasted on Bala, while the other hissed and pounced on Prabhakar, managing to chew off his leg before a guilt-ridden Archana clubbed the crocodile to death and rescued the boy.

It was all a bloody, screaming mess and Sankhar had just stood there, watching in horror.

"Please understand that I do not judge you, Bapu. I have seen my mother during many lifetimes since then. But I feel very sad for *your* mother. She suffered greatly during your last journey. I hope you will see her again."

My mother.

Elm was remembering Glorie. She was remembering her funny hats and her mermaid cane and the way she would snort sometimes when she laughed.

And then she remembered all the pain she had inflicted and began to cry.

"Yes, let them flow," Prabhakar cooed, stroking her hair. "No worries for me. This is a wonderful occurrence."

"What do you mean?" Elm sniffed, embarrassed that her son should see her in this state.

Prabhakar smiled. "I mean only that water is a good thing. It is the best cleanser. You are indeed blessed!"

"I despise water," Elm snarled. "It messed up my life and I don't trust it. Water killed my father, it destroyed my home, and it killed me—and I can't believe those Inn Lak'ech people didn't take all that into consideration when they gave me Water as my guardian element!"

"So, are you ready to continue?" her son queried,

ignoring her outburst. "I only ask because the movie stops each time you are busy in thought."

Like a pause button, huh? So I guess I'm gonna be stuck watching this movie, no matter what.

"Stuck? Oh, no one is ever stuck, Bapu. There are always new choices. Look, I will make things fun for you. Watch this!"

With their feet on the empty seats in front of them, Prabhakar initiated a good-natured game of "pummeling". He threw popcorn at the screen and encouraged Elm to follow his lead. During Elm's "bratty" scenes, they jeered and pummeled the screen with popcorn. By the time the movie had ended, they were laughing and pummeling each other, although the popcorn bag they shared was still full.

"Exciting lifetime, Bapu," said Prabhakar. "Lots of surprises. I enjoyed your many character flaws and conflicts, which always makes for a better cinematic experience, don't you agree? I cannot wait to watch the next one."

If there's even going to be a next one.

Despite her son's eagerness to entertain her, watching each scene from her life had been agony for Elm, particularly when she saw just how short her life had been.

"So now what?" she asked, trying her best to sound enthusiastic.

"You will see," said Prabhakar, mysteriously.

That's just great. First, these aura people entice me by giving me a luxury suite and a nice father-son reunion, next I get to beam down to the hot place with the devils and pitchforks. As Grandma might say: 'Here's where that devil girl gets her comeuppance!'

Prabhakar laughed. "Devils and pitchforks? That is funny, Bapu. You must tell that joke to the family."

"Whose family?" she asked, looking behind them and seeing nothing but empty seats.

"*Our* family, of course!"

Elm hoped this new development didn't mean she would be confronted by Sankhar's wife and mistress. Perhaps she would be ambushed by a horde of Prabhakar's less compassionate siblings. Or maybe she would spend the rest of eternity being yelled at by relatives or eaten by crocodiles. There were a lot of uncertainties and she wasn't ready to face any of them.

Prabhakar squeezed her hand. "I understand, Bapu, but uncertainties make experiences more interesting, yes? No matter what happens, I do hope there will be no yelling because anger is a very negative emotion and that makes me sad."

Elm felt a twinge of guilt, realizing that anger had been her modus operandi during the last years of her life in Little Blessing. As much as she enjoyed being with Prabhakar, she was weary and yearned for a reprieve.

I wish I could just curl up into a ball and be left alone.

Her wish was granted.

Elm's body jumped right out of the theater's roof, through the clouds and the cosmos, and bounced down onto the Earth's moon. She bounced past two golf balls, a camera, several moon buggies, a pair of moon boots, and the flag of the United States of America.

"Stop!" she screamed. "Oh-my-god, please stop!"

Then she rolled a few yards more and came to a sudden halt at the edge of a moon crater.

At first glance, the terrain resembled an abandoned set of a science fiction movie. But as haunting as this moon "stage" appeared, Elm was more disturbed by the silence. There was no sound at all, not even the beating of her own heart.

If I even have a heart. I forgot to ask if they let me keep my organs. And unless a grisly moon monster is lurking nearby, there's nobody around to ask.

Since she couldn't move her body, Elm had no choice but to watch and wait.

She noticed she was facing the flag. The sight of its beautiful red, white and blue colors made her homesick, triggering a memory of the first time she had shared the podium with her parents during the annual July 4 celebration.

Elm was proud to be the mayor's daughter that day, so proud to be an American and to have the honor of singing a patriotic solo. Ruth had insisted she sing "America the Beautiful" because its lyrics had been written by the daughter of a Congregational pastor on Cape Cod. Elm never understood why "America the Beautiful" hadn't been selected as the national anthem. The song certainly captured the beauty of her country, and it was much easier to sing than the battle-themed anthem written by Francis Scott Key.

> "America! America!
> God shed His grace on thee…"

But where was God? Was He listening? Was He watching her right now? What did He want from her anyway?

"Look, I'm tired of this!" she hollered. "Stop torturing me!"

It felt so good to scream that she decided to keep up the momentum and screamed some more. She screamed because she was afraid, because she was dead, because she didn't know if she was going to heaven or hell. She screamed because she wanted her father. She screamed because she never had a true romance with Noah. She screamed because she was stuck on the moon with no food, no bed, no company whatsoever. And she had changed into a ball, so she found it easy to scream about that, too.

After a long bout of screaming, Elm felt surprisingly calmer. Incredibly bored, she entertained herself by singing all the songs she could remember, beginning with the letter *A*.

She was just finishing the last stanza of the television theme song to "Gilligan's Island" when she realized that another voice had chimed in.

"Hello? Is there someone here? Hellooooooooo?"

"Are we having fun yet?" replied a disembodied voice, each word echoing like a chorus of clanging cathedral bells. "Are we having fun yet?"

Elm didn't enjoy being a ball with a limited vantage point.

"Whoever you are, I can't see you," she said. "Where are you?"

A human hand scooped up the Elm ball and tossed her high into the air.

She came down fast, bouncing off a moon buggy and falling deep inside a crater.

Whoa!

Each time she bounced up, she was smacked down again, like someone playing a seriously aggressive game of handball.

"So, how does it feel to be tossed around, Miss Sea Priestess?"

CHAPTER 34

THE VOICE SOUNDED FAMILIAR. *EXTREMELY* familiar. *But how is it possible?*

"Oh, it's possible, all right. How does it feel to be completely helpless?"

Elm thought she detected a shadow moving towards her. "Who's out there?"

The shadow grew closer. "Why, Elm, are you afraid?"

"No," Elm lied, hoping the voice did not belong to someone disgustingly gruesome like Leatherface or Freddy Krueger.

A huge shadow fell upon Elm's rotund body, which was rising from the ground.

Am I gonna get thrown across the moon again?

Elm was being examined from all angles. At every rotation, she spied something different—a nostril, half a lip, an eyebrow, a chin, a green eye. By the time a strand of red-gold hair came into view, her anxiety lessened and she was able to speak.

"I know you!"

"Well, you should," the young girl snapped. "I *am* another yourself!"

Elm was relieved that her captor wasn't a pitchfork-wielding demon.

"Are you real, Mercy-Faith, or am I just imagining this?" She didn't even care if she was hallucinating. At least she had someone to talk to.

Mercy-Faith did not reply. Instead, she carried Elm to one of the moon buggies and placed her on the seat, holding her steady so she would not roll. Then she stepped back, revealing her entire physique.

Elm was looking at herself at age nine, a period in her life when she was completely and ecstatically happy. It was a time when she could not wait to begin her day, antici-pating all sorts of new adventures with her best friend in the world, Snow Whitedove. It was the year she had discovered real mermaids in the cove and the only thing that ever irritated her was when Holy Cow Sundaes ran out of her favorite chocolate ice cream or Forbidden Passionfruit gelato, which almost never happened.

"Have you figured out why you are here, Miss Sea Priestess?"

"Sorry," said Elm, "but I have no idea why I'm anywhere. Or why I'm a ball. Or why I'm dead. I figure it's some kind of joke."

"A joke? Do you see anything funny about this?"

"Not really."

"You destroyed our life," Mercy-Faith insisted. "You chose your own selfish needs above the needs of all the people who loved you. So how is that funny? What do you have to say about *that*, Miss Jokester?"

Elm didn't want to say anything about it. As far as she was concerned, the past was the past and she could care less what Mercy-Faith had to say about it. In fact, if she wasn't a ball and still had her fingers, she would have gladly put them in her ears and sing: "La-la-la, I can't hear you!"

"That's *so* childish," said Mercy-Faith, reading Elm's mind. "No wonder you got into so much trouble."

"Hey, I don't need a lecture from you, Mercy-Faith," said Elm. "You were the golden child. Everybody in town loved you and you never had to worry about where you were going to sleep or how you were going to pay for your next meal or if your boyfriend was going to slap you around that day. You never worried about anything. Well, my life was much different and you just don't get it."

"You just don't get it," Mercy-Faith taunted. "You just don't get it. You just don't *get* it!"

"Now who's being childish? Can you get me out of here or not?"

Mercy-Faith was defiant. "Why should I? Do you have somewhere else to be? Are you in such a hurry to learn your fate?" She climbed aboard the buggy and held Elm in her lap. "Shall I throw you again and see where you land?" she laughed.

Shall? When have I ever said 'shall'? And I remember being super sweet when I was nine. Nothing like this girl!

"I really wish you wouldn't," said Elm, pretending to be calm. "I don't know if balls can throw up, but—"

"Oh, I just want to curl up into a ball and be alone— that's what you said!" said Mercy-Faith, holding Elm up to her eyeball. "You did this to yourself, Miss I-Hate-Every-body. You are a ball because you asked the Universe for it. And now you are discovering just how it feels to be completely powerless. As a ball, you've realized that you cannot progress without the aid of another."

"Progress to where?" Elm spluttered.

"Well, that's really up to you, isn't it?"

Sheesh.

It had been torturous enough watching her life movie with the son she had failed. She just wanted to let it all go.

"And curl up into a ball and be alone!" Mercy-Faith blasted, clutching the ball a little too tight.

No damn privacy.

"Look," Elm said, angry that she had to defend herself. "I don't know why this is such a big deal anyway. Except for a few situations which were really not my fault, I think I was actually a pretty good kid."

It was the wrong thing to say. Mercy-Faith jumped off the buggy seat and drop-kicked the surprised ball across the moon.

"You abandoned me!" cried Elm's other self. "You swore! You lied! You plotted! You hated! We were having so much fun and then you went and ruined it by being so hateful!"

Elm bounced around for what she guessed were a few thousand times before Mercy-Faith caught her and returned her to the buggy seat.

"Hey, are you trying to scare me?" Elm challenged. "Because I don't scare easy."

"You're lying, Elm Sunday," Mercy-Faith said, her face red with anger. "You *are* afraid. And I'd like to feel sorry for you, but you make me so mad. And you know I *never* get mad. Except when Noah's teasing me."

Mercy-Faith plopped herself down on the hard moon surface, glaring at Elm with snake eyes.

"Look," Elm said, trying to appear sympathetic. "I didn't abandon you. I just grew up."

"No, you grew *away*," Mercy-Faith hissed. "Away from me, away from our family, away from the Light."

Now Elm was mad.

"Well, excuse me, Miss Know-it-all Fancypants, but did it ever occur to you that maybe living in the Light wasn't so great? Like, maybe it's actually scarier because you're totally exposed and there's nowhere to hide and everybody can see who you really are?"

"But I thought nothing frightened you, Miss Sea Priestess?"

"Not usually."

Mercy-Faith sighed. She stood and dusted herself off and said, "I'm sorry I lost my temper, Elm. Wanna play a game with me?"

Wow, that was a switch.

"I'm too old for games," said Elm.

"Look, do you want me to throw you around again?"

"No, thanks."

"Right. So here's how the game goes," Mercy-Faith explained. "I will give you the beginning of a sentence and you will finish that sentence with the first thing that pops in your mind. And it has to relate to something from our life in Little Blessing. Get it?"

"Yeah, I guess."

Mercy-Faith muttered something unintelligible, then continued. "Okay, complete this sentence: *I hate.*"

I hate stupid kid games.

"I can throw you anytime, you know!"

"Alright, alright," said Elm. "Okay, I hate, uh, broccoli."

She really didn't, but she couldn't think of anything else to say.

"No, you don't," Mercy-Faith corrected. "Now be serious, Elm. What is it you really hate?"

You really want me to go there?

"Yes, I do, and I want you to imagine that whatever it is

you hate is right here, right now. Can you handle that, Elm?"

"Maybe."

So this kid is going to keep picking at my scabs until I'm bleeding again.

"Okay, I hate my mother," Elm blurted. "Are you happy now?"

"Are *you*?"

"No," Elm replied, "because I said I don't want to talk about it."

"But that's against the rules," said Mercy-Faith.

"The rules *you* made up," Elm reminded her.

"Whatever. So now, say 'I hate my mother because...'"

I hate my mother because she ruined my life.

Mercy-Faith wrinkled her nose. "No. Be more specific."

"Okay, I hate my mother because she stuck her big fat nose in my business!"

"Good. Now keep going," Mercy-Faith urged.

"Um, I hate my mother for making me wear pink."

"Oh, I love that color," said the younger girl. "What else?"

"Uh, I hate my mother for making me decorate my bedroom with mermaids?" Elm wasn't really sure that was true, but it sounded plausible and she had a lot to prove.

Mercy-Faith seemed to enjoy egging her on. "Come on, you've gotta hate her for more than that. If not, what was the point of your I Hate Mermie campaign?"

Elm felt an inner boiling, like she was about to erupt into steam.

"Okay, you really wanna know? I hate my mother for her stupid laugh and for embarrassing me at my birthday parties with her stupid stories about being a professional mermaid. I hate my mother for making me go to church when I didn't want to and I hate her for not letting me get an octopus. And I hate my mother for getting as fat as a pig and I hate her for getting sick."

There. I said it.

"So you blame Mermie for her illness?" Mercy-Faith queried. "That doesn't make sense."

"You're darn right I blame her because I think she brought it on herself," Elm snarled.

"You sound like Grandma," the girl giggled.

"Yeah? Well, maybe The Pray Lady was right," said Elm. "Mother's always liked being the center of attention —that's why she became a mermaid entertainer in the first place. And she's always been so needy. Like, she can't do anything without Daddy's help."

Mercy-Faith scooped up the ball and said gently, "Did you forget how she was before she got sick? She was happy and fun. We adored her."

"Whatever," said Elm. "Anyway, you asked and I told you. And since you asked, I also hate Mother for getting rid of our dogs and for getting sick when I needed her to be well. I hate her for not being able to properly take care of Daddy when *he* needed her. I hate her for not letting me grow up and for judging me and for not accepting my relationship with Royce. I hate her for wearing stupid hats and I hate her for causing Daddy to die, all because she lost her stupid hat!"

"So you blamed all your troubles on poor Mermie," said Mercy-Faith. "You know what? That's just sad. And then you devoted the rest of your life to getting revenge and power. Real smart, Elm."

Elm was tired of being judged. "So what if I did? What do you know about life, anyway? You're just a little kid."

"I *know* I am not just *any*thing," said Mercy-Faith. "I know I am another yourself. And I also know that you cannot truly love others if you do not love yourself. It's that simple. And when you don't love yourself, you get scared. And I also know that you wrote your own darn movie, Elm Sunday, and that you don't get the prize until you've faced your fears, one by one. You have to ask for forgiveness, forgive everybody for everything you think they did to you. If you don't, you will always feel pain. You will always be sorry. Get it?"

Elm wanted to say something smart-alecky, but before she could reply Mercy-Faith had already transformed into a thin, cotton-haired man wearing the dark garb of a Puritan clergy.

With a stern face and a crooked finger pointing at Elm, he barked, "Repent, ye sinner! The kingdom of God has come near. Repent and believe the good news!"

Elm thought the man might be the first Reverend George Sunday, her ancestor and the founder of Little Blessing. He sure looked like the pictures she had seen in her local history books.

"Well, if I do repent, can I finally leave this stupid place?"

"Whoever conceals their sins does not prosper," he responded. "But the one who confesses and renounces them shall find mercy."

Elm hoped the "mercy" included a nice warm bath.

"Repent of this wickedness, Child, and pray to the Lord in the hopes that he may forgive you for having such evil thoughts in your mind and heart!"

I still don't think I did anything that bad.

The reverend's voice rang through her mind like a grandfather clock that wouldn't stop chiming.

"Thou shalt not have strange gods before me! Thou shalt not steal! Thou shalt not take the name of the Lord in vain! Thou shalt not kill! Thou shalt not steal! Thou shalt not bear false witness against thy neighbor! Thou shalt not covet thy neighbor's goods!"

As the reverend faded into nothingness, his words continued to echo through Elm's mind. Apparently, she had two choices: to continue to exist in her boring, lunar prison or to get busy and purge her soul.

She decided the latter would be less torturous.

CHAPTER 35

L ESS TORTUROUS? THE UNIVERSE LAUGHED, sending a deck of cards to float before her like falling leaves. They settled on the moon's surface and spread into the shape of a fan, as if Elm was about to conduct an oracle card reading.

"Well, how about starting with me?"

Elm glanced at the cards, realizing that each depicted someone she had known in her last life. One of the images was waving at her.

"Snow?"

"Yeah. So you're a ball now, huh?" Snow looked exactly the same except she was carrying a water bucket. "Funny how things work out 'cause you were sure bouncing around a lot when you were alive."

"I guess," Elm said. "Where are you, anyway?"

The card portrayed Snow against a sunset backdrop.

"Dad let me take off work to go out west and join other Native people at a reservation, trying to protect the water from an oil pipeline that threatens to pollute it. My water protector family and I will probably get arrested today."

Elm didn't know what else to say, except "Really? Wow. Well, be careful."

Snow set down the bucket and dug her fists into her hefty waist. "You know what, Elm? It's really interesting you should worry about me *now*. I mean, considering you abandoned me to run off with that Garrett guy. Considering we were like sisters!"

"Sorry about that."

But Snow was defiant. "Are you *really*, Elm? Because the day you left Little Blessing, you threw away everything and everybody who ever mattered to you. Not to mention leaving poor Mermie to fend for herself."

Here we go with Poor Mermie again.

"Look, I said I was sorry, Snow. What do you want from me?"

The card next to Snow coughed for attention but Snow had not finished, shaking her finger at the ball.

"And who knows what might have happened to your mom if *we* hadn't been around to take care of her. She was *your* mother, Elm, *your* responsibility. You were her only flesh and blood!"

"Snowshoe is right," said Noah, sitting in the office at Sunday's Marina and looking as handsome as ever. "It's not like the rest of us weren't grieving for Big Dave, too—we all loved him. But you never thought about that, did you, Elm? You were too busy pining away for that dead guy."

Another card—Garrett, leaning against the outside of his trailer—decided to weigh in. "Oh, boo hoo! You people got off easy. This girl was no prize when she was with me. And I took her in when none of you wanted her, so don't forget that. But how did she show her appreciation? She lied, she stole, and she left the place looking like a dump—I couldn't wait to get rid of her!"

"But you lied to me, too!" Elm countered. "And you hit me!"

More cards jumped into the conversation—Ruth, Jason, Kat, even some of the kids Elm used to babysit. Their voices were emotionally charged and everyone was talking at once. Elm felt like she was being pelted by snowballs with no letup.

Finally, one voice was louder than the others, a gentle voice of reason that Elm loved so well.

"My daughter has heard all of your grievances," said Big Dave, wearing his Sunday's Marina cap and floating in a boat-shaped cloud. "Let's all be kind enough to give her the opportunity to address them."

One by one, Elm faced her accusers. And for what seemed like an eternity of complaints, something inside her finally clicked.

The cards are right. I did cause a lot of a pain. And I regret it.

"I'm so sorry, Daddy," she wailed. "I'm so sorry that I disappointed you!"

She was overtaken by remorse. After a long and painful process, Elm managed to apologize to each of the cards, even the smirking Garrett.

But there was still one card she had yet to address. Since its background was totally black, she had previously ignored it.

"Is there somebody in there?" Elm asked the card.

Silence.

"Hello?"

"I am here," said the card, "but I am lost in the shadows. Even so, you know me well. And you certainly know how you hurt me, Elm Sunday."

"Mermie, is that you?"

The voice sighed. "Thank you for calling me that. It's been a long time."

To Elm's surprise, the cold hatred she had reserved for her mother transformed into regret.

"I am so, so sorry, Mermie," Elm cried. "I was selfish and you needed me. Please forgive me, Mermie. Please, please forgive me!"

The cards dissolved into nothingness, leaving Elm alone with her sorrows of a wasted lifetime. She finally understood that the hell she had lived was of her own creation. She had forgotten to love her neighbor. She had forgotten to send love to the ocean. Most of all, Elm had forgotten that she was created from love and was love herself.

After more tears and repenting, Elm still felt she was doomed.

"Am I gonna be here for the rest of eternity?" she cried.

Splash!

"Well, you asked for it, Suite 8—and the Universe always happily delivers!"

Elm was elated. "Flo! Is that you?"

"Of course! As your personal guardian element, I am always with you. And if you turn around, you will see me."

Elm was confused. "But how? I'm a ball and I can't move by myself."

"Of course you can. Just think about it."

Okay, I am turning around to see Flo!

Elm was now facing a water puddle—Flo!

"Congratulations, you did it!"

"Yeah, I did," Elm agreed, but still not satisfied. "Did you say you have you been here all along?"

If that was true, wasn't she perfectly justified for being angry at Flo? After all, Water had turned on her before!

"Absolutely," Flo admitted, sounding quite proud. "I

was very quiet so you could fully enjoy your lunar experience."

Enjoy? Are you kidding me?

"What the hell kind of guardian are you?" Elm challenged.

"The best kind," said Flo. "But I won't interfere with your progress."

Elm still felt betrayed. She had many questions but was mostly curious about how she ended up on the moon. "I was just sitting peacefully in the movie theater when I got zapped into outer space," she said.

Flo chuckled. "Well, I told you we communicate through water, remember? So now you understand that thoughts become things. When you were human, you had choices. Here you will learn what those choices created."

Definitely not the pleasant afterlife I imagined.

"Perhaps not," said Flo, "and now you have curled up into a ball—per your request, I remind you—and so I will be quiet for as long as you wish."

Elm panicked. "Wait! Don't go!"

"But you said—"

Elm longed for company, even if that company was a talking water puddle.

"Look, I know what I said before, but I changed my mind. Please, Flo. If being stuck on the moon is to be my punishment, would you at least stay and talk to me? I need to hear a voice that's not mine."

"I love to talk," Flo gurgled, "but is that all you wish?"

Elm thought carefully, realizing that an innocent musing might easily transport her into a lion's den or worse.

"Actually, what I really wish is to get out of this rubber ball outfit and sleep in a warm, fluffy bed for a thousand days. Oh, and would it be bad if I said I hope I never have to say I'm sorry *again?!*"

SINCE TIME DID NOT EXIST, ELM HAD NO WAY TO KNOW how long she had slept in her suite. But she thought the transparent decor matched her brand new attitude because she felt cleansed and hopeful, as if all the dark clouds had parted and replaced with sparkles and Light.

"Welcome back, Suite 8," Flo bubbled. "I trust you enjoyed your exotic moon vacation?"

Exotic? That's not the word I would have used. But I'd better watch my thoughts because I sure don't want to go back there.

"Oh, it was delightful," Elm lied, wondering if water elements understood sarcasm. "Actually, I'm glad to see you, Flo, because I need to apologize, even though I hoped I wouldn't have to."

"I'm intrigued," said Flo.

"Well, the Reverend Sunday said I broke, like, seven commandments. But one of the worst things I did in my last life was to pollute the water with my negative thoughts. I forgot to send love to the ocean. So I'm really sorry about that, Flo."

"Apology unnecessary," said Flo. "Of course, I am happy to accept it if it helps your spiritual growth. You will find that nothing ever annoys me—I continue to go with the flow, no matter what. That's one of the benefits of being water. Of course, it is my great privilege to guide you, Suite 8—I am happy to. But you might wish to remember that your power lies within your own water. In the end, the direction you take towards your ultimate desti- nation remains *your* choice. You have always had the power of choice. It is a great gift."

Elm nodded. "I see that now. Hey, I've got a question for you. Those cards I was talking to on the moon—were they real?"

"The souls are real," Flo replied, "but you don't need oracle cards to communicate with them. Just think—and do so with love."

Elm wondered if so much thinking might cause her one gigantic headache. It was all too fantastic to digest.

"So what's on the agenda for today?" she asked.

A few drops of water sprinkled on Elm's nose. "How about a swim?" Flo suggested. "Maybe a guided water tour of Inn Lak'ech?"

"Sounds good," said Elm. "As long as I don't have to face another mob of angry people."

She stepped into the water and instantly merged with Flo.

"Wow!" she exclaimed, as they drifted from the suite to the ocean. "Now *I'm* going with the flow! Get it? You're Flo and I'm going *with* you?"

It was a corny joke but Elm couldn't remember the last time she had truly laughed and the release felt amazing.

"It's good for me, too," Flo said. "Laughter releases the vibration of joy. By the way, you don't need to speak out loud if you have a comment or question because we are both pure water and I can read your thoughts."

Okay. Can you hear me now?

"Loud and clear," Flo chuckled.

Great. So across from us is Inn Lak'ech. It looks like a bunch of white caves—all connected—like something you'd see on Santorini in Greece.

"Very similar," said Flo. "And each guest has their own cavern, like you. But we call them suites. It sounds much more luxurious, don't you think?"

Sure. I like the balconies with all the green plants and orchids. I like purple.

"It's a spiritual color. So you've seen the reflection pool —that's me—and the singing gardens—"

And the lighthouse.

"Yes, the lighthouse. It's not really a part of the main inn, but—"

The movie theater.

"Yes."

But where are the restaurants?

"Restaurants? For what?"

Well, for eating, of course!

"Why? Do you think you're hungry?"

I guess I should be starving because I don't think I've eaten anything since Seraphina fed me in the lighthouse. Oh, wait. I did have that popcorn at the theater. But honestly? I don't have any desire to eat anything. Do you think I'm sick?

"Not at all," Flo assured her.

That's a relief. But I thought maybe I should fill up on food before I get booted out of here.

"Booted out? That's a funny expression," said Flo. "Where do you think you're going to be booted *to*?"

I have no idea.

"Besides," Flo continued, "you don't require food anymore. That's why you have no appetite."

Interesting. Okay, I have another question.

"Ask away!" said Flo.

Why is it so quiet around here, Flo? I mean, there's got to be people in these caves—I mean, suites. So far I've only met three—my son, the Pink girl, and Seraphina.

"Thank you for such an easy question," Flo replied. "There are many guests at Inn Lak'ech, but—like you— each has their own journey. So you will not reunite with them all at once."

Okay. But this is where Archangel Zadkiel hangs out, right?

"Yes, it is his retreat. All the archangels have one—elsewhere, of course."

I guess being an angel tires you out, huh?

"I can only imagine," Flo agreed.

I've heard of Michael, Gabriel, and Raphael, but not Zadkiel, until Pink Girl mentioned him. I've never seen his name in the Bible. Who is he?

"Everyone wants to know the answer to that question," said Flo. "For your understanding, I will refer to our beloved angel patron as 'he,' although angels are really androgynous beings. Archangel Zadkiel is the angel of purification and wisdom. He helps people find diplomacy and tolerance, helps them through the grieving process. It was Zadkiel who stopped Abraham from sacrificing his son, Isaac."

I think he's called the Angel of the Lord in the Bible.

"That is correct, Suite 8, although other angels have been identified with that name as well. And you are also correct that the Bible does not mention him by name."

Do you ever see him, Flo? Or does he keep to himself?

"Zadkiel? I see him all the time," said Flo. "For instance, I see him in you."

Elm thought it was a curious statement but did not remark. They were moving closer to the shore, flowing past a round, open-air temple with a bright golden dome.

And then it called to her. Literally.

CHAPTER 36

"I T'S THE ARCHANGEL'S RECEPTION," SAID Flo, "which means we'll have to stop the tour now. It's too bad because I know you would really enjoy the steam caves. Oh, well—no worries!"

Elm was hardly listening because she was captivated by the melodic messages that she amazingly understood.

They are waiting for me.

In an instant, she was inside the temple, standing next to a sparkling fountain. Curious, she leaned over to see her reflection in the water, but it did not appear.

"What are you trying to do?" Flo gurgled in amusement.

I'm trying to decide if I need to change my clothes for this party. But now that I think about it, do I even have a body?

Flo was forever patient. "You have an astral body, so clothing should not be a concern. Everyone you meet will see you as the soul they remember."

Okay. I mean, it's weird, but I'll try not to stress about it.

"I'll be right here in the fountain if you need me," said Flo.

Cool. Thanks, Flo.

The temple was breezy and surprisingly empty. Elm wandered the length of the building, past white Grecian columns and marble benches, all the while entranced by the domed ceiling. Looking up, it appeared to be a giant Mother-of-Pearl seashell outlined in gold.

"It is a Chambered Nautilus, Sister."

Elm turned around to see a familiar face smiling up at her, a petite nun with a violet aura.

"Mother Hildegard!"

Even without a physical body, Elm could feel the loving energy of hugging her old friend.

"It is good to reunite with you, Sister Anna," the nun beamed. "I understand that you lived by the sea during your last life, so you must be familiar with the message of seashells. Have you ever read the poem, *The Chambered Nautilus*, by Oliver Wendell Holmes? It is very lovely. I had the opportunity to memorize it during one of my twentieth century lives on Earth. I particularly like the last stanza: 'Build thee more stately mansions, O my soul—'"

Elm joined her former abbess, reciting:

"As the swift seasons roll! Leave thy low-vaulted past! Let each new temple, nobler than the last, shut thee from heaven with a dome more vast. Till thou at length art free, leaving thine outgrown shell by life's unresting sea!"

The two laughed with joy and sat on a bench, chatting about their life in the abbey. Eventually, Elm realized the temple had filled with people.

"Actually, they're souls," Flo corrected. "But you may call them 'family.'"

So this is the reception.

One by one, people of all different colored auras lined

up to greet Elm, even those she had despised or treated unfairly. No one seemed to hold a grudge, not even the Confederate brother she had shot to death during her stint in The Civil War as a Union soldier.

Elm remembered them all, including the stout, middle-aged Englishwoman wobbling towards her, encircled by a sunny yellow aura. She hugged Elm and exclaimed: "Welcome back, Mrs. Tinsdale! I am so excited to see you again. What a blessing you are!"

During their early twentieth century lifetime as neighbors in a tiny town in England, no one had ever called Mrs. Louise Tinsdale a blessing. As the proprietor of *The Dog's Breath* tavern, her calling was to serve bowls of hearty soup and tankards of ale to the local working class.

According to Elm's recollection, the woman with the yellow aura—Miss Patsy Fairweather—was the true blessing of the town. The kindly woman ran a boarding house next door to the tavern and whenever Mrs. Tinsdale's patrons were too inebriated to get home, Miss Fairweather would take them in, free of charge.

Miss Fairweather's life was full and devoted to service, whether she was volunteering at the hospital or tending to her roses and lavender-filled Hildegarden, which she grew for the benefit of St. Mary's Catholic Church. The garden was a tribute to Mother Hildegard, the nun she had helped raise in a parallel life. So Elm knew Miss Fairweather from the abbey, too.

As Mrs. Tinsdale, Elm also appreciated how the spinster had never ostracized her for smoking a pipe behind the tavern. It was extremely unladylike and it remained their little secret.

Ting-ting. Ting-ting.

Ethereal bells chimed and Prabhakar appeared at Elm's side.

"Two o'clock and all is well!" her son announced with glee. "Grateful greetings, Bapu."

"Hello, my son," Elm said, giving him a quick hug. "What time did you say it is again?"

"You are teasing me, Bapu, for surely you remember that time does not exist. It is irrelevant, but I still like to pretend to be human. It is a fun game."

Elm pressed for more details. "What do you mean, *pretend* to be human?"

Her question went unanswered because Prabhakar recognized someone he knew and skipped away, leaving Elm's attention solely on a bouncing fruit basket. As it drew closer, she realized it was attached to Seraphina's head.

"Snow!"

She was dancing the cha cha with Mother Hildegard.

"Join us, sweet girl!"

Elm wondered how the women could dance without music.

"Think *music*," Flo sputtered from the fountain.

Music!

And then Elm heard the Latin rhythm and began to sway.

One, two, cha-cha-cha.

"You're catching on," said Seraphina, in mid-cha cha. "Feeling better?"

"I guess," Elm said, wondering how long it would take before Seraphina's wobbly fruit "hat" toppled to the floor. "It kind of feels like I decluttered my brain."

Everyone in the room laughed, nodding with familiarity.

In addition to the fruit basket hat, Elm was fascinated by the necklace Seraphina wore around her neck. The charm was dangling from the silver chain, which appeared to be the number *8* on its side. It rested on a bed of lilac-hued sea glass.

"Pretty," she said, feeling nostalgic about her own sea glass designs.

"It's the Infinity symbol," Seraphina replied, reading Elm's mind again. "It was a gift from someone I love very much. He gave it to me as a hostess gift, of sorts."

"That's nice."

Elm noticed that Miss Fairweather was dancing with Teresa, Elm's sister from her life in Mexico.

"Hey, hermana!" said Teresa. "You're dancing!"

"Si, Teresa," Elm responded. "I thought I'd forgotten."

But she hadn't forgotten that Teresa had once stolen her husband and she had retaliated by sleeping with Luca, Teresa's spouse. At the time, Elm had threatened the impregnated Teresa with a knife, but that seemed to be all water under the bridge now.

"Conga!" Seraphina announced.

Elm had just joined the end of the line, laughing and dancing, when a yellow-haired woman with no aura rushed at her, shoving her to the floor.

"You!" the woman cried. "You left my family to perish in Atlantis. You stole our boat!"

"My apologies," said Seraphina, helping Elm back to her feet. "Number 9 shouldn't be here."

Elm was shaken but not injured. "Who is Number 9?" she asked, noting that the angry woman had disappeared.

"Well, in one life she was an Atlantean scientist and mother of eight children. But you may better remember her from your own life in Little Blessing when she appeared to you as a tempting young sailor."

Royce!

To clear the negative energy, Seraphina broke into song.

"We are Love. We are Loved," she trilled, urging the others to join in unity. "We were created from Love…"

The dancing resumed and Elm wandered alone to the temple's scenic deck, overlooking the exquisite ocean. She needed to be by herself to think, despite knowing it was virtually impossible.

So let's pretend nobody can read my mind.

The incident with the woman who was Royce bothered her. She remembered his arm tattoo. It was a mimic octopus, a shapeshifter. From what she had read online, octopuses were fierce, protective mothers. Had the tattoo actually been a clue to his real mission? A mission of revenge?

Jeez, I need to sit.

A turquoise beach chair magically appeared. In the sky was a parade of colorful kites, flying at varying heights in the breeze. Elm sat for a while, wondering where their pilot was but detected no one on the beach.

A tall man with a trim silver beard and a brilliant silver violet aura was watching her with interest from the temple archway.

"Do you like kites, Dear One?" the man asked, suddenly standing next to her.

Elm thought he had an incredibly sexy voice, deep and resonant like the lanky cowboy actor her mother used to swoon over.

"Doesn't everybody?"

"And what is your heartsong?" he queried.

My heartsong?

The man sat in the chair that materialized next to her. He was graceful, like a dancer.

"I could watch the waves forever, couldn't you?" he said, staring out to sea. "They have so much to teach us."

"I fear it would be a waste of time," was Elm's response.

Whoa, did I just say 'I fear'? Which life is that from?

"You did not always feel that way. As already explained to you, there is no time, Dear One. It merely is a human invention which limits you from manifesting what you truly desire."

Elm said nothing, but wondered if they knew each other.

"Would you like to try it?" he asked, handing her the kite strings that suddenly manifested between his smooth hands.

"Wow. I haven't done this kind of thing since I was a little kid."

"I was a bit older," he laughed. "My heartsong is Kiel. It is the name I resonate to. And yours?"

"Um, Snow," she said, jerking the strings. The kites were acting very strange, like they were dancing a group cha cha. "Yeah, Snow. Snow Moonwater. That's me."

"Is that so?" said Kiel, visibly amused.

A giant pink and gray octopus kite seized the sky and Elm gasped, realizing she was holding its string in her hand.

Wow! I'm an octo-pilot!

Ecstatic, she turned to Kiel and found him staring deep into her soul, a faint smile on his lips. Then he took her hand with incredible gentleness and kissed it, slipping an *I swim past obstacles to find new treasure* mermaid card in the palm of her hand.

"Are you really bold enough to lie to an angel of God, Miss Mercy-Faith Sunday?"

CHAPTER 37

"**D**ADDY?!"
   Their chairs pitched forward, scooting off the deck and floating downwards to the ocean.

   Bouncing along the waves like wooden toy boats, the chairs slowly turned to face each other. Elm's joy was nearly too much to contain because the white-bearded Kiel had metamorphosed into her beloved, blond-haired father!

   "Hey, Babycakes," said a grinning Big Dave. He was sitting across from her in his familiar white shirt and Sunday's Marina cap, healthier than she had ever seen him.

   "Daddy Lighthouse!" Elm cried, leaping to her father's chair and smothering him with kisses. Her abandoned chair floated behind them, but she didn't care. She just wanted to crawl into her father's lap, ask a million questions, and never, ever let him leave.

   Big Dave chuckled, hugging and rocking his weeping daughter. After some time, Elm wiped her tears to look into her father's face, seeing a flash of shared memories in his twinkling blue eyes.

"Are you an angel, Daddy?"

"I am," he said. "Now what do you think about that?"

"It's pretty cool," Elm said, thrilled to hear Big Dave's voice again. "Have you always been an angel?"

"Always."

"Have you seen God?" she inquired.

"Definitely," said her father.

"Do you still like dogs, Daddy?"

Elm was afraid if she stopped asking questions her father might disappear.

Laughing, Big Dave said, "Yes, I still *love* dogs, Elm. I sometimes visit Numbers *One* thru *Seven* and I've been told that there will be an eighth dog soon."

Now it was Elm's turn to laugh. "I guess angels never run out of dog bowls, huh?"

"Never," said Big Dave. "So what do you think about my little retreat?"

Elm realized the chair had traveled a great distance because she couldn't see the temple dome anymore.

"It's beautiful, Daddy. I haven't seen it all yet but I like your singing garden a lot. I wish Mermie could see your flowers."

"Maybe she will someday."

Was it possible? Would they one day be a happy family again, living at Inn Lak'ech for the rest of eternity?

As Elm and her father continued sailing towards the horizon, they joked and reminisced about happy times: Elm's first boat ride, the Christmas Eve the dogs ate Santa's cookies and spilled his milk, the day Big Dave told her about Miss Vi and tree mail. It was strange how the memories seemed so recent and yet ancient at the same time. Eventually, Elm got serious and the tears flowed.

"Daddy, do you have other families, too?"

His answer was not what she expected.

"As an angel of our Divine Creator, I have been blessed with many gifts, Dear One. I can be thousands of places with thousands of souls at one time. Even so, I have but one human family in the Third Dimension."

Elm was relieved. "So, even though you are an angel—an archangel, I mean—I am your only *real* child, the only one you have. Is that right?"

"Bingo!" her dad said.

There was something satisfying about learning she was a half angel. Elm wondered if Glorie knew, but her father read her thought and shook his head.

Elm was happier than she had ever been. With nothing but sea and sky around them, their chair continued sailing at a leisurely pace. She had no fear about where they were heading because Big Dave was the best sailor in the world.

"So, Dad," she teased, "if you're really an angel, can you make this chair go faster? Like *real* fast?"

Her father winked. The chair sped across the waves, making huge figure eights, and then flew in the air with sprouted angel wings.

"Yahoo!" Elm cried.

When they landed safely on the water, a purple dolphin raced with them. It jumped high in the air and did a back flip, then rubbed its sweet face against Big Dave's shoulder.

"Hello, Elm."

With everything Elm had experienced since arriving at Inn Lak'ech, she was hardly surprised to meet a talking purple dolphin.

"Uh, hello," she said, shyly.

"You never met me but I was your father's twin brother, George," said the dolphin. "Others know me as Lady Amethyst, Zadkiel's twin flame."

At that moment, the dolphin revealed itself to be a beautiful woman, emanating a soft violet glow.

Elm felt a bit threatened by the intrusion. Did this mean that Daddy had married again? Was Lady Amethyst her stepmother? And what the heck was a twin flame, anyway?

Not wanting to deal with it all, Elm closed her eyes and buried her face against her father's chest. "I love you, Daddy," she whispered. "I love you so much. Please don't go away again."

When she opened her eyes, the ocean waves had parted and the chair had transformed into the aqua and gold mermaid chariot from the Seashell Carousel! It was sailing toward a watery archway in the shape of a heart.

"Where are we?"

Big Dave smiled. "You are in *my* dream now, Sweetie."

Elm didn't understand. "Angels have dreams?"

"Sure we do," said her father. "And the one dream that I would have dearly loved to witness while in human form is your wedding."

"That's funny, Dad," she laughed. "I'm way too young for that. And who would I have married?"

"Can't you guess?"

In the distance, she saw Noah, waiting for her at the arch. He was filled with light and looked like a prince in a fairytale.

Big Dave helped his daughter from the chariot to where Noah was waiting.

Oh-my-god! Noah's standing on the water! I'm standing on water! We're all standing on water!

Elm and Noah held hands as Big Dave beamed with tremendous love. Lady Amethyst served as officiant, addressing the happy couple in her melodic voice.

"Noah Skyfeather Smith, do you take thee Mercy-Faith Sunday, to be your wife? To have and to hold, in sickness and in health, for richer or for poorer…"

≈

THUMP! IT WAS A CRUEL TRANSITION AND ELM DID NOT appreciate the joke.

One moment she was saying "I do" to Noah (whom she had just discovered had always been her one true love) and the next moment she was back in Suite 8, hugging her bed pillow.

"Did you have a nice time? Did you meet anybody special? How was the wedding?"

Flo was bubbling with questions and Elm wanted to throw something.

"Are you kidding me? What the hell am I doing here, Flo?" she screamed. "I just found out my father is here— he's *the* Archangel Zadkiel—and he took me to my wedding—it was absolutely beautiful—and right when Noah and I were saying our vows I got zapped back here. What's going on, Flo? Tell me everything you know or I swear—"

"Let's try to stay calm now."

Elm hadn't been angry in a long time and threw her pillow across the room. "Don't you dare tell me to be calm! Are you gonna tell me what's happening or what?"

"Well," said Flo, softly. "You're a special situation. An angelic experiment, you might say."

"Experiment? You mean, like a lab rat?"

Elm was hysterical. She ran around the suite, searching for things to throw because she planned to have a full-out temper tantrum. Grabbing one of the angel figurines from the mantel, she threw it against a wall but it did not smash, so she reached for another one.

"You can't take them away from me again!" Elm cried. "Send me back to Daddy and Noah—right now! Send me back, Flo—or I'll tell Seraphina that I want a new guardian!"

Splash!

A water wave slapped Elm across her face and she collapsed on the floor.

The next thing she saw was a row of pulsing, colored lights and several beings huddled over her, including one with a fruit basket on its head.

In the corner stood Archangel Zadkiel, watching her with great concern.

AFTER A DEEP SLEEP ERASED ALL MEMORY OF MEETING KIEL and everything thereafter, Elm awoke in an excellent mood. Flo was right there to greet her, careful not to divulge anything about Elm's recent meltdown nor her subsequent trip to the lighthouse for an emergency color tune-up.

"Flo, I've been curious about something," said Elm, relaxing in the reflection pool.

Oh, wait. I need to practice my telepathy. Can you hear me now?

"I can hear you."

Great. So why don't I have an aura? I know I've lived many lives, so shouldn't I have an aura by now—or at least a pretty pink one?

"Excellent question," said Flo. "The answer is you have always been afraid to progress, so you never completed your lessons. Instead, you kept returning to Earth and other planets, making the same mistakes over and over. Of course, that was your choice, Suite 8. You always have a choice and no one judges you for it."

I think Seraphina told me that, too. Well, I believe I'm ready now.

"Are you sure?" Flo asked. "Because you still must release your negativity and fears first. That prerequisite hasn't changed."

I didn't think it would. But I want a pink aura, Flo, I really do. It's the first color I can earn, right? So please tell me how to get it. The sooner, the better.

"I'll do my best, Suite 8. Do you remember when you were a Girl Scout? You had to perform a variety of tasks before you were awarded your badges, correct?"

Yes, and I actually liked Girl Scouts, especially when I was a Brownie and a Junior Scout. My mom was our troop leader back then and we had a lot of fun. She helped me earn my water awards and my Jeweler badge. And now that I think about it, that's probably what inspired me to create my own sea glass jewelry line.

"Well, there are many challenges you must complete before you can earn your pink aura. As I mentioned, they are required. But I must advise you that these challenges will be more difficult than anything you have ever experienced before."

No problem, I'm ready! So how much time do I get?

Flo gurgled. "You have all the time in the world, Suite 8, since it does not exist. It's completely up to you how quickly you progress."

Well, unless there's something else you've already got scheduled, I'd like to start my first lesson right now.

"Excellent," said Flo. "For your warm-up exercise, we'll go to The Bubble Room first, then come back here to rest before heading over to the steam caves."

The Bubble Room?

Elm imagined a fun place with a great bubble machine or communal bubble bath. Or maybe she would be given her own pipe to blow, creating hundreds of soapy, rainbow bubbles that she could chase.

That sounds like fun, but I do have one more question before we leave.

"One question, one thousand questions. It's all the same to me," Flo said. "How may I serve?"

Well, I'd like to learn more about this place, this sacred retreat of Archangel Zadkiel. Like, what does he look like? What does he do here? And do you think I'll ever get to meet him—or is he away a lot?

CHAPTER 38

ELM FOUND THE ENTRANCE TO The Bubble Room at the end of a long corridor past the Inn Lak'ech reception desk. It was identified only by a tall door with a large peace sign painted in Day-Glo red, green, turquoise, and purple.

Walking inside, patchouli immediately offended her nostrils. Hanging from the middle of the ceiling in the dark entryway was a neon sign, reading:

Be cool now.

An arrow flashed, pointing to a large beanbag chair. Elm sat, giggling at the squishiness, as her eyes focused upon a six-foot lava lamp, glowing brightly in the corner.

Cool. I could watch this all day. Maybe this is what the sign means!

Dancing in its mystical, aquamarine liquid was a shape-shifting white blob, rising slowly from the bottom of the lamp. As it rose, it met with another white blob which magically appeared at the top. Elm kept watching the lamp, fascinated with how several white blobs would suddenly appear and then merge into one.

Very cool.

"Peace, Baby Soul Sister! I see you've been diggin' on our community lava lamp."

Flashing the *V* sign was an old hippie with scraggly gray hair, untidy goatee, striped bell bottoms, and flowery sunglasses. He was shaking a tambourine covered in hot pink and orange ribbons and his smile was as radiant as the lamp.

"Pretty groovy, eh? Check out those white blobs with the green, the orange with the pink, the pink with the white, the green with the orange, the orange with the white, the pink with the green. Just like our soul family, every color blob is unifying into one total mind-blowing harmony!"

"Cool," she responded.

"Right on," said the man. "My heartsong is Love Child. Are you Snow?"

She suppressed a giggle, wondering if the man had looked into a mirror recently because he was way older than a child.

Unless he means that he is illegitimate, which is really not my business.

Regardless, Elm had a confession to make.

"You know, I think I should tell you something," she began. When I came here, I didn't want to give out my real name, so I lied. My real name is Elm. Elm Sunday. Snow is my friend. So you can just call me Elm."

"Yeah, I can dig it," said Love Child. "We all cop out sometimes."

The hippie's love beads jingled as he led Elm through a rainbow-beaded curtain to The Bubble Room. The room itself was dark, although Elm could see the faint outline of auras sitting on colorful, floating pillows.

But absolutely no bubbles in sight.

"This is The Bubble Room?" Elm was disappointed.

"The one and only," Love Child croaked. "So what's your bag, Sister?"

"I don't have a bag," said Elm.

In fact, I don't have any personal stuff anymore.

"Well, don't flip your wig, Elm," said the hippie. "Everyone's got a bag."

"You mean like a purse?"

"Negative. Like, you know, what you're into," Love Child explained. "Your bag is your purpose, your mission, your goal—you dig?"

Dig what?

"Hmmm," Elm said, "so are you saying that maybe my bag is to find out what my bag *is*? Sorry, but I never learned this Sixties lingo."

"I'm hip. Well, have a blast in The Bubble Room," said Love Child. "Be there or be square is my mantra!"

Whoa!

A shiny, purple pillow materialized beneath Elm, catching her off guard. As she attempted to steady herself, the pillow floated slowly across the room to a vacant spot.

I still don't see any bubbles.

Love Child laughed, settling on a long fuchsia pillow at the front of the room. "Chill, Baby Sister. This happening will blow your mind!"

But patience was never Elm's strong suit. She waited for a long time for something—anything—to happen. Every once in a while, she would glance at Love Child (who was reading *Alice Through the Looking Glass*) and the other souls in the room.

What's up with these guys?

Not one had moved or made a noise since she had arrived. Were they meditating? Was she supposed to be meditating, too? Elm couldn't think of anything more boring than sitting and waiting. In fact, she hated it.

And where the hell are those bubbles?

The Universe responded by manifesting pearlescent orbs around her head, containing all the thoughts she had been thinking just seconds ago. She watched them float upwards, merging with the other bubbles like the lava lamp in the entryway.

Then a different kind of bubble emerged. Inside was the word *HELL*, flashing in bold red letters. It floated just above her head, then moved over one of the silent souls, which Elm could now see was an elderly man who looked an awful lot like Reverend George Sunday. Then the *HELL* bubble burst, releasing a sour milk stench and spilling red goo all over the man, shrinking him to the size of an ant. Dwarfed by his pillow, he looked up at Elm with a quizzical "Why me?" expression, but said nothing.

Elm's pillow quivered and pitched forward, slamming into the pillow people as if she was a renegade bumper car.

Oh shit.

A *SHIT* bubble materialized, spilling more sticky goo, this time on a skeletal dark woman wearing a ragged farm dress and a kerchief around her curly black head.

"Oops, did I do that?" Elm asked the woman.

"You know you did!" the woman hissed, pushing Elm's pillow away.

This is weird. And what's the point?

Confused, Elm glanced at Love Child. He was in his own little world, making daisy chains out of thin air. Then the answer came to her.

My thoughts are booby-trapped. Damn, it's just another stupid lesson!

Up floated her thoughts and the word *DAMN* showed in a bubble, which crashed into *STUPID* and splattered angry red goo over Love Child. Surprisingly, the old hippie did not flinch, but continued his chain-making and humming, "I'd Like To Teach The World To Sing."

"Sorry, Mr. Love Child!" Elm cried, dismayed that she was the only one getting thought bubbles.

Love Child nodded. "You've got to tune out what everyone else is doing or receiving and do your own thing, Baby Soul Sister," he instructed. "If you want a groovy pink aura, you've got to free yourself from your own negative vibes. Even curse words can hold you back. It's poison, dig?"

The hippie's comments made no great impact because Elm was more interested in controlling her restless pillow, which was still smashing into walls and souls. Unable to keep her balance, she fell off the pillow and released a string of profanities for all to enjoy. Her punishment was swift, colorful, and extremely messy because every one of the pillow people was covered in goo.

"Oops! Sorry! Darn! My fault! Sorry again!"

At that moment, a movie screen appeared on one of the black walls. Clutching her pillow, Elm floated to a space in front of a projected image of three puppies in an Easter basket. She immediately brightened.

Aww, puppies! Aren't they cute.

The word *CUTE* became a thought bubble and floated over the first man whom Elm accidentally shrank. It showered him with colorful posies and he returned to his full height.

I think I've got it now. Someone gets clobbered every time I think of something bad and gets flowers when I'm thinking something good.

Elm watched thousands of images. Whether they were friends, family members, neighbors, celebrities, politicians, food, places or animals, she had an opinion about each and her thought bubbles acted accordingly. It was like being a contestant in some rapid-fire quiz show, except there was no new car or dining room set if she won. Just flowers.

"Pssst! How's it going, Suite 8?"

Flo was whispering from within the liquid remnants of the latest *CUTE* bubble.

"Well, not great," said Elm. "I'm not making any friends around here, Flo. I must have apologized, like, a hundred times."

"That was very wise," said Flo, "especially since they are members of your soul family. Do you want to meet them?"

"I guess."

But do I really?

Flo was giddy. "Oh, yes! This is so exciting, isn't it? And all you need to do is just float up to each one and ask who they are. Don't be shy now!"

Elm thought *First Man!* and her pillow floated next to the man she had miniaturized.

"Hi, I'm Elm Sunday," she said, pretending confidence. "Are you Reverend George Sunday, my great, great, great grandfather?"

The man smiled, happy to be back to his original size. "Give or take a great," he laughed. "But thank you for acknowledging me, my child."

Elm was relieved that this version of Reverend Sunday wasn't as frightful as the one she had encountered on the moon.

"Look, I didn't mean to shrink you, honest I didn't. Actually, I'm not even sure how I did it."

The reverend's smile quickly faded.

"Every thought you think affects another, don't you

see? Even those in other realms whom you have never met. It's simple spirituality, my child."

"Oh. I didn't know that."

Bump!

A large red-haired woman on a silver pillow crashed into Elm.

"I didn't know that, either," she drawled in a syrupy Southern accent. "But I always did things my way. And you see how poor Gloria turned out."

"I'm Elm. Are you my grandmother?"

"Ha! Not hardly," said Sophie Mae, a bawdy, loud woman with cauliflower ears and a deep, smoky laugh. "I'm your great great grandmother. Looks like my bad karma trickled way down to y'all, too."

Elm had no idea what she meant. "What bad karma?"

"Well, you're here because of your anger, right?"

"I guess so."

"And your mama done you wrong."

"Definitely."

"Well, y'all can thank me for that lovely gift," Sophie Mae laughed.

Bump!

"And me!"

"And me!"

"And me, too!"

Suddenly, Elm was surrounded by women, swooping in like pigeons attacking a handful of bird seed.

"Wait a minute!" she cried, getting bumped on all sides and trying to think her way out of the pillow gridlock. "Stop! Wait!"

Love Child tossed some daisy petals into the fracas. "Peace, my children," he purred. "Everything is beautiful!"

The ancestors quieted and Elm was relieved to see

them float back to their respective places, leaving her alone with her thoughts. Except for Reverend Sunday.

"Sorry, Rev. I forgot I was in your spot."

And then she returned to her own space, simply by thinking about it.

Wow. I guess I need more practice controlling my thoughts because this bubble stuff is way too messy.

"Kind of a bummer, huh?" Love Child was hovering over Elm, playing with a column of white light.

Elm nodded, wishing she had known about the power of thoughts while living on Earth.

"But you always knew your thoughts were powerful," Love Child reminded her. "You just didn't use them for the greatest good. You dig?"

It was true. Anger had taken over her life, just as it had apparently rattled so many female branches of her family tree.

"Perhaps it would increase your understanding if you climbed your mother's branch and saw for yourself," said Love Child, shedding his funky beads and glasses to reveal that he was actually Seraphina, the chameleon innkeeper.

"Wow," said Elm. "You sure like to play dress-up. So where's the tree? And how high do I have to climb?"

"Oh, we're not going to climb a tree, Dear Girl," Seraphina chuckled. "We're going to a spa!"

CHAPTER 39

E LM HAD NEVER HAD AN interest in communicating with her ancestors. That was Snow's department.

She recalled one summer at Girl Scouts when she had helped Snow create a medicine wheel to communicate with her long-departed mother, Debra. It took them several hours to collect and move stones before Snow was satisfied the wheel was energetically complete. After briefly explaining the purpose of the center stones and the "spokes," Snow had stepped inside the center circle to await maternal guidance.

Back in the afterlife, Elm and Seraphina stood at the mouth of a cave. The eccentric innkeeper had changed her attire for spelunking: a khaki shirt, pants, boots, and helmet. Elm thought she resembled a character from an Egyptian mummy movie.

Eeeek!

A swarm of bats flew past them and Elm screamed. She had heard of spas offering bizarre treatments like using fish to eat off the dead skin from feet. But bats seemed a bit extreme unless you were a vampire and she fervently hoped none existed at Inn Lak'ech.

"Please tell me this isn't the spa!" said Elm.

"It's the entrance to it," said Seraphina. "We'll start off with the steam caves."

The first chamber was a profusion of light and as big as a cathedral, a geological jungle with crystals jutting from every surface.

"I hear music," said Elm.

"They're from the crystals," Seraphina replied. "It's a crystal sound bath—so enjoy!"

Red, orange, yellow, green, blue, indigo, and violet rays swirled around the cavern, emanating sweet tones. Elm felt giddy and flew to the ceiling.

"Wow, this feels great!" she said, twirling to absorb the full spectrum's cleansing vibrations. "I wouldn't mind just staying here all day."

But Seraphina had other plans.

"A little longer, then we must continue. There are seven smaller rooms in this part of the cave. Why don't you think *'Fly to red'* and investigate?"

Elm nodded, detecting a red glow to her left.

Fly to red!

She flew into a room made entirely of red rubies, feeling an immediate warmth and energy. A disembodied voice said, "You have received the gift of red, the color of courage and stability."

Elm flitted from room to room like a bumblebee gathering nectar in a garden. The second room glowed of bright orange carnelians and the joy Elm felt as she touched the stone was tremendous. "You have received the gift of orange," the voice said. "Orange is the color of joy and creativity."

Upon entering Room Three, Elm was greeted with radiant yellow citrine. Said the voice: "Your gift from yellow is knowledge and confidence."

Room Four was a treasure of gorgeous, sparkling emeralds. The ambience was balanced and loving. "You have received the gift of green, the color of love and good health," said the voice.

Elm continued onward to Room Five, a space brimming with cool, watery blue topaz. "You have received the gift of blue," the voice announced. "Blue is the color of peace and integrity."

The next room was filled with indigo-colored iolites, appearing rather mystical, like the night sky. Elm held up one of the tingling iolites to her Third Eye, which sparked the voice to say: "Your gift from indigo is imagination and intuition."

Tears flowed as Elm entered the violet room, an exquisite lair of rich, gorgeous amethyst. "Congratulations," said the voice. "You have received the gift of spirituality and wisdom."

Elm had enjoyed her time with the colors. In gratitude, she knelt on a huge amethyst tablet, thanking the Divine for all that she had received.

THEY WERE HEADING TO THE SECOND CHAMBER, WHERE THE walls were black with silvery sparkles and a noxious gas assaulted the air.

"Um, this is different," Elm said, wishing she was back in the color rooms. "I hope we don't have to stay here too long."

Somewhere in the darkness, Seraphina said, "The word you're looking for is *chiroptophobia*."

"What's that?"

"Fear of bats," said the woman, matter-of-factly. "Come sit next to me."

Seraphina!

The ground was hard, damp, and bumpy. "Okay, so now what?"

"We wait for the drummer," Seraphina replied.

The drummer?

The old woman smiled, taking a book from under her helmet and began reading *The Divine Comedy* by Dante Alighieri.

"Are you sure this is the right place? I can't see a thing and it's creeping me out."

"What may appear dark also harbors the light," Seraphina said, not looking up from her book. "So ask me."

"Ask you what? And why am I still surprised that you can read my mind?"

"I've been wondering that myself," Seraphina chuckled. "Why don't you try practicing your telepathy?"

Okay. Well, I've been thinking about, uh, hell.

"How synchronistic!" Seraphina exclaimed. "I was just reading about that."

She assumed the guise of a priest sitting in a confessional. Lowering her voice to a compassionate tone, Seraphina said, "So what has been bothering you, my child?"

Elm hesitated. She had heard that confession was good for the soul, but was it too late to save herself?

Okay, I'll just say it. Inn Lak'ech seems like a nice place and all, but it could be all smoke and mirrors. I've done a lot of bad things, so here's what I'm wondering. When are the devils coming to stick me with pitchforks?

"Pitchforks?" whispered the voice behind the screen. "Is that what your Christian faith taught you?"

It's what my grandmother told me to believe. She said I was a sinner.

"I see. Would you be surprised to learn that hell is merely a religious tactic to control you through fear?"

Not really.

"It has always been imaginary. So no, Sister, you will not go to hell for stealing or killing or any other so-called infraction. Would you say that hell is the feeling of being separated from our Creator?"

I guess so.

"And have there been times when you hated your fellow human?"

Oh, yeah!

"And did you suffer during these times?"

Yes.

"Like you were living in hell?"

Absolutely.

"So do you think it is possible that what you perceive to be punishments were actually created by your own angry thoughts or actions?"

Maybe.

"Then maybe you have your answer," said Seraphina, who had changed back to her wise woman self, minus the confessional.

No, it couldn't be that simple. Elm needed more answers.

Are you saying that I created hell in my own mind? That the world is not really evil and painful and I always had the power to change things by changing my thoughts? Because if that's what you're saying, Seraphina, then why couldn't my life be, like, heaven all the time? I don't remember sitting around thinking, gee, I've had too good a life and now I'm ready for some hell! Sorry, but this just doesn't make sense to me.

Seraphina smiled, knowingly. "When you open to the energy of Trust, it will make all the sense in the world. Ah, the drummer has arrived!"

Prabhakar was practically out of breath, as if he had been running a marathon. "I am here, Seraphina! I am here to drum for my father!" He was holding a large drum, nearly as large as himself, but managed a quick wave and a huge smile. "Hello, Bapu!"

Elm waved back. She wondered why he did not approach her, staying by the opposite wall. And then she heard the rushing of a waterfall and saw a stream of water flow past her.

"Yes, I am here as well, Suite 8," said Flo. "I will help make the steam."

"I'll explain," said Seraphina, responding to Elm's quizzical expression. "Our steam treatment is a very special way for you to release toxic fears from your soul."

"Like a fear of bats?" said Elm, looking above her.

"Perhaps," Seraphina said, "for you cannot experience real love, Sister, until you release what frightens you."

"Okay," Elm said, still not convinced that bats weren't lurking close by. "And how do you do that?"

"Actually, *you* do the hard part, with the aid of the greatest fear extractor that has ever existed anywhere!"

"You mean a wizard or masseuse or something?"

Seraphina winked at Prabhakar, who laughed with her. "No. Something much larger."

"Like a giant?"

"Compared to most creatures," Seraphina said. "In this case, I'm speaking about a black dragon."

Elm snorted. She didn't want to sound argumentative,

but dragons were a myth and she was surprised Seraphina believed in such nonsense.

"You're kidding, right? I mean, a *dragon*? Like in fairy-tales and *Harry Potter* and *The Hobbit*? That kind of dragon?"

"Yes," said Seraphina, "but you look a bit worried, Sister."

"Not me," said Elm, matter-of-factly. "Because everybody knows that dragons don't exist."

"Is that so?" Seraphina challenged. "Let's see."

The cave walls echoed with heavy breathing. The next sound was something being dragged across the floor, followed by a loud thump. Finally, a pair of blazing, red-orange eyes pierced the blackness.

I…believe…you.

"And that is my cue to depart," said Seraphina, cheerily. "But I leave you in good hands with Char, our resident fire keeper."

Elm panicked. "Wait! Don't go!"

But Seraphina had disappeared.

Great. So now I'm stuck here in the dark with a boy, a puddle, and a dragon. Just great.

Char's face was so close to Elm's that his hot breath nearly knocked her over.

Maybe Prabhakar knows what to do. Why doesn't the kid say something? And that dragon is way too close. I wonder what would happen if I threw a rock at it?

"I suspect I am the *it* you wish to harm," said Char. "It's sad to hear your thoughts, Elm Sunday. Do you not know that humans once considered dragons as their best friends?"

"I never heard that," Elm said aloud. "Listen, I don't want to be rude but could you back up a bit? Your breath is pretty hot."

Her son beat excitedly on his drum. "And it's going to get hotter, Bapu!"

"You are correct, my little friend," Char agreed, backing up a little. Then he said to Elm: "I'm curious. Why did you once display dragon replicas in your sleeping space if you did not wish us to be friends?" He was referring to Elm's bedroom.

"I guess I was going through a phase," said Elm. "I wanted power objects around me and I thought dragons were destructive and cool. I just never thought I'd get to meet one for real."

Char and Prabhakar exchanged glances. "Then what did you think when you met my cousin, the one you call Nessie?"

"I was thinking that Nessie was a dinosaur," Elm replied, looking for a more comfortable place to rest. "Are you telling me that she was really a dragon?"

"*Is* a dragon," Char corrected.

"But you two look so different," said Elm, astonished. She had found a pile of large, flat stones and climbed to the top to sit.

"Perhaps, but is it not true that most humans look different, despite their commonalities of a nose, two eyes, two ears, and a mouth?"

Elm nodded. "I guess so. Okay, let's say I believe you. Nessie's a dragon and she's your cousin. But how does that help me?"

"We help you to purge," Char replied. "As you can see, I am a black dragon. I will assist you with cleansing your thoughts of fear to help you accept the creative power of the Divine Feminine. Without it, you cannot be reborn."

The Divine Feminine.

Where had Elm heard that term before? And then she remembered Kat, the energy healer.

"Hey, I used to know someone who was into all that Divine Feminine jazz, but it didn't excite me. Why should I care about it now?"

"That's a good question, Suite 8," interrupted Flo. "And the answer will come to you soon. In the meantime, we have a firepit to build so I suggest you climb down and stand back."

Boom. Boom. Boom. Boom.

While Elm waited on a slab bench against the wall, Prabhakar pounded his drum, loud and steady.

Boom. Boom. Boom. Boom.

Char piled dry river rocks to make a firepit and placed a mouthful of sweetgrass in the center.

"I am the firekeeper," Char announced. "I am the light of the Violet Flame."

Purple fire spewed from the dragon's mouth, igniting the sweetgrass into one fiery heap. Then Flo doused water on the blaze, causing steam to hiss and rise from the pit.

I'm feeling dizzy, Flo. I think I might be sick.

"Just close your eyes, Suite 8. Let whatever you're thinking come naturally."

No, I really think I'm gonna be sick.

Boom. Boom. Boom. Boom.

As Elm watched Char and Flo repeat their fire and water routine, another type of fire was rising inside her. Like emotional kindling, every fear she had ever imagined in any lifetime was added to the blaze: her fear of falling from a mountaintop, fear of being suffocated, fear of losing loved ones on the battlefield, fear of drowning, fear of rejection, fear of embarrassment. Even her peanut butter phobia.

Boom. Boom. Boom. Boom.

It's hot. So hot. Does Prabhakar have to keep beating that drum?

Elm thought she might need to vomit, but she didn't get the chance because there was a painful eruption inside her.

"Yowwwwwwwwwwwww!" she screamed.

Boom. Boom. Boom. Boom.

CHAPTER 40

W HEN ELM REGAINED CONSCIOUSNESS, SHE was alone and shaking, staring at a pile of stones that had scorched black in the firepit.

Still in pain, she assumed her phobias were gone because there were some bats hanging from the ceiling and she wasn't frightened at all. She wondered if the enormous charred stone lying nearby had anything to do with her excruciating experience.

But why am I able to see in the dark?

Since there seemed to be no one around to answer her question, Elm fixated on a glimmer of pink to her far right. It was exciting to see a color that wasn't red-orange or black.

Pink!

She was at a door, encrusted with rose quartz, singing to her in cosmic tones. Elm turned the pink doorknob and walked in.

The room was immersed in a dreamy pink light, which was a welcome contrast from the dreary Steam Caves.

Instead of bats, Elm was greeted by a radiant pink being with luminous rainbow wings.

"Welcome to the Soul Spa," she said, softly. "My heart-song is Re-sa. Here we specialize in the four *Re's*—re-lax, re-fresh, re-join, and re-flect. Today we will be serving a full menu of Divine Feminine treatments for your party of eight."

"Eight?" Elm checked to see if anyone was standing behind her. "Nope, it's just me," she said.

Elm was escorted to a private spa room, a bright and sunny space with pale pink walls, lush green plants, and a heart-shaped skylight overhead.

Wow.

The room also displayed a rose quartz fountain and a spa massage chair with a golden pedicure bowl. Next to the chair was a tall table with a built-in sink and a pink face towel, pink jar, and pink bottle resting on a small, golden tray. Alongside one of the walls, a stack of plush, pink towels had been placed on a bench, accompanied by a pair of pink slippers and a fluffy pink bathrobe. In the corner opposite from the bubbling fountain was a full-length mirror.

"Is everything to your satisfaction?" Re-sa whispered.

"It's pink, but nice," said Elm. "And your pink aura goes well with the decor."

"Yes, I am very blessed," said Re-sa. "So I believe you have everything you need?"

"Um, I think so."

"Good, then I will leave you now."

Wait a minute!

"What about my Divine Feminine treatments?" Elm asked. "I mean, aren't you supposed to stick around to give me a facial and manicure and stuff?"

Re-sa shook her head. "I am sorry you are confused.

This is a love-yourself salon. Begin at the mirror for instructions. Your reflection will guide you from there."

Re-sa vanished, leaving a cloud of pretty pink sparkles.

Go to the mirror, huh?

Elm smiled at her reflection, seeing a translucent version of her last self. Then she made funny faces.

"Are you dissatisfied?" asked the mirror.

"Yes, because I don't have a colored aura."

"That is true," said the mirror, "but why should it bother you? You no longer have fear so you do not need to compete, not even with yourself. Stop judging how you think you should look and focus on the beauty of your own soul."

"I'll have to work on that," said Elm. "What's next?"

Her reflection told her to go to the bench and put on the robe and slippers. "It is time to prepare for your first spa treatment, a cleansing meditation that will help you get rid of your mental impurities."

To Elm's surprise, there was something lovely about wearing pink. Why had her teenage self always fought it?

"First, walk over to the table," said the mirror. "Open the pink bottle and empty the contents into the copper pedicure bowl below the chair."

"Done," said Elm, after following the mirror's instructions. "And I smell roses!"

"Roses have a high vibration," the mirror said. "From this point on, it will be easier for you to use telepathy to communicate."

Okay.

"Now open the pink jar and apply its smooth, pink cream all over your face. Sit in the chair and stick your feet into the pedicure bowl, which is filled with moisturizing rose water. Then, just press the pink button on the side of the chair and watch the water bubble and swirl around like a whirlpool."

Ahhhhhh. Now, this is a spa!

Her reflection giggled. "Almost heaven, yes? So while your face and feet are receiving their special beauty treatment, imagine you are sitting on a white sandy beach. The sun is directly overhead and its rays are brilliant and warm as they flow from the top of your head and down, throughout your body. Can you visualize that?"

Not only could Elm visualize it, all she had to do was think it and she was there!

"Good. Now let your toes feel the cool, blue water. See yourself staring out to sea, mesmerized by the dancing rhythm of the waves. Watch the seagulls fly above you and see them dive into the sparkling water. You feel so at peace here."

At peace. Yes. Absolutely.

The meditation continued for a while and when it had ended, the mirror said, "Now just relax. Listen to the birds...enjoy the floral aroma...the sun through the skylight...the water trickling in the fountain...and focus on nothing but being loved."

Elm focused and was surprised to find how easy it was to feel loved.

"Yes, your deep cleansing is going very well, Sister. But there are still more toxins to release. So I'd like you to open your eyes and write this sentence: 'I believe the main reason I am afraid of letting myself love again is...'"

But I don't have anything to write with.

A pretty pink fan spread open on Elm's lap. It was heart-shaped, resembling a valentine. It was accompanied by a pink pen covered in sparkly hearts, which Elm used to write on the fan:

I believe the main reason I am afraid of letting myself love again is because every time I do I lose that person.

"Understandable," said her reflection. "Now imagine that your greatest dream has become reality. Perhaps your book has become a bestseller or you are onstage accepting an award for bravery from the President."

But I'm dead.

"You have transitioned, but do not let that distress you. See your family and friends joining you to offer congratulations for a job well done. Do you see them?"

Yes. I see Daddy and Mermie. Snow and Noah and Jason are there, too.

"Yes, they are. They are hugging you, praising, and encouraging you. They are telling you to keep persevering. They are saying 'You are loved, Elm Sunday! We support you in everything you do!' For the first time in a long time, you feel truly loved and understood! Gone is your pain, your sadness, your fears. You can see clearly now and you are free to share your light and love with the Universe!"

After a few minutes, Elm rinsed the pink cream from her face and dried her feet with the pink towel.

Basking in the glow of self-love and compassion, she stepped out onto the terrace to absorb the rays of the glorious sunshine and the sights and scents of a spectacular pink garden.

Everything looks so beautiful here. Beautiful and new and pink.

"Yeah, yeah, it's all pinky keen. Hey, Miss La-tee-da! Are you finished loving yourself yet? Come on out here, Gal, so we can get a good look at ya!"

CHAPTER 41

THE BOISTEROUS VOICE BELONGED TO Sophie Mae and "out here" was an enormous hot tub in the middle of the garden. Elm had to walk down a lovely pathway of shimmering rose quartz and through a labyrinth of pink roses, begonias, tulips, carnations, chrysanthemums, and hibiscus to find it.

There were seven naked women of different ages, leaning against the inside perimeter of the hot tub. Their heads were wrapped in pink towels and they were chatting and drinking from long-stemmed glasses of bubbly pink champagne.

Wow. They're colorless, like me.

"Who ya callin' colorless, Peanut?"

Elm was looking down at the bawdy Sophie Mae, who was wearing a diamond choker around her thick neck and nothing else.

"Sorry," Elm stammered, "I just happened to notice you don't have auras."

"Hey, I was just funnin' with ya—jump in!"

But you're all naked.

Sophie Mae snorted. "So? Have you taken a gander at yourself lately? Not a stitch on ya under that pretty pink robe, I'll guarantee ya. Besides, it's not like we've never been naked before. That's how we all came into this world, remember?"

"Maybe she's shy," said Frances, a reddish-blond woman who looked a lot like Glorie. "Don't push her, Sophie Mae. Not everybody likes to show off."

Sophie Mae was not a fan of mollycoddling. "Shy about what? We're not gonna judge and we're sure as hell ain't gonna gawk. Except maybe Matilda," she snickered.

"Are you implying something, Mother?" accused the lanky, scowling woman next to Frances.

Okay, I'll do it. Just please stop arguing.

Elm disrobed and jumped in the water, squeezing between two of the women. Something live and rubbery wrapped itself around her middle, but she could see nothing through the whirling bubbles and decided to ignore it.

"It is good you are not afraid," said a Native American woman with two black braids peeking out from under her pink turban. "You must take after me. Strong. Brave."

A glass of champagne floated to Elm and she took a sip, the bubbles shooting up her nose.

"So, who are all you lovely people, uh, souls?" she slurred. "Hey, you know what? It doesn't even matter because I know—I know I love you!"

Sophie Mae laughed. "Your first pink champagne, Dearie? Seriously, one sip and you're tipsy?"

Guess so.

"Never mind that, Daughter," said Hard Winter, the Native American woman.

Matilda interrupted. "Is someone going to tell this girl why she's here?"

Why am I where? Boy, this tastes good! I wonder if they'll let me take some back to my suite.

"I'll tell her," blurted Ida June, the skinny black woman Elm had offended in The Bubble Room. "We're the reason why you hate your mother." She shot Matilda a scornful look. "Happy now?"

Matilda nodded.

"Did you know my mother?" Elm asked.

"Frances was her mother in that lifetime," added Petit Fleur, a sophisticated mulatto with a slight French accent. "But we have always been connected. And *you're* the reason why we are able to spend this lovely time together getting beautified."

"And the only one who can break our stupid, colorless curse," Matilda said, pointedly.

"Amen, Sister," said Ida June.

Elm took another sip of her champagne and stared at each of the women.

They all look so serious. Don't they know that love is the answer?

"Sure, I'll break your little curse," Elm giggled. "Just point me in the right direction and I'll make it all disappear—just like that!" She tried to snap her fingers but nothing happened. "Wow, that's embarrassing."

"She's had too much champagne," said Frances.

"She's a lightweight," Sophie Mae snickered.

"And she's not taking any of this seriously," Matilda interjected. "This is Mercy-Faith's chance to right a wrong for the sake of our soul advancement."

"What about me?" Elm blurted.

"You, too," said Matilda.

"Then we must make her listen."

Speaking from the opposite side of the hot tub was Deka, a large African woman with a powerful baritone voice and a penchant for storytelling.

"Since I am the elder here, I will speak from my perspective first. My name is Deka, which means 'pleasing'. In my home in Somalia, I was the perfect good girl. I never knew my mother—she died by my father's hand when I was three. I was raised by my stepmother who was actually my sister, but I did not learn that for many years. Like my father, my stepmother was very strict so I did what was expected of me or I would be punished. So I was always pleasing people. That was my life and the end of my story."

"Well, it wasn't the end for me," chided Ida June. "My hell was only beginning. You sold me into slavery, Mother. Do you know what it was like to be on a slave ship for six months and to be whipped nearly every day of your young life?"

"I did what I had to do, Ida June," said Deka. "I bear no shame. It was the price you paid to enjoy an adventurous life."

Ida June was furious. "Adventurous life? The life of a *servant*?"

"You forget that I was a slave, too," Deka huffed. "A slave to my family. I was always serving and I never wandered outside of our village. I never saw new people, new things. But you, My Daughter, you saw many things. And did you not enjoy many children in the new land?"

Petit Fleur cleared her throat. "I am one of those children, Grandmother. They call me Petit Fleur, meaning Little Flower. I am the slave they brought in from the fields. The master called me his Pet. He had red hair like your mère's, Mercy-Faith. Well, it wasn't until the mistress died and the master took me to Paris as his companion that I learned he was my very own père. He told me the truth when we were in bed, like he was proud of the fact. I wasn't so proud. I hated him and I hated my mother, but it was too late for me to escape. I was already carrying his son and the master still owned me. When we returned to the Americas, Ida June said taking up with the master was the right thing to do. The *only* thing, she said. She said she was protecting me, but I never believed her. It was unforgivable and she knew it was a sin."

Hard Winter spoke next. "In my youth, I often wondered why The Great Spirit chose Petit Fleur to be my mother. I am Hard Winter, from the Arapaho tribe. Petit Fleur married two times before she met my father. She left us shortly after I was born, taking my older brother with her. I don't think she ever loved my father, even though he was very respected. Without a mother to guide me, the women in our tribe taught me how to be obedient. Sometimes they hurt me. One day I met a white man in the woods and we fell in love. He took me to his village where the whites called me Winnie. Sophie Mae is my daughter. It is not the name she was given when I bore her."

"It's the name I liked, Old Lady," Sophie Mae reminded her.

"I can relate," said Elm.

"You ran away from yourself!" said Hard Winter, ignoring Elm's comment. "You invented a new story, a new name, and you brought shame on our family by killing your husband!"

"And where did you get that Southern accent?" Frances added. "You were born in Wyoming!"

Wow, my family tree is like a bad soap opera!

Sophie Mae snapped her fingers and more champagne appeared in everyone's glass.

Sophie Mae turned to Elm and said, "Honey, I spent all my time looking good for my man 'cause that's the way my mama taught me. She never said it outright but she always had on a clean dress and wore her hair with something pretty in it, like a ribbon, whenever my father came home from trappin'. So I saw that and I knew I wanted more than Mama ever had. And I found me a fancy man to pay for it all—the jewelry, the furs, the clothes, the makeup, the traveling—all of it. Did you know I was a stage actress? Honky-tonk saloons out west, mostly. Well, all the time I was singing and dancing my big ol' ass off, my *loving* husband was out spending my money on liquor and gambling and whores. Mama never taught me how to handle that, so I found me a gun under the bar and I shot his ass. Mama never visited me. Not once. She raised my daughters and called them her own and that's all I know. Matilda, you're next."

Matilda stiffened. "I was a late bloomer, Mercy-Faith. I didn't get involved in the Suffragettes until I was nearly forty. That's right before Mama Winnie died. She told me she was my grandmother and my real mother was in prison. When my sister and I traveled to California to visit Sophie Mae, she refused to see us. It broke my heart, even though I didn't remember my mother at all. But I knew she was my mother and a strong one, too. At least, we had that in common. So I continued to fight for the rights of all women, even the incarcerated ones. And then I got raped by a politician who said he would sure as hell make me like men. He was entirely wrong about that but he did leave me with my precious Cady Susan, whom I tried to protect and never let out of my sight. I took a job as a secretary to support us and raised her to not ever need a man. Or so I thought. Then one day she ran off with some fisherman, just as fast as she could. Can you believe that? A fisherman!"

"But why did I disappoint you, Mama?" protested Frances. "Because I insisted on being called Frances? Because I didn't want to be paraded onstage every night while you stood at a podium, shaking your fist, and preaching to any woman who would listen that all men are evil? Because I happened to fall in love with a good man who earned an honest living and took care of me? If I'm not mistaken, most of Jesus' disciples were fishermen."

"Amen, Sister," said Ida June. "Which brings us to poor Gloria. We expect she'll join us one day but you will take her place until then, Mercy-Faith. In fact, we've made you an honorary member of The Bad Mothers Club."

What?

"But I'm not a mother," Elm insisted.

"The hell you ain't!" said Sophie Mae. "Didn't you just lay a big ol' dragon egg of fear in the Steam Caves? We could hear you wailin' all the way out here!"

"I have no idea what happened," said Elm, still sipping her champagne. "It was very dark in there. But I'm feeling much better now, thank you!"

Everyone laughed and then Petit Fleur raised her glass in a toast.

"To Mercy-Faith. Many blessings for all you are about to do for us—and good luck!"

"To Mercy-Faith!" the women toasted.

As each woman raised her arm, a giant tentacle rose with it until Elm could plainly see that they were all being held by an enormous octopus.

So that's what's been clutching me all this time. I always wanted an octopus. I guess I finally got my wish.

"Yes, she is the octopus mother," said Deka, nodding at Elm's thoughts. "We invited her for support."

"Sort of like having a big rubbery mascot, Honey," said Sophie Mae.

Frowning, Frances said, "She has been telling us about her role as a mother, how she takes care of her children at the risk of her own life. My daughter, Gloria, does not appreciate the message of the octopus because she believes I failed to protect her and she failed to protect you, dear granddaughter. It has been a continuous cycle. And Gloria lives in darkness to this very day because she has not forgiven herself."

"And she cannot heal until she remembers who she really is," added Deka. "As you are learning."

Ida June agreed. "None of us forgave our mothers, so we are depending on you, Girl. Help our Gloria break this curse so we can all get ourselves a pretty pink aura."

"Please, Granddaughter," Frances urged.

Elm looked at each of her ancestral mothers with compassion and love. Of course, she wanted to help them, but she was no longer in the Third Dimension. For all intents and purposes, she was dead.

How on Earth can I save Mermie when I couldn't save myself?

CHAPTER 42

"WHAT DO YOU THINK OF this class, Bapu? Very interesting, yes?"

Where are you, Boy?

"I'm looking down at Gaia. Do you see her yet?"

They had been flying through galaxies at light speed alongside other soul members, many of whom were repeating the class as a training refresher.

Not yet. Which way should I be looking?

From her vantage point, Elm could see faraway stars and planets and it reminded her of a time when she visited the High City planetarium during a school field trip.

I see it now! Wow, it looks like a big beach ball! And look at all that water!

"Did you know that over seventy-five percent of Mother Earth is covered in water, Bapu?"

I think my father told me that. The whole planet looks great from up here, doesn't it? Like a postcard.

Elm enjoyed this way of traveling. She was one with the air, the stars, the Light—heck, she *was* the Light. And she most definitely was Water. Her merging experiences with Flo had taught her that.

"Bapu, I have a question."

Yes?

"What did you like about your last life?"

It was a tough question.

Well, I liked being a sea priestess.

"And why is that, Bapu?"

It made me feel important, I guess. And I didn't have to be such a goody-goody mayor's daughter all the time. It was my own identity, the one I chose for myself.

"Very interesting," said the boy. "I am sorry you did not remember who you are."

The class was descending upon Earth, scattering in various directions for their next Oneness assignment.

"Now pick a spot and unify with a tree," ordered Wing-caw, their instructor. He was a twitchy male who bore a striking resemblance to a black crow.

I thought the word was 'merge'.

Wingcaw heard her thought and said, "We are not driving on a road, Sister. Our objective is to unify. Please do so now."

Got it. Tree!

Elm was in Vermont during autumn, looking out from the hilltop of a red-gold apple orchard. She shook a little as sparrows flew in and out of her vibrant leaves, delightfully aware that a red-capped woodpecker was tapping at her trunk and a few pale pink worms tickled her branches. Elm noticed that she wasn't the tallest tree in the orchard, but she certainly had a good view.

I wonder how old I am.

"If you're so curious, why don't you just split yourself open and count your circles?"

The voice was coming from another tree and caught Elm off- guard.

"That's rude," said a gray-brown squirrel.

"I agree," said another tree. "I'm over five hundred years young and I never felt better."

"Oh yeah?" said the first tree. "How do we know you're not lying about your age?"

Um, hi. I'm Elm.

"Elm? An apple tree named Elm? Now I've heard everything!"

The entire orchard was laughing at her. The old Elm would have said something sarcastic, maybe threaten to unleash a tidal wave from the duck pond. Instead, she sent love to everything around her.

Elm was watching a haywagon. It was carrying nine chattering passengers, bouncing along a muddy country road and past the giant "Pick Your Own Apples" sign. It parked a hundred yards away and a group of excited children jumped off and raced towards her, swinging their wooden buckets.

"Let's have a contest," said a woman in patchwork overalls. "The one who picks the most apples in an hour wins a prize."

"Yay!" the children exclaimed, jumping up and down.

Two men set up ladders against the trees and the children climbed like ravenous monkeys. Elm wasn't sure she enjoyed this sensation of being pulled at but she also had no choice. She was there only to observe, to experience, and not be attached to the outcome.

After the assignment, Elm returned to Inn Lak'ech, where she attended her first AquaAura Yoga class in the Ascension Pool. She was surprised to learn that Flo was one of the instructors, teaching the class how to stand and kneel on the water.

Seraphina also made a surprise appearance and the class cheered. Dressed in the garb of an ancient mariner, the innkeeper was sitting in a lotus pose, reading *Moby Dick* by Herman Melville, while her aquamarine yoga mat sailed the length of the pool to where Elm was floating.

"Ahoy there, Sister," called the innkeeper. "I see you survived your Oneness lesson. Tell me, what was your overall impression of your Vermont experience?"

"Well—"

Seeing that Elm was desperately attempting to maneuver the downward-facing dog pose with her right leg up, Seraphina suggested she respond telepathically.

Okay. Well, Vermont was as beautiful as I expected it to be in the fall. I'd never been there before but Mermie used to get those New England wall calendars and there was always a picture of Vermont foliage on the October page. But the apple-picking could have been organized differently. The kids didn't stay on the ladders, some began climbing me and didn't seem to care at all where they put their feet or how hard they were bending my branches. It was as if I was completely invisible and not a part of them in any way. The only thing they were concerned about was beating their competition.

"And how did you feel about this competition?"

Elm gave up on the downward-facing dog and settled for a camel pose.

Honestly? I felt that it was a total waste of energy. They could have collected enough apples to make a pie through the spirit of unity, through cooperation. The way I saw it, the adults didn't have to orga-nize a competition to get the kids to pick apples. The eating of the apples could have been the reward itself. And it looked like the kids were afraid they would be losers if they stopped. A few of the kids got ugly, you know, calling the other kids names or throwing twigs at the ones who were going too fast for them. One girl scratched her knee on my bark and a boy fell off the ladder, while the rest of the kids either laughed or just kept picking my apples. The adults told the kids to stop being babies and to keep their eyes on the prize. But they hadn't even been told what that prize was! So it wasn't about Oneness at all, Seraphina. More like Won-ness.

"An interesting perception, Sister," said the innkeeper. "Your father once gave you an affirmation card of a flower. Do you remember what it said?"

I do! A flower does not think of competing to the flower next to it. It just blooms!

$$\sim$$

FOR HER NEXT ONENESS EXERCISE, ELM CHOSE TO BE A scallop shell on a beach in Aruba.

As her energy unified with the shell, Elm was conscious of the turquoise ocean waves, flowing in and out, and the hot sun beating down upon her. She listened to the occasional laughter and loud voices from the cocktail bar on the beach and the metallic tones from the steel drums.

Like all the other times, Elm was aware of everything around her during the unification —the pebbles, the seashells, the sand, the occasional plane or seabird flying overhead, even the insects. They were all sharing the same air, the same space.

We are all connected. I see that now.

With her new perspective, Elm was truly enjoying her unification lessons. She had unified with a baby elephant in India and a toucan in an Amazon rainforest. She had even traveled to other planets in other galaxies and unified with beings there.

The process had become quite fun and one day Elm was on such a high that she enthusiastically asked Seraphina if she could unify with her. At the time, the woman was sprawled across her bench near the lighthouse, engrossed in *1984* by George Orwell.

"That's very sweet, Sister, but I must humbly decline."

Elm was disappointed. "I just thought it would be interesting because you're able to do and be whatever you like whenever you want. And because you run this inn and everything."

Seraphina's eyes twinkled. "I thank you for the offer but I have an alternate idea. Do you like to read, Sister?"

"You mean, like, books?"

"Exactly. I know it's been awhile, but think back to your last life. Do you remember the name of your favorite children's book?"

Elm thought of her book collection in Little Blessing, recalling her most treasured tomes in her white wicker bookcase next to the window.

"Well, probably *The Wizard of Oz*."

"Good choice," said Seraphina, transforming into a pig-tailed Dorothy Gale, carrying a barking Toto in her basket. "How would you like to unify with an important character from literature?"

"Maybe. But how can I? They're not real."

"They're not?" Seraphina teased, changing from Dorothy to Humpty Dumpty wobbling on a wall.

They both laughed. If Elm had learned anything during her Inn Lak'ech adventures it was that everything was possible because everything was energy.

"Okay, I'll try it."

"Excellent. But let's give it a twist," Seraphina suggested. "Select your *least* favorite character and unify with that person."

"You mean like the Wicked Witch of the West?"

The thought of unifying with Dorothy's nemesis was appealing, especially the part about riding a broom and cavorting with flying monkeys.

"No, too easy," said Seraphina, "although someone did

write a book about her perspective and a hit Broadway musical."

Elm wanted to please her mentor, so she cleared her mind and received a vision of her grandfather delivering a sermon from his pulpit at the Grace Church of the Ascension.

"Can the character be a real person, like from the New Testament in the Bible? I remember I never liked Judas—he was the bad apostle who betrayed Jesus. What do you think? I mean, considering how my family tree mothers thought their mothers betrayed them and how I felt about my own mother and all."

For good measure, Elm remembered a negotiating tactic she would sometimes use on her parents. "And it would be educational, too!"

Seraphina's response was to morph from the cracked egg in a nursery rhyme to a gospel choir singer. "Oh, Happy Day!" she sang excitedly, twirling her long purple choir robe and shaking a tambourine. "Glorie Hallelujah—I feel the *power*!"

Elm giggled at the reference to her family's boat.

"So, you really like it?"

"I do," Seraphina agreed. "And it makes perfect sense."

"I think so, too," Elm said happily. "But how do I do it?"

Seraphina returned to her old self again. "Why, you're going to *think*, of course. You already know how to unify, so think about the era. The people. Jesus. Judas. Think of everything you have ever read or heard about Judas and his life. And when you unify with him, Sister, remember that you are there only to observe the world through his perspective. Do not interfere with the outcome of his actions."

CHAPTER 43

JUDAS ISCARIOT LEFT HIS SURPRISED brethren sitting in disbelief in an upstairs room in his father's house, just outside Jerusalem. Teacher had accused him of being a traitor and the uproar it created was all the proof he needed to retreat into the night.

He scurried like a rat, past modest houses lit with oil lamps, hearing an occasional loud snore through an open window or a growl from a scavenging dog. His heart pounded, knowing that nothing would ever erase the events of the last supper from his mind.

Teacher had held up a loaf of bread and said it represented his body, handing a piece to each of his apostles. Eat this, he had told them. And then he had raised a cup of wine, proclaiming it to be his blood, which would be shed for the sins of all humanity. He passed the cup and each apostle drank from it. It was an uncomfortable ceremony, including the part where Teacher washed his apostles' feet.

Why are you bothering, Lord? I have committed the most heinous act and can never be cleansed.

Judas recalled the first time he had heard Teacher speak. Not even Jesus' cousin, The Baptist, was as eloquent. Judas had been one of The Baptist's followers and he wondered why Jesus had never bothered to use his magic to save John from death. He certainly had the power to do so. Jesus had performed many miracles in Judas' presence, one of which was the healing of his father Simon Iscariot, who suffered from leprosy. So why had The Baptist not been spared?

As much as he had grown to love Jesus, Judas doubted that Jesus would ever redeem the Jews, despite the prophecy. He saw no evidence that Teacher was building an army to conquer the Romans and this angered him. As much as he'd like to believe otherwise, Jesus was nothing but an amazing healer, a poor dreamer who preached unconditional love.

And the world is overcrowded with dreamers.

Nevertheless, it had been a fascinating journey. Everywhere Teacher and his apostles went they were joined by throngs of people, all clamoring to get a glimpse of The Messiah. Happily, some people would give donations and it was ironic that Judas should be entrusted as the group's treasurer since he found the handling of money a powerful experience.

Of all the apostles, Judas believed himself to be the smartest, taking his role as one of Jesus' chosen companions quite seriously. Unlike the others, Judas thought it was demeaning for Teacher to ride upon the back of an ass for his processional through Jerusalem. He also found it irksome when Mary anointed Teacher with spikenard.

Imagine that—spikenard! Everyone knows that spikenard is costly. Why didn't someone in the group have the good sense to sell the oil to make a profit instead of wasting it on ritual?

As he made his way through the dark, Judas heard the

silver coins jangling in his purse. Interestingly, it was exactly the amount a man would have received had his slave been accidentally killed.

Small payment indeed for such a supreme sacrifice.

But Judas was certain that Teacher wanted him to carry out this great deed, to fulfill the prophecy. And he knew Jesus would forgive him.

And I've played my part well, so why shouldn't I accept the money for my many inconveniences?

Besides, thirty pieces of silver made him a happy man for only a moment, not a lifetime.

Judas wished he could take back some of the things he had done, but it was far too late for that. Everything was in motion now. His father (a devoted Pharisee, despite his healing from Jesus), had arranged for the secret meeting with the priests and now he had arrived at the destination.

After some discussion, he led the priests and soldiers to the Garden of Gethsemane, where Teacher had taken the apostles on many occasions. There he found his beloved Jesus, betrayed him with a "friendly" kiss and watched the drama unfold from behind an olive tree.

I am sick to my stomach. I can't wait for this sordid ordeal to be over.

Sweat poured through his modest clothes as the soldiers bound Jesus and took him away.

It had all gone according to plan, but seeing the actual arrest was devastating to Judas. His heart was heavy and he did not sleep well that night. When night became day, he learned that Teacher had been condemned to death. This discovery was a shock because he thought the priests only meant to interrogate and frighten Teacher. Indeed, he did love Jesus and never wished him harm, despite their philosophical differences.

And now they brand me a traitor.

Judas' hopes of a triumphant uprising against the Romans were dead and so was Teacher. Consumed with intense shame and agony, he attempted to return the silver to the priests but they laughed, refusing his money.

At that point, he saw no way to live with the magnitude of his sin. With tears streaming down his tormented face, Judas went into a field, found a tree, and hung himself.

Forgive me, O Lord.

◈

ELM THOUGHT IT WOULD BE A SIMPLE PROCESS, BUT SHE was so distraught after unifying with Judas that Seraphina suggested she recuperate in her suite.

The girl couldn't stop thinking about Judas' ego and all of the repercussions and misunderstandings from his actions. She cried, consumed with empathy for his soul and cried for the rest of the apostles, too. She cried for Jesus and all of his followers. And then she thought of Glorie and the foremothers and cried for them, too.

One day, Elm was swimming underwater in the reflection pool, exchanging thoughts with Flo.

You know how everyone says that they wish they knew then what they know now? It's really true.

"Is it? And what else have you learned?" asked Flo.

Oh, so much! Like the fact that everything is energy and we need to remember that if we want to heal ourselves.

"That's a good one," said Flo.

Yes, and another thing I learned is that I don't need anyone to save me because I have the power to do that myself. I always have. We all do.

An apparition from the concierge desk interrupted their conversation, floating just above the water. Elm was cordially invited to attend a special Ice Crystal Concert on the Planet Kalt.

"Oh, you'll love that," said Flo. "It's held in a crystal ice cave where all the musicians play instruments they carved from the ice. It's very pretty because a rainbow shines through the instruments while they are playing them. Perhaps it will inspire you."

Flo was right about the concert. It not only uplifted Elm's spirits, it also sparked an idea that she couldn't wait to share with Seraphina.

When she returned to her suite, the innkeeper was there, wearing a floppy garden hat and a dirt-smudged apron.

"Nice concert? I've been doing a little gardening," she said, holding a copy of *The Secret Garden*. "I was also enjoying this book by Frances Hodgson Burnett. It's a classic, you know."

"I had a coloring book about secret gardens," Elm said, "but I don't think it was by the same author."

She hoped that ended their discussion on books and gardens because she was excited to share her plan.

Seraphina received the message. "Your thoughts indicate that you now wish to become an Earth Ambassador. To help a soul achieve their Ascension."

"That's my goal," said Elm. "The concert was great, by the way. It made me think about the healing power of sound and water and how it might help someone I used to know. Can you guess who that is, Seraphina?"

"It is your mother, the woman you call *Mermie*."

Elm nodded. "I can do it, right?"

"Of course. You have no fears and you have mastered unification and telepathy. But remember that she must make her own choices," Seraphina reminded, fastening her own Infinity symbol necklace around Elm's neck. "Please wear this as a reminder of our Oneness, with my blessing."

"Thank you for the necklace, Seraphina. I'll try not to lose it."

"You won't," said Seraphina. "But I have another gift for you. In a moment, you are going to meet our wonderful Archangel Zadkiel."

Finally!

"Oh, thank you, Seraphina. I am very grateful. Is there anything I need to know before I go?"

"Just think, Sister."

Zadkiel's Temple!

As much as Elm enjoyed the sweet pinkness of the Soul Spa, nothing could have prepared her for the euphoria she felt when she reached the temple.

"Come closer, Dear One."

Elm was confused because the voice seemed to be surrounding her from all directions.

"Step forward."

She found herself face-to-face with a radiant being of beautiful violet light. In fact, the light was so intense that the angel's facial characteristics were obscured.

"Are you the Archangel Zadkiel?"

"I am Zadkiel."

Elm was in awe, like she had been granted a backstage pass to meet her favorite rock star. "You mean, the *real* Zadkiel?"

"The real one."

"Well, it's good to meet you, Sir."

Sir? That was dumb. He's an angel, for cryin' out loud. I probably should be calling him Your Highness or something. I'm not even sure that he's male. How could I be so stupid not to know these things? It's a good thing I'm not afraid.

She winced, expecting the angel to be splattered in red by her *STUPID* thought bubble.

"Zadkiel is fine," said the angel.

Elm thought she detected a hint of amusement in Zadkiel's voice and was relieved that no thought bubble materialized.

"Zadkiel."

"Seraphina tells me that you have learned how to love and to forgive, to release your anger and your fears, and that you have also shown accomplishment in unifying with plants, minerals, and animals," said Zadkiel. "As one might say in the Third Dimension, this makes my heart sing."

Elm loved listening to Zadkiel's resonant, melodic tones.

"Yes, Sir—Zadkiel. And I can't wait to become a Pinkie!" she blurted.

Flo had told her that Pinkies were souls who had successfully completed all the tasks of the Pink Level. Elm thought it sounded very cool.

"And wait you shall, because there is an assignment on Earth that is reserved for you only. It means that you will need to return to Little Blessing."

This pleased Elm. She immediately thought of her female ancestors and how certain they were that she could help them.

"Is this a mission to break through the resentment that runs through my mother's side of the family?"

"It is," said Zadkiel, sounding impressed. "And to help your loved one remember what is most important. Do you know what that is?"

She did. "Love and forgiveness?"

"Correct again," said the angel. "But you must allow your mother to make her own decisions. She must take the responsibility for her own good health—emotionally, physically, and spiritually."

"I agree," said a beautiful white unicorn, suddenly appearing beside Zadkiel. "And once she has released her resentment, a new purpose shall be revealed to her."

Prompted by an inner nudge, Elm touched her Third Eye to receive a vision of a unicorn purifying the ocean with its spiral horn.

Cool.

"You must return to your suite now," Zadkiel said, petting the unicorn's neck.

"Uh, okay," said Elm. "Well, thank you, Zadkiel. I enjoyed meeting you. And I think you have a lovely temple here. I like the violet light. Just lovely. Oh—and Seraphina is a great innkeeper, too! Really great."

Sheesh, I'm stammering. Suite 8, please!

"Go with the love and protection of our Divine Creator, my daughter."

Once Elm had left, the unicorn transformed into her true nature—first as the innkeeper, then as a seraphim. She stretched her mighty wings to embrace the archangel whose head was bowed.

"She will be just fine, Kiel," Seraphina sang in the language of angels. "She is ready to serve."

Back in her suite, Elm prayed to the Divine Creator for guidance. Her adventures at Inn Lak'ech were over, at least for now. She didn't understand everything she had experienced, but she did know that Love and Forgiveness had fully prepared her for this important assignment.

She was going back to Little Blessing to save her family tree, to save Mermie.

I can do this, Daddy. I can swim past obstacles to find new treasure!

CHAPTER 44

CHOOSING A 3-D IDENTITY WAS like walking into Holy Cow Sundaes after not eating for a month and trying to decide on one flavor. There were so many choices! Fortunately, Elm knew exactly which body she wanted.

She found Glorie sitting in her bedroom in the dark, wearing a gray sweatsuit and pink knit booties. She was staring at the television but not watching it, holding in her hand one of the few belongings recovered after the hurricane: a framed picture of Glorie, Big Dave, and nine-year-old Elm on their trip to Florida.

So here we go!

Elm had forgotten how dense having a physical body could be. The first thing she felt after the merge was a sadness that consumed her, coupled with the belief that her life was meaningless.

She heard a key turn in the front door lock, followed by the sound of footsteps. The lights switched on and a pretty Easter basket containing daffodils and tulips was placed on the bedroom dresser.

"Hey, Mermie. How are you feeling today?"

"Fine," whispered Glorie.

The young woman touching Glorie's frail arm wore a miniature dreamcatcher dangling from a leather cord.

"I brought you a little Easter garden," said Snow, pointing to the basket. "Maybe you'd like to plant it later in your window box."

"Maybe," said Glorie. *But probably not*, she thought.

Elm wondered why Glorie had been left alone. Then she spotted a Care Schedule on the table next to the bed. She was pleased to read that someone from Little Blessing Caregivers would be visiting Glorie three times a day.

Snow retrieved a wooden hairbrush from the top drawer of Glorie's dresser. She sat next to Glorie on the bed, brushing her thinning gray hair.

"So, remember the time I went out west to protest the Government's mistreatment of the Native tribes there and the contamination of their water? Well, I've been asked to set up a satellite office here in Little Blessing, to help raise funds for the water carriers. Most of what I'll be doing is answering people's questions online and posting on social media. Of course, I'll still work at the clinic with Dad but I'm really excited about working with this organization. No living thing can survive without water, so it's very important that we treat water with respect. Don't you think so, Mermie?"

Glorie said nothing. Then Snow talked about how she had lived at a prayer camp, what happened when the camp shut down, and how she almost got arrested.

"We were very peaceful in our demonstration. We drummed and chanted and prayed to save the water. Do you remember me telling you about that, Mermie?"

Elm watched with admiration. Snow was good

company for her mother, even though Glorie had pretty much tuned her out.

Since it appeared that Glorie was in good hands and Snow was going to chatter for some time, Elm decided to leave her mother's body and go sightseeing.

ONE CLEAR THOUGHT AND ELM WAS ROAMING THE MARINA again, sniffing the geraniums in the flower pots, jumping in and out of boats, and rolling on her back in a water puddle made by someone washing their boat.

She was having a lot of fun in her new guise, but eventually stopped playing to saunter over to the Sunday's Marina office. Then she saw someone she remembered and ran to him.

Noah!

Her former crush was walking towards her, accompanied by a young woman with long red hair. Elm didn't recognize the woman, wondering whether she was Noah's girlfriend or employee. Like Noah, she was wearing a navy Sunday's Marina cap, white shirt, and khaki shorts.

"Hey, Pup," said Noah, stopping to pat Elm's furry brown head before entering the office. "Where did you come from?"

My mother. And you?

Elm barked a greeting while Noah's companion frowned. "Ewww, don't touch it, Noah," the woman warned. "It's all wet and dirty and it might have rabies."

Rabies?

Noah continued to rub Elm's curly-coated fur. "She says you're wet and dirty, but we don't care, do we, Boy? We don't care at all!"

Wow, I could get used to this. Thanks for the back rub, Noah Skyfeather.

The phone was ringing in the office. The woman rushed past Noah, then called out, "Noah, would you leave that filthy dog alone! Johnson's on the phone about a potential customer needing a mooring."

"Hey, I think this guy's a Spanish Water Dog," said Noah. "I've seen pictures of them in one of my dad's books, but never saw one up close before. Look, put Johnson on hold. I'm curious about something."

He ran his hand over Elm's necklace, tracing and retracing his finger over the Infinity symbol. "Hmmm, this is different. Instead of a collar, you're wearing a necklace with sea glass and an *8* charm. Is that your name, Boy? Are you *8*?"

From the angle the Infinity symbol was hanging, Elm understood why Noah thought it was an *8*.

"Noah!"

I think he'd rather play with me, Lady. But you're right. We both have important things to do.

"I'm coming, Tracy," said Noah. "See you around, *8*. Don't get into any trouble!"

ELM SCAMPERED ALONG UNTIL SHE HAD REACHED THE front steps of the Grace Church of the Ascension. Since the big doors were opened, Elm accepted it as an invitation to investigate.

She hadn't been inside since Big Dave's funeral. Noting there were white ribbons tied to the pews and numerous vases of white lilies around the pulpit, Elm assumed it was Easter-time, when Christians throughout the world celebrated the resurrection of Jesus Christ. She immediately thought about Judas' sacrifice and felt a wave of empathy.

Elm ran up the aisle to the steps of the elevated pulpit. She looked down upon an imaginary congregation, pretending to deliver a heart-pounding sermon that invoked a chain of "Hallelujahs." It was a pretty church with white walls, mahogany-stained pine trim and pews, and clear glass windows.

As a child, Elm had always wished there were at least a few colorful statues or stained glass windows because the church was dreadfully plain. She had mistakenly mentioned this to her grandmother one Sunday, after which Ruth scolded her for not realizing that color was vulgar.

Years later when Elm was reading about the Puritans in her history class, she learned that the original Puritans had banned the use of color in their church. They also believed that singing and music were sins, compared to the present time when Grace Church had an organist and award-winning choir.

"Darn shoelace!"

Hearing the pastor's voice outside, Elm ran down the steps to the aisle and out into the sunshine. The pastor was tying his shoelace on the front steps when Elm jumped over him.

Whoops!

"No dogs allowed in the House of the Lord!" he exclaimed, making another attempt at his shoelace.

Elm sent him love and continued her jaunt through town.

She was pleased that little had changed. Moonwater Beach was still there, of course, and so was Hallelujah House, the tearoom, ice cream shop, and most of the other businesses she had known. But there was also something new on Charity Street. Apparently, Carousel Boutique had gone out of business and, along with its Sea Angels neighbor, had been converted into one larger space called HeartWaves Books & Wellness.

Wow. A self-healing center in Little Blessing!

Elm barked with approval, jumping up and down on the sidewalk.

There was a framed sign in one of the shop windows, announcing that the store's owner, Katrina Corrente Smith, would be giving a book signing and Q&A session about her newly published book, *My Choice to Heal*, on the first Saturday in April.

People were coming out of the store with HeartWaves shopping bags, so Elm assumed the business was doing well. But she wanted a closer look.

"Wait a minute there, doggie."

Elm looked up and immediately recognized the woman blocking her way.

"Sorry, but I can't let you in there," said Kat.

The healer held the door open for two elderly women, exposing an aromatherapy counter with huge glass decanters and seashell bottle stoppers. Elm tried to slip between them, but Kat pulled her back.

"Go home, little guy," said Kat, bending down to inspect Elm's charm. "An Infinity symbol on violet sea glass. I wonder how you got that? Well, I'm sure somebody's missing you, so go on home now."

Kat walked inside, closing the door behind her.

Fortunately, Elm had no limitations.

Aromatherapy bottle!

She quickly unified with the deep blue liquid inside the bottle marked *German Chamomile*.

HeartWaves had a wonderful ambience. In addition to the uplifting scent of oranges and Native flute music playing softly in the background, Glorie's old store had been completely transformed. The walls had been painted a soothing mint green, all of the bookcases and furnishings were new and white, the floor was a polished brown teak, and rainbows danced constantly from the crystal suncatchers in the window.

Wow. There's a lot of stuff in here!

The first room contained crystals and gemstones, dried herbs, essential oils, soaps, candles, color therapy lights, suncatchers, angel figurines, chakra clothing, jewelry, writing journals, oracle cards, and books. And even though there were many products on display, the store managed to project a clear, uncluttered flow.

And so many books!

They were categorized by healing modalities like Aromatherapy, Bach Flower Remedies, Color Therapy, Crystal Healing, Energy Healing, and Sound Healing. There were also books about angels, Native American traditions, and self-help manuals on how to heal relationships, depression, and grief.

A six-foot rainbow bridge over a live fish pond led into the next room, the former Carousel Boutique. Elm caught a glimpse of a crystal singing bowl and thought *Bowl!*, joining a set of chakra-colored crystal singing bowls that were displayed on a multi-tiered shelf. From her new vantage point against the wall, she saw gongs, chimes, a crystal harp, and a didgeridoo. And what was that in the corner? A collection of drums and, yes, a sea drum, too!

Three rows of white folding chairs had been set up for a lecture. A young Native woman was arranging a book display on a pink draped table, then placed a vase of white lilies on a pedestal in the center and left the room.

By this time, people were crossing the bridge from the other room and being seated. Elm recognized most of the audience, which included Jason and his daughters Autumn and Lily in the back row. She was also happy to see Cassie (her one-time Sea Gypsy sister), who stepped up to the table with a silver angel handbell. She rang the bell three times to announce the lecture.

"Welcome to HeartWaves," said Cassie, setting the bell gently on the table. "I am very pleased to introduce our guest author, Katrina Corrente Smith. Of course, we all know her as the owner of HeartWaves—not to mention our new First Lady of Little Blessing! Well, today Kat will give us a sneak peek into her new book, *My Choice to Heal*, and she will take your questions and do a book signing afterward."

There was a round of applause. Jason waved to his bride as she entered the room, a vision in a blush pink and white goddess gown.

"Thank you, Cassie," she said. "I'm so grateful you all could be here today during this sacred weekend of rebirth."

Taking a moment to clear her throat, Kat began her story.

She had been raised by religious blue collar parents in Baltimore. An ambitious girl, Kat received her Bachelor of Arts degree in English literature, then met and married a young attorney. They moved to Philadelphia where her husband pressured her into becoming a high society "trophy wife". The day she discovered she was pregnant, he threatened divorce if she did not get an immediate abortion, saying that he did not want to be married to a fat pig.

Up until that point, Kat thought they had both wanted children. The subsequent abortion sparked a deep depression, which she tried to overcome with drugs and alcohol. During that difficult time, her husband fell in love with another attorney and flaunted the affair in Kat's face.

After their divorce, Kat moved to Boston where she found some work as a substitute English teacher. She fell into another toxic relationship—this time with a drug-dealing Copley Square bartender—which resulted in a baby daughter, born deaf.

Wanting to connect with her widowed mother, Kat returned to Baltimore with the child but was rejected because her mother was ashamed to have a disabled grandchild. The baby was given up for adoption and Kat moved to High City to escape her painful past.

"I soon learned that it didn't matter how far away I ran, I couldn't escape my history," said Kat. "But in High City, I was exposed to many new possibilities."

She first learned of self-healing after accepting a minimum wage job working as a cashier in a small natural foods store.

"I was drug and alcohol-free by then, but I also suffered from a serious lack of self-worth. And I felt guilty about giving up my daughter. In fact, it was guilt that made me drink and do drugs in the first place."

One day at the store, Kat met a woman who was presenting a workshop about the Divine Feminine. Kat was intrigued and attended the workshop, amazed to discover that she had the power to heal her life. After that experience, she signed up for every self-healing course she could afford, including Reiki, color therapy, aromatherapy, and EFT.

Kat received a scholarship from an unknown benefactor to further her studies at a prestigious holistic school and obtained her certification as an energy healer practitioner. On the day she received her degree, her angels guided her to move to Little Blessing to set up her healing practice.

Listening to Kat's courageous story for the first time, Elm was surprised to receive an angel nudge herself—and Kat was the key!

CHAPTER 45

N o Dogs Allowed.
      The sign at Moonwater Beach surprised Elm
but she was not discouraged. After all, she was a dog with
extraordinary powers. No dog catcher on Earth could
capture her!

Near her paws in the water was her next unification
subject. Elm had never been a fan of jellyfish because they
stung, but she did admire the fact that they had survived
multiple mass extinctions, despite having no heart nor
brain.

Jellyfish!

She floated out to sea in her new gooey body, while
excitedly discussing her intentions with Flo.

"It's an excellent plan, Suite 8," Flo agreed. "And
you're right to include Nee-nah. Perhaps all of the
mermaids in Little Blessing can help you. Of course, you
will need to repay their efforts with some sort of gift. It is
expected. Do you have any ideas?"

Oh yes, Flo. I absolutely do.

≈

UNIFYING WITH GLORIE PROVED MORE DIFFICULT THAN Elm had expected. Even though Elm could easily flit from one body to the next, her mother's despondency was overwhelming. Yet she was determined to help Glorie heal and one way to achieve that goal was to understand her mother's fears through her dreams.

The evening's first dream featured Glorie as a seventeenth-century Spanish priest named Padre Tomas, whose sole vocation was to bring Jesus to the heathens. The priest taught Catholicism to the Pueblo children in a small settlement near Santa Fe, New Mexico, renaming his Christian converts to reflect names from the Bible. It was just one of numerous atrocities resented by most of the Pueblos, who revolted in 1680, intent on destroying all symbols of Christianity.

Knowing there were armed warriors stationed at the community well, Padre Tomas had a difficult choice to make. Which one of his Pueblo students should leave the mission church schoolhouse to fetch their drinking water?

Normally, the task would have been assigned to Juan, the eldest, but he had broken his leg in a fall and was still hobbling, using a gnarly tree limb as a crutch.

"I'll go," Santiago volunteered.

"Me, too!" said his twin brother, Mateo.

Padre Tomas tried not to show his fear. He knew it was a great risk and an innocent child could be killed. But water was crucial for their survival, so someone had to go.

"I propose a spelling contest," he said, his voice quivering at the sounds of gunshots outside. "And the prize is having the honor of fetching our water."

That's where the dream ended.

Glorie sipped the water from a glass on her bedside table, then fell immediately back to sleep.

Her next three dreams were snippets, like astral movie trailers. She dreamed about a red-haired Celtic queen fighting the Romans on her land. She had torched London and was screaming hysterically as Roman soldiers retaliated by flogging her and molesting her daughters.

Dream Number Three featured Glorie as a mermaid. She was swimming in the ocean, diving for pearls in the deepest, darkest part. A black bag hung from her waist and each time she discovered a pearl, she was subjected to some form of pain and anguish before she placed it in her bag. When the bag was full, Glorie rose up to the surface where she sunbathed on a large rock, stringing the white pearls on a chain to create a necklace. It was her badge of honor. A necklace of pain.

Glorie's final dream that night had her floating in a cocoon in the blackest of outer space. She heard the voices of people—her caregivers, Snow, Noah, even Elm and Big Dave. But she had no strength nor will to break out of the cocoon.

Elm was so moved by her mother's torment, she gave Glorie an inner nudge to wake up.

Groggy, Glorie reached for her phone. "Hello, Kat? Glorie Sunday. I'm sorry it's so late, but you told me to call anytime."

She told the healer about her disturbing dreams and how she was afraid to go back to sleep.

"Do you think a Reiki session and some time on the crystal bed might help me?"

Kat thought it was a good idea and promised to see Glorie the next morning. In the meantime, Kat suggested that Glorie do some color breathing, with emphasis on the colors pink and blue.

That night, Kat received guidance in a dream that she was to lead a special ceremony on Mother's Day.

It was imperative that Glorie should attend.

EVER SINCE ELM COULD REMEMBER, RUTH ABBOTT Sunday had organized an annual Mother's Day buffet brunch from 11 a.m. until 3 p.m., so having a competing event from Kat was not appreciated by the cranky octogenarian.

While Glorie ate her simple Mother's Day lunch at home, Elm was curious about her grandmother's event at Hallelujah House.

She slipped inside the kitchen of Thanksgiving, the new second-floor restaurant, where she immediately unified with a silver-plated tray. She felt the weight as a server covered the tray with a white linen cloth, arranging an assortment of scones and pastries before carrying it out to one of the buffet tables.

Wow, Grandma really went all out this year.

There were platters of Eggs Benedict, Belgian Waffles, Quiche Lorraine, Seafood Crepes, Prime Rib, Baked Scallops, New England Clam Chowder, Shrimp Cocktail— even a dessert station with Strawberry Shortcake and Chocolate Mousse.

If I still ate food, I think I'd be in hog heaven.

There were well over one hundred women and their families in attendance. The dining room was lovely with pristine white tablecloths and a fresh floral bouquet of pink and yellow blooms in the center.

And there's a woman playing Broadway show tunes on the piano. Very nice.

Ruth sat at the head table, wearing a white orchid

corsage and picking at her plate of Maple Glazed Ham and Thyme Roasted Potatoes and Carrots. To be closer to her grandmother, Elm unified with Ruth's empty champagne glass.

"I'm telling you, Elizabeth," said Ruth, gabbing to the silver-tressed woman sitting next to her, "I think she deliberately planned it for the same date. She's even in the same building!"

Okay, I've seen enough. It's time to get back to Mermie.

It was unseasonably warm for the second week of May, but Glorie draped a sweater around her shoulders, expecting it to be chilly sitting next to the water. She had no idea what else to expect. She just knew that it was Mother's Day and she had no child to mother. *At least, I can walk again,* she thought.

Thanks to regular energy healing visits with Kat, Glorie was feeling much better, which is why she had canceled her caregiver service.

Snow dropped her off in front of HeartWaves Books & Wellness, then drove to the Moonwater Beach parking lot. As Glorie stood in front of her old Sea Angels door, she panicked. *Why am I here?* she thought. *I don't know anything about this Divine Feminine thing. Why didn't I just tell Snow that I was sick and had to stay home?*

Unbeknownst to Glorie, she was not alone because her only child was sharing her body, observing everything she was seeing and feeling. And what Glorie was feeling was sadness, from the moment she stepped inside HeartWaves.

"That's a good one," said Cassie, startling Glorie, who was skimming through angel books. "It's about the seven most well-known archangels. The pictures are really beautiful."

Glorie smiled shyly. She was happy that Cassie was still working in the old space. Cassie was a good girl. Elm had been a good girl, too, until she changed. *Why does everything good in my life have to die or change?*

Glorie found that each of the archangels featured in the book had their own chapters: *Ariel. Chamuel. Gabriel. Haniel. Jophiel. Michael. Raphael. Uriel. Zadkiel.*

She turned to the last chapter in the book and began reading about Archangel Zadkiel, whose name meant "The righteousness of God." According to the book's author, Zadkiel had an etheric retreat in Cuba and was associated with the color violet, the amethyst gemstone, and lavender.

It's true, Mermie, but there's more!

Reading on, Glorie discovered that Zadkiel was the angel of transmutation and responsible for some mystical energy called the Violet Flame. But the most exciting thing she read was about Zadkiel's work with people suffering from neurological disorders. Could Zadkiel help rid her of Lyme?

The little bell over the door chimed and Snow entered, walking up to the counter.

"Hey, Cassie. Kat said you've got some burden baskets in the back and I want to see if they're authentic. Can I take a look at them?"

Snow passed Glorie on the way to the storeroom and grinned. "Just one of the cool perks of having your step-mother be the owner!"

Glorie waited for Snow to reappear, then the two stepped over the bridge into the next room where Kat was scheduled to lead a Divine Mother tiara-making workshop at 1 p.m.

There were two long tables draped in pink. At each of the ten places was a bag of rose quartz points, jewelry wire, a metal headband, glue bottle, and pink ribbon. Four of the chairs were already occupied by women whom Glorie knew from her old Girl Scout leader days and they waved to her.

During the workshop, Kat showed the group how to glue and wrap a pink ribbon around their metal headband, then wire-wrap the rose quartz points around the front.

"The rose quartz represents self-love and compassion," said Kat, placing her finished tiara on her head. "Whenever you wear this tiara, you will be reminded of the gift of the Divine Feminine."

Okay, I'm wearing my silly crown, Glorie thought. *What do I win?*

"You all look beautiful," Kat said. "Now, that you've finished your tiaras, are you ready to go to the water?"

CHAPTER 46

K AT LED THE ROYAL PARADE across Charity Street to Moonwater Beach, where the tiara-wearing women were guided to a small bonfire, encircled by a ring of pink beach blankets.

In her unified form, Elm thought of her foremothers and how they were depending on her. She hoped her plan would succeed, especially since Glorie had become an aquaphobe and wasn't used to exposing her soul in a public setting.

Autumn was waiting for the group, holding her tribal drum. When everyone had claimed a blanket, Kat turned on her portable loudspeaker. "Welcome to our sacred circle. Please be seated, remove your shoes and your tiaras, and place them on your blankets."

So I'm already dethroned, Glorie thought.

While the women got situated, Glorie scanned their faces, all desperate for a transformation, a revelation, a miracle of some kind. Not Glorie. She was only there for Kat, a nice young lady who had helped her through some dark times.

"In honor of Mother's Day, we celebrate all mothers," said Kat. "Whether you have given birth or not, every woman has an etheric womb."

Etheric womb, thought Glorie. *Never heard that one before.*

"Let us invite the love of the Divine Mother into our hearts this day. Let us reclaim our power, to awaken to our Divine Femininity, to release the emotional pain of our lives, to forgive, to love, to heal our wombs and our memories through the gift of water. We were born of the water within the wombs of our mothers. Water is a blessing."

Except if you're afraid to drown. Elm wasn't sure if that was her thought or her mother's.

"A Course in Miracles says 'forgiveness is the key to happiness' and that is what we are going to concentrate on first—to forgive our mothers."

It's not that hard, Mermie. Really.

"To quote Rumi, the mystic poet," said Kat, "'There is a sacredness in tears. They are not the mark of weakness, but of power. They speak more eloquently than ten thousand tongues. They are messengers of overwhelming grief and unspeakable love.' And, of course, our tears are comprised of cleansing, powerful water."

Glorie thought: *And maybe if I cry, Snow will take me home.*

Kat asked the group to think of their mothers. "Can you do that? Good. Now, remember one thing she did that you have not forgiven her for. Just one thing, Ladies."

At that moment, a seagull walked boldly across Glorie's blanket. Someone once told her that gulls were just big rats with wings because they were forever scavenging. *The bird's smart,* she thought. *Sometimes the only thing you can do is grab what you need and get out fast.*

That's exactly what happened when Glorie decided to leave Humble Shores, Georgia to study marine biology in Florida.

While Kat continued the ceremony, Glorie remembered the day she took her belongings to run away from the constant reminder of the man who had raped her in the high school gymnasium. She had told Frances about it but her mother responded as she always had during difficult situations—she denied it.

A quiet, mousey woman who did not covet the spotlight, Frances begged her daughter not to breathe a word about it to anyone, not even their parish priest.

"You'll just have to live with it," she told Glorie.

I never knew that, Mermie. I am so sorry for you.

There were other mother-daughter issues, too. As soon as Frances learned about Glorie's mermaid gig, she sent her a scathing letter, writing that she was ashamed of her daughter for flaunting her body in public.

Unlike most mothers Glorie knew, Frances never told her daughter about periods or sex or how to shave her legs. And Glorie never asked. She had to learn it from her girlfriends.

Religion and politics were other issues. Even though the War Between The States ended in 1865, Southerner Frances never forgave Glorie for marrying a non-Catholic Yankee. She also refused to attend Elm's baptism in Little Blessing, claiming it wasn't a real sacrament in God's eyes because it was a Protestant ceremony.

"Now try to picture your mother as a little girl," Kat continued. "An innocent, sweet little girl. She has no idea that she has so much power to cause you pain. Do you see her?"

Not really, thought Glorie. *I've never seen a photo of her from childhood. I'm not even sure she was a child!*

"It has been said that holding onto anger is like drinking poison and expecting the other person to die," said Kat, passing out paper and pens. "What I'd like you to

347

do now is to write all the things that your mother did to make you angry. And when you are finished, fold the paper and throw it in the fire."

Glorie wrote: *I am angry at my mother because…*

Surprisingly, once she began to write, it was difficult to stop. One thought morphed into another and another until Glorie had filled the page and flipped it over to write more thoughts. She grinned, imagining little Frances peering over her shoulder and being aghast at the comments.

Finally, Glorie walked over to the fire and tossed her folded paper into the crackling orange, blue, and white flames, watching it burn into angry ashes. Was it her imagination or did she just see Frances' adult image walk through the flames?

"I know this has not been easy, Ladies," said Kat. "So now that you have accomplished the difficult part, I'd like you to give yourself a big hug!"

Glorie glanced at Snow, who was rocking back and forth and hugging herself.

"The rocking reminds us that we are all waves of love," said Kat.

It's just a little rocking, Mermie. You can do it!

But Glorie was having nothing of it. She sat on her blanket, unyielding, staring at the bonfire.

"Don't worry if you get emotional," Kat assured the group. "It's necessary to open the old wounds to heal. Even the ones that have been dormant. Just let it go."

Some of the women began to moan, others wailed, and Glorie nearly laughed out loud.

"Good. Very good," said Kat. "Now, everyone please lie down on your blankets and close your eyes."

Kat led them on a guided meditation where they were embraced by the Divine Mother. This was difficult for Glorie, who tried to visualize the Virgin Mary statue from her church in Humble Shores. Mary was the only Divine Mother she could relate to and that was hardly at all.

After the meditation ended, Kat said, "Let us all place our tiaras back on our heads and go to the water for our blessing."

As the women lined up at the water's edge, Glorie's heart pounded. She had stopped swimming after Big Dave's disappearance and now she was afraid the water might swallow her up, too, just as it did with her husband and daughter.

Autumn stayed on the sand to maintain the fire while the women lined up along the water's edge.

"Good," said Kat. "Now, let us hold hands and feel the cleansing energy of the water on our feet, imagining that loving, cleansing energy is pulsating from our feet, going up through our legs, through our torso, through our chest, our arms and legs, our neck, and our head. Is everybody feeling that?"

"Yes," the women echoed.

Kat continued. "We are fortunate to have this beautiful water to swim in, to bathe in, to cleanse us from all our worries."

Glorie's thoughts broke her mind's protective wall like a determined bulldozer. *But I don't want to remember. You took my husband. You took my baby girl. I will not forgive you. I don't want to swim in you. I'm afraid of you!*

"Remember that we are all divine mothers," said Kat, ending the ceremony. "So let us remember this day when we awoke to our power to create, to collaborate, to speak our truth, and to bless each other. Let us tap into our well-springs of love and joy and forgiveness. Happy Mother's Day, Sisters!"

The group cheered, then returned to their blankets to collect their belongings.

Snow had just turned to ask Glorie a question when she realized her friend's blanket was empty. She saw Glorie standing on the shoreline, motionless, as if she was stuck in the sand.

Then Snow noticed a funnel-shaped cloud in the distance.

"Run, everybody!" Snow cried. "It's gonna hit land!"

The women screamed, scrambling in all directions while Snow and Kat struggled against the fierce wind to reach Glorie.

"Mermie!" Snow shrieked. "Mermie!"

The surprise tornado tore through the beach, inhaling everything in its path: seaweed, seashells, blankets, paper cups—and Glorie.

CHAPTER 47

GLORIE WAS SPINNING INSIDE THE dark funnel, the fury of the wind churning in her ears.

She was high above land with Little Blessing blurring around her like she was riding the Seashell Carousel at warp speed. Bits of debris pelted her body as she fell into the ocean, her lungs filling with the salty fluid.

And then she blacked out.

When she opened her eyes again, she was swimming effortlessly through a shadowy world in motion.

Don't worry, Mermie. I'm still with you.

At that moment, a red light broke through the darkness and Glorie found herself staring into the wide, ferocious jaw of a dragonfish. *Jesus, help me!*

Help came in the form of a silver harness, dangling within her reach. She grabbed it, holding on tight as she sped from the deepest part of the ocean, pushing through a bioluminescent show of yellow-ringed octopod, golden coral, and flashlight fish.

~

THE WATER HAD CHANGED TO A HAZY GREEN. GLORIE WAS glad to be out of the pitch blackness, but she wondered how she was able to breathe so long underwater. As she wrapped the harness securely around her waist, she glanced down at her sides and yelped when she saw the gills.

Pretty cool, Mermie.

At first thought, the possibility that she had died and returned as a fish was ludicrous. Then Glorie glanced behind her. *Good gravy, I have a tail!*

She looked forward again and thought she saw another tail in front of her. *Is this for real? Because from the back they look just like mer—*

She didn't finish her thought because she was rear-ended by a gray dolphin. *What the heck?*

He raced alongside her until they were joined by a larger, white-colored dolphin. Glorie felt her head turn to the right so that she was facing the white dolphin. The "cow" gently head-bumped Glorie and her pineal gland opened, unleashing a wonderful rainbow energy.

It's a gift, Mermie. Now you can see things differently.

Glorie's Third Eye was indeed open because she could clearly see seven mermaids swimming ahead of her in single file. They were connected by a separate silver harness, not dissimilar to a locomotive coupled to its freight cars. In fact, Glorie was the "caboose" in their swishing, mermaid train!

She watched the mermaids pass through an ancient archway but when it was her turn, she came to a sudden halt. *Something is blocking me,* she thought. *And I can't see what it is.*

The archway began to revolve so that whenever she moved, Glorie would see a different water scene from her life: her baptism, the first time she was given a bath, her first swimming lesson, her mermaid debut at the water-park, even the time she and Big Dave went skinny-dipping in the marina pool.

Now, that's something I didn't know!

Soon, Glorie was free again. The mermaids resumed their tour, leading her past ancient ruins, statues, and large pyramid structures. *What is this place?* she wondered. *Some sort of underwater city?*

There were more marvels ahead. Passing through another archway, large golden harps appeared on either side, spraying their sound vibrational waves of peace and healing. There were many of these archways and each time Glorie arrived at one she would close her eyes, receiving a cleansing concert for her body, mind, and spirit. *Is that Mozart or Bach?*

The experience was so uplifting that Glorie would have happily continued swimming from one harmonic carwash to the next and back again. However, the mermaids continued tugging Glorie's harness and her blissful sound healing session ended. *So are we just gonna swim all day or do you have an actual destination in mind?*

The answer came in the form of roaring cheers from a large arena with three performance rings and an audience of hundreds of mermaid spectators. It was directly ahead and Elm was more excited than her mother when it appeared before them.

Mermie, look! It's a mermaid circus! Can you believe it? I mean, for real! How cool is that?

Glorie was fascinated. Inside the first ring was a mermaid performing aquabatics on a trapeze. The larger center ring was empty. A team of mermaids riding sidesaddle on seahorses was the third ring act.

The mermaid train pulled in to the center ring station. The harnesses broke and the mermaids swam freely. They tossed and swam through large silver hoops, inviting Glorie to join their show. She was thrilled to be able to perform again, managing to successfully maneuver some backflips, barrel rolls, and handstands.

You're having fun, Mermie. And look at you—you're not afraid anymore!

The fun was short-lived because the earth suddenly shook and the water clouded, sending the mermaids swimming in all directions.

Hold on, Mermie. Hold on!

GLORIE WAS DRENCHED AND SPUTTERING WHEN SNOW AND Kat found her lying naked on the shore.

"Oh, my gosh, Mermie," said Snow, covering her with a pink beach blanket. "Are you okay? We were so scared for you."

"Water, please. Water!"

While Kat ran to get drinking water, Glorie attempted to find her center. Except for being thirsty, she felt more than okay. She felt—what was that word? *Renewed!*

That night, Glorie had a dream that she was on a television show called "What's Your Legacy?" Along with two other contestants, she was quizzed about her lifetime achievements. While her competitors scored big in the "Relationships", "Artistic Contributions","Charitable Work", and "Spiritual Living" categories, Glorie had no personal accolades and ended the game with zero points.

"I think I've spent enough time drowning in my own pain," she admitted to Kat during a Reiki session the next day. "Some people look at their children as their greatest legacy. I lost my Elm, but I'd still like to leave some sort of legacy. Something more than an empty life."

~

THE DIVINE FEMININE BLESSED GLORIE IN A MYRIAD OF ways. After the Mother's Day ceremony, she accepted her true power and (with the support of Kat's newly formed grief support group) sought to live a happier, more productive life. This included regular Reiki sessions, color therapy, meditation, swimming at the high school swimming pool, and lessons in A Course In Miracles. She also practiced the sacred virtue of listening.

Eventually, Glorie's health improved so much that Snow convinced her to resurrect the Sea Angels Beach Cleanup event on Earth Day, volunteering to serve as co-organizer. It was the first thing that had excited Glorie in a long time, especially the mermaid underwater trash cleanup.

There were more changes on the horizon. One day during meditation, Glorie furiously scribbled the names of *Deka, Ida June, Petit Fleur, Hard Winter, Sophie Mae, Matilda,* and *Cady Susan.* She had no idea who they were nor why she was unable to control her pen, which appeared to be writing without her. But something (or maybe someone) kept nudging her to research her ancestors, so she wondered if the names had any connection. She eventually learned they were family!

It took nearly a year of self healing before Glorie was able to completely forgive her mother, Cady Susan aka Frances. When she decided she had, she contacted her old high school in Humble Shores to help institute a Frances DuPriest Rape Victim program for teenage girls.

"It felt good doing this in Mom's name," she told Kat later. "I think if she were alive today, she would have approved."

From her unique perspective, Elm knew her grandmother was thrilled and probably already popping champagne corks with the rest of The Bad Mothers Club.

As for Elm, she was grateful to witness Glorie's magical awakening. It wasn't the kind of magic where you snapped your fingers, said "Abracadabra!" and fantastical things happened. It was a process. And every positive step that Glorie took to heal herself brought her one step closer to helping Elm on her soul's journey.

I'm gonna be a Pinkie. I'm gonna be a Pinkie!

CHAPTER 48

I T WAS A GOOD DAY for wearing pink. Glorie stepped out of her lacy gingerbread cottage in her best pink floppy hat and sunglasses, happily breathing the clean exhilaration of pine.

By her calculations, she would reach Grace Church in less than fifteen minutes if she didn't *dilly-dally*, a word that had never existed in her mother-in-law's no-nonsense vocabulary. Ruth had told her that she always took long, swift strides because "There are only twenty-four hours in a day and The Lord's work is never done."

Ruth Abbott Sunday had passed away in June, leaving her friend Elizabeth Townsend to organize the arts festival. Hearing that Glorie's health had improved, Elizabeth appointed her to oversee the church venue. Excited to participate, Glorie wanted to do a quick inspection before the volunteers set up the art exhibit in the lobby.

Like the other venues, the church had been trimmed in red, white, and blue bunting to commemorate the Independence Day celebration. As Glorie climbed the front steps, a brown and white dog rushed past her, nearly knocking her down.

The dog was waiting at the closed door. He appeared friendly enough, so Glorie bent down to stroke his matted fur, speaking in a cutesy voice reserved for pets and babies.

"Where did you come from, Sweetie? Did you lose your way?" She checked his unusual collar and tag. "What's this? Some kind of fancy eight design?"

The dog licked her hand.

"Do they call you *8*?"

Elm barked in response.

Glorie laughed. "So where's your owner, *8*?"

The dog barked twice.

"Okay, okay," she said. "Stop barking. You're in God's house now."

Indeed, the cuddly pooch had followed her inside. For a second, Glorie thought that maybe Big Dave had sent her the dog as a present from the Great Beyond. It sounded like something he would do and she could imagine him having quite the chuckle over it. She missed his chuckling. She missed everything about him. He was a good man. An angel.

The next day Glorie awoke to find *8* lying at the foot of her bed.

"Oh, no, Doggie," she said. "I've always had this stead-fast rule that dogs should sleep in their own beds."

But Glorie couldn't resist those gentle brown eyes.

The two became an inseparable pair and one day they returned to Moonwater Beach to hunt for sea glass and deliver a special gift. Glorie had added a few seashells and rose quartz beads to her original Divine Mother tiara and cupped it in her hands, visualizing the color pink while transferring her gratitude into the piece.

Standing at the shoreline, she said aloud: "To my

mermaid friends who assisted me during my journey underwater, I thank you for helping me see life from a new perspective. And for helping me make peace with the water."

With that pronouncement, she tossed the tiara into the water.

$\sim$

"Happy Re-birthday, Mermie!"

To celebrate Glorie's "grand awakening," Snow and Kat held a mermaid party by the Seashell Carousel. As she sat in the mermaid chariot with 8 on her lap, Glorie was content.

"I haven't been here in so long. Snow, do you remember when we had the mermaid birthday party for Elm?"

"Yeah," said Snow. "And do you remember when Noah tossed his football into that humongous mermaid cake, and Elm got so mad she hid his jacket under the carousel?"

Glorie laughed. "I seem to recall there was plenty of mischief that day."

After a few more minutes, they left the carousel and strolled over to the yellow and white-striped tent for cake and appetizers.

Jason came over to give Glorie a quick peck on the cheek. "Happy Re-birthday, Mermie! Seeing that you brought a special friend with you and this happens to be a special day, I hereby declare that Moonwater Beach shall be open to 8 until sunset!"

Kat leaned down to pet the dog. "Oh, I'd say he is *very* special. Right, boy?" And then she winked.

"Glorie!"

"Yes?"

Glorie looked at Snow, who was precariously balancing a paper plateful of seashell pasta, flip flop sandwiches, crab croissants, deviled egg sailboats, sanddollar cookies, and mermaid cupcakes. "Did you want something, Snow?"

"Not me," said Snow, reaching for her cup of Seawater, which was actually lemon blueberry punch. "I've been too busy grabbing the good stuff before Hungry Noah gets here."

"Glorie!"

"Maybe I'm hearing things," Glorie said to *8*.

She glanced at the party guests, all engaged in various conversations.

"Glorie!"

As if in a trance, she and *8* walked toward the shoreline. She still carried her cane, but only as a fashion accessory because the Lyme had gone dormant and she had little trouble walking these days.

Suddenly, *8* barked excitedly, pawing at an object on the sand. Glorie bent down to look at his treasure and gasped.

"Grandma Matilda's mirror!" she exclaimed, picking it up by its ornate handle. "I thought it was lost forever!"

With one arm wrapped around the dog, she sat on the sand and wept.

"There you are!" said Snow. "We thought we lost you, Re-birthday Girl! What's that in your hand?"

"My mirror," said Glorie, trembling. "It's been missing since before the hurricane."

As Snow and *8* watched, Glorie used her cane to write a heartfelt message in the sand:

Thank You

EPILOGUE

Like every town, Little Blessing had its legends. Perhaps the most famous of all was the tale of a dog named *8*, whose spirit was said to have returned to Glorie's side on the day she died at age ninety-seven.

Some of the local residents, including the minister, reported seeing *8* at Grace Church during the funeral, lying next to her closed casket, and even the *Little Blessing Observer* wrote a story about it. The story was embellished over the years until the local children swore that *8* visited them in their dreams whenever they had been naughty.

Glorie was buried at Purity Park, not far from the spot where Jason had performed her marriage ceremony with her beloved Big Dave. It had a pleasant view of the water and the town council marked the spot with a little fenced-in garden and a special plaque:

Gloria Frances DuPriest Sunday
First Lady of Little Blessing

One month later, there was an international news

report that a dog wearing an Infinity symbol was on the battlefield in a war-torn Middle Eastern country, carrying emergency supplies to wounded soldiers.

A few years afterward, a brown and white Spanish Water Dog was heralded for pulling out a little boy from the shark-infested waters in Cancun, Mexico. The scruffy canine hero was proclaimed "Valiente" for his bravery and immediately adopted by the appreciative family. It was unfortunate that he had lost a leg in that rescue, but the dog (formerly known as Mercy-Faith "Elm" Sunday) was loved and eternally grateful.

Back in Little Blessing, Noah renovated the treehouse for his grandchildren before he became too elderly to climb. Snow had kept Elm's metal box of tree mail and made Noah promise to keep it in the family after her death. Had they known that one letter was missing, they would have been understandably surprised by its contents. But they were never meant to find it because it was no ordinary letter. It could only be accessed through the Hall of Akashic Records.

Dear Miss Vi,

I'm not really writing this—I'm thinking it—but I know you'll still get it because thoughts are things. Anyway, I saw you today. Did you notice the dog that was peeing on your trunk? Yes, that was me and, yes, I'm male! I didn't really have to go, but I wanted the experience, you know? So I did a little manifesting. Anyway, I died (but not really) and then I came back to Little Blessing to help Mermie. It's been quite the adventure. Maybe they'll make a movie about it someday. Wouldn't that be cool? I know I'd watch it.

You're not going to believe this but Mermie is teaching swimming lessons to people who are afraid of the water and I helped her do it! Every Saturday she gets up and rides her bike to the high school. Do you know how far a drive that is? Well, pretty far from where Mermie lives now. So you can tell that she is doing much better with her Lyme. I mean, the doctors say it's still there, but she's not letting it overtake her entire life. Good thoughts matter, you know?

Now that Mermie is happy again, I feel my journey to remember who I am is really just beginning. If all goes well, I will have "aced" all of my challenges and earn myself a beautiful pink aura! And wouldn't it be nice if Mermie got to reunite with all the other mothers, having a nice hot tub party with pink champagne and an octopus?!

Flo tells me I'm doing a great job here on Earth, but I admit I'm also looking forward to going back home to Suite 8, hanging out with Prabhakar and Seraphina. I wonder which book she's reading now? I also hope to speak to Archangel Zadkiel again. Wow, can you believe I know a real angel?

Anyway, I'm off to Mexico, but I have a few stops to make first. Seraphina said we all have parallel lives, so I'd like to check out a few more of mine. Did you know that I visited another dimension while I was on the plane to England? I was a reverend and I was married to Noah! I think I'd like that.

I've been thinking a lot about Water. My opinion has changed so much! Like, I started out being curious, then I got angry and tried to capture its power, and now I am a Water Messenger.

So you just never know how things are going to turn out, Miss Vi. Anyway, I hope I get to meet you in one of my other lives because you've been a great friend in this one. Until next time, I love you and hope you still love me.

In Lak'ech,

8

ACKNOWLEDGMENTS

This book was born through the blessings of the Divine Creator and the teachings of Dr. Masaru Emoto, Jesus Christ, Laarkmaa, and Archangel Zadkiel. Thank you for helping me see the bigger picture.

I am beyond grateful to my handsome husband, Nicholas G.F. Sharp, for being my Number One Fan and loving me unconditionally, especially when I wrote and researched until the wee hours of the morning.

Special hugs to Michelle Hanson, Diantha Smith Harris, and Marie Lukasik Wallace—all wonderful teachers and healers—for encouraging me and for bravely reading my first draft.

Much gratitude, too, to the awe-inspiring Visionary Fiction Alliance and to the writers in Ascension Cabin for their illuminating words of wisdom and support.

And to the element of Water, my muse, I send a tidal wave of thanks for your messages. *I love you!*

ABOUT THE AUTHOR

Eleyne-Mari Sharp has been a professional writer since 1980. *Inn Lak'ech: A Journey to the Realm of Oneness* is her first visionary fiction novel for young adults.

Born in St. Louis, Missouri, she is a former Air Force brat who lived in Texas, Alaska, Mississippi, Italy, and Germany during her first seventeen years.

Ms. Sharp is also a certified color therapist, spiritual aromatherapist, crystal worker, jewelry designer, events organizer, radio show host, and radio show producer.

She lives in New England with tons of crystals, her yacht captain husband, Nicholas, and their mischievous little furbabies.

For information about Eleyne-Mari's books, courses, and podcasts:
www.writelighter.com
writelighter@yahoo.com

"In the story of *Inn Lak'ech*, we follow a bright young girl named Elm as she undertakes an Odysseus-like voyage away from an idyllic seaside village. The catalysts for her journey are the deaths of her first love and her father. Loss ignites a dark fire in her soul that leads her into a marine otherworld where she devolves, using wizardry to wreak havoc and eventually self-destruct. This is a touching and dramatic story, told through whimsical settings, delightful characters, and a quick pace. As was true in Odysseus' tale, what makes the journey away from home most meaningful is the return.

Elm is rescued by a woman named Seraphina, who takes her to the remote Inn Lak'ech. There Elm undergoes a series of activities designed to awaken her from the seeming nightmare in which she finds herself. These experiences involve psychological, physical, and spiritual transformation, with respect to New Age modalities. Elm's story can be a map for struggling young adults, but also to those of us who have lost our way later in life, who have wandered away from 'home' and yearn to return to a brighter outlook on life, for freedom from grief, isolation, and negativity."

— **ROBIN GREGORY**

"Sharp weaves a coming-of-age tale of forgiveness and love. Fans of personal development fables and all things metaphysical are sure to be drawn in to this beautiful story."

"This book made me weep! In all my years of hosting Angel Talk Cafe, I have never felt so emotional after reading a guest's book. But *Inn Lak'ech: A Journey to the Realm of Oneness* is not just any novel—it's a *healer*.

Unfortunately, my relationship with my mother was extremely difficult for many years and she made her transition without us reconciling. My childhood was very difficult. I thought the deep emotional pain, abuse, and betrayals would never heal.

I laughed and cried my way through this book. It's mystical, magical, and full of insights and spiritual understanding. For me personally, *Inn Lak'ech* is spiritual medicine. I am no longer tethered to the emotional pain, anger or resentment—I feel inner peace, joy, and gratitude!"

"Eleyne-Mari Sharp is taking evolutionary concepts into the teenage market, with her new book, *Inn Lak'ech*. Each young adult who reads this book will be inspired to learn more about possibilities and other realities. She has woven together an intriguing story, full of enlightened concepts!"

— PIA ORLEANE & CULLEN BAIRD
SMITH

"In *Inn Lak'ech*, Elm Sunday is a teen living in the seaside town of Little Blessing. We get to know this town and its inhabitants intimately (and for anyone who has lived in a small town, it just feels right). Elm's life is shattered when her boyfriend is murdered and later her father dies. Young adult defiance and rebellion send Elm spiraling down. How does the Universe respond? Elm is about to find out. This is a story of connection, loss and grief, and redemption. Well imagined and well executed! Ms. Sharp brings her experience and understanding of the metaphysical to a work that teens and adults can both enjoy. The book allows for deep questioning and searching. Nicely done!"

— ELLIS NELSON

"Lovely and affirming story about death, loss, and finding one's way. I found this very charming and emotional, and would definitely recommend it to anyone looking for a positive, reflective journey as they follow Elm along on hers."

— CECILY WOLFE

ALSO BY ELEYNE-MARI SHARP

Mad About Hue: A Memoir in Living Color